God's Maidservant

Anna Chant

Cover image of St Cyriakus Church: Borisb17/ shutterstock.com

Cover image of woman: faestock/shutterstock.com

Prologue: The Year of our Lord 937

Adelheid clung tightly to her mother's hand, daunted by the fear in her eyes. She whispered a few prayers, although she was unsure what she should be praying for. The last time she had prayed so earnestly was when her father was ill earlier that year. Those prayers had not been answered and she had spent the months since his death at an abbey.

"It will just be for a little while, my child," Bertha had promised when she sent her there. "I have some matters to attend to."

Adelheid had expected to hate the abbey, but instead she had enjoyed every moment. The Abbess had taken her in with a warm smile and Adelheid had become a favourite with the nuns, impressing them all with a piety and intelligence they regarded as remarkable for a girl of just six years. She had wept bitterly when her mother had summoned her back to Orbe Castle where her sorrow was quickly overwhelmed by dread.

It was not just her mother who looked worried. Her older brother, twelve year old Konrad, greeted her without even a hint of a smile to lighten his pale face.

"Come, Adelheid," Bertha said. "There are some noble guests waiting to greet you."

Wishing more than anything she was back at the abbey, she accompanied her mother to the hall. A dark-haired man was sat in a chair, his feet on the table, making a laughing comment to another man. They both stopped their conversation as

Adelheid entered, but neither rose.

"I see, Bertha, this is the child, is it? She has not grown much since last I saw her." He bared his teeth in what she supposed was a smile. "You should curtsey to me, Adelheid. I am King Hugh of Burgundy and Italy, your stepfather and father-in-law."

It had not occurred to Adelheid to wonder who the King of Burgundy was, now her father was dead and she glanced in confusion at her mother as she dropped into the curtsey the man had commanded.

"King Hugh and I are wed," Bertha explained. "He is now your stepfather, but he has long been your father-in-law." She stretched out a hand to a boy who looked to be slightly younger than Konrad. "This fine young man is Lothair, your betrothed."

Adelheid had always been aware she was betrothed to the son of the King of Italy. It was an arrangement her father had made when she was two as he gave up his own pretensions to the Italian crown, but such a matter had always seemed too distant to overly occupy her thoughts. She looked at the boy, who stared back, appearing just as uninterested.

"What a charming pair they will make, will they not, Berengar? A fine future king and queen," Hugh said to the other man.

Adelheid's eyes widened, certain he was mocking her. This belief was strengthened when Berengar got lazily to his feet to sweep her a low bow. "How honoured I am to greet you, Queen Adelheid. Although, Hugh, you and the fair Queen Bertha too make a fine pair."

Hugh laughed again, putting his arm around Bertha's waist and pulling her to him. Bertha smiled at the action, but to Adelheid the expression was very different to how she remembered her mother's smile.

As his father's gaze was distracted, Lothair elbowed the boy standing next to him in the ribs. "Adalbert, watch this." He reached out to yank hard on one of Adelheid's blonde plaits. From shock rather than pain, she burst into tears.

"What is the matter, my child?" Bertha asked, turning back to her.

"He pulled my hair," Adelheid sobbed.

"I did not," Lothair said hotly. He and Adalbert looked down to hide the smirks spreading across their faces.

"Your daughter is a liar, my lady," Hugh said. "She should be beaten."

Bertha took Adelheid by the shoulders. "Adelheid, you must not cause trouble with your future husband." She looked pleadingly up at Hugh. "Adelheid has always been a good girl, wise beyond her years. The nuns were impressed with her understanding."

"My son does not require wisdom and learning from his wife. He requires obedience and many sons. I trust you will raise your daughter with that aim in mind."

"Of course," Bertha murmured.

"Adelheid, apologise to my son."

Adelheid looked up at him, her blue eyes narrowed in rage. "I did not lie. He hurt me."

Bertha moaned as Hugh scowled. He took Adelheid roughly by the shoulders and shook her. "Apologise to Lothair or you will be beaten."

Adelheid pressed her lips together, but Bertha knelt down, looking earnestly into her eyes. "Adelheid, you must do as you are bidden."

Almost speechless at the injustice, Adelheid muttered, "I am sorry if I falsely accused you."

"That is better," Hugh said. "One day you may be queen of Italy and Burgundy. I expect you to learn to act with some decorum."

Bertha and Konrad gasped. "Not Burgundy," Bertha said. "Burgundy is for Konrad. It was his father's realm."

"But now it is mine by dint of marrying King Rudolf's widow. Of course, I shall leave my realm to my son."

"That is not fair," Konrad cried. "I am the King of Burgundy."

"A monastery might be appropriate for you, Konrad," Hugh

said. "Otherwise I may have to find some other way of disposing of you. You will never be King of Burgundy."

There was a clatter of footsteps. "Are you certain of that?" said the man striding in the door.

"Who are you?" Hugh demanded.

The man gave a slight bow. "I am Hermann, Duke of Swabia and stepfather to Queen Bertha. I am here on behalf of King Otto of Germany."

"What do you want? Queen Bertha is my wife."

"I am sure that is a great honour for you," Hermann replied with a smile. Adelheid stared at him from wide eyes, taking a definite liking to this man who was so obviously annoying Hugh. "But I wish to see my wife's grandson on the throne of Burgundy and King Otto is in full agreement."

"Otto?" scoffed Berengar. "That young puppy? He has no influence here. He has enough problems with his own lands."

Hermann smiled pleasantly. "You are wrong. The King is no puppy. He may be young, but he is as skilled a leader as any I have come across. He wishes Konrad to be king and is quite prepared to use force if necessary." His smiled widened. "Forgive me, I thought I had explained. I am accompanied by a sizable force and the King will send more if needed. I strongly advise you not to fight."

"Why does King Otto want to help me?" Konrad asked, looking stunned by Hermann's announcement.

Hermann put a hand on his shoulder. "King Otto has barely been on the throne a year. He needs allies, as do you. He believes you can come to a mutually beneficial arrangement."

"Mutually beneficial?" Berengar snorted. "He sees a young boy ripe for exploitation. This arrangement will not benefit Burgundy."

Konrad looked from Hugh to Hermann in a bewildered fashion.

Hermann smiled again at Konrad. "Do not be afeared. King Otto is a sensible man. He will not exploit your youth. He knows you will not always be a boy and would not come to any arrangement which might later breed resentment. You can be assured he will not interfere in your rule."

"Nonsense," Berengar muttered.

Adelheid shivered at how powerless her brother was. He would either lose his throne to Hugh or risk finding himself dictated to by this Otto.

"I think I will be grateful for any assistance King Otto cares to offer me," Konrad said in a wavering voice.

"Sensible lad," Hermann replied.

"You fool," Hugh cried. "Do not let German power into Burgundy. Listen, my boy, we can come to some arrangement. Perhaps I was too hasty saying Lothair would be my heir."

Konrad glared at him. "I do not trust you." He turned to Hermann. "I have no reason to trust King Otto either, but I have as yet no reason to distrust him. What must I do?"

"Once Hugh has returned to Italy, we shall appoint someone to oversee matters here, while you come with me and your grandmother, Regelind, to King Otto's court. You will receive a warm welcome from him and the fair Queen Eadgyth, do not doubt it." Hermann glared at Hugh. "How soon can you depart?"

Hugh scowled, shuffling his feet. "Soon enough. I shall take my wife's daughter with us. She is betrothed to Lothair, my son, so I trust there is no objection to that."

"None at all," Hermann replied. He glanced around, his gaze alighting on Adelheid with a smile. "I have a daughter named Ida about the same age as you. She has dark hair, but other than that she looks quite like you. You be a good little maid for your mother and stepfather. I do not doubt that one day I shall hear many great things of the fair Queen of Italy."

"Thank you, my lord, for helping my son," Bertha said, only a slight tremble betraying she had noticed Hugh's furious glare. "I know I can rely on you."

Hermann kissed Bertha's hand. "You can and you can rely on King Otto too." He gave a slight bow to Hugh and Berengar. "A good day to you both. I will not keep you from your departure.

I trust you will guard well your queen. And you too, young Lothair, should truly value your wife. If she grows as prudent and devout as her grandmother, you will have a fine wife indeed."

Lothair squirmed under the man's gaze. "If she is obedient, I shall value her well enough."

Hermann looked steadily back. "I hope you will value her for more than that. Queen Eadgyth of Germany is greatly revered by all for her wisdom and charm and her presence has enhanced Otto's status. The King values her very highly."

Hermann bowed once again to Bertha. "I wish you and Lady Adelheid every happiness in Italy. I shall keep you both in my prayers."

Part One: The Year of our Lord 947-8

Chapter one

Adelheid followed Father Warinus out of the church, eagerly firing questions which the grey haired priest was delighted to answer. Adelheid's piety and extraordinary understanding had made her a favourite of all the clergy attached to the household of King Hugh of Italy, which had been based for the past two years in Arles. However her questions stuttered to a halt as she saw Hugh coming towards them along the passageway. Repressing a sigh, she dropped to her knees.

Hugh was still the King of Italy, but in name only. A vicious quarrel with Berengar had seen the man briefly exiled to the court of King Otto, only for him to return with a force capable of driving Hugh out. Nonetheless Hugh insisted on being accorded all the respect due to a king, so Adelheid remained on her knees, hoping not to provoke his notorious temper. For the most part she kept out of his way and only wished that Bertha could do the same. Instead her mother had to listen to endless monologues on the betrayal of Berengar and the ingratitude of his son.

Lothair had remained in Italy and was now the king, although as Hugh often contemptuously mentioned, he was no true king. Berengar controlled everything. Adelheid had reached a marriageable age, but Lothair had never shown her any affection, and when she left Italy with her mother and stepfather, he had simply bidden her a curt farewell.

As Hugh approached, she bowed her head, hoping he would

stride on past her. He rarely spoke to her except when he found fault.

"A good day to you, Adelheid."

She glanced up, realising to her dismay that he had paused in front of her. "Good day, my Lord King," she replied. Beside her, Father Warinus stirred slightly and Adelheid knew he found Hugh's pompous manner distasteful.

"Please rise, Adelheid."

Obediently she got up, but kept her eyes down as she waited for him to announce what she had done wrong this time. But Hugh put his hand under her chin, tilting her face upwards. He gave a smile, but it was not one which brought her any joy. Although she was unsure why, she would have preferred a scold to this look.

"You have become a very beautiful young woman, my dear."

"Thank you, my Lord King," Adelheid murmured, feeling anything but grateful. Over the last few years many had told her she was beautiful, but the compliment meant little to her. She knew what a sin it was to indulge in vanity and much preferred it when she was complimented on her piety.

"Yes, very beautiful. Much too good for that young puppy." His hand was still under her chin, his thumb stroking her face. Lothair had sided with Berengar in Italy and the betrayal infuriated him. Adelheid stood still, wishing he would stop touching her and move on. He had struck her on many occasions for some piece of perceived insolence, but somehow that was less threatening than this gentle caress. She sent a frightened look at the priest.

"Is there some matter I or Lady Adelheid can help you with, my Lord King?" Father Warinus said.

Hugh looked irritated. "No, you may move on, Father. I am sure Lady Adelheid will accompany me a while." He laid a possessive hand on her shoulder, sliding it slowly down her arm to take her hand. He smiled back at Adelheid. "That boy took what was mine. It is not right."

Adelheid froze, wanting to pull her hand from his grasp, but he held tight.

"My Lord King, I trust you are not thinking of taking something which belongs to your son," Father Warinus said urgently. "Consider your soul, my lord."

Hugh let go of her hand as he rounded on the priest. Adelheid took a step back against the wall, her heart thudding. She was confused by her fear, but the attitude of the priest confirmed she was right to feel it.

"I do not know what you are insinuating, Father," Hugh snapped. "But I have no further use for you. Please leave us."

Father Warinus stood his ground. "I do not think that is appropriate, my lord."

"Rubbish. She is my daughter. Get from my sight this instant."

The priest's face fell. He could hardly refuse a direct order. Hugh turned his back on him, not waiting for him to leave before moving closer to Adelheid. His body was almost touching hers, as he again took hold of her hand.

Father Warinus was still watching them in a helpless horror. He was a very lowly priest, with no power against the King. As Hugh pressed a kiss against her hand, a sound made Warinus turn his head. Relief lit up his face. "My Lady Queen," he cried, his voice far louder than it needed to be. "A good day to you."

Hugh muttered a curse, stepping back sharply from Adelheid. She let out a long breath. Hugh had never showed her any hint of affection before and she was certain his actions that day had not been affectionate, however gentle they had been. Never had she felt so relieved to see her mother coming towards her. She wanted nothing more than to fling herself into her arms, but instead she looked down.

"My lord husband, is there a problem?" Bertha asked, looking nervously from her daughter to Hugh.

Hugh straightened himself with a scowl. "Indeed there is. That girl of yours remains insolent. I am continually having to reprimand her for her rudeness. I will not tolerate it."

"I am sure Adelheid does not mean to be impertinent, my

lord." Bertha's face flushed with distress. "My child, beg your stepfather's pardon."

Over the years Adelheid had been made to apologise many times for sins she was certain she had not committed. When she was a child she had resented her mother as much as anyone else for her continued blame. But as she got older, she realised this was her mother's way of protecting her. The resentment was replaced by pity that her mother was so powerless. "Forgive me, my Lord King, for any insolence I have shown you," she said in a low voice.

"You should be stricter with your daughter, my lady," Hugh snapped. "I know my son will not stand for such an attitude."

He did not wait for a reply before stalking arrogantly away. "Mother, I..." Adelheid started, but Bertha put her arms around her. Gratefully she snuggled closer, the warmth of her mother's embrace more comforting than ever.

"Hush, child. I know what a good girl you are. I have never known you be impertinent to any, but it does not do to anger him."

"I do not think I did anger him," Adelheid said slowly. "I am not sure what he was thinking before you arrived." She could still feel the pressure of his fingers on her and she buried her face against her mother's shoulder, uncertain why the touch distressed her so much.

"My lady," Father Warinus said. "I can vouch for the fact that Lady Adelheid did not behave in any way impertinently. She always shows the King the utmost respect. More than he deserves in my opinion."

"I know, Father," Bertha replied.

Warinus looked uncomfortably down before taking a deep breath. "My lady, I wonder if I might discuss a matter with you."

"Of course, Father. What is it?"

"My lady, it is a most delicate topic. Perhaps we might go somewhere we will be unheard. I ask you in advance to forgive me for this, but I have this day seen something of grave concern."

Chapter two

"That is impossible," Bertha said. "He would not do such a thing. Adelheid is his daughter twice over, by his marriage to me and her betrothal to his son."

"My lady, I know what I witnessed. Lady Adelheid is no longer a child. She has become a beautiful young woman and the King can see that. I do not think he cares what a great sin it would be."

Bertha rubbed her eyes wearily. "Everyone knows he is not faithful to me. The number of bastards he has sired are testament to that, although in truth I care little. But Adelheid?"

"Mother, have I done something wrong?" Adelheid had been listening to the hushed comments between her mother and the priest in increasing concern.

Bertha took hold of her daughter's hand. "My child, I have told you what to expect of the marriage bed."

Adelheid nodded in bewilderment.

"Not everyone saves such an act for marriage, which of course is very wrong. Hugh is one of those and he thinks nothing of indulging in such sinful desires. Father Warinus is concerned he has turned his attentions to you."

Adelheid crossed herself, shuddering at the memory of his hands on her. "I would never do such a thing, Mother."

Father Warinus nodded. "Lady Adelheid, we know you would not willingly participate in such a sin, but it could be forced on you. The piety of your heart and soul is an inspiration to us all, but a woman's body is not so strong and can be easily over powered."

Adelheid stared at him, completely speechless. It had never occurred to her that she might have to physically fight for her virtue.

"Do you really think he would force himself on her?" Bertha asked, looking close to tears. "For him to take a willing mistress is bad enough, but…"

"For the sake of his soul, I pray not," Warinus said. "But you did not see him. There is such a rage in him. Lady Adelheid's beauty, combined with the chance to take revenge on his son, makes her a prize indeed. My lady, your daughter is not safe."

"What can I do to protect her? I could entreat Konrad, but no act has been committed yet against her and Hugh would undoubtedly deny everything."

"She is old enough to be married," Warinus said. "I know you had hoped to delay a little longer, but I think it would be wise to proceed with the union."

Bertha sighed. "I received a messenger from Konrad saying Lothair is demanding his bride. I had intended to ask Konrad to refuse for now, but perhaps I should not."

"I do not think you should, my lady. It is time for Lady Adelheid to take her place as Queen of Italy."

Adelheid looked down to hide her fear. During their years in Italy she had never warmed towards her betrothed. As a boy, he had continued to be spiteful, revelling in causing trouble for her and as a young man, he had ignored her. She knew it would be her duty to love him, but unless he had changed, it would be a hard emotion to force.

"You are right, Father," Bertha said. "I shall tell Konrad to invite Lothair to Burgundy." She smiled reassuringly at her daughter. "To be Queen of Italy is a fine destiny and you will most certainly grace the office."

"Must I, Mother?" Adelheid asked. "I would prefer to take holy vows. It is what I have always wanted."

"Adelheid, we have spoken of this. The marriage was planned

by your father long ago. It is your duty to honour it."

Adelheid sighed. She had expected her mother's answer. "I know. Is it wrong of me to be afraid? The Italian court has changed much since we were there. I have heard how Berengar and his wife control all."

"I fear your life will not always be easy, my lady," Warinus said. "But you will bring some much needed piety to the court. In time King Lothair will recognise what a blessing he has in you and I am sure you will find contentment in your role. I understand how an abbey calls to you, but as Queen of Italy you will carry out God's tasks."

Adelheid nodded, trying to smile. She knew it was God's will for her to honour the wishes of her father. With an effort she suppressed the undutiful wish he had not made such a decision. "I shall miss you, Mother. I will feel so alone in Italy among strangers."

"God will be with you, my dearest child," Bertha said, tears welling in her eyes. "And you will always be in my prayers."

Warinus' brow was creased as he watched them. "My lady, may I make a suggestion? I am confident Lady Adelheid will fulfil her role to perfection, but it is daunting to one so young, even someone as great spirited as your daughter. It would be appropriate for her to take her own priest to her new home."

"You would go with her, Father?" Bertha exclaimed.

"If both of you ladies agree."

"I most certainly agree," Adelheid said, relief surging in her. "To have one friend and trusted advisor will be the greatest of blessings."

Bertha nodded. "But Adelheid, remember your first duty is to your husband. Father Warinus' guidance will greatly aid you, but you must follow your husband's rule."

"Of course, Mother. I hope to be the very finest of wives, but such trusted spiritual guidance will help me in my duties to my husband and my new land."

Bertha smiled. "I must confess, it will be a relief to know you will watch over her, Father. I agree to the plan. I shall inform

Konrad this day."

Chapter three

Bertha kept Adelheid closely guarded for the remainder of her time at Hugh's residence. The days passed quickly as they busied themselves preparing her raiment for the wedding. When Konrad sent for her to be married from his court, Bertha barely concealed her relief and broke the news to Hugh that night.

"Konrad has arranged for Adelheid's marriage. Lothair is on his way to Burgundy."

Hugh looked up. "Why was I not informed?"

"I believe Lothair prefers to deal directly with Konrad," Bertha replied calmly.

Hugh cast a contemptuous look at Adelheid. "I trust you will not expect me to attend your nuptial, Girl. I'll have nothing to do with that puppy."

"Of course, my lord," Adelheid replied. "I understand." She hesitated, hating to lie, but knowing what was expected of her. "I shall regret your absence very much."

"Humph." Hugh took another mouthful of his dinner. "You will not attend either, Bertha."

Adelheid's eyes widened, but Bertha remained unfazed. "Forgive me, my lord, but Konrad has made plain he expects me to be there. I do not think it wise to disregard him."

Hugh scowled and he returned to his dinner. Adelheid watched him, suddenly overwhelmed by pity. He had once been King of Italy and part of Burgundy, but now he was an exile, clinging desperately to what little remained of his position. At the end of the meal she curtseyed deeply before him, determined to honour him as befitted a king. He barely glanced up.

"My Lord King, I wish to thank you for your care and guidance over the years. I am sure it will stand me in good stead for my new role."

Hugh did look up at that, staring at her as if he suspected mockery. Adelheid looked back, her eyes clear and honest. She had never loved him as a father, but at least she could respect him as one. Hugh patted her clumsily on the hand. "You be a good and obedient wife to my son, Adelheid. I hope he will appreciate his fortune, but I suspect he will not."

It was not encouraging, but Adelheid dropped into another curtsey, quashing her relief that she would not have to see much more of her stepfather.

∞∞∞∞

The atmosphere at Konrad's residence was very different. Guests had been summoned to the Burgundian court to witness the marriage of the King's sister and the meals each night were full of laughter and music, growing ever greater as each new set of guests arrived.

"Mother!" Bertha's face lit up when the latest party arrived. Away from Hugh, her manner had turned as joyous as Adelheid remembered from her childhood. She rushed forward, pulling Adelheid with her to fling her arms around a woman, whose face was lined, but lit up by a warm smile. "Adelheid, this is your grandmother, Regelind."

Regelind studied Adelheid and kissed her. "So this is the young bride. How beautiful you are, my child. Why, she has a look of Ida, does she not?" She turned to a man with grey streaked hair.

"She always did," the man replied.

Adelheid stared at him, recognising the man by his smile.

"Hermann! Oh, forgive me, my Lord Duke. I am delighted to see you again."

Hermann smiled. "You may call me Hermann, Adelheid. I am pleased to see you. May I present my daughter, Lady Ida."

He took the hand of a girl, whose face did indeed bear a resemblance to her own. Adelheid smiled shyly. Ida looked to be slightly younger than her, but already she wore the mantle of a married woman. "I am honoured to meet you."

Ida smiled back. "It is good to meet you. Your brother has told me much about you over the years."

There was a handsome, fair-haired man stood with Ida, who appeared only a little older. Hermann put an arm around his shoulders. "As you can see, I have acquired a fine son this last year, as Ida is now married. May I present Lord Liudolf of Saxony."

The young man bowed. "It is an honour to be here."

Bertha smiled at him. "So you are King Otto's son."

"I have that honour," Liudolf replied, the sparkle fading slightly from his clear blue eyes.

"We have heard much of you," Bertha said. "I am delighted to meet you at last."

Konrad joined them at that moment, bowing before Regelind and Ida, but flinging an arm around the two men. "Hermann! Liudolf! Greetings and welcome." He smiled at Liudolf. "Is all well with Otto?"

Liudolf shrugged. "He was in good health last time I saw him, but that was some months ago now."

"Otto wants you to become familiar with the duchy, Liudolf, that is all. You are after all to be my heir as well as his," Hermann said, resting his hand on Liudolf's shoulder.

"I do not think it is that at all." Liudolf's face set into angry lines. "Mother was scarce cold in her grave before Father rushed the plans for my marriage and my sister's. It seems he no longer wants either of us often at court."

"I suppose it was a shock to you," Bertha said.

"The marriage wasn't. Ida and I were betrothed as children."

His face brightened as he glanced at his wife. "Even before Mother died, I had been asking Father to let us wed. Naturally it is no hardship to be at Hermann's household, but I assumed I would divide my time between Swabia and the court. We did remain with the court for a while after the wedding, but then he suddenly sent us away and will not tell me when I am to return."

"The court is not the merry place it once was," Hermann said, shaking his head sadly. "The Queen is much missed by all and Otto avoids company. He is more often away campaigning in West Francia on behalf of his sister. I think he does not overly care if he returns from the fights."

"He still sees William," Liudolf muttered. "He has not turned away from all his children."

"William?" Bertha said. "I did not know you had a brother."

"He is my half-brother, my lady," Liudolf explained. "Father sired him before he was wed to my mother."

Adelheid frowned. For many years she had heard of King Otto as the saviour of her brother and regarded him as a great hero, but this bastard son told a very different story. Evidently Otto was no better than Hugh.

Fortunately Liudolf misunderstood the disgust she was sure was apparent on her face and smiled at her. "Forgive me, my lady. We are here to celebrate your wedding, not dwell on such sad matters. I am honoured to attend the nuptial of my wife's kinswoman, but I believe we have another kinswoman in common. Was not Lord Ludwig of Burgundy your uncle?"

"Yes, he was," Adelheid said.

"He was wed to Lady Elfgifu, I believe, my mother's sister."

"Of course. I remember Lady Elfgifu very fondly, my lord," Bertha put in. "I do not think you saw her often, except as a very young child, Adelheid. Her beauty was much admired in Burgundy."

They were startled from their conversation by a bout of coughing, as Hermann suddenly fought to regain his breath. Regelind put her arm around him. "Sit down, my love. The ride has wearied you."

"I am fine," Hermann protested, but allowed himself to be led to a chair, objecting even more at how Ida and Liudolf fussed around him. Adelheid smiled as she watched them, thinking briefly of her own father who she scarcely remembered. She wondered if he were alive that day, whether they would have enjoyed the affection both Ida and Liudolf so clearly felt for Hermann.

∞∞∞

There was no news of when Lothair and the Italian party would arrive, but no one in Burgundy cared, as the court remained in a festive mood. Adelheid spent her days pleasantly with her mother, enjoying getting to know her grandmother and Ida. At times she almost forgot about her impending marriage.

"Lothair will be with us this night," Konrad announced one noon. "We must prepare a welcome."

Konrad gave orders for a magnificent feast, while Regelind, expressing her delight at the news, immediately surveyed Adelheid's clothing, determined she should make a good impression on her husband. She selected a tunic of a pale blue with an overdress of a deeper shade, while Bertha herself combed her blonde hair into a shining golden cloak. Ida and Regelind speculated happily on the looks and character of the King of Italy, but Adelheid was silent as she did her best not to think of the disdainful youth who had so delighted in taunting her.

"You will be the most beautiful bride any of us have seen," Regelind said, as she admired their handiwork.

Adelheid blushed and disclaimed, shooting a quick glance at Ida, hoping she wasn't too offended.

Ida laughed. "Oh, I know I am not as beautiful as you."

Regelind patted her hand. "Nonsense. You made a very

pretty bride, my child. You certainly brought a smile back to young Liudolf's face. I do not doubt King Lothair will be similarly aware of his good fortune."

"He certainly will," Bertha said. "Come, my child, let us be ready in the hall for when he arrives."

Adelheid was not fooled by her mother's cheerful tone and was all too aware of the concern lining her face. Lothair's attitude towards his stepmother had ever been insolent, so it was no wonder Bertha had not liked him. She could only hope the responsibility of ruling Italy had worked some considerable improvement on him. The mood in the hall was high, as everyone anticipated the magnificent feasting which would take place over the next few days, but Adelheid stood nervously between Konrad and her mother. Her heart thudded loudly as Lothair strode into the hall.

Chapter four

Lothair had changed little in appearance since she had last seen him. With his dark hair and eyes set off by a vivid green riding tunic, he was a handsome twenty year old, but in his thin features, Adelheid could see the resemblance to his father. Muttering a prayer he was not like his father in character, she sank into a low curtsey.

He raised her up and bowed over her hand. After staring at her for a moment, he nodded his head in a curt but not disapproving fashion. "Greetings, Lady Adelheid."

"Greetings, my lord," she replied trying to force her face into a smile.

Lothair did not reply, but glanced at Konrad. "Greetings, my Lord King of Burgundy."

"Welcome to Burgundy, my Lord King of Italy. Allow me to present my guests."

"Never mind about that," Lothair said. "I am not here to meet all of your supporters. I am here for my bride. How soon can the wedding take place?"

Regelind gave a faint gasp at this rudeness and Hermann stepped forward. "Now then, young man, we all understand your eagerness to claim so fair a bride. But the wedding cannot take place this night, so allow Konrad to introduce you to us."

Lothair shrugged, his face setting into the sneer Adelheid remembered so well. "Very well, my Lord King, present me to your most illustrious guests."

Konrad frowned, but maintained his pleasant manner as he

presented the others. Lothair looked bored, until Liudolf was presented to him.

"Lord Liudolf of Saxony? King Otto's son?"

"I have that honour, my Lord King of Italy," Liudolf replied.

"He who granted refuge to my good friend, Berengar until he could drive my father from Italy. Your father has my eternal gratitude."

"Indeed," muttered Bertha.

"My dear Stepmother," Lothair cried, suddenly in great humour. "How delightful to see you again. Is my father also here?"

"He is indisposed," Bertha replied.

Lothair grinned. "Couldn't face seeing me, I suppose. Well, he will not be missed."

Adelheid felt bewildered. Lothair's rudeness had confirmed all her worst fears, but his attitude towards Hugh gave her hope. Anyone who disliked Hugh could not be so bad.

∞∞∞

Lothair got his way and the wedding was planned for just two days later. The excitement at the Burgundian court was immense, but for Adelheid there was nothing but dread. Never before had she known such an atmosphere as the one at Burgundy. Konrad maintained a relaxed court and the guests had all been merry. Accustomed to the strained relations between her mother and Hugh, the gentle affection between Hermann and Regelind had been a revelation. She wondered if the arrogant young Lothair would ever show her such deferential respect.

On the morning of the wedding she dressed silently in a pink dress, with wide sleeves revealing the fine linen of a white tunic. Regelind and Ida chatted excitedly, Ida commenting on Lothair's good looks, but Bertha was as silent as Adelheid.

"You look beautiful, child," Regelind said, smoothing back

Adelheid's hair. "Italy is gaining a fine queen."

"Is she ready yet?" Konrad called from outside the chamber. "Lothair is becoming impatient."

Bertha opened the door. "You can come in, my son."

"Who can blame the lad for his impatience?" Regelind commented with a smile.

"He will be so proud of you," Ida exclaimed. "You will make such a handsome couple."

Konrad and Bertha exchanged glances. "Let us hope so," he muttered.

Regelind gave her a hearty kiss. "I wish you every happiness, my dear child." And after an embrace from Ida, the two left her.

Adelheid looked helplessly as her mother's eyes filled with tears. Konrad shrugged. "Just because the father is a poor husband, it does not follow that the son will be."

"Of course he won't be," Bertha said, forcing a smile. "Indeed there is much that is fine in Lothair. Come, my child, we must not keep him waiting."

Fearfully Adelheid rested her hand on her brother's arm. If only they had permitted her to be a Bride of Christ, she would have attended such a union in joy. A brief vision of herself dressed in a grey habit, kneeling at an altar flashed before her eyes. That would have been a fine destiny, but it was not the one planned for her, the one it was her duty to accept.

At the church door Lothair made a handsome figure in his fine blue tunic or he would have done were it not for the faint frown on his face. It cleared into a look of appreciation as Adelheid drew closer. She looked frantically around. Regelind and Ida had taken places next to their husbands. Hermann gave what was no doubt meant to be a reassuring smile, but with the worry obvious in his eyes, it offered no comfort. She looked back at her bridegroom and took the hand he had stretched out to her. He raised it to his lips and looked expectantly at the Bishop of Arles.

"Say the words to bind yourself in matrimony with this woman, my Lord King," the Bishop stated.

"I, Lothair, King of Italy, take you, Adelheid, daughter of the late King Rudolph of Burgundy as my wife from this day, until death parts us."

"Say your vows, Lady Adelheid."

She took a deep breath to steady herself as she made the vows she had no wish to make. "I, Adelheid of Burgundy, daughter of King Rudolph of Burgundy, take you, Lothair, King of Italy as my lord and husband from this day, until death parts us, with the permission of my noble brother, King Konrad of Burgundy."

"King Lothair, Lady Adelheid, I declare you wed," the Bishop pronounced, his voice as solemn as when he performed a requiem mass.

Lothair pressed his lips briefly against Adelheid's. She shivered, already disliking the sensation. Looking anxiously into her new husband's face, she hoped he had not noticed her reaction and prayed she would be a good wife to him.

There was no time for any private conversation together, as the day followed with a mass before the magnificent feast Konrad had arranged. Lothair was in excellent spirits at the feast. He laughed with Konrad and Liudolf, raising no objections as his cup was filled again and again with fine wine.

At length the women rose from the table and Adelheid knew it was time she retired to the bridal chamber. She had eaten and drunk sparingly, but her stomach churned and for a moment she thought her nerves would overwhelm her.

"Do not fear, my Lady Queen," Liudolf called, as she paused for a moment to compose herself. "We will not keep your husband from you for too long."

Adelheid started. It was the first time any had used her new title with her. She straightened her back in pride, concealing her fears as she was escorted to the bridal chamber. Her mother sat on the bed, giving her a tight embrace. "All will be well, my child," she said, trying to smile.

"Of course it will be," Regelind said. "Really, Bertha, you are scaring the girl half to death." She gave Adelheid a warm hug. "There is no need to fear, Adelheid. I have had two wedding nights and I could not say which was finer."

"Of course." Adelheid smiled back, ashamed of how obvious her fear must be. "I shall be honoured to receive my lord husband this night."

"Exactly and God willing there will soon be a little Italian prince in your arms," Regelind replied. "I wish you every happiness, my dear granddaughter."

As her mother and grandmother left the room, Adelheid tried to steady her racing heart. It felt like an age, yet far too soon before Lothair entered clad only in a robe, his face still flushed. His eyes glittered in the candlelight as he sat down on the bed. Without saying anything he gave her a long kiss, his lips tasting of wine. As he released her, his face appeared more flushed than ever.

"You are very beautiful, Adelheid," he muttered. "Very beautiful indeed."

"Thank you, my lord," Adelheid replied, trying not to shrink from the wet kisses he was pressing against her neck. Nervously she kept talking. "But it is of course a great vanity and a sin to take pride in such things."

Lothair's blow to the side of her head was not hard, but none the less Adelheid cried out. His face had gone crimson, but this time obviously with anger. "Do not contradict me, Adelheid or prate on about such nonsense."

She looked down to hide the tears in her eyes. "Forgive me, my lord."

He gripped her shoulders tightly, forcing her to bite her lip so as not to cry out again. "You and I will deal much better with each other if you remain obedient. I trust that is clear."

"Of course, my lord."

He relaxed his grip and pulled off her robe, casting a

contemptuous look at her body. "Your role is to be an obedient wife and to bear me a son. I trust you will manage that, Adelheid."

"I pray I shall, my lord."

"Good." Lothair threw off his own robe, climbing into bed next to her. Adelheid closed her eyes, wishing she could also shut off all feeling against the hands which squeezed every part of her body, each touch seeming more impatient than the last.

Chapter five

Adelheid spent the night lying very tensely in her determination not to disturb her husband. As soon as she was sure he was asleep, she had edged away from him, huddling her body to the far side of the bed. Her fear she would anger him further made it impossible to sleep deeply. Only the occasional doze gave a brief respite from her turmoil, but always she swiftly awoke again, uncomfortably aware of the deep breaths of the man in her bed.

Dawn had already broken before Lothair stirred. He rolled over to look at her and she tensed, expecting him to grab her again.

"Try to make your disgust a little less obvious, Adelheid," he said, his eyes narrowed. "I have already instructed the Archbishop of Arles to arrange for some transfer of lands as your morning gift."

"Forgive me, my lord. I am most grateful," she whispered. "I do not mean to-"

"Never mind that now," Lothair said impatiently. "Unfortunately I promised your brother and Lord Liudolf a day's hunting and it doesn't do to offend King Otto's son. So you may have one more day with your family. Tomorrow we go to Italy."

"Yes, my lord. Thank you."

Lothair kissed her so hard, she could feel his teeth against her lips, before he rose from the bed with no further words. Adelheid lay still, as he dressed and only after he left the chamber, did she let out a shaky breath and allow a few tears to flow.

Impatiently she wiped at them, knowing she must not worry her mother or grandmother. Her mind focussed on Ida. They were the same age and she too had been wed just a short while. If anyone could help make sense of what she had endured that night, it would be her. Ignoring the twinges of pain, she dressed quickly, hoping Lothair had already left.

She found Ida near the doorway to the hall. Adelheid held back, watching how Liudolf was kissing her just as Lothair had done. Except it wasn't quite the same. It took a moment for her to realise what was different. Ida's arms were not hanging by her side, but were around Liudolf's waist. Liudolf's actions too seemed to be different, his hand drifting gently down her back. To Adelheid's astonishment, as Liudolf pulled away, smiling at his wife, it was Ida who stood on tiptoes to press one last kiss against his lips. She too was smiling as she turned away from him.

"Adelheid!" Ida ran over, giving her a swift hug. She looked at her anxiously. "Is all well? Marriage can be strange to start with."

Adelheid was flooded with relief. From their conversations over the previous days, it was obvious Ida was a contented newlywed. It felt good to know such contentment could come from an unpromising beginning. "Was marriage difficult for you in the beginning?"

Ida sat at the table, filling up their cups with weak ale. "Not difficult exactly. I had known Liudolf for years. As we were betrothed, it was not improper for us to be alone and we had shared many a kiss by the time it came for us to wed. Eadgyth caught us once and was not impressed. At least, she said she was not impressed, but her scold was very mild." Ida laughed at the memory. "I think secretly she was pleased I cared so much for her son. In truth, by the time we wed I was very curious about the marriage bed. It was strange, but never unpleasant. Liudolf was always so caring."

Adelheid's shoulders slumped, realising how different Ida's experiences with her childhood friend had been. No doubt Ida had always shown Liudolf due respect and never annoyed him, as she had so quickly angered Lothair.

Ida looked at her in concern, squeezing her hand. "Adelheid, was last night very bad for you?"

Adelheid forced a smile, too ashamed to admit how she had disappointed her husband. "No, not bad. Like you said, it is strange, but I shall become accustomed."

"Are you sure? You do not look happy."

"My husband says we are to go to Italy in the morning. Of course, I am eager to take up my place, but I know the life there will not be easy. I shall miss my mother. You are fortunate that you have remained with your family in Swabia."

"I know. Although I would be happy if we were more often at court. Otto has always been very kind to me. After the wedding he honoured me almost as a queen. Eadgyth too, when she was alive, always treated me as a daughter." Ida sighed. "I miss Eadgyth."

The two sat in silence for a while, until more entered the hall. "Father?" Ida cried in surprise as Hermann came in. "Are you not hunting this day?"

"No, my child. The feast went on late last night. I feel a little weary today and do not want to tire myself before our return to Swabia."

Ida poured her father a drink, watching him anxiously.

Hermann took a mouthful of his drink and smiled kindly at Adelheid. "And how is the young bride this morning?"

"I am well. I was just telling Ida how eager I am to take up my new role, although a little apprehensive too."

Hermann took another mouthful, the concern in his eyes suggesting to Adelheid he had not been fooled by her cheerful tone. "That is natural. I think Italy is fortunate indeed to be gaining so fair a queen, but it is true the role may not be an easy one. If you ever need assistance, Swabia will be ever honoured to provide it."

∞ ∞ ∞

The hunt seemed to have been a successful one, judging by the high spirits Konrad and Liudolf displayed as they arrived in the hall. Liudolf spun Ida exuberantly off her feet, before starting an animated conversation with his father-in-law. Adelheid watched them wistfully, wondering if she and Lothair would ever be so at ease with each other.

Lothair entered the hall and bowed politely to her. "Good evening, Adelheid. I trust you have passed a pleasant day."

Adelheid flushed, knowing how everyone was watching her. Konrad's court was in a sentimental mood following the wedding and would be hoping for some sign of affection between the bride and groom. "Yes, thank you, my lord. I trust you also did."

Lothair snorted. "I have had better."

Adelheid's heart sank as she took her seat beside him, bowing her head for prayers. As they ended Konrad rose to his feet, bidding everyone welcome to the night's feasting.

"Thank you, my friends, for such a fine day's hunting," Konrad continued. "Although, Liudolf, I think I shall never hunt with you again!"

"That was not my fault," Liudolf cried gleefully.

"It was your suggestion to ride that way," Konrad retorted.

"How was I to know you and Lothair would ride so fast?" Liudolf's face was a picture of innocence. "How can it be my fault you both tumbled from your horses into the mud?"

Konrad grinned. "Be quiet, Liudolf, before I dump the contents of my cup over your head."

"Very well," Liudolf replied. "I shall never again describe to any the sight of two fine fools sat in the mud."

The hall descended into laughter as Konrad shook his head in mock anger.

"And certainly I shall never again mention my mirth as

Lothair tried to rise, only to fall flat on his face again, looking more mud than man."

The laughter increased and Adelheid joined in, not noticing the scowl deepening on her husband's face. She was too busy watching the scuffle between Konrad and Liudolf, as it ended in a good humoured embrace between the two. The merriments continued throughout the meal, Konrad and Liudolf carrying the lively conversation so no one noticed how Adelheid and Lothair said very little. When she rose from the table, he got up with her.

"I shall retire too, I think. I thank you for your hospitality, my dear Konrad."

"Cannot wait to be alone with your wife, is that right?" Liudolf called. "I know that feeling only too well." He pulled Ida onto his lap. She screeched, descending into giggles as Liudolf kissed her. Hermann was shaking his head in amusement, although he glanced at Adelheid to nod at her as she left the hall with Lothair. Silently she followed him along the passageway, determined to be a good wife for him that night, hoping she could soon relax with her husband as Ida did.

"The Queen will not require your assistance this night," Lothair snapped at the two serving women who were waiting in the antechamber.

Adelheid looked nervously at him as he pushed open the door. He did not wait for it to close before delivering a stinging blow to the side of her head. She stumbled back, crying out loud, staring at her husband.

"Do you find it amusing to join that little Saxon puppy in laughing at me?" He struck her again.

"No, no." She held up her hands to cover her head. "Please, my lord, no offence was intended. I thought it merely a jest in good humour."

Lothair seized her arms, shaking her harder than ever, as tears began to stream down her cheeks. "Stop contradicting me, Adelheid. Either this insolence stops now or I shall beat it out of you."

Chapter six

Adelheid was glad her mantle covered the bruise to the side of her face the next morning. At least no one would see how she had angered her husband. It was fortunate too that it was a hurried departure, with no time to exchange confidences. She maintained a calm manner, which seemed to ease the mind of her mother, as they shared a last embrace. She turned to see Hermann nodding curtly at Lothair.

"I told you once before to value your wife, my Lord King. I trust you will do that. She may only be my granddaughter by marriage, but I most certainly consider her a kinswoman."

Lothair's face was frozen into a courteous smile. "I am sure as my sweet Adelheid grows into her role, she will prove to be truly valuable indeed."

"Farewell, Adelheid." Hermann smiled at her reassuringly. "Remember, Swabia will always be honoured to aid you. I am sure I not only speak for myself, but for my heir."

Liudolf bowed. "Of course. Are we not related twice over, through both my wife and my aunt? I can certainly echo Hermann's words."

Adelheid smiled gratefully at them, keeping her tears back with an effort. As she looked at her family for the last time, her eyes stung at how close they all were. Konrad was stood with her mother, while Regelind and Ida's arms were entwined. Hermann and Liudolf were linked only by marriage, but with Hermann's arm draped around Liudolf's shoulders, they seemed closer than many a father and son.

"Perhaps we could be on our way, Adelheid," Lothair said, his even tone not concealing his impatience.

Adelheid nodded calmly at him. He was her family now. "Of course, my lord. Let us most certainly be on our way."

As Lothair helped her onto her horse, she glanced back at their entourage. Somewhere in the group was Father Warinus. That knowledge enabled her to smile brightly at her family. However hard it was to leave them, at least she was not completely alone.

There were many cries of farewell, as Lothair ordered them to start. Adelheid swallowed the lump in her throat, giving what she hoped looked like an airy wave, as they started on their way to Italy.

∞ ∞ ∞

It was a long, lonely ride to Pavia through hills which grew ever steeper. Although he rode alongside her, Lothair rarely spoke to her, which was something of a blessing. If she said little, the chances of her saying something wrong were at least lessened. She managed a light conversation with their entourage but kept her words only on topics of a general nature which were unlikely to offend him. But even so she awaited him each night in the guest chambers of the abbeys they stayed at with trepidation, wondering if he would punish her for some perceived slight.

Only in those moments when she knelt in prayer with Father Warinus did she feel able to speak freely.

"I am failing my husband, Father," she whispered to him one night. "I try to be dutiful and obedient, but it is not enough. He finds me ever insolent."

"I have never known you be insolent, my child," Warinus replied. "No doubt the King has much on his mind which makes him less patient."

"Perhaps, Father." Shame prevented her from telling him how Lothair had struck her. "But I feel I should do more to please him."

"Continue to show him your love and respect. In time he will appreciate it."

Adelheid's eyes filled with tears. "I do not love him, Father. I know what a sin that is, but my heart will not be moved."

Warinus took her hand, the smile on his face remaining sympathetic. "Show him respect and affection. Perhaps in time the love will grow, although it not an emotion which can be forced."

"I shall try, Father."

He laid his hand on her head in blessing. "My child, your path is not an easy one, but your love for God will guide you through your troubles."

"I hope so, Father."

"It is your duty to serve your husband, but remember he is but a man. If he is dissatisfied with the marriage, he must remember that he too is a sinner. I have known you since you were a child and I have always considered your faults to be far fewer than most. The responsibility for contentment in the marriage lies with you both."

Although she had never been particularly happy in Italy as a child, she had none the less grown to love the country. Pavia was a fine city which Hugh had helped rebuild after Magyar raids had all but destroyed it. As they rode through the city gates, Adelheid managed to feel a little happier. This was journey's end and it was a fine one.

Of all the buildings in Pavia, the finest was the royal palace. People swarmed from the doorway to greet them and urge refreshment upon them, before she was conducted to the royal bedchamber.

"I trust you will be comfortable here," Lothair said, his tone kinder towards her than she had yet heard.

"I feel sure I will be, my lord," she replied. "I had forgotten how fine your residence is."

Lothair looked pleased. "It is indeed. Adelheid, I consider your manner much improved. You must not feel the need to be formal with me when we are alone. Please use my name."

Adelheid summoned up the courage to meet his eyes, suddenly hopeful they could become more comfortable together. She smiled shyly. "Thank you. I shall strive ever to please you."

Lothair folded his arms. "Make sure you do. The Margrave of Ivrea is on his way to join us. Dress finely for tonight. We shall have a grand feast to celebrate our nuptial."

The Margrave of Ivrea. Berengar. Adelheid's heart sank. She had loathed him even more than she had hated Hugh. And no doubt his avaricious wife, Willa would be with him. But she murmured her assurances to Lothair and he managed a curt smile, as he left her alone.

∞∞∞

Adelheid dressed as finely as she had been instructed in a blue dress, edged in bands of scarlet silk and fastened jewels around her wrist and throat. A blue mantle completely covered her fair hair, but it served only to enhance the intense colour of her eyes. When Lothair arrived so they might enter the hall together, he looked her up and down, nodding approvingly.

"Your appearance is very pleasing."

"Thank you, although I fear I am not as fine as you."

Lothair was magnificently dressed in a green tunic edged in jewels, the iron crown of the Lombard's gleaming against his dark hair. He stretched out a hand to her and for once she took it willingly, pleased to be on better terms with him. The warmth of his hand felt reassuring as she prepared to enter the hall for the first time as Queen of Italy.

Everyone rose to their feet as they entered, bowing as they passed. Adelheid caught many murmured comments on her beauty and Lothair's dark good looks. Her spirits rose as she was suddenly sure she would make a success of her new role as Lothair's wife and queen.

However they plummeted again as she saw the people sat near the head of the table. They had not yet risen, but did so slowly as they drew near. Alone of everyone in the hall, these three did not bow. Adelheid's spirits crashed to new depths, as she realised that not only had Willa accompanied Berengar, so had their over indulged son, Adalbert.

"Greetings, my Lady Queen," Berengar said, nodding his head, in the merest sketch of a bow. "Welcome to Pavia."

Adelheid smiled the most gracious smile she could manage. "Thank you, my lord. I am glad to see you again." She turned her smile to Willa. "And you too, my lady."

"Indeed," Willa replied. "You have grown much since we last saw you. I do not doubt you are missing your mother. Naturally I shall be happy to take on that role, should you need it." She was smiling, showing most of her teeth. Adelheid could not imagine anyone less like her mother.

It took a moment or two for the meaning of her words to sink in. "Do you intend to remain in residence with us at Pavia?" she asked.

"Of course, my lady," Berengar replied. "I am always in residence with the King."

"The Margrave is of the greatest assistance to me," Lothair added tersely. "I am sure you will find the Margravine to be similarly valuable."

Willa's smile widened. "Of course I will."

Adelheid stared at them, despising Lothair for how he had turned against his father to help this man into such influence. She had heard much of how Berengar controlled all, but never had she realised how bad it had become.

Chapter seven

"You have indeed grown, my Lady Queen," Adalbert said, looking her up and down.

Adelheid shrank closer to Lothair, not liking the gleam in Adalbert's eyes. When she had previously lived in Italy, her pretty face had been much admired, but in the few years she had been away, her figure too had blossomed. As his eyes swept over her, Adelheid regretted fastening her girdle so tightly. Reluctantly she extended her hand for him to kiss, having to fight the urge to pull it away as his lips lingered far longer than necessary against her skin.

"You remember my old friend, Adalbert, do you not?" Lothair asked, embracing the other man.

Adelheid pressed her lips angrily together. It was a fine husband who had done nothing to protect her from such obvious lechery. The affection she thought might be growing for Lothair, waned rapidly. In that moment she realised how she would have to depend only on herself.

"I think it is time we dined," Willa announced.

Adelheid raised her eyebrows. It was hardly the Margravine's place to make such an announcement. She gave another gracious smile. "Indeed, I approve your suggestion," she said. "Please take your places, my lords."

A faint frown marked Willa's face at Adelheid's regal manner. Determined to press home her advantage, Adelheid looked at the man in episcopal robes, who was clearly waiting to say prayers.

"My chaplain will say prayers this night," she said, gesturing to Father Warinus.

"The Bishop always says the prayers whenever he is present," Willa replied. "You have much to learn of our ways, my Lady Queen. Be guided by me."

"I shall be most grateful for your suggestions, but naturally I shall make some changes."

Before Willa could reply, Lothair leaned forward. "Adelheid, I am sure your chaplain is wearied after the ride here. Allow him to take his place at the table." He nodded at the Bishop. "Father, we will be glad for you to say prayers."

Adelheid flushed in humiliation, furious with Lothair for not supporting her. It was no wonder Berengar controlled all, when he showed so little resistance in even a trivial matter.

$\infty \infty \infty$

The next day Adelheid knelt in the Basilica of Saint Michele, so Bishop Litifredo could crown her as Queen of Italy. Although she gave no outward sign, she was struggling to hold back her tears as she looked up at the bishop intoning the blessing. This was a sacred rite, but with Berengar and Willa controlling both the realm and the court, the ceremony was a mockery.

"I do not know what to do, Father?" Adelheid whispered to Father Warinus a few days later, as it became obvious she would have no say in even the most basic of household affairs.

"Matters are bad," Warinus replied. "I can see that."

"I am queen merely in name," Adelheid said. "Just as Lothair is king merely in name. He does nothing to challenge it."

"He has lived with this situation for some years now. Perhaps the King does not even realise how bad it appears to your fresh eyes. Or perhaps he does not care."

"I suspect he does not care." Adelheid could not keep the bitterness from her voice. Since their arrival in Pavia he had spent most of his days hunting and drinking with Adalbert.

"It is not appropriate to criticize your lord and husband, my daughter."

"I know. Forgive me, Father. I endeavour always to show him respect. But my heart cannot help wishing he would do more."

"Perhaps once you have given him a son, matters will change. Becoming a father will force him to become a man. And as a man he will feel the humiliation and long to rule so he may bestow honour on his son."

"I pray that happens, Father." Adelheid longed desperately for a child, so that he would no longer share her bed. Since their arrival in Pavia he had inflicted no further violence on her, although he remained impatient. "But such an event could be a long while off. Even if I were to conceive this night and all goes well, it will be almost a year before such a child is born. And it might not be a son."

"I know, my child. But you can do nothing on that. Such matters are in God's hands. What do you want to do now? It is clear the King will not assist you."

"I know. What I want is to have never been wed," Adelheid said, tears filling her eyes. "I want to serve God."

Warinus took her hands. "Oh, Adelheid, it is a tough burden to be unable to follow the path you believe is intended for you. I pray you become reconciled with your life here. But, my daughter, is there any reason why you cannot serve God as a queen?"

∞∞∞

Adelheid followed the priest's advice. She stopped trying to assert herself at the court. Instead of appearing for their evening meals dressed regally and dripping with jewels, she instead opted for fine, but plain garments with only simple jewellery adorning her wrists and throat and the golden diadem on her head. On the first evening she appeared in such fashion, Willa looked at her suspiciously, but said nothing, while Lothair, if he noticed, was too busy laughing over a drink with Adalbert to comment.

The following day, accompanied only by Father Warinus, she began a visit of the churches of Pavia. Many of these were humble institutions, overwhelmed to receive a visit from the Queen, but once they saw the warm garments and food she had brought to dispense to the needy, the priests welcomed her eagerly. Admiration for her grew in these lowly parts of the city, as she listened to what was needed with no hint of arrogance in her bearing.

She returned to the palace, her heart lighter than it had been for a long time.

"You see how well suited I am for God's service?" She looked up at the columned façade of the palace, dreading entering the building. "I should have been permitted to enter an abbey."

"But, my daughter, an abbey should not be an easy path. I think it is because it would be so easy for you, that God requires you to take a more testing route."

Adelheid came to an abrupt halt, her face lighting up. "You are right, Father. I have never seen it that way before. If I can retain my faith even in such a loathsome life, I shall truly earn my salvation."

With her head high she entered the palace, now welcoming the challenges it presented. Over the next weeks she made no comment on her charitable endeavours and her visits to such humble parts of the city went unnoticed. She continued them daily, her popularity in those areas growing stronger by the day. Among the poor, the sight of the beautiful young queen, accompanied only by her priest became a familiar sight and they adored her. Even in dangerous areas, where thieves abounded, she went unmolested.

After some weeks of this, her confidence soared to the point where she felt ready to make her move at court. As Bishop Litifredo finished the prayers one night, instead of starting to dine, Adelheid got to her feet.

"Father, I thank you most humbly for your service. We are fortunate indeed to be able to listen to the words of so wise a man as yourself."

The Bishop looked startled, but nodded courteously. "Thank you, my Lady Queen. It is an honour."

"I beg you accept this gift from the King and myself as a small token of our very deep gratitude." Knowing of the Bishop's love for fine things, Adelheid had embroidered an elaborate altar cloth in silken threads on fine linen. Out of the corner of her eye she could see Lothair's puzzlement at being included in her speech.

The Bishop was delighted. "My lady, this is a very fine token indeed. It shall adorn the high altar in the basilica." He held up the cloth, so the golden threads glinted in the torchlight. There was a murmur of appreciation from the court. "My Lord King, I thank you for this gift. How fortunate for Italy that you married such a queen."

As Adelheid had hoped, Lothair's puzzlement turned to pride. With a flicker of contempt, which she swiftly quashed, she reflected how quickly he had accepted credit for the gift. She nodded gravely at the Bishop. "I am honoured you consider my poor efforts worthy of such a place, Father."

"That is very fine, Adelheid," Willa said, her voice sharp. "I do not know how you find the time for such endeavours, when you seem to be absent from court most days. Tell me, my dear, where do you go each day?"

"I make some small steps towards easing the lives of those unfortunates of the city. It is a small matter, which would seem paltry indeed compared to the fine works of such esteemed men as Father Litifredo." Adelheid smiled calmly at the assembled court. "Forgive me. I did not mean to delay our meal this night. Let us dine."

As they ate Lothair immediately turned his attention to Adalbert, while Berengar spoke to the envoy who had arrived that day from the Pope. But Willa watched Adelheid out of narrowed eyes as she talked quietly with the Bishop. As

Adelheid had hoped, the man was intrigued by words and eager to hear more.

Chapter eight

A ided by the Bishop, Adelheid's charities increased. For the first time she began to enjoy her life in Italy and her popularity in Pavia grew even greater. When she rode through the streets, the cheers were deafening, as the people showed their adoration for the young queen.

"Your wife is eclipsing you in popularity, my boy," Berengar said to Lothair one day as they returned to the palace. "It seems they see nobody but her."

Adelheid looked down, as Lothair frowned at her. "I agree," he said. "It is most inappropriate."

"I do not crave their attention, my lord," she said. "Please tell me what I should do to stop them cheering me. I do not wish to displease you."

"Perhaps you should stop visiting the poor so often," Lothair snapped, obviously squirming under Berengar's eyes.

"You wish the Queen to curtail her pious charities?" The Bishop sounded shocked and Adelheid kept her eyes lowered to hide her satisfaction. "My lord, I must protest this."

"Well, I require her more at court."

Adelheid looked up. "What do you wish me to do at court, my lord? Dear Willa handles matters so well there for me, I fear I would grow idle."

"I don't care," Lothair said, growing ever more flustered under the reproving glare of both the Bishop and Berengar.

"My lord, I fear it would reflect very badly on you if the Queen's endeavours were stopped. She makes plain everywhere she goes, that she does these duties on behalf of you both. The people are so grateful for your largesse."

"Mine?" Lothair's mouth dropped open.

Adelheid nodded. "Naturally, my lord. I ensure the people understand I can only dispense such charity because of your great generosity and regard for your people."

Berengar and Willa visibly ground their teeth, as Lothair stared at his wife, obviously suspecting her of mockery. But Adelheid met his eyes respectfully.

"I see. Perhaps you should continue," Lothair said.

Adelheid lowered her eyes, murmuring her thanks, while the Bishop took his hands. "Thank you, my lord. Such generosity will most certainly help secure your salvation."

∞∞∞

Lothair did not mention the matter again, even on occasions basking in Adelheid's popularity. She hated implying to the people that it was Lothair generosity she was dispensing, when she knew he cared only for wine and lazy days with Adalbert, but boosting his popularity was essential. Only then would he find the strength to force Berengar from power.

Her status rose too at court, as the nobles showed her increased respect. Willa was furious as they sought Adelheid's favour rather than her own.

"I am sure it is very fine for you to have such freedom, while I have to deal with the management of the household," she snapped.

"My dear Willa," Adelheid replied, taking hold of her hands. "I had no idea you were finding it so hard. Please forgive me. I shall be happy to take over the running of the household."

Willa scowled. "I am not finding it hard."

"There is no shame in this, Willa." Adelheid's voice was full of concern. "Of course I can take over. Indeed, as I am the queen, it would be most fitting."

The two women stared at each other, Willa's eyes narrowed, Adelheid's steady and clear. Willa's eyes dropped first. "I do not care to annoy the Bishop, my dear. He has made it plain how valuable you are to him."

"Of course," Adelheid replied. "But I must not fail in my duties here if I am needed. I would be ashamed to take advantage of your willing nature. Please, Willa, do not exhaust yourself."

Afterwards she went down on her knees to beg God's forgiveness for such a deception.

"Compassion should be a true emotion," she whispered. "I am the most terrible of sinners to pretend it."

"I do not think God will judge you harshly, my child," Warinus said. "It will be better for this land and indeed for your husband if their power is reduced."

However Willa need not have feared. Their grip on power continued as strongly as ever. Adelheid's efforts had boosted Lothair's popularity, but he showed no desire to oust Berengar and as the spring came, the situation in Pavia remained unchanged.

It was news from Germany which brought matters to a head. An envoy from the court of King Otto dined with them, bearing news from that realm.

"The King is to formally announce his son, Lord Liudolf of Saxony as his intended heir. The nobility of Germany will have to agree, but I do not think there will be any detractors. Naturally Saxony will oblige and Franconia too has long been in the King's possession. No nobles there will oppose the King."

"Of course Swabia will also support him, will it not?" Adelheid said. "Lord Liudolf is wed to my kinswoman, Lady Ida of Swabia."

"Naturally, my Lady Queen." The envoy turned away from

Berengar, seeming pleased to discuss the matter with her. "Lord Liudolf is well known to be as a son to Duke Hermann."

"What of Lotharingia?" Berengar asked, pulling the attention back to him. "They have never supported the Saxon upstarts."

The envoy frowned. "Duke Conrad of Lotharingia is a brother to Lord Liudolf through his marriage to Lady Liutgarde of Saxony, daughter of King Otto. He has long been a firm supporter of the King."

"I suppose that just leaves Bavaria," Berengar said. "I do not suppose that fool, Duke Berthold, will put up any opposition."

The disgust of the envoy became more obvious. "The noble Duke Berthold died some months ago. King Otto is intending to enfeoff his brother, Lord Henry of Saxony there."

Berengar scowled. "Otto has Germany quite under his thumb, it seems."

"The rule of King Otto sounds wise indeed," Adelheid said with a smile. "How fine it must be to enjoy such harmony in his realm."

The envoy brightened at her praise. "It was not always so harmonious, but King Otto's wisdom has prevailed. He hopes Italy will send a representative to the ceremony to invest his brother as Duke of Bavaria as well as the elevation of his son. Can I assure him you will, my Lord King?"

Lothair glanced up from his talk, giving a vague nod. "Of course."

"Most certainly you can assure the noble King Otto representatives from Italy will be there," Berengar said. "I shall give the matter some thought and appoint someone suitable."

The envoy sent a shocked glance at Lothair and Adelheid could only imagine what reports he would take back to his powerful king. She was not certain what she made of the German king. This was, after all, a man who thought nothing of flaunting his bastard son at court, even expecting his legitimate son to consider him his brother. But at least he ruled his own realm. If King Otto turned his attentions to Italy, there would be little to stand in his way.

Adelheid took a deep breath and laid her hand on Lothair's arm. "My lord, I am sure you have some thoughts on a suitable man to witness such august events."

There was a tense silence at the top of the table. Lothair's mouth dropped open at Adelheid's actions and he looked swiftly from her to Berengar. Eventually he gave a hearty laugh. "My dear Adelheid, I am sure my good friend Berengar has the matter well in hand."

"Indeed I do," Berengar replied with an icy glance in Adelheid's direction.

Berengar had directed a charming smile at the envoy, but Adelheid was certain it was not possible for the man to appear any more disgusted. Her own face had flushed crimson in shame at Lothair not even pretending to rule the land.

Awkwardly the envoy smiled at her. "I shall inform King Otto of your interest, my Lady Queen. I am sure he will be most grateful."

Chapter nine

"**A**delheid, your actions this night were unacceptable. Keep your concerns to your charities and do not meddle in matters which do not concern you."

Adelheid shivered, pulling her robe tighter around her. She had awaited Lothair's arrival in her chamber with dread. "But, my lord…"

The blow she had been expecting stung her ear, but she had endured worse. "The envoy from King Otto was horrified at your boldness."

In her mind Adelheid muttered a prayer, knowing how she was going to anger her husband. "No, Lothair. He was disgusted by the way Berengar controls all. He wished to discuss the matter with the King. With you."

His fist shot out, causing Adelheid to scramble backwards, ducking her head to avoid it hitting her eye. "I said, do not meddle," he screeched.

"Please, Lothair. I am begging you to listen to me." She backed up against the wall, knowing his next blow would hit her. There was nowhere she could escape to. "Berengar is not popular. If you assert yourself, you could take power. You could be a great king, like King Otto of Germany."

"Otto?" Lothair scoffed. "Do I have to remind you of how Otto's actions cost me the throne of Burgundy?"

Adelheid was bewildered by the change of topic, but as he had not hit her, she lowered her arms. "Truly it was right

Konrad inherited."

She heard the sound of the slap against her face before the pain shot through her body. "Be silent. You understand nothing of such matters."

"I understand more than you think," she cried, as the blows stopped. Her cheeks stung as she summoned up the last remnants of her courage. "Perhaps King Otto's actions did cost you the throne of Burgundy, but it is your own which are costing you the throne of Italy. You do nothing but drink with Adalbert, while Berengar rules in your place. It makes me ashamed to be your queen. Lothair, you do not have to be so weak. Together we could take a stand against him."

For a long time Lothair stared at her, giving her a brief hope he would listen to her words. "Have you finished?" he asked.

Nervously she nodded.

The first blow caught her lip, sending a salty taste into her mouth, while red drops fell to her robe. The second to her stomach caused her to double up in pain. She cried out both from the agony and the ferocious expression on his face. Her mind scrambled for prayers as it appeared almost as if he wished to kill her. "I told you once I would beat the insolence out of you, Adelheid. You should have listened to me."

He seized a handful of her hair, yanking her head back to where it cracked against the wall. There was an instant of merciful blackness which gave way to a ringing in her ears as the pain tore again through her body. In her daze she lost count of the slaps against her cheeks, not even realising when they had stopped.

"Do you now understand your position?" he demanded.

It took a moment for her terrified mind to register he had spoken, causing Lothair's face to suffuse with crimson. Seizing her by the shoulders he forced her back against the wall.

"I said, do you understand?"

Her lip was so swollen, it was hard to speak. "Yes, my lord," she whispered.

"Good." He picked her up and flung her on the bed, looking

down at her contemptuously. "I suggest you remain there a few days, Adelheid." His tone was calm. "You cannot face the court in such a fashion. I shall tell everyone you have been taken ill. Spend that time reflecting on your manner towards me."

He strode to the door, banging it hard behind him. Adelheid lay still, not even moving to pull any covers over herself. Her body shook violently as one by one the candles flickered and died, leaving her in blackness.

∞ ∞ ∞

It was the shocked whispers of her women that drew her from her stupor the next morning.

"I fell," she whispered.

The two women exchanged glances. "We know, my lady," Orsa, the elder of the two said. "The King informed us."

The other, a girl named Gilia, was holding a basin of water. "Let us bathe your wounds, my lady."

The woman was gentle and the cloth was soft, but nonetheless each touch stung as sharply as if it were stuffed with needles. Adelheid lay motionless, enduring the agony patiently until she was done.

"It is not so bad, my lady," Orsa said, trying to smile. "A few days and your beautiful face will be restored."

Adelheid reached out a stiff arm to pick up a mirror. It showed a chalk white face smudged in black bruises. Swollen lips added a crimson slash in the only colour other than the tear filled blue eyes. Wearily she lay the mirror down and closed her eyes.

"Take some food and ale, my lady," Orsa begged, tucking a blanket around her.

"Leave me alone now."

"At least some ale."

But Adelheid did not move. The soft sound of the door

closing as the two women followed her instructions made her open her eyes again. The jug of ale and a platter of honeyed cakes lay on a nearby table, but her stomach turned at the thought of them. She pulled the covers over her aching body and allowed the blackness to take her once again.

∞∞∞

She awoke with a start sometime later to find Father Warinus sitting by her bed. She sat up, sending sharp slices of pain throughout her body.

"I fell, Father," she said quickly.

The priest shook his head sadly. "Oh, Adelheid, my poor child."

The tears she had been holding back, trickled out at last. "You are right, Father. I should not tell such a lie. I angered my husband. I did not show him the proper respect. I was insolent and disobedient and he was right to chastise me. I am the worst of sinners. Perhaps you too now hold me in contempt."

Again the priest shook his head, taking hold of her hands. "My child, we spoke some time ago as to why you had been placed on this path and how in following such a hard path, you might find God's salvation."

"Yes, Father. Are you telling me now how I am failing on this path?"

"No, my child. You did not ask me whether I had found my path hard."

"Do you, Father? You appear most contented on it. I know you chose to renounce women. Was that a hard burden for you to bear?"

"Perhaps, in the beginning," Warinus replied. "But soon I found I did not miss carnal desires. Over time it was not the absence of a wife I found hard. It was the absence of a child. For many years I would baptise the newborns of other men, concealing the regret I would never see my own offspring."

"I did not know that."

"No, it was my private burden and I accepted it as God's challenge. Then I was appointed to serve your stepfather and I met you. And you, Adelheid, became as a daughter to me. I thought it would ease my burden but instead it is now many times worse."

"Because it is not acceptable for you to love any as your child?"

"There is no shame in that. But it is my sacred duty to love the sinner. To forgive men for their transgressions. To hold all men in love and compassion. But you are the child of my heart and I hate the man who did that to you. Even if he were here on his knees, begging for forgiveness, I do not think I could grant it."

"Oh, Father." Adelheid wiped at her tears. "You must not think like that. I am a terrible sinner. My husband has the right to guide me."

"I have never known you be insolent, my child. You have shown your husband greater respect than he deserves. He should cherish you, but instead… Yes, I know I should not cast such judgement upon him, but I do. May God forgive me, I hate him as I have hated no man."

"I do not know what to do, Father," Adelheid whispered. "How can I endure this life?"

"Do not look too far ahead, my child. For now let your body heal. Your women said you will not eat or drink. Come, you must. Perhaps it is hard, but it will help."

Obediently Adelheid sipped at the cup he held out. The cut in her lip stung, but he was right. The cool liquid did give her strength. Resolutely she took a bite from a cake and then another. She looked up at the lined, worried face of the priest, gaining comfort from the affection in his eyes. However hard she found this path, at least she was not alone.

Chapter ten

"It is good to see you, my dear. I trust you are quite recovered." Willa's smile at Adelheid when she at last left the seclusion of her chamber left her in no doubt that she knew exactly why Adelheid had absented herself.

Adelheid smiled calmly back. Over the last days she had made many decisions and one was to no longer fight the situation at court. "Thank you, Willa. I am much recovered."

Lothair made no comment on either her manners or his own actions. Certainly if she had hoped for an apology, she was disappointed.

"I assume you are well enough to receive me," he said as he arrived in the bedchamber that night.

"Of course, my lord." She kept her face expressionless, knowing how he was angered by her reluctance, but unable to make herself show any welcome. Another resolution she had made was to only speak with Lothair to agree with him.

It was a relief when he and Berengar departed to attend to some matters in Milan. Despite the continued presence of Willa and Adalbert, who took it upon himself to preside over the court in Lothair absence, Adelheid felt as if a weight had been lifted from her. She continued to dispense charity to the poor, allowing herself to be warmed by the cheers of the humble people, but the task no longer brought her the joy it had once done.

With the court much scaled down in the absence of the King, Adelheid took to retiring early to spend her evenings in the church or alone in her chamber.

It was on one such night that Lothair returned. He did not hasten to his wife, but drank late into the night with Adalbert, bursting into the bedchamber, his face flushed, long after Adelheid was asleep.

"Wake up." He seized her roughly.

Still half asleep, Adelheid forgot her resolve to be obedient. "Leave me alone. I am tired."

Lothair frowned, pulling her upright. "Do not talk to me like that, Adelheid. It is your duty to receive me."

"I have done my duty," Adelheid bit back. "I am with child."

Lothair's mouth dropped open and he relaxed his grip as he stared at her, wonder lighting up his face. "With child? Adelheid, this is the most wonderful news."

It was Adelheid's turn to feel shocked, touched by the joy in his expression. She nodded. He slipped an arm gently around her and just as gently pressed his lips against her forehead. "When will it come?"

A sudden burst of affection flared in Adelheid's heart. "Towards the end of the year, I think, if all is well."

"All must be well." Lothair ran his hand almost reverently over her stomach. "We shall take good care of you. Are you feeling well? Is there anything you need?"

She smiled, letting her head sink against his shoulder, surprised how good it was to know such tenderness from him. "At this moment, only sleep."

Lothair frowned. "I suppose I shall have to seek my pleasures elsewhere?"

The flare of affection flickered uncertainly and died. "Yes, you shall."

Lothair stood pettishly up. "I expect a son, Adelheid. I trust you will pray for that."

∞∞∞

"The Queen is with child," Lothair announced proudly at the meal the next night.

Willa's face froze and she exchanged a swift glance with Berengar before managing a beaming smile. "How wonderful, Adelheid. I cannot believe you have said nothing to me these last weeks, even when I commented on how pale you were."

Adelheid smiled calmly, feeling more secure. Now she knew how Lothair longed for a child, she was certain he would do nothing to harm her. She reached for his hand. "Naturally I wished my husband to be the first to know."

"We shall all pray for your good health, my dear Adelheid," Berengar said, but his smile was forced.

Lothair's own smile rapidly lost some of the shine from when he had made his announcement. To Adelheid's satisfaction she realised the child was already opening his eyes to the situation at court. She looked around, her eyes meeting those of Father Warinus. In spite of her words to Willa, the priest had been the one to first hear her news. He nodded, murmuring his own pleasure at the news, but Adelheid could see that he too was pleased with how matters were changing.

∞ ∞ ∞

However it was news of a death which hastened the change. Adelheid's pregnancy was going well. She delighted as her body swelled and a few faint flutters stirred inside her. Lothair's manner remained courteous. For the most part she only saw him at meal times or at prayers, where he never failed to enquire to her health, although their conversation rarely went beyond it. To her disgust, she learnt he was spending his nights with other women, but she realised it was no better than she had expected from Hugh's son.

One evening as they dined, a messenger was ushered in. He knelt before Lothair. "Greetings, my Lord King. I bring a message from Arles."

Berengar snorted. "Oh, what does the great King Hugh want now?"

The messenger remained down on his knees. "I bear a message from Queen Bertha. She begs to inform you that her husband, your father, the noble King Hugh of Italy has died and was buried this day. May God have mercy upon his soul."

There was silence. "It is of no loss," Berengar muttered.

Lothair looked stunned. "Then I am truly the king."

Adelheid kept her face expressionless, but the attitude of everyone repulsed her. She had not liked Hugh, but never would she celebrate his death. As the messenger was taken to refresh himself, Adelheid followed him, eager to learn how her mother was. But when she returned to the head of the table, she found only Willa and Adalbert had remained.

"My father and Lothair have much to discuss now," Adalbert said.

"Of course." Adelheid inclined her head. "Perhaps you will excuse me. King Hugh was my father twice over. This news is disturbing."

She did not wait for a reaction, before leaving the table. Feeling genuinely unsettled, she made her way to the church, thinking somebody should say prayers for Hugh's soul. After all, he needed them more than most.

But when she arrived in the church, she found she was not alone in wanting to say some prayers. Lothair was kneeling before the altar, his head bowed. Adelheid stared at him, shocked he was there. Never had she seen him so intent on his devotions and she realised his father's death had after all affected him.

For a moment she was tempted to leave him to it, but in spite of everything that had gone between them, she was overwhelmed by pity. Tears filled her eyes as she realised how it was now too late for him to ever reconcile with his father. She went softly forward and knelt beside him.

He glanced sharply at her, looking embarrassed to be caught there. "I thought to say some prayers. He was my father."

"Do you wish to be alone?" Adelheid asked, the pity increasing as she saw the bleak look in his eyes.

Lothair shook his head. "No, I do not think I do."

Gently Adelheid smiled. "Then I will stay."

The two knelt in silence for a while. "Fathers and sons should not fight," Lothair said at last. "I pray I never fight with our son. Perhaps I did wrong in supporting Berengar."

Inwardly Adelheid cheered that statement. "Such quarrels are never good, but the reasons are complex. I know your father did not always treat you as kindly as a father should treat his son."

"No," Lothair said, gazing up at the crucifix.

There was silence again before Adelheid plucked up the courage to say the words she had so wanted to say. "You do not need to keep supporting Berengar. You are the king."

"I know. Perhaps..." Lothair shook his head. "A woman knows nothing of such matters. Go to your rest, Adelheid. Bear me a son."

In spite of his words, Adelheid felt hopeful. "These matters lie in God's hands, but I hope I will. I shall remember your father in my prayers."

She paused at the door, looking back to where he had bowed his head once again. Tears stung her eyes. Matters would be so different between them if only they had always been able to speak like that, but she did not know how to forget the pain he had caused. She slipped out of the door, thinking perhaps one day, even if she could not forget, she would at least forgive.

She walked slowly along the corridor, her gait ungainly with the extra weight she now bore. The couple standing in the shadows of the hall did not notice her and she froze, realising it was Berengar and Willa.

"This news changes matters, Willa. You heard him. He sees himself now as a true king."

"And she is with child. If it is a boy..." Willa's voice trailed away.

"It must not be a boy," Berengar said.

Chapter eleven

"Of course I will attend to you when you give birth, Adelheid," Willa said, taking her hand in what appeared to be an affectionate manner. "You should have someone who cares for you at such a time."

"You are too kind," Adelheid stammered. "But I cannot put you to such trouble. My women will care for me."

"It is no trouble, my dear. I shall be there."

Adelheid's heart thudded. She had never forgotten those sinister words she had heard a few months previously. "Lothair, tell Willa she does not need to trouble herself."

Lothair barely looked up. He seemed to have been in a stupor since his father died, no longer even drinking and wenching with Adalbert. "Such matters do not concern me. Willa has birthed several children of her own. I am sure she knows what should be done."

As always she turned to the one man who listened to her. "Father, I have tried to attach some other meaning to her words, but I am so afraid of what she will do if she attends the birth."

"Murder is a heinous sin. Do you really think she would blacken her soul in such a way?" Warinus asked.

"Is it still murder if the child does not even draw breath? Oh, Father, I know not. All I know is I am so afraid for her to be the first to handle my child."

Warinus frowned. "I do not want to believe your fears, but a mother's protective instinct is a powerful one. Do you think you can conceal your confinement from her?"

"If I did not tell her when the birth starts and I do not draw attention by crying out..." Adelheid's voice trailed off.

Warinus took her hand. "My poor child, it is a tough burden to not even be able to cry out with the agony of birth."

"Oh, Father, I am so afraid. And if I give birth with no one to attend me, the child could easily die anyway."

"Of course you must have someone with you. Your women, Gilia and Orsa are devoted to you. Let them attend you. I shall speak to them, impressing upon them the need to say nothing."

Adelheid nodded, remembering how in the days after Lothair had so savagely punished her, they had indeed shown a genuine devotion. She breathed a sigh of relief that there were still some people she could still trust.

"If the Margravine does find a way to be present, ensure one of those two are at her side throughout."

She smiled gratefully at him, thinking for probably the thousandth time since she had arrived in Italy, how fortunate she was to be able to rely on the priest's wisdom.

∞∞∞

The pains struck when she was alone in the dark of the night, still some hours before dawn. Initially they were mild and she remained in bed, her mind running over the day. To her relief she remembered how Willa had promised to help the Bishop prepare the Basilica of Saint Michele for the feast day of Saint Syros. If only she could conceal her pains until she left, she might be able to give birth without her realising.

By the time she rose from her bed, the pains were increasing. But none the less, Adelheid managed to dress and calmly make her way to the palace church. She told no one that the birth was imminent, not even Lothair when he made his usual brief enquiry to her health. Only as the church emptied did she confide in Father Warinus.

"Remain here for now, my child," he said. "The Margravine will soon depart."

Adelheid nodded her agreement. It was not unusual for her to spend time in the church in prayer or repairing the fine cloths. Covering her lap in such a cloth she sat, praying the waters would not break or that she give any other sign her labour had begun. But as the severity of the pain increased, she was unable to help the odd gasp.

Warinus came over to her, taking her by the hand. "Courage, my child."

He was still beside her when Willa swept into the church. She looked surprised to see them together in such a familiar fashion. "Adelheid? Is all well?"

Adelheid managed a calm smile. "I was discussing with the Father whether I should change this design to cover the stain. With Christmas tide so close upon us, I wish the church to look its finest."

Willa lost interest. "Father, where are the cloths I am to take to the Bishop?"

"I shall fetch them, my lady." He nodded in a friendly fashion to Adelheid. "Make such changes as you think appropriate, my Lady Queen. Your cloths are always most fine."

As he moved away, Adelheid struggled to keep her composure with Willa standing so close.

"Is all well, Adelheid? You look a trifle pale."

"I feel a little tired. It is hard to sleep comfortably at present."

"Indeed. Well, I am sure it will not be much longer now."

Adelheid did not answer. To her horror she could feel another pain building. With Willa's eyes boring into her, she did not know how she would conceal it. At that moment came a clatter from the altar, followed by an exclamation of annoyance.

Willa turned sharply. "Really, Father, how can you be so careless?"

Although she had screwed up her eyes in pain, Adelheid

could see the finely wrought candlesticks rolling on the stone floor.

"Forgive me, my lady," Warinus said. "I am truly a clumsy fool. Thank you, most kindly for your assistance. Here are the cloths for the Bishop."

As Willa looked back at Adelheid, the pain was subsiding and her expression tranquil once again.

"Well, I must be away. But really, Adelheid, do not be a fool and sit here all day if you are tired."

"You are right. Perhaps I will rest myself this afternoon. Please pass my greetings to the Bishop."

Willa nodded curtly, gesturing to Warinus to carry the cloths out for her.

"She has gone," he said, as he returned. "Come, I shall help you to your chamber. You will be in my prayers this day."

∞ ∞ ∞

The word in the palace was simply that the Queen was resting and the mood was excited, as many suspected the birth would be likely in the next few days. In her chamber, Adelheid paced around, grateful to the two women who were with her. The heavy scent of the oils they were rubbing into her body filled the space, the odour clogging up her nostrils as she tried to avoid making a sound.

As the pains increased, she took to muffling her voice in a pillow, determined no word would be sent to Willa, encouraging her swiftly back. She had no idea how much time was passing. All she was aware of was each pain sweeping through her more severely than the last, before again releasing her body from the agony.

"Not much longer, my lady," Gilia murmured, holding a cup of wine to wet her dry lips. "Praise God it is happening so quickly."

It did not feel quick to Adelheid. She was certain she had

been in pain for ever and there seemed no end to it. She clung onto Gilia, pushing with all her might.

"Nearly there," Orsa cried.

Again she bit into the pillow, not certain how she could bear it and then came a strange feeling. Orsa cried out in delight and Adelheid raised her face from the pillow to see a baby in her arms.

"A girl, my lady," she said.

The flood of disappointment that she had not born a son, vanished as the infant was put into her arms. The baby was perfect in every way.

Adelheid did nothing but gaze at the baby suckling eagerly at her breast, as the women dealt with the afterbirth and gently sponged the blood from her legs until, with relief, she was helped into bed. She relaxed her body against the pillows, closing her eyes in a swift prayer of thanks that the ordeal was over.

"Inform the King if he has returned," she said to Gilia.

"He will have returned," Gilia said. "Night has fallen."

Adelheid blinked in surprise that the day had already passed. No doubt everyone was gathering in the hall. She began to laugh as she imagined the look on Willa's face when she learnt the baby had arrived without her knowledge.

∞ ∞ ∞

"What use is a girl to me?" Lothair demanded, as he peered down at the baby.

Tears came to Adelheid's eyes. Evidently the days of him enquiring solicitously to her health were over. "She is strong and healthy, Lothair. We are fortunate for this blessing and we are young yet. There will surely be many a child to follow."

"I suppose so." He stretched out a hand, a flicker passing over his face as the baby's hand curled around his fingers.

It was not much of a welcome for their daughter, but it was

something. "What shall we call her?" Adelheid asked.

"Emma," Lothair said.

Adelheid was surprised. She had expected the baby to be named for Lothair's mother, but she did not argue. "A fine name."

Lothair kissed the baby. "For a fine girl. Pray our next one is a boy."

Adelheid breathed a sigh of relief when he left them alone. With her baby snuggled in her arms she lay down, already overwhelmed with love for the little girl. She drifted off to sleep, but woke a little later to the sound of whispered voices outside her room.

"Just as well it is a girl, Willa. What if she had born a son?" It was Berengar's voice.

"How was I to know the little fool would conceal the birth from me?" Willa whispered back.

"Lothair is a fool, but Adelheid is not. We must be careful."

The muffled voices moved away, leaving Adelheid dry mouthed in fear at the words. The baby whimpered and she brought her to her breast, smiling through her tears as she began to suck.

"Oh, my little one. What cruel world have I brought you into?"

But as she lay back against the pillows, a nervous happiness filled her. She had a daughter. No longer did she feel so alone.

Part Two: The Year of Our Lord 950-51

Chapter one

Lothair bashed his cup on the table, ignoring the wine splashing over his sleeve. "Stop telling me how to run matters in my realm, Berengar. I am the king. If I wish to reward Lord Azzo with some lands, who are you to say otherwise?"

Adelheid sent a sympathetic glance to Lothair's vassal, Lord Azzo, guessing how awkward he felt to be at the heart of such a quarrel.

"He has done nothing to earn them," Berengar insisted. "There are others more deserving."

"Lord Azzo has served me well. He is loyal to me as his king." Lothair narrowed his eyes. "Do you consider that a fault?"

"You are a fool," Berengar cried. "You mismanage everything. Stop this foolishness and listen to me, my boy."

Lothair stood, glaring down at Berengar. "I am not your boy, I am your king. I expect you to start showing me some respect."

Over the previous year Lothair had slowly pushed at the restrictions Berengar had placed on him, trying desperately to oust him from the court. Conferring additional power on men loyal only to him, was his latest strategy and one Adelheid applauded. Knowing her help would not be welcomed, Adelheid ignored the disputes and turned her efforts to seizing control of the household from Willa. She had been aided in this by Willa's pregnancy, which had proved to be troublesome, leaving her with little energy. Little by little, Adelheid had edged her way into control. Willa's new daughter was not yet a month old and as she had not yet re-joined the court, Adelheid for once had no rival for her position.

Adalbert got to his feet, standing with his father. The friendship between him and Lothair too had soured. "After all my father has done for you, you should show more gratitude."

"He has done nothing for me." Lothair tossed the remains of his drink at his erstwhile friend. "Everything he has done, he has done for himself. My good friend Azzo shall have those lands and that is the end of the matter."

With no further words Lothair stormed from the hall. Adelheid tried not to look too interested, but the sight of Adalbert with wine dripping down his cheeks was a delightful one. Furiously he wiped at his eyes, cursing Lothair. Keeping the smile from her face, Adelheid handed him a cloth, her thoughts racing. This scene was the most open hostility she had witnessed.

Lothair was still in a temper when he came to their chamber that night. "I want to move the court to Turin," he snapped.

"Of course. How soon do you wish to depart?"

"As soon as possible. And, Adelheid, it will be us only. Berengar and that fool, Adalbert, will not be welcome."

Adelheid lowered her eyes to hide the joy. "Naturally. Willa is not yet well enough to travel in any case. I shall start making the arrangements in the morn."

"Good." The temper eased out of Lothair's face. More to himself than her, he muttered, "I need to muster my support. Berengar has enjoyed his influence too long."

"Why not ask for help from my brother?" she asked.

Lothair looked irritated. "Why would I do that? Your father was once King of Italy. I do not want your brother having any ideas of a claim."

"What of Swabia? The Duke swore he would aid us." Adelheid's expression changed to sadness. A few months before, they had received word of the death of Duke Hermann of Swabia. Although she had only met him a few times, Adelheid had wept as she remembered his wisdom and kindness. It had been a peaceful ending by all reports but her heart ached for her grandmother and Ida, who she guessed would be deeply missing him.

"That Saxon puppy is the Duke now."

"I know, but he too promised me aid. Liudolf is my kinsman by marriage twice over. I feel sure he would help."

"Don't be a fool. Think who his father is. We do not want King Otto's son and heir meddling in Italy."

"But you need allies and…" Adelheid got no further words out before Lothair seized her by the shoulders. He shook her, rage twisting his features.

"Stop prating on about matters you know nothing about. Under no circumstances can the Germans be allowed into Italy. Is that clear? If I find you have gone behind my back…"

"No, Lothair, of course not," Adelheid cried. "I know your wisdom is superior to mine."

He pushed her away so hard she stumbled backwards. "All I require from you is a son. Are you with child yet? Emma is over a year now."

Adelheid shook her head. "I pray to be blessed."

"Make sure you do," Lothair said curtly, starting to disrobe.

Wearily Adelheid got into bed, already dreading the night ahead. He was never gentle with her, but when he was in a temper it was worse than ever. She focused her mind on her daughter. Rather to her surprise Lothair doted on the little girl. When she saw the two together, she was reminded that under the weakness and cruelty, there was good in him, but shivering at the look on his face she found it almost impossible to believe.

The move to Turin could not help but be a positive one. For the first time Adelheid had a completely free hand over her household. Away from Berengar, Lothair too was in a much better humour and although she could never feel truly at ease with him, he was easier to deal with. For the first time in an age, Adelheid dared to believe her marriage could become a happy one.

It was not to be expected that Berengar would easily let his grip slip on power. Despite the men congregating at Lothair's court, power remained firmly in his hand. Adelheid was unsurprised when he too moved to Turin, guessing he would want to keep Lothair under his eye. But with Lothair steadfastly refusing to allow him at court, Berengar was forced to take up residence in his own magnificent household, although he continued to act as if it were he, not Lothair who was king.

Throughout the summer this continued, with foreign envoys and bishops visiting both households, their reactions ranging from bewilderment to amusement at the ludicrous situation. In the autumn Lothair pulled off a triumph when the papal envoy stayed in his household, before returning to Rome without even seeing Berengar. Lothair was jubilant, convinced the balance of power was shifting.

That belief was strengthened as the tone of Berengar's messages changed. No longer did they make demands, but instead brought enquiries to his health and respectful greetings. Eventually Berengar requested a meeting to discuss the division of power. Flushed with triumph, Lothair waited a few days before signalling his acceptance.

He dressed magnificently for the meeting, determined to display his regal bearing in every item he wore. His red tunic was edged in fine silks with a jewelled belt circling his waist. More gems hung around his neck and the Iron Crown of the Lombard's adorned his head.

"You look very handsome, Lothair," Adelheid said, as he took a punctilious leave of her. The admiration in her voice was genuine.

"Thank you. I shall show that fool Berengar how to appear a king, shall I not?"

"You shall indeed." Adelheid smiled. "But remember, there is more to kingship than appearance. Show everyone how you act as a king."

She immediately regretted those words. As they were in public, Lothair did not strike her, but his eyes narrowed and he gripped her hands tightly, his nails pressing into her skin. "I know that, Adelheid."

Managing to avoid wincing in pain, Adelheid maintained her smile. "Of course you do, my lord. Forgive a foolish wife for her anxieties. Be careful. I do not trust Berengar."

Lothair let go of her hands, his eyes meeting hers in a mischievous gleam. "Nor do I, my dear."

Adelheid smiled too, as he bowed and kissed her hand. Lothair could be very charming when he wanted to. She sighed as she watched him leave the hall, his entourage forming around him. When he smiled at her like that, for an instant she would forget all the cruelty, but only for an instant. Tears filled her eyes as she reflected on how different everything could have been. As so often before, she wondered what she should have done to bring more harmony to their marriage.

When Lothair returned at noon a few days later, Adelheid's first impression was one of disgust. He was riding pillion, slumped on the horse. So much for him impressing everyone with his kingliness. He was drunk. She watched as he stumbled towards the doorway. He was very drunk.

"The King is taken ill, my lady," the man supporting him said.

"Indeed," Adelheid replied. "Take him to his chamber, where he can sleep it off."

Lothair raised his head at her voice, his eyes darting wildly around. He stared at her, his pupils tiny black specks in his eyes. "Adelheid," he whispered, his voice almost unrecognisable. "Is that you?"

"Of course it is me," Adelheid replied, bewildered at the question for he was looking directly at her.

Lothair cried out in pain, vomiting suddenly all over the floor. Adelheid jumped back. Never had she seen him in such a state.

"How much did he drink?" she asked the man.

"This last day he has drunk only weak ale, my lady. He complained of an excessive thirst and quenched it often. He took some wine yesterday, but he did not drink more than was reasonable."

"Take him to his chamber," Adelheid said. "Make him comfortable."

She stared after her husband as the man supported him. She knew Lothair had not got himself in that state through drinking weak ale.

Chapter two

As Adelheid entered the chamber, Lothair let out a desperate howl, his voice hitting a note which sent shivers through her spine into her heart. His eyes wide with terror, Lothair struggled to the side of the bed, pointing behind her. She tried to put an arm around him, but he pushed her away, clawing frantically at the blankets.

"The demon!" he screamed. "The demon is coming for me."

Adelheid went white and crossed herself. Terrified of what she might see, she turned to look in the direction he was pointing. But the corner of the chamber simply held a finely carved coffer, just as it always had.

Father Warinus hurried forward, kneeling beside the bed. "My son, this sickness is causing you to imagine such sights. There is no need to fear."

The priest's soothing voice worked and Lothair calmed into slow, juddering breaths, allowing Adelheid to kneel beside him and take hold of his hand. Even holding it lightly, his racing pulse vibrated through her fingers.

"I drank the wine, Adelheid," he mumbled. "Do not drink it."

"Hush, Lothair, you are ill. This is not the effect of the wine." Adelheid forgot the cruelty he had so often shown her and instead gently smoothed his hair, just as she did when meeting the sick of the city. "Rest. I am sure you will recover soon."

Lothair immediately became agitated again. "Do not drink it. Let no one drink it. Throw it away."

"Hush, Lothair. I shall do as you ask."

Lothair slumped back against the pillows, his eyes dropping shut. His doze was an uneasy one, his body twitching but at least he was resting. Adelheid gestured to the priest to leave the chamber.

"He is concerned about the wine," she commented, afraid of the direction her thoughts were drifting.

"He is rambling, my child," Warinus replied. "I do not think he knows what he says."

"I am not so sure. I must speak to someone who was with Lothair at the meeting."

A man was quickly summoned and questioned about the events. "The Margrave of Ivrea presented the King with a fine wine as a gesture of his good will, my lady. The King was most grateful and sampled a cup immediately."

"Did anyone else drink any?" Adelheid asked.

"I am not sure, my lady. The Margrave poured himself a cup, but I do not know how much he drank before it was spilt."

Adelheid stared at him, the scene flashing through her mind. Berengar, all smiles, no doubt cursing his clumsiness as he spilled the wine, so Lothair alone would drink it.

Warinus put a hand on her shoulder. "My child, what do you think?"

"I do not know what to think," she said. "Where is this wine? Did it return with him?"

"Yes, my lady," the man said.

The cask was brought to her and she opened it, admiring the dark red colour. Breathing in deeply, Adelheid inhaled the rich fruity aromas drifting upwards. If such a wine was poured for her, she would be delighted to drink it.

She looked at the man, seeing the suspicion on his own face. "We must test it. Give some to an animal. I am sure we are being foolish."

The dog they selected was an elderly one, which since an accident had occurred to its paw was of little use in hunting. It limped over, sniffing at the bowl of wine. Adelheid found it hard to watch as it lapped it up.

She turned away. "Keep me informed as to the state of the dog," she said and returned to her husband.

Lothair was no better, tossing around in his agitation, mumbling terrified words. When Adelheid held cups of water or weak ale to his lips he gulped at them eagerly, only to vomit them back up again shortly after. All night she sat by his bedside, dozing only intermittently, praying for him to recover. Late the next morning Orsa came to her.

"My lady, one of the men requests your presence in the courtyard."

She already knew what she would see, but even so the sight brought tears to her eyes. The dog was stumbling in a manner which could not be explained by its injured paw. It blundered into a wall, yelping in pain, but seemed to learn nothing as it repeated the action. Slumping to the ground, it coughed, bringing up a mixture of water and mucous before struggling back to its feet. It raised its head, howling at the sky, the noise an eerie echo of Lothair's own cries of terror.

"You were right," Warinus said quietly.

"Lothair was right," Adelheid replied. "He knew what they did to him."

∞∞∞

After the fresh air from the courtyard, the stench of Lothair's chamber was more pungent than ever and the incense they were burning made little difference. Swallowing back the nausea, Adelheid knelt again by his bed, taking his hand. His eyes flicked open, the piteous expression in them driving her own fear and disgust away.

"They are evil, Lothair. They shall not escape their crimes. Once you are recovered we will take action."

"Too late," he mumbled.

"No, Lothair. It is not too late. We are all praying for your recovery."

"Let me see Emma. Please."

Adelheid's eyes filled with tears. She would have preferred to have kept her daughter away from the sick chamber, but she could not refuse Lothair a last glimpse of his only child. She nodded, rising to her feet.

Emma was only two years old, a merry dark haired child. She had on occasions accompanied her mother on visits to the sick, so did not seem unduly upset at the sight of her father. Lothair even managed a smile as she babbled happily to him. The pain in Adelheid's chest grew as she watched them, the love he felt for his daughter so obvious in his expression. As his eyes grew heavy, Adelheid stood up.

She forced a cheerful tone into her voice. "Come, Emma. Father is tired. You can see him again in the morn."

A tear ran from Lothair's eye as he laid a trembling hand on his daughter's head. Desperately keeping control of her own tears, Adelheid returned Emma to her nurse, the lump in her throat almost strangling her.

"She will not even remember him," Adelheid said to Warinus, as she tried to calm herself again before entering the sick chamber. "I barely remember my father and I was four years older when he died."

Lothair's eyes were shut when she returned to him, but they flickered open as she again took her place by his side.

"Adelheid," he whispered.

"Do not try to speak. Save your strength."

"I must. I... should... have listened...to you. Berengar... evil. Protect... my little Emma."

"I will. Do not worry about her."

"And Italy... Protect... Italy. Do not... let them... prevail."

"What can I do? I am a mere woman."

"You... can..."

"My child," Warinus put in. "A king's widow is an influential figure in the selection of the new king. You may be able to stop Berengar."

"Please... Adelheid... try."

"I will, Lothair. I promise."

Lothair thrashed around, becoming agitated once again. "Anyone but them," he shouted, his voice suddenly strong. "Not Berengar. Not Adalbert."

With difficulty Adelheid pulled him back down, keeping her arms around him. "Lothair, I promise I will do whatever I can to stop them. Please do not concern yourself."

As Lothair slumped back against the pillows, he appeared more peaceful and she thought he was sleeping, but the eyes suddenly shot open.

"Adelheid, forgive me..." he whispered. "I did not... treat you... as I should... please, forgive me."

Numbly Adelheid nodded. "Of course I forgive you, Lothair. I hope you can forgive me if I ever failed as a wife."

"Never," Lothair mumbled and Adelheid shivered, thinking he was saying he would never forgive her. But his eyes were swimming with tears. "You... never... failed."

Adelheid put her head in her hands and wept bitterly for the waste of a marriage. Lothair, so young and handsome, should have been an ideal husband. They could have brought such happiness to each other but only now had he realised it.

Warinus laid his hand on her shoulder. "My child, I think I should administer Last Rites, so his soul goes blameless to God."

Adelheid nodded, watching through her tears as Lothair kept his eyes fixed on the priest, mouthing the sacred words of the creed. With each word his eyelids dropped further, but his face relaxed and she knew the words were bringing him peace.

When Warinus finished, marking his head with holy water, Lothair shut his eyes. He never opened them again.

Chapter three

Dressed all in black, Adelheid spent most of the next days on her knees in the church praying for Lothair's soul. Grief consumed her although she had no idea what she was truly grieving for.

"I suppose I never gave up hope that one day we would be at ease with each other," she said. "But now that hope is gone. He had so many faults, but Lothair was still young. I feel sure he would have improved, as would I."

"We can never know what might have been," Warinus said. "But he died in the full possession of the sacraments. His soul will be blessed."

"I pray so, Father," Adelheid replied, gazing at the crucifix. "But what of my soul? Marriage was given to me as a path to follow. But I failed. I failed so badly. I did not show my husband the proper respect. I angered him so often. How will God judge my sins?"

"My child, you will receive God's mercy for any sins you truly repent of."

"What if I do not repent?" Adelheid asked, tears again brimming in her eyes. "I was right on so much of what I said to Lothair. Even now I am angry that he did not listen. He might still be alive if he had."

"I told you long ago that the responsibility for the success of your marriage lay with you both. I saw how you strove to succeed but I saw no such signs from him, until his last moments. At that moment I witnessed a genuine affection between you. At the end you both succeeded."

Adelheid shook her head. "I felt no affection for him, Father. Even as he lay dying, I could not feel it. May God forgive me, but what you witnessed at the end was pity."

"Compassion is one of the finest emotions, as is forgiveness. You displayed both of these."

Adelheid got to her feet. "I hope so, Father. But in any case, my marriage has now ended. I shall enter an abbey and devote myself to God."

"I think that is very wise, my lady."

Adelheid whirled round to see Berengar standing in the doorway to the church, Adalbert at his side. Both men were dressed in black, but the sombre colours did not conceal the satisfaction on their faces.

"What are you doing here?" she demanded. "Leave my residence immediately."

"I came, naturally, to convey my condolences and deep sorrow at the death of the King."

"Indeed," Adalbert said, trying to force his smirk into a solemn expression. "I loved dear Lothair as a brother. This sad event is terrible indeed."

Adelheid clenched her fists in her efforts to control her anger. "Do not prate of grief. You killed him."

"My dear lady, I feel your grief has most overset you. Such accusations." Berengar shook his head sadly.

"I suppose you were a party to it, Adalbert," Adelheid spat. "For years Lothair trusted you, regarded you as his closest friend. You both disgust me. Get from my residence."

Berengar gave a soothing smile. "Naturally I have no wish to distress you, my lady. Please do not worry yourself for anything. We shall protect you now."

"I do not need your protection and you are in no position to offer it."

"Oh, but I am," Berengar said. "Who do you think will be proclaimed King now dear Lothair has so sadly died?"

"By Lombard tradition I have the right to a say in the

successor. You shall not be king and nor shall you, Adalbert."

"Who else is there?" Berengar's eyes narrowed although his voice remained even. "Take my advice, my lady. Enter an abbey as you planned. We shall be happy to act as guardians for your fair daughter."

In both fear and anger Adelheid ran towards them. "Get from my dwelling, you murdering fiends. I will never entrust Lothair's daughter to you. And I will not rest until the crown is away from your grasp."

Berengar laughed mockingly as he and Adalbert left. Adelheid stared in a helpless panic at Father Warinus.

"Now what do I do, Father?"

It was a hasty return to Pavia. Adelheid made a tragic figure, dressed in her black widow's weeds as the gates opened before her. She was more popular than ever, the people cheering her with tears in their eyes. It felt strange to be arriving back at the royal palace a widow. Always when she had resided there, she had been under the dominance of Willa or Lothair. But now she was in charge.

She was not alone in making a return to the city. Berengar, Willa and Adalbert returned two days later, accompanied by an enormous entourage. He wasted no time in demanding that the Bishop of Pavia crown him.

"It has been agreed, my lady," the Bishop said, when Adelheid registered her protest.

"But I have the right to a say," Adelheid replied. "I wish to name my brother, Konrad. Our father was once king. He has a true claim."

"Your father renounced his claim, my lady."

"That was in an agreement with the noble King Hugh," Adelheid said. "He made no such agreement with the Margrave of Ivrea."

"King Konrad is far away, my lady. He has stated no claim."

"How can he? He has probably barely been notified of King Lothair's death. I state a claim on his behalf."

The Bishop shook his head. "My Lady Queen, I sympathise how hard it must be for you, so young, to have lost your lord and husband. But Italy needs a king now. I am here to request you hand over your husband's crown, so that it may now be placed upon the head of a worthy man."

"I consider no man more unworthy than Berengar," Adelheid snapped but she knew she had no choice. Power had always resided with Berengar. If Lothair had lived longer and wrested more control from him, her position would have been so much stronger.

"And the Queen's crown, my lady," the Bishop said, looking ashamed to be making such a demand.

Adelheid's eyes flashed. "Never. This crown was granted to me by the grace of God. It is mine until I die or renounce all worldly possessions."

"I had understood from the Margrave that this was your intention, my lady."

"It is an option I am considering," Adelheid replied with dignity. "But I shall make no hasty decisions. My daughter needs me to make the correct one. It may that I should wait until she is older before renouncing my worldly life."

It was a hollow satisfaction to see the Bishop depart without the Queen's crown. Lothair had begged her to prevent Berengar's accession, but already she had failed him. Nor did Berengar give up on the Queen's crown, when the Bishop summoned her to bring an agreement between them.

"I wear this crown by the grace of God and only God will take it from me," she maintained.

"We shall see about that," Adalbert muttered.

Adelheid looked sternly at him. "Are you threatening me, Lord Adalbert? Do you intend to slay me as you slew my husband?"

"My lady, I will make allowances for your grief," Berengar put in, with an anxious eye on the Bishop. "But I cannot allow you to make such comments."

"I understood the late King died of a sickness, my lady," the Bishop said, looking distressed.

"Indeed he did," Adalbert said.

"So if I had the wine you presented to him, brought here, would you drink a cup?" Adelheid demanded.

"I would be delighted to, my lady," Berengar said with a smile. "Provided you also drank a cup so I could be assured you had not tampered with it in any way."

Adelheid threw him a black look, but did not continue the argument. It was worthless anyway since she had given the order for the wine to be discarded.

"Now, about the Queen's crown..." the Bishop started.

"It is mine," Adelheid replied. "They can try to wrest it from me by force, if they wish, but I shall ensure everyone knows of their actions."

Given Adelheid's popularity in the city, Berengar clearly realised such an act would not help. "Very well, my lady. We understand your attachment to the crown. Now, concerning the Lady Emma, daughter of the late king. I am sure you understand she will now pass into the guardianship of the new king."

"Never," Adelheid hissed.

"My lord, given the child's tender years, I think she should be left with her mother," the Bishop said. "Naturally you will be consulted when it is time for the young lady to wed."

"Naturally," Adelheid said through gritted teeth. Any marriage for Emma would be years off and was not the immediate issue.

"Indeed," Berengar replied, also through gritted teeth. He bowed to Adelheid. "My crowning is in a few day's hence. I trust you will attend. Adalbert is to be crowned alongside me."

Adelheid stared at the smug look on Adalbert's face. For both father and son to be crowned was Lothair's worst fear coming true. Her fingers twitched as she longed to claw the satisfaction from his face.

"No. I shall never show my support for your rule." Adelheid walked from the church with her head held high, her shoulders only slumping once she was alone with Father Warinus.

"Yet again I have failed Lothair."

"No, my child. You did not. Remember, his first request to you was to keep his daughter safe. You have achieved that."

The weight in Adelheid's heart eased a little as she remembered Lothair's trembling hand on Emma's head. "That is true. But what of Italy?"

"That may take a little longer."

Chapter four

Adelheid spent the day of the crowning on her knees, praying for guidance. But many others brought details of the splendour of the ceremony. Descriptions of the sumptuous scarlet robes Berengar and Adalbert had worn, bedecked in jewels, tortured her mind, as did images of Willa's blue dress, said to have been even more lavish than the robes of the kings. But worse than the reports of this finery was hearing of the triumph on their faces as they were anointed and crowned, the cheers of the loyal echoing throughout the basilica.

For all her prayers, she was unable to help the bitter tears flowing into her pillow that night. The plans she'd made for Christmas that year went forgotten, as her household remained in the deepest of mourning. The solemn mood stood in stark contrast to the merriments they heard were taking place in the residence of the new king.

As the shock wore off, Adelheid began to pick up her customs again, visiting the poor and the sick, glad to forget her own miseries while she eased those of others. Berengar had ignored her since her refusal to come to his crowning, so the first time she saw him was during Lent when she had been dispensing alms. It was a damp day and he did not initially notice her, as he rode towards the basilica on a fine black steed, accompanied by a magnificently dressed entourage. The people watched him in silence with expressions ranging from disinterest to hatred.

"He does not appear to be liked," Adelheid commented.

"His rule is strict and his donations to the poor are miserly," Warinus replied. "The people have no reason to like him. It is said they like Willa even less."

Adelheid could not help the dart of satisfaction. She knew she was wrong to feel such pride in her popularity and vowed to seek penance for it later, but at that moment she enjoyed the feeling and even more the hope that Berengar's unpopularity might make him easier to topple.

"The Queen!" the people called, as they noticed Adelheid. "God's blessings on you, my lady."

Berengar reined in his horse sharply, wheeling it round to face her. The fury at the warm greetings the people were calling was obvious in every line on his face. He nodded curtly at her before urging his horse into a brisk trot.

"Fancy not offering the poor, sweet queen the use of a horse on a day such as this one," a man nearby muttered.

A stout woman elbowed her way through the crowd, curtseying before her. "My dwelling is far too poor for a great lady such as yourself, but it is not right you are out in such weather, my lady. I beg you come inside."

Adelheid smiled at the woman. "A dwelling can never be poor, when the welcome is so warm. Thank you, I shall be glad to wait for the rain to stop."

"That man," the woman muttered, busying herself with cups of ale. "He is no true king to us. You are our queen."

∞ ∞ ∞

"Could I be a reigning queen?" Adelheid asked Warinus after their return to the palace. She had given much thought to a suitable man to rule Italy, but since Konrad had no wish to stake a claim, she had been unable to come up with any.

"It would be most unusual," Warinus replied. "If you had a son, it would be reasonable for you to act as regent, but I do not know if the nobles would accept you on your own. If you married again…"

"Never," Adelheid replied. "I will remain chaste from this day."

"I do not know if you could be accepted. Certainly your wisdom and piety is much admired, but for all his unpopularity, the King is a man of great experience in both battle and administration. Besides, it is no easy matter to topple an anointed king."

Adelheid continued to dwell on the possibility and perhaps Berengar did too. Certainly he felt threatened by her popularity. He sent demand after demand, that she should curtail her charities and stop drawing such attention to herself.

Adelheid replied that she would not halt God's work and that she did nothing to draw attention to herself. It was true. She dressed always plainly in the dark colours befitting a widow and was accompanied usually by just the priest and one of her women. Yet in spite of that, the welcome for her was always jubilant.

Eventually Berengar decided he could tolerate it no longer. He and Adalbert arrived, accompanied by a huge entourage of armed men. Although her body trembled, Adelheid simply raised an eyebrow at the sight.

"Do you need so many men to force me to curtail my charities, my lord," she said, a mocking smile on her face. "I had no idea I possessed such strength."

"I am not here to ask you to curtail your most Christian work, my lady," Berengar said. "Indeed such work is fitting indeed for a queen of Italy."

Adelheid looked at him suspiciously. "I am relived you see it that way, my lord. I have heard little of dear Willa's efforts in this matter, but I am sure they are admirable."

Berengar reddened with annoyance and Adelheid hid her smirk. The descriptions of Willa's avarice had reached her and it was known she would part with little no matter how worthy the cause.

"May we sit and take some refreshment, my lady," Berengar said, recovering his good humour. "We have a matter of grave importance to discuss with you."

The sight of Adalbert's smile made her uneasy, but she sat down, calling for some wine.

Berengar took a mouthful, before smiling at her. "My dear lady, we are most concerned for your situation. You are so young to be unprotected and unguided."

"I thank you for your concern, but I am surrounded by people who would give their lives for me."

"It is not enough, my lady. Of course you must most grievously miss your dear lord, King Lothair. My son and I too continue to mourn."

Despite her trepidation, Adelheid could not restrain an incredulous look, as Adalbert sagely nodded his agreement.

"Poor Lothair. I loved him as a son," Berengar continued. "I feel I owe it to him, to protect you as if you were my own child."

Completely bewildered by this, Adelheid forced a smile. "I am sure that is a great comfort to me, my lord. If I ever need your assistance, I shall be glad to inform you."

"As a woman alone, you need my protection now, my dear," Berengar said. "Fortunately I have a fitting solution. My beloved son, the noble King Adalbert has a very great regard for you."

"Indeed I do, my lady," Adalbert said with a leering smile. "I have long admired you for your beauty and sweet nature."

Adelheid's heart thudded. "My lords, such comments are flattering, but truly I am in no need of protection."

"But, my dear, it is surely the logical answer. You are an unprotected queen of Italy. My son is a strong and noble king of Italy. I have decided that you shall be wed and Adalbert has made me most proud by his willingness to take on your protection."

Adalbert stretched out his hand to place it over Adelheid's. She shivered as the clammy fingers entwined with hers. Snatching it back, she leapt to her feet.

"My lords, your proposal is most flattering." Her voice trembled. "But I have been so recently widowed. I have no intention of marrying again. Besides, I am truly unworthy of your son."

"Don't talk nonsense, Adelheid," Adalbert snapped. "You have always made it plain how much better than us you think you are."

"No, no, I am a sinner indeed. I am not worthy."

Berengar also got to his feet. "I agree. You are not worthy. But my son will make you worthy. He will succeed in moulding you into a good wife in a way poor Lothair could not."

"I will not marry him," Adelheid cried. "Not this day. Not ever."

Berengar seized hold of her hands, squeezing them tightly. "It seems I have not made the position clear. I was not asking for your opinion. I have made my decision. You will marry my son."

Chapter five

With difficulty Adelheid wrenched her hands free, backing away from them. She held her head high to glare at Berengar. "I will not marry your son. Leave my residence immediately."

"You will marry me, Adelheid," Adalbert snapped. "You have no choice."

"There is always a choice," she cried. "You cannot force me to say the words to bind myself to you. And if you lie and say I have, I shall go to the Basilica of San Michele. Perhaps I shall even go to Rome and swear by the most sacred relics that I have not. I will be believed."

"Who would believe a foolish woman over the word of a King?" Adalbert said, narrowing his eyes.

Adelheid laughed scornfully. "I will be believed."

Berengar shrugged. "She is well known for her piety. She will be believed."

"Exactly. Now leave." Adelheid gave no sign of relief.

Berengar strode over to her, taking her by the shoulders. He shook her impatiently. "You will say the words to bind yourself to my son. Say them now."

"No. You cannot make me."

"I can. It will take time that is all." Berengar brought his face so close, the spittle showered her. "You are now forbidden to leave this residence. And we will strip you of everything you value."

Adelheid's mouth went dry, as she imagined little Emma

born away to their residence, screaming for her mother. Her mind raced, trying to think of a solution, but all she could see was Lothair's dying eyes, pleading with her to keep their daughter safe. With a heavy heart she realised how little choice she would have.

As she turned to speak to them, wondering if she could just beg for a little more time, she noticed what Berengar's men were doing. They were gathering up the costly silver platters and finely wrought candlesticks. Almost she laughed. She did not care how many of those items she lost. Determined to keep the men's thoughts away from her daughter, she ran to her treasury and stood before the doorway.

"These treasures are mine. You have no right to take them from me."

The men stared at her, looking uncertain of what to do. Berengar strode over. "What are you doing, you fools? Of course her finest jewels are in there. Take them all."

"I shall not let you enter," she cried, pressing her back against the door.

The men continued to stare, none of them willing to force aside a woman and a queen at that.

"Do not stand there." Berengar strode over, pulling Adelheid roughly away. Contemptuously he shoved her and she stumbled to one side. Before she could fall, Adalbert caught her in his arms. They enclosed around her as the cruellest of prison walls.

"Let go of me," she cried.

"You will be my wife one day, Adelheid. Why not agree to it willingly?"

"I will never marry you," she hissed through clenched teeth, as he tried to kiss her. She struggled to get away, but all she achieved was a tear to the sleeve of her dress as he grabbed her once again.

A splintering sound made her turn. Too impatient to wait for the keys to the treasury to be fetched, Berengar and his men had wrenched the door from its hinges. With cries of glee they dove into the room, seizing coffers and bags of coins.

"Take everything," Berengar ordered. "This woman deserves nothing. This is royal property and it belongs to the King."

Adelheid watched them, indifferent as the jewels were carried from her. Only the bags of coins she had intended to distribute to the poor over Easter brought any pain. Good men and women would starve that year, while Willa would no doubt buy herself ever more jewels.

"God will damn you forever for this."

Berengar laughed. "I do not think so. All this is mine by right." He strode over to her, looking down into her white face. "And so is something else." He pulled the golden crown from her head.

"That crown is mine by the gift of God."

"It is time it graced Willa's head. I was patient with you over this matter for too long." Berengar's lips curved into a cruel smile. "It will look much finer on the head of a noble woman, than an arrogant, disobedient little hussy such as you."

Adelheid's eyes filled with tears. "You can take my crown, Berengar, but I am still an anointed queen. You can never take that from me."

"You have nothing now," Adalbert said with satisfaction, relaxing his arms around her at last. "So, will you marry me?"

"Never."

∞ ∞ ∞

Adelheid waited until Berengar had left before returning to the hall. Gilia ran to her. "My lady, are you harmed?"

She tried to smile, looking nervously around the wreckage of the hall. Chairs were upturned and food lay dumped in heaps on the table as the platters had been emptied. On the walls blank stone showed where the rich tapestries had been torn away. But it was not these which concerned her. Father Warinus was sat on a chair, holding a cloth to a swollen lump on his forehead.

"Father, what did they do you?" Adelheid dashed to kneel beside him.

"I am fine, my child." He managed a smile and his eyes twinkled slightly. "At my age I think I should not have tackled armed men."

Adelheid shook her head. "Oh, Father, you should not have risked yourself on my account."

"They have taken everything of value," the priest said sadly.

But as Emma hurled herself into her mother's arms, Adelheid smiled. "Not everything. Not the most valuable of all." She smoothed back her daughter's dark hair, overwhelmed with relief she was still with her. Cradling the frightened child close to her, she managed to smile brightly at everyone. "Come, my friends. We do not want to live in this mess. Let us set the hall to rights."

Adelheid ignored the protests of the others as she insisted on helping with the work, but her mind whirled. It was clear she was no longer safe in her own residence, not even the one in the city which loved her.

"I doubt very much whether the King will give up on his scheme," Warinus said when at last the task was completed. "He needs your popularity."

Adelheid clutched Emma tighter to her. "I know."

"Would marriage to him really be so bad, my lady?" Orsa asked. "Italy would be glad to regain you as a reigning queen."

"It is what I intend to do," Adelheid said. "But not married to Adalbert. I do not wish to marry again, ever. But even if I did, it would most certainly not be to the son of my husband's murderer. Emma cannot be raised by the ones who slew her father."

Warinus nodded. "I agree, my child. Such a marriage must be avoided."

"I need to escape from here," Adelheid said. "The estates King Lothair granted to me are to the south. If I can get there, loyal men can gather to me, although escaping may not be easy..."

"But not impossible, my child. Even with guards on the gate, some coming and going is to be expected. We shall smuggle you out, perhaps under the cover of darkness."

Adelheid nodded, feeling better now they were formulating a plan, but her mood was brought abruptly down by the priest's next question.

"What will you do with the child?"

She looked down to where Emma was sleeping in her arms. "She comes with me, of course. I cannot leave her here. They would take her immediately."

"I agree she cannot stay here," Warinus said. "But to raise a rebellion against a king is a perilous task. It may be dangerous for her."

"I know," Adelheid whispered, tears forming in her eyes. "Tell me what to do, Father. As a mother I cannot make a judgement in these circumstances."

"My advice is that she is placed for safety in an abbey. I know of one, not far from Pavia. It is a humble foundation, not well known, but the Abbess is a kindly woman. Emma would be cared for simply, but with love."

The tears rolled down Adelheid's cheeks at the thought of being parted from her precious daughter. So often it was only her bright smile which had given her strength. Besides, the little girl had just lost her father. Was she now to be taken from her mother? But she knew Warinus was right. Taking a child into a conflict would be foolish.

"Very well, Father. I shall pray it is not for long."

Chapter six

Somehow Adelheid managed to stay dry eyed as she bade farewell to her daughter. The previous few nights she had taken the child into her own bed and lay, watching her sleep, memorising every detail of her tiny features. As she awoke on the last morning, Emma's beaming smile almost destroyed her and she had to turn away several times to hide her tears while she was dressed for the day.

She embraced Father Warinus. "We shall meet soon on my lands, Father. Please, take these." She thrust a heavy pouch of coins and some of the few jewels she still possessed. "Reward the abbey for caring for Emma and if anything goes wrong, donate what is left to the poor. At least Berengar will take nothing more from me."

The priest nodded. He was unwilling to leave Adelheid, although he knew logically he needed to be the one to take Emma to the abbey. "Such jewels may be useful for rewarding your followers."

"Agreed. Father, if you hear I am slain or have been married to Adalbert despite my efforts, please take Emma to my brother. They murdered her father. I cannot let them raise her." She crouched down taking the child into her arms one last time. "You be a good little maid for Father Warinus, my child. Whatever happens, Emma, remember how much I love you. Your father loved you too. He was ever proud. You will be in my prayers."

Emma looked bewildered, but her mother's smiling face

seemed to reassure her as she snuggled into the priest's arms.

"May God be with you, my child," Warinus said, as he turned away.

Adelheid kept smiling as the priest, accompanied by Emma's nurse left the hall. She waited tensely for shouts from the gate, reporting they had been discovered. But the sight of the priest, his head bent as if in silent penance, drew no attention and it seemed none looked behind the sack he was carrying to see the child.

"They are away," Adelheid said, releasing her breath and letting the tears run down her cheeks.

"It will not be for long, my lady." Orsa put an arm around her.

"Who knows how long it will take?" Adelheid replied. "Weeks, months. It could be years before I see my daughter again. Perhaps I will never see her." A sudden memory of the pain in Lothair eyes as he said his final farewell to his daughter turned the trickle of tears into a river. She put her head in her hands and sobbed as she had never sobbed before.

∞ ∞ ∞

After Emma had gone there was an agonising wait before they could make their own departure. It had been decided they would escape under the cover of darkness. Although it seemed risky, she intended to slip from the palace accompanied only by Gilia and Orsa. Once they were safely away she was confident she could surround herself with strong men to form a more impressive entourage.

As dusk fell she called for the meal to be brought to the table as usual, determined no spies in her household would report anything amiss. At the end she retired at her normal hour, but in her chamber she and the two women changed into plain woollen garments. Her valuable possessions were now much diminished, but what little she had she divided among the three of them.

Adelheid looked around the bedchamber. "Next time I lie here, it will be as queen, free from the threat of Berengar."

"I pray so, my lady," Orsa whispered nervously.

"Remember, if matters do not go as planned, try to escape anyway and inform Father Warinus of what has happened."

The two women nodded and Adelheid embraced them warmly. "I am fortunate indeed to have such loyal friends. Come, let us depart."

Silently the three passed through the darkened palace into the torchlit courtyard. They kept to the shadows, edging towards the gateway. As she had expected, the guards Berengar had appointed were dozing, a flagon of wine on the floor beside them. They barely stirred as the three women slipped through into the city.

This was the risky part. Three young women alone in the city after dark could easily stray into danger, but as they moved swiftly through the streets, they encountered few people and none who threatened them. Their progress was rapid, bringing them to the city gates some time before dawn where they huddled nearby, drinking sips of wine, waiting for them to open.

Orsa and Gilia slept a little, but Adelheid kept her eyes fixed on the eastern sky, watching as it lightened. Her mind went over what she would need to do once they were free of the city. She wondered if it would be possible to acquire horses, so as to put some distance between them and Berengar. She looked down at the wedding and betrothal rings still on her fingers. It seemed wrong to sell them, but she was certain Lothair would want her to do so, if it meant taking power from Berengar and Adalbert.

As the sky lightened still further she heard noises, both animal and human, from the other side of the gate. Traders and farmers would be gathering, ready to bring their goods into the city. It sounded as if there were a goodly number, which was useful. Surely as such a throng entered, it would be easy for them to slip out unnoticed.

When the first rays of sunlight struck the gate, the watchmen sprang into action. The wood creaked as it was hauled open and the carts rolled in, laden with produce. Adelheid looked at her companions. "Are you ready?"

The two women nodded nervously, pulling up their hoods to conceal their faces. They moved towards the gate, Gilia slightly in front as all three kept their heads bowed. Adelheid's heart thumped. If all went well in just a few moments they would be free of the city before anyone had even missed them.

With her head bowed and whispering a few prayers, she did not notice the man coming in and stumbled over his foot. He caught her.

"Forgive me, Lady," he cried jovially.

Adelheid caught her breath, tying to swiftly replace her hood.

"It's the Queen!" one of the men cried.

"The Queen, the Queen," joyful voices called.

Adelheid shook her head as her popularity suddenly became her bane. "Of course I am not. You have made a mistake."

Disturbed by the noise, the gate guards came over and looked at her. Adelheid looked defiantly back, her heart sinking. One of the men had previously been used as a palace guard and he recognised her instantly.

"My lady, I had not heard you were leaving Pavia," he said uncertainly. "And it is most improper for you to be travelling in this fashion."

Adelheid lifted her head. "Stand aside, my man. I am making a private penance which I cannot discuss. Of course I am not leaving Pavia."

"My lady, forgive me, but I must check this matter with the King."

Orsa came forward, holding out a handful of coins. "Take these and let us pass through," she begged.

"I cannot. Please, my lady, you must wait with me. I would be grieved to restrain you by force."

Helplessly Adelheid and Orsa looked at each other,

overwhelmed by failure. As they were escorted away from the gate she suddenly remembered Gilia. She glanced back to see the woman was coming towards them. Hastily she shook her head. Gilia stared at her and for a moment Adelheid was sure she would disobey. But the woman gave a slight smile and a nod before darting out of the gate.

With as much dignity as she could manage, Adelheid sat down, clasping Orsa's hand and awaited Berengar's men. She clung onto the hope that Gilia would find Father Warinus. It was a faint hope, but as she saw Berengar himself riding towards them, his expression thunderous, that faint hope was all she had left.

Chapter seven

"You, my lady, will accompany me back to my residence," was all Berengar said. "It is not fitting that you are out here in the city with just one attendant."

Adelheid glared back at Berengar, trying to appear far braver than she felt. "What will happen if I do not?"

"I shall force you if necessary, but I would prefer not to make a scene. If you compel me to such an action, I shall have your attendant stripped and beaten for abetting you in this plan."

Orsa gasped, shrinking closer to Adelheid. To her great pride the woman made no protest, but Adelheid guessed how frightened she must be. All Orsa had ever done was serve her with kindness. She did not deserve to be repaid by such a fate.

With curt courtesy Berengar helped her onto a horse and they rode together through the streets of Pavia. Adelheid's cheeks burned in shame that she was riding apparently willingly beside her husband's murderer. As people stopped to stare at them, she realised that for the first time there were no cheers.

"What plans were you hatching?" Berengar demanded once they were back at his residence.

Alone with him, Adalbert and Willa, Adelheid looked defiantly back. Orsa had been locked up, no doubt terrified, but at least so far she had been left unharmed.

"I do not care to remain in the same city as you, Berengar," Adelheid snapped.

"I suggest you show me a little less insolence. Face facts, Adelheid. You have no choice but to marry my son. Accept it with a good grace."

Adelheid looked into Adalbert's gloating face. "Never."

Adalbert's smirk changed to a look of rage. He took her by the arms, shaking her. "You have no choice," he shouted.

"There is always a choice and I choose not to say any words to bind myself to you."

Adalbert spat in her face. "You are a fool. You should have accepted me when we first offered. I would have been a reasonable husband to you. Now I see why Lothair complained so often of your manner."

"It was not my name he cursed as he lay dying. He was your friend, but you helped your father murder him."

"Be silent," he shouted. "You will not say such words. You are to be my wife and that is the end of the matter." He slid his hands down her body, gripping her firmly around the waist. "Perhaps if I force you to share my bed for a while, you will understand what you must do."

Adelheid's body trembled and her mouth went dry. The scream building up in her throat stuck fast, as fear froze her. These people would do anything. They cared nothing for the abhorrence of such an act. Already the touch of his hands sickened her. She could not endure a lifetime sharing his bed.

Adalbert looked down mockingly. "Well, do you wish to say the words to bind yourself honourably to me before we retire to my chamber?"

She was unable to help the tears in her eyes as she shook her head. "No. Nothing you can do will force me to say those words." Her voice came out in a trembly whisper, but somehow she forced strength into it. "Do what you will with me. I have not the strength to fight you, but there will be no marriage. Even if you force me to bear your child, I shall parade my shame through the streets of Pavia so everyone knows how you have treated me."

Berengar pulled Adalbert away. "Don't be a fool, Boy. The

people would tear you apart if you did such an act."

Adelheid was trembling so violently, she was not sure how she kept standing. But the relief of being away from Adalbert was short lived as Willa strode forward, shoving her hard against the wall. "How dare you think my son is not good enough for you," she shrieked.

Slap after slap followed. Dimly through the pain she heard Berengar laugh, as Willa wrenched the mantle away from her head. She grabbed a handful of blonde hair, causing Adelheid to scream at the agony suffusing her scalp.

"Marry my son."

"No." Tears poured down her cheeks. "I will not."

"Then I shall make sure no other man will ever want you." Willa's finger nails slashed at her face, narrowly missing Adelheid's eye. She dug it into her flesh, raking it downwards. The skin tore, sending a trail of torment to race down her cheek.

This time it was Adalbert who came to her rescue. "Stop it, Mother. I do not want a disfigured bride."

"She has said she will not be your wife," Willa panted, straining to get back to Adelheid. "What difference does it make?"

"We are going to change her mind," Berengar said, glaring through narrowed eyes. "She cannot stay here, winning the people to her."

"What will you do, Father?" Adalbert asked.

"She can go to our stronghold at Garda. A spell in captivity away from her child will, I am sure, make her much more amenable to our plans."

Berengar and Adalbert laughed, but Willa narrowed her eyes. "Where is the child?"

The laughter halted as they all looked accusingly at Adelheid. Her face bloodied, she smiled calmly back, determined they would not seek Emma out. "I sent her some days ago to my brother, Konrad in Burgundy. I should imagine she is almost there by now."

The look of rage on all three faces filled Adelheid with triumph. It was a small victory, but at least it was something.

∞ ∞ ∞

It was under the cover of darkness that they started their journey to Garda. Adelheid was ordered to travel in a cart, her hands bound and a hood pulled firmly over her head. She was ashamed of the relief when Orsa was shoved into the cart next to her. The woman was wide eyed and shaking. She should never have been caught up in this, but Adelheid was glad not to be alone.

"Are you unharmed?" she said in a low voice.

"Yes, my lady," Orsa replied. In the flickering torchlight she caught a glimpse of Adelheid's face. "Oh, my lady, what have they done to you?"

"It is not so bad," Adelheid said, amazed how calm she felt, as with a jerk the cart started to move through the streets, arriving at the gates just before they closed for the night. It was a rough journey, as nothing had been added to provide any comfort. With every bump the cart passed over, her body jerked, adding fresh misery to the injuries she had already suffered. The pouch containing the few coins she had left had been taken from her, but they had not thought to search Orsa and she whispered to Adelheid that she still possessed hers.

Such tiny triumphs helped as huddling close to each other, they made themselves as comfortable as they could for the long trip.

∞ ∞ ∞

It was several days later when they were ordered from the cart to stand before a vast expanse of water, surrounded by towering hills. It was a fair spot with the sun still peeping over the crags to sparkle against the lake. Set in the shimmering water was an island upon which she could just make out a castle.

Adalbert came up behind her, grabbing her roughly by the arm. "Get in the boat."

She stumbled into the shallow water, causing raucous laughter from the men. She made no reply, determined to show no emotion as she took her place in the boat with Orsa thrust in just as roughly beside her.

Adalbert said nothing more as they were rowed across, but as they stepped onto the island he took her by the shoulders.

"Take a look at your new home, Adelheid." He gestured at the rough looking castle of crumbling stone. "How long you stay here is up to you. I care not if it is for the rest of your life." He turned her to face him. "But you can still say the words now to bind yourself to me in marriage and we will merely spend our wedding night here and start our return to Pavia in the morn."

Adelheid shuddered at the thought of a wedding night with him. "I will not marry you. Not this day. Not ever."

"As you wish, but this decision confines your woman also to this prison," Berengar put in.

"I am honoured to serve the Queen in whatever way I can," Orsa said quietly.

Both guilt and pride filled Adelheid's heart at this comment, but she pressed her lips together, refusing to answer.

"You are both fools." Berengar turned to Orsa. "I suggest you persuade your mistress to comply."

"Send word when you are ready to wed me, Adelheid," Adalbert said. "But until the day you are to become my wife, farewell."

Adelheid and Orsa were shoved into a dark, bleak room, their few belongings thrown after them. The two sat in silence, clasping each other's hands and listening to the sound of the boats rowing away, leaving them imprisoned on the island.

Chapter eight

"What will become of us?" Orsa whispered.

Adelheid put an arm around her. "You should hate me for everything I am putting you through."

"Never," Orsa replied. "Truly I am honoured to serve you. But what happens now?"

"I know not, but Father Warinus is still free. I pray Gilia has reached him, but even if she has not, I know he will find the truth. We will soon be missed in Pavia. I know it is likely that few know we are here, but I suspect word will soon spread. Do you think all the guards here will be discrete?"

Orsa managed a laugh. "I have never met a guard who manages to be discrete beyond a week or two."

"Exactly." Adelheid got resolutely to her feet. "We may be here a while, but it will not be forever." She began to unpack their meagre belongings. "We shall at least make ourselves comfortable while we wait."

∞ ∞ ∞

For all her brave words, Adelheid was not as confident as she maintained. They were so far away in Garda that even if the guards did talk of their prisoners, it would take a long time for word to filter back to Pavia.

Through long days she kept cheerful, spending much time in

prayer or talking in a bright manner with Orsa as they stitched. The bare room they were incarcerated in did at least become brighter as the hangings they made adorned the walls.

But at night Adelheid often wept silently, wondering what was happening with her daughter. Her arms ached to hold her again. Sometimes she dreamt of her beaming face and the way her dark hair flew when she spun around. For an instant as she woke, happiness filled her until the bitter memories struck and she realised her arms were empty.

But worse than those nights were the ones she dreamt Adalbert had returned to make good his threat to force her into marriage. Never, even in the darkest days of her marriage to Lothair, had she felt such fear and loathing as during those dreams of his body pressing into hers. With the weeks of captivity drawing into months, she feared that when he returned she would no longer have the strength to resist him.

As the summer began, their chamber became stiflingly hot and nights were too unbearable to sleep properly. It was on one of those sleepless nights that Adelheid sat up, looking curiously at the wall. There was a scraping sound fixed in one point, low down near the ground. She held her breath. The noise did not stop, but continued steadily on.

"Do you hear that?" she whispered to Orsa.

"Yes, my lady. I heard it last night as well. I think it is the wind blowing a branch against the wall."

"Probably," Adelheid agreed. But she was puzzled. The night was not, as far as she could tell, a windy one, but nonetheless the scraping was almost continuous. "Or perhaps it is an animal, a rat most likely, in the walls."

"It could be. Perhaps it is stuck there," Orsa said.

"Trapped as we are. I never thought to feel sympathy for a rat." Adelheid turned over, trying to find a cooler part of the pallet she slept on.

She could only doze on such a sticky night and every time she woke, she could hear the relentless scraping on the wall. It stopped at dawn, leaving Adelheid more puzzled than ever.

When it started up again the next night, Orsa became alarmed. "What if it is some demon sent to torment us?"

Adelheid clutched her cross to her breast, wanting to say something reassuring. If it had been daylight she could probably have managed it, but on that heavy, oppressive night the scraping took on a sinister tone. All too clearly she could imagine a taloned apparition, ready to drag her to hell for all her sins. For another night she lay staring into the darkness, muttering prayers and terrified of what might appear in her chamber if she dared to close her eyes.

∞∞∞

The men and women who brought them food were mostly a taciturn bunch. Occasionally there would be a murmured greeting, but often the food was set down without so much as a glance. It was strange when one day the boy who brought the food gave them an odd look. He said nothing, but he stared at them both for a moment before scurrying away.

Feeling lethargic from the heat and sleepless nights, Adelheid barely looked at the food. The scraping had continued every night, apart from when a thunder storm had roared around them. As no demons materialised in her chamber, the noise had become an irritation rather than anything to concern her.

Orsa picked up a platter of bread and smoked fish. She was about to bring it over to her, when she stood still, staring at the tray.

"What is wrong?" Adelheid asked.

Orsa set down the platter, lifting something which had been lying underneath it. It was a flat stone. "My lady, there are marks on the stone. What does it mean?"

Adelheid stared at it, not sure whether to believe her eyes as she took in the ink, slightly smudged against the stone. Her face grew radiant. "It is the answer to our prayers."

Orsa's own face lit up, as she took in the first real smile she had seen on her mistress's face in a long time. "What does it say?"

"That noise we have heard each night is Father Warinus coming to our rescue. Listen. 'My dearest child, I am close by and am trying to come to you through the wall. It is a long task, but I am making progress. Stay strong, my child. Warinus.' He is tunnelling through the wall."

"We shall escape," Orsa said in an excited whisper.

"God willing, yes, we shall. We must help him. The task will be quicker if we break through the wall to meet him."

"But the guards will surely notice such a thing. Indeed it is a miracle they have not spotted the Father's efforts."

"He must be concealing it in some way and we shall do the same." For the first time in months, hope surged in her. She picked up the cloth they had been stitching. "We shall hang this on the wall and tunnel behind it each night."

Orsa nodded and with no further words the two women began to eat from the platter with gusto, the hope in their hearts giving them strength for the task ahead.

∞∞∞

Adelheid and Orsa took to dozing through the hot, languid days, so they might be fresh for their work each night. As Warinus had said, the tunnelling was a laborious task, although the rock was soft and crumbling in places. During the day a fine cloth covered their efforts, but night after night they worked steadily by candlelight, delighting as the hole grew ever bigger. Although she had not yet heard his voice, the scraping from the other side filled her with joy and as the noise grew louder each night, she rejoiced as she realised how close they were becoming.

It was an emotional moment when after many days they finally broke through. The hole was tiny, only large enough for a few fingers, but as they met the callused fingers of Father Warinus on the other side, tears poured down Adelheid's cheeks.

"Is all well with you, my child?"

His whispered voice caused the tears to flow even faster and for a moment she could not answer. "Yes, Father," she managed eventually. "I am unharmed."

"God be praised," Warinus said. "I was so afeared when young Gilia told me what had occurred."

"These months have been long and would have been lonely, were it not for Orsa," Adelheid said. "How soon can we escape?"

The priest gave a soft laugh. "Patience, my child. I do not think you will fit through this hole. Let us continue our efforts."

Chapter nine

Although it did not feel that way to Adelheid, their progress from that point became rapid. Before long she was able to grasp the priest's hand and look through the hole into his eyes. Eventually Father Warinus tested the hole by slithering into their chamber. He arrived covered in dust from head to toe, but with a triumphant smile. Adelheid flung her arms around him, overjoyed at their success. He looked around their prison, shaking his head at their efforts to brighten it with their work.

"My poor children, what confinement is this?"

"It has been a dull one," Adelheid said. "It could easily have been worse."

"Your spirit is truly an inspiration, my child." He turned to Orsa. "As is yours, Orsa. God will most certainly reward you for your loyalty to your mistress."

"What now, Father?" Adelheid asked.

"It is almost dawn. Endure this prison for one more day while I make some arrangements. Rest yourselves as much as you can and pack whatever you need. God willing, you shall escape this night."

Adelheid was barely able to contain her excitement, as she again embraced the priest. Certainly she was too excited to rest. It was an effort to maintain her downcast lethargy when a serving man brought them food. They both ate well, packing what remained for their journey. The day passed in excruciating slowness, as Adelheid feared some unexpected event. Every sound made her fear their tunnel had been spotted or that Berengar had returned. But as dusk fell, nothing untoward had happened. She and Orsa exchanged looks of relief as they were left alone for the night.

Everything was ready and the two sat in silence for what felt like an age. Adelheid mouthed prayers until the soft voice called from outside. "My children, are you ready?"

"Yes, Father," Adelheid whispered, pushing the packs to him, before slithering through. Her tunic tore slightly on the rough stone, but she did not care, as she emerged into the shrubs which had concealed the exterior of the tunnel. Orsa was not long in following her and the three slunk through the shadows towards the water's edge.

A boat was waiting on the lake, clearly lit up by the moon. Adelheid wondered whether it was wise to escape on so bright a night. The moon would light their path, but would also make them easier to see. Nervously she took a seat beside Orsa as Warinus gave the boat a hard push, before scrambling in himself.

The splash of the water sounded deafening and she glanced back in trepidation at the castle, expecting to see men streaming out. But all was still and her racing heart steadied as Warinus' swift, strong strokes pulled the boat ever further from their prison.

They spoke little as the boat glided across the lake, eventually bumping along the shallow ground of the shore. As they scrambled out, Warinus tossed their packs to them. He too leapt for the shore, pulling the boat onto the land, but just as Adelheid was muttering a prayer of thanks for their escape there was a shout from the island.

"The Queen! She is escaping."

"What now, Father?" Adelheid cried, horrified at the thought of being returned to prison and even more frightened of the punishment which would follow.

"Run, my child. Quick!"

Never in her life had Adelheid run so fast, following the

priest away from the lake. The ground was rough and they stumbled often in the darkness. Their packs slowed them down, but they did not dare discard them and leave some clue as to their direction. As they went on, the ground became marshy and full of tall reeds.

Warinus slowed. "We must go carefully," he said. "The ground here is treacherous."

"Perhaps we should go another way," Adelheid suggested, longing to run ahead.

"No, my child. I do not think you can outrun those men. This way may be slow, but the reeds will provide cover."

Her feet already soaking wet, Adelheid shivered, but she took hold of Orsa's hand and followed the priest onwards. The slow pace was agonising, but there was no sound yet of pursuit. By the time they paused for a furtive drink, they were starting to hope they had eluded their captors.

The lightening sky was a blessing, as they could see their way more clearly, although Warinus cursed, as he realised how close they still were to the lake. As the sun peeped over the hills, they at last stopped for a proper rest.

With thudding hearts they listened carefully, but the only sound was the faint squawking of marshland birds. At length they relaxed enough to take some food.

"Do you think they have abandoned the chase?" Adelheid asked in a low voice.

"I doubt it, my child, but these marshes are a very maze of paths. We will not be easy to find. But we are too close to the lake at present. Once we have rested ourselves we must change direction."

It was with trepidation they did that, taking a treacherous looking path through the thick reeds. They had not gone far when Warinus came to an abrupt halt.

"What is it, Father?" Adelheid asked.

"I heard something. Someone is not far behind us."

"Should we run, Father?" Orsa breathed.

Warinus shook his head. "Such a noise would alert them

immediately. Come, this way."

To Adelheid's horror he led them off the path, deep into the reeds. He pressed firmly ahead of himself with a stick, checking the ground which squelched and sank beneath their feet. As they reached a pool of water he sank down, gesturing sharply for the two women to do the same. The sound of footsteps and voices had come closer as Adelheid and Orsa too lay on the wet ground, their bodies trembling with fear and cold.

"Do not move," Warinus whispered.

"Someone has been this way," came a voice. "Look how the grasses are flattened."

"It might not be them," said another.

"Could be anyone. The fishermen use this path and boys come out here hunting for fowl," a younger voice said.

"Be silent and keep checking."

The sound of sticks and weaponry thrusting through the reeds made Adelheid hold her breath in terror as she wondered how deeply into the reeds they would come. She realised Warinus had made a wise choice when he had led them to this bleak spot. The waterlogged ground would have quickly swallowed up their footsteps, leaving, she prayed, no sign of their presence.

The thrust of weaponry came closer and closer. She could see the reeds bending beneath the flash of metal. The rushes perilously close to their hiding spot swished to one side and fell back. Adelheid closed her eyes, waiting for the shout of triumph and prepared herself to be dragged back to captivity. But nothing happened. The stick thrust through the reeds a little along from them, but again they bent back. Slowly the footsteps moved away, the swish of reeds continuing but growing ever fainter. She raised her head, staring at Warinus in hope.

He gave a slight smile, but no one dared move. Even after the last sounds had faded away, they remained flat in the mud until Warinus gave the signal to rise. They pushed through the reeds cautiously, pausing often. Even the sound of the wind stirring the grasses was enough to make them drop back to the ground. Warinus peered out of the rushes, beckoning the two women on as he saw no threat.

Back on the path they looked at each other. Almost Adelheid laughed, as she took in the bedraggled aspect of her companions, guessing she looked no better herself. Warinus led them back the way they came, until they found yet another path. The sun was high now, swiftly drying their damp clothes, but however hot it became, they dared take only the shortest of breaks, not resting until nightfall.

∞∞∞

With the darkness enveloping them and no sounds other than the occasional rustle of an animal, Adelheid and her companions finally relaxed. Nibbling on some bread and smoked fish, they described their captivity.

"Never have I felt such admiration," Warinus said. "You have both been through so much, yet your spirits remain undaunted."

"How did you find us, Father?" Orsa asked. "We were not sure if anyone knew where we were."

"After Gilia told me you had been caught in your escape, I returned to Pavia. I hoped to find you at the palace so you can imagine my alarm when I realised no one knew where you were. But a guard remembered a royal cart, appearing almost empty, leaving the city that night, so I knew which direction you had taken. The rest was guesswork. It was obvious Berengar would have taken you somewhere secure and I knew of this stronghold of theirs. Once I arrived at the lake, I heard from some fishermen that two ladies were imprisoned here. It had to be you."

"I cannot thank you enough, Father. I was truly starting to think I would have no choice but to accept Adalbert's offer."

"I need no thanks, my child."

"What do we do now, Father? Do we make for Burgundy or my grandmother in Swabia?" Adelheid's heart almost failed her at the thought of such a long journey through the mountains.

"I think not. It would be too far and we would have to pass through Berengar's territory. Do you remember Lord Azzo? It was your late husband who granted him his lands and he is well known for his dislike for Berengar. I think he will grant us refuge."

"Yes, I remember him. The stronghold is still some distance I believe, but not as far as Burgundy. Very well, Father, I agree."

Warinus looked at her sympathetically. "You have not asked me about Emma."

"I dare not," Adelheid whispered, a painful lump forming in her throat. "I scarcely dare think of her."

"She is well, my child. She took a liking to the abbess immediately and of course she has her nurse. The abbess will take good care of her and, God willing, we will soon reunite you."

Chapter ten

They lingered on in the marshes, allowing themselves to be lost in the network of paths, confident it would only be the merest chance which could lead Berengar's men to them. As their food supplies ran low, Father Warinus spent many an afternoon fishing. Determined not to be a burden on her companions, Adelheid insisted that Orsa teach her how to skin and cook the fish and took pride in smelling it roasting on the fire each night.

Occasionally, if a settlement was nearby, Father Warinus ventured in to beg or barter for more food. Adelheid was always nervous that such excursions might lead to her discovery, but the priest was confident.

"A priest is almost invisible," he told them. "So many people see the robes, but not the face. On three occasions I was seen on the island and no one did more than murmur greetings, not even realising I was not one of the castle chaplains."

He proved to be right and always they were able to continue on their way unmolested. When eventually they broke away from the marshes, Adelheid worried they would be spotted in the settlements along their way.

"I do not think any would recognise you as a queen, my child," the priest said, looking at her ragged, travel stained apparel. "If any ask, we are pilgrims on our way to Rome."

"I hate to tell a falsehood on such a matter, Father, but perhaps it is not truly a lie. I do intend one day to go on such a pilgrimage."

"I pray you will. It is a place of marvels indeed."

Their journey was a wearisome one and as they drew further away from the mountains, the weather became stifling. Often Adelheid wondered how much longer she would be able to continue, but felt ashamed as she looked at her two companions. Warinus and Orsa were on this lengthy trek for her sake and so even when her feet blistered and her shoulders ached, she made no complaint. Instead she made every effort to keep spirits high and in the evenings when the three shared a flagon of ale around a fire, there was even laughter among them. They had come so far now from Garda, she had begun to feel confident all would be well.

After some weeks in the dusty heat, the land started to rise again. "These are the hills we have been aiming for," Father Warinus said with satisfaction. "Lord Azzo's stronghold is among them."

They employed a boy to guide them through the hills until one afternoon he pointed out the fortress. Adelheid stopped, looking at it wonder. The settlement was small, but sturdy looking with thick stone walls. However it was not this which had made Warinus recommend it as a safe refuge. It was the location, perched high on a pinnacle of rock so steep that Adelheid could not comprehend how anyone could scale it, let alone build on it.

"You are right, Father. Such a fortress will be safe indeed." She glanced up at the sky. "Will we make it by nightfall do you think?"

"I think we will," Warinus said, tossing the promised reward to the boy.

The thought of a hot meal at a table and a proper bed spurred them on into the dusk, arriving at the foot of the rock just as the last light was fading.

"We are wearied travellers," Warinus said to the man at the gate. "We have heard the lord is a god-fearing man, who will not turn such people away."

A priest and two women were no threat and the gatekeeper

waved them through, a guard guiding them up the steep path to the castle. A knot of anxiety twisted itself in Adelheid's stomach. If Azzo turned them away, she did not know what they would do.

They were shown into a hall, where the aroma of roasted meat and stewed vegetables rose to meet their empty stomachs. The guard pointed at a space near the foot of the table, but to everyone's bemusement Adelheid walked past it. She could see Lord Azzo on a finely carved chair. He had not looked in their direction, presumably considering such lowly guests beneath his attention. It was only as she drew closer that he glanced up at her in a puzzled fashion.

At his chair Adelheid sank to her knees, her clear voice ringing out, "My Lord Azzo, I am the Queen of Italy and I beg most humbly for refuge from my enemies."

The shocked silence was broken by a ripple of laughter as all wondered what lunatic had strayed in, but Azzo was staring at her face, his mouth wide. He leapt up, pulling Adelheid back to her feet. Then he knelt, bowing his head.

"My Lady Queen, I pledge my loyalty and bid you most welcome to my residence."

There was another shocked silence as everyone present fell to their knees.

Adelheid let out a shaky breath. "I bid you all rise. You must not kneel to me. I am here as a humble supplicant."

Around the hall whispered conversations started up, as everyone absorbed the news that the Queen had appeared in their midst. Azzo's wife swiftly rearranged the top table, bidding Adelheid and her companions to be seated and urging cups of wine and dishes of food upon them.

"My Lady Queen, I cannot tell you how heartily glad I am to see you," Azzo said as his hungry guests started to eat. "No one knew what had become of you. It seemed as if you had simply vanished from this earth. Pray tell me what has occurred these last months."

As they ate, they described everything which had happened.

Azzo listened attentively, his face changing from dismay as he heard of their imprisonment to admiration as they described their escape.

"That is truly a marvel," he said. "For two women and a priest to outwit the King's army. My lady, I am honoured you have come here. It will be from Canossa that you start your fight back, until, God willing, we have removed the pretender kings from the throne."

"Thank you, my lord. In truth I did little. The credit for the escape must go to Father Warinus for his plan and indeed Orsa for serving me so well. I humbly thank you for pledging your support."

"I remember your late husband with the very deepest of gratitude for granting me these lands," Azzo said, his face growing sadder. "There are rumours his death was not a natural one."

"That is what I believe," Adelheid replied. "Of course Berengar denies it, but I am certain Lothair met his end at his hands."

In the sorrowful silence which followed, Adelheid reflected on what a wise move Lothair had made in rewarding Azzo with lands. If only he had lived longer, he might have emerged into a capable ruler and as he grew in wisdom, he might too have become kinder. For a moment she allowed herself to dream of taking her place beside a truly strong king, but such thoughts were useless. No one knew how matters would have gone if Lothair had lived. Her focus had to be on gaining support so she might rule Italy.

That night, as she enjoyed lying in a proper bed, knowing she was free and surrounded by loyal men, she vowed that no matter what it took, she would keep her final promise to Lothair. She would not rest until Berengar was driven from the throne.

∞∞∞

They knew word of Adelheid's whereabouts would leak out and were not unduly concerned. Indeed they hoped it would encourage loyal men to flock to their aid, but Berengar moved quicker than they had expected, sending a large company of men towards them.

There was concern at Canossa when scouts brought the news and Azzo moved quickly, bringing in livestock and supplies from the area, declaring the castle to be at siege. So when Berengar's men arrived, led, to Adelheid's disgust, by none other than Adalbert they found the gates barricaded and the pinnacle of rock inaccessible. The demand Adalbert made of Azzo to surrender the Queen was sent back with contempt.

"Do not be afeared, my lady," Azzo said to her. "This castle was built to withstand a siege. We will keep you safe until our allies gather."

"I fear I am putting you all in danger," Adelheid said.

"My lady, Canossa remains honoured to defend you. I gained this castle only because of the generosity of your late husband. It is fitting I use it to defend his widow."

Adelheid smiled faintly, thinking on the irony that Lothair who had shown so little regard for her when he was alive, was protecting her from beyond the grave.

Several weeks passed and no new allies came. Adelheid had hoped Italy would flock to her, but however strong the dislike was for Berengar, it seemed no one was prepared to go to war for her.

"I believe for Italy to depose Berengar, they wish first to know which man will replace him," Warinus said.

"What can we do?" Adelheid asked. "This siege is intolerable. How long can we endure it?"

"We are well stocked," Azzo reassured her.

"But the supplies will not last for ever. I cannot be responsible for everyone in the castle starving to death." Adelheid paced around, seeing what seemed to be an endless stretch of armed men gathered below the rock.

"We are a long way from that, my lady. But I think we must

plan further. We need help."

"I wonder if we could get a message to my brother in Burgundy. He could aid me. He could be crowned king, could he not?" Adelheid looked hopefully at the other two.

"It is possible," Azzo said. "But I am not certain Italy would accept him. They cast out your father."

"Burgundy has need of its own men," Warinus said. "I am not certain King Konrad could spare enough to make much difference here."

Adelheid sank down, putting her head in her hands. "I cannot marry Adalbert."

"My lady, we have already sworn we will do everything we can to avoid that," Azzo maintained, but his gaze, as he looked down from his fortress, was concerned. "What of Otto?"

"Otto?" Adelheid looked up. "Do you mean the King of Germany? Why would he aid me?"

"He might. He aided your brother," Warinus said. "He is a wise ruler who likes to have amicable relations with the realms on his border if they are good Christian realms. He has done much to ease the situation in West Francia."

"Then I suspect he will wish to cultivate an alliance with Berengar," Adelheid muttered. "Indeed did he not aid Berengar once before?"

Azzo shook his head. "He welcomed Berengar as an exile, but he refused to take sides in the struggle between him and Hugh, declaring it a matter for Italy to sort."

"Then I expect he will say the same in this matter," Adelheid said with a shrug.

"That depends on what is on offer for him," Warinus said. "He did not aid Berengar or Hugh last time, because there was nothing in it for him. He aided your brother because he gained an ally when he needed it most and he helped in West Francia because of the marriage of his sister and a pledge they would withdraw their claim to Lotharingia. If he had something to gain from helping us…"

"No," Adelheid said. "Lothair did not want German power in

Italy. It was matter he felt strongly on."

"He also begged you to do whatever it took to stop Berengar," Warinus pointed out. "The help of King Otto may be your only hope."

Adelheid shook her head, fearing that whatever she did she would be failing him. "What of the Pope? Could we not implore him for aid?"

"My lady, the Pope does not want to invite trouble to Rome. Our cause is too uncertain for him to involve himself. But King Otto is the most powerful man probably in all Christendom. He would be certain to take up the challenge if there was something to make it worth his while."

"What can I offer him?"

Azzo and Warinus exchanged glances. "Yourself."

Part Three: The Year of our Lord 951-2

Chapter one

"**N**ever," Adelheid cried. "I will not marry again."

"My lady, it would be a fine match," Azzo said. "You would be a queen twice over."

"Why would he want to wed me?"

"Because of your lands and that by right of marriage, he could gain the title of King of Italy. I do not doubt he has also heard of your beauty." Azzo looked taken aback by Adelheid's attitude. "He has been a widower himself now for several years. I am certain he will have been considering a new marriage."

"Is he not rather old?"

"Not very, my lady. I believe he has not quite seen thirty-nine years."

"Perhaps at a mere two decades, that seems old to you, my child," Warinus said with a twinkle in his eye.

In spite of herself, Adelheid laughed. "Forgive me. Of course that is not old. Indeed I am sure King Otto is in his prime, but..." She looked despairingly at Warinus. "You know why I cannot marry again."

"My lady, your devotion to your late husband does you credit," Azzo said. "But it is not improper for you to marry again. Indeed I feel sure King Lothair would not have wished you to go unprotected."

Adelheid bit back the words she wanted to say of Lothair. Azzo clearly though highly of him and it seemed churlish to deprive Lothair of that.

"All marriages are different, my child," Warinus said gently. "And in truth, I think you are out of other choices."

"I do not want to marry again. I wish to rule Italy alone."

Warinus smiled. "You are most certainly wise enough, but I fear you would be vulnerable at any time to a strong man who wished for the crown."

"What I truly want is to enter an abbey and devote myself to God. If King Otto were to aid me, could I do that?"

"In that case King Otto would be seen as an invader and Italy would flock to Berengar. Indeed I doubt very much whether a ruler as wise as King Otto would come under such circumstances." Azzo shrugged. "My lady, I believe another marriage is essential. Whoever you marry will have a claim to the throne. Better it is done at a time of your choosing."

Adelheid walked away from them, staring bleakly out at the hills, wishing she could hurl herself from the cliffs and end her life. Warinus put his hand on her shoulder. "After the King died, you felt you had failed in the task God set you when he placed you on the path of marriage. It seems you have another chance to succeed. The question is, who will you marry? Otto or Adalbert?"

"Is there much to choose between them?" Adelheid asked, turning back to the others.

Warinus and Azzo looked at each other. "I have never had the privilege of meeting King Otto, but his reputation is good," Azzo said. "He is merciful to his enemies and generous to his friends. His efforts against the heathens on the borders of his realm have been impressive indeed."

"And as a husband?"

"The late queen was much revered. Upon their marriage she was given extensive lands in Saxony, which she controlled herself. Indeed her influence in Germany was known to be considerable. It is said the King was truly devoted to her."

"I believe he would always recognise he ruled Italy through you," Warinus put in.

"From what I have heard of his morals, marriage to him

would be like marriage to Hugh," Adelheid snapped, irritated at hearing such praise heaped on the licentious king.

"His morals, my lady?" Azzo looked genuinely puzzled. "I have heard nothing ill on that."

Adelheid blushed. "Forgive me. Perhaps it is not common knowledge, but I heard he has a bastard son who he flaunts, much as Hugh flaunted his illegitimate children."

Azzo's face cleared. "Oh, you mean William. He is said to be an excellent young man."

"He is intended for the church, I believe," Warinus said. "From what I hear, he will be a fine addition."

Adelheid stared at them both in shock. "You condone this?"

"Not condone, exactly," Warinus said slowly. "But…"

"King Otto was very young when he sired William," Azzo said. "Of course it is still a sin, but it is not an uncommon one among young men. He was married to the late queen not long after William's birth and there was not another scandal about him. Not even since her death."

"My child, such matters are not ideal, but it seems wrong to condemn him for one sin so long ago."

"I suppose so," Adelheid replied. "What if we do nothing? Perhaps good men of Italy will still come to us."

"Perhaps," Azzo said. "Indeed, if that is what you command, my lady, that is what we shall do."

"But you may have to watch the good men and women of Canossa starve, my child. Can you do that, when a single action of yours could save them?"

Adelheid bit back a sob, realising it would yet again be her duty to marry. "No, I cannot. So it is Adalbert or Otto. The traitor or the German. Lothair wished for neither of these. But his last request was to stop Berengar, so if King Otto is truly our only hope…"

"I believe he is," Warinus said.

"Very well. What can we do? How do we get a message to him?"

"I will bear it," Warinus said. "A priest will easily slip

unharmed through the lines."

"Oh no, Father. Such a journey is so long. I cannot ask you to make such a perilous trip."

"Of course you can, my child. I shall not undertake it on foot. I am sure Lord Azzo will grant me the use of a horse."

"Absolutely and anything else you need. I think this plan is truly wise, my Lady Queen."

Adelheid felt as if she were being dragged back to prison, but forced a smile. "Let us hope so. Father, will you take down a message? State, 'Most noble Otto, King of Germany, I, Adelheid, by God's grace Queen of Italy and by herself a poor sinner, implore for your aid from my refuge at Canossa, where I am besieged by the enemies of myself and my late husband, the noble King Lothair. If you can liberate me from my desperate situation, I pledge myself to you in marriage. Such a union will join the fair lands of Italy to your realm.'" Adelheid bowed her head, wishing she could wake from the nightmare. From her pouch she took one of her last jewels. It was a ring which had belonged to her father. "Present him with this token as proof of my pledge."

"I shall, my child. I feel sure he will be honoured by your offer."

Adelheid wept bitterly that night, wishing more than anything there would be an alternative to the plans. When she arose early the next morning to bid Warinus farewell, she scanned the horizon, praying for some men to aid her without the need of marriage. But the hills remained stubbornly empty.

"You will be in my prayers, Father," she said as she hugged Warinus farewell.

"And you will be in mine, my child. Try not to fear. King Otto will come and your enemies will surely flee. You will be reunited again with Emma."

The pain in her heart eased slightly at the thought of that. She would bear anything, if she could be with her daughter once again.

Chapter two

The weeks which followed were long and anxious. She worried for Father Warinus, the number of possible accidents seeming never ending. He could fall from his horse or be overcome by the heat. He might encounter thieves who would attack him for the single jewelled ring he bore and the plain crucifix around his neck. Then there were the remote mountains he would have to cross. It was a long journey for a man, who although not yet old was not young either.

The summer was hot and even high in the hills as they were, it was often unbearable. Their food supplies grew lower and eventually had to be strictly rationed. Adelheid was consumed with guilt as she watched the people eat their meagre portions while the aromas of roasting meat and fish drifted up from the army camped below.

"How much longer can we hold out?" Adelheid asked, as the first hint of autumn filled the air.

"Not much longer, my lady. Another few weeks perhaps."

Adelheid shook her head. "I will not let you starve. If there is no word from the German king soon, I shall have to give myself in marriage to Adalbert."

"I pray it will not come to that," Azzo said. "Father Warinus should have reached Germany some time ago by now. Help is surely on its way."

"He may have befallen some accident and never reached his destination," Adelheid said, the familiar anxiety gnawing at her once again. "Or perhaps the German king does not wish to marry me. Why should he risk his men in such a venture?"

"I would be surprised indeed if that is the case," Azzo said. "I pray it is not."

But the days passed with still no sign of aid. At last came the night when the meal was more meagre than ever and she realised they must be down to their last scraps of food. Silently she scraped her bowl, not even tasting the contents as she came to a decision.

"Lord Azzo, I thank you most humbly for your hospitality, but I cannot take advantage of it any longer. In the morn I shall surrender myself to Adalbert's forces and you shall all dine well at my wedding feast."

"But, my lady," Azzo protested. "Wait another few days, I beg you. We can last out a little longer."

Resolutely Adelheid shook her head. "There is no point. I will bid you good night, my lord. I beg you not to try to sway me."

In her chamber Orsa was in tears, as she added her entreaties. Tears stung Adelheid's eyes. After everything Orsa had been through to keep her from marriage with Adalbert, it was cruel that in the end it had proved useless. Warinus too had sacrificed so much. Perhaps he had even sacrificed his life for her.

"If I had accepted Adalbert's offer when it was first made, Father Warinus would still be with me," she said. "I would have spared you all so much and not have endured these months away from my daughter. Please leave me."

She wept often throughout those dark hours, as a wretched future of life with Adalbert stretched before her. Her defiance of Berengar would not be easily forgiven. By day she would be treated with contempt and at night... Adelheid's mind veered away from those visions, praying she would have the strength to endure them. Bitter tears flowed at how miserably she had failed Lothair and when she bore Adalbert a son, her failure would be complete.

It was a long night, yet it seemed that all too soon light had touched the sky. She rose from her bed and dressed neatly.

Even if she was preparing herself for execution, she could not have been more afeared.

She left the chamber, moving solemnly to where Azzo was waiting.

"Can I say nothing to dissuade you, my lady?" he asked.

Adelheid smiled, her face in a mask of serenity. "No, my lord. Your kindness will never be forgotten. Will you escort me down?"

Azzo swallowed, looking close to tears. "It will be an honour, my lady."

There was similar sadness on the faces of all who had gathered to bid her farewell. Adelheid nodded graciously at them all, as she made her way to where the entrance had been blockaded, preparing herself for the descent.

Only one bolt had been removed, when a murmur of surprise and excitement came from the men on look out. Azzo paused, frowning up at them. "What is happening?" he called.

"We are not certain, my lord," a man cried. "But it looks as if the King's army are packing up."

"Replace that bolt," Azzo snapped.

"But..." said Adelheid.

"No, my lady. I will disobey you, so do not ask me to unbolt the gate. We can hold out for a little longer while we see what is occurring."

Adelheid slumped in a corner of the hall, not joining the others at the look out. She did not think she could bear the disappointment if it turned out the army was staying after all, but when Azzo returned to the hall his broad smile told her the news was good.

"They are moving away and moving swiftly," he announced.

"God be praised," Adelheid murmured, feeling as if she would weep with the burden lifting from her. "But why? Is it the German army?"

"I know not. There is no sign of another army, my lady. They must have received a message telling them to move on."

Azzo sent men down for fresh supplies and they came back

laden, reporting that the army had moved on so quickly they had left much in the way of provisions.

"Even if they return, we can hold out for a long time," Azzo said, gleefully tossing hunks of bread to everyone.

∞∞∞

Although the army had gone, they did not dare lower their defences as nervously they awaited the next development. It did not take long before the lookouts reported a large company of men approaching.

When the company arrived at the foot of the hill, their actions were not aggressive. The guard sent down to ask their intentions returned quickly with a smile on his face.

"The Duke of Bavaria begs admittance," the man said. "He comes in peace and brings instructions from King Otto of Germany."

"Please bid the Duke most welcome," Azzo replied.

"The Duke of Bavaria. The King's brother, I believe," Adelheid said slowly. Her face lit up. "It must mean Father Warinus reached journey's end without mishap. God be praised."

It was not long before a tall, fair haired man strode into the hall. Azzo went forward to take the man by the hands and drew him over to her. He dropped to one knee.

"I am honoured to meet you, my Lady Queen," he said. "I am Henry, Duke of Bavaria."

"Welcome, my Lord Duke," Adelheid replied properly.

The man got to his feet and studied her. He grinned. "My brother is fortunate indeed. Another beautiful wife."

Adelheid blushed, taken aback by the forward nature of the man. He looked to be around thirty years of age and in spite of his bold manner, she could not help liking him. She found herself smiling back.

"What are the King's instructions?" Azzo asked.

"He wishes me to escort the Queen to Pavia, where they can

be wed." Henry winked at her. "I do not doubt that once he sees her, he will be eager indeed for the wedding to take place at all speed."

Adelheid smiled faintly. The relief she would not be forced into marriage with Adalbert now overtaken by a new fear.

"Is it safe now?" Azzo asked. "I am reluctant to allow the Queen out of my protection until it is."

Henry nodded. "We faced little resistance. As soon as the former king heard Otto was in Italy, he fled south. A sensible man – facing Otto is a fight few men have any stomach for."

"The former king?" Adelheid asked.

"Otto has been crowned King of Italy."

Although she gave no outward sign of her irritation, Adelheid ground her teeth, feeling she should have been consulted before the German crowned himself king. As she smiled graciously at Henry, she was also annoyed Otto had not come for her himself. Such actions did not bode well for the influence Azzo and Warinus had assured her she would have.

"Lord Azzo, I admire your devotion to the Queen's safety," Henry said. "I shall be glad for you to also accompany her to Pavia, so you can assure yourself of her wellbeing. How soon can you be ready to depart, my lady?"

It was as if she was being returned to prison. "As soon as you give the word, my lord."

Chapter three

As she mounted a horse for the ride to Pavia, she looked up for the last time at the Fortress of Canossa. They had been trapped there by the siege, but ironically she had felt freer that summer than she had been for years and perhaps ever would be again. She shivered in the crisp autumn air, not certain if it was from the cold or fear.

Henry urged his horse to her side. "Please tell me whenever you need to rest, my lady. This journey shall progress at your pace."

Adelheid inclined her head, touched by the respect the German men were showing her. "Tell me of the family, my lord. I believe the king has another brother."

"Bruno, the wisest of us. He is Otto's chancellor and chaplain. You will meet him at Pavia."

"I know the King has a son and daughter, but what of you, my lord? Are you wed?"

It was obvious from Henry's face that she had asked a question which pleased him. "I am wed to Judith, daughter of the late Duke Arnulf of Bavaria. We have been blessed with two fair daughters, although I may have another child by now. Judith was not far from her time when I left."

"No doubt you are hoping for a son this time."

Henry gave a slight frown. "I am hoping to hear Judith has come safely through her ordeal, but yes, we will be overjoyed if it is a healthy son."

Adelheid smiled at his obvious concern for his wife. She had been trying to work out who Henry reminded her of, but she suddenly realised now that it was Liudolf, Ida's husband. It was not surprising since Liudolf was Henry's nephew and, it suddenly struck her, soon to be her stepson.

"My lady, forgive me if I am being too forward, but for the most part Otto maintains an informality in the family. Please call me by my name and if I may, I will use yours."

"Of course. Is that all the family?"

"Well, our sisters are wed and both in West Francia. You mentioned Otto's son. I assume you meant Liudolf, but Otto has another son, William. And there is our mother, the Dowager Queen, Mathilda."

Adelheid had no wish to speak of the bastard son, but she was surprised by his last words. "Your mother? I had not realised she still lived."

"She does indeed and enjoys excellent health."

"I hope she likes me," Adelheid murmured, her thoughts on Willa. The last thing she wanted was another rival queen.

"I expect she will." Henry grinned. "As a general rule she has a much higher opinion of her sons' wives than she does of her sons."

They were still a day's ride from Pavia when the King's messengers swept up to them in a cloud of dust. Henry laughed as he saw them.

"You can tell the King he will get his bride soon enough," Henry called. "I will not wear her out just to curb his impatience."

The messenger grinned as he saluted Henry. "The King is indeed eager to meet the fair Queen of Italy, but that is not why I am here. There is news from Bavaria."

Henry tensed, sucking in his breath. "Is it Judith? Is all well?"

"Yes, my lord. Your most beautiful duchess was safely delivered of a fine son. With your blessing, my lord, she wishes to name him Henry."

Henry stared open mouthed at the messenger before his face

lit up into a huge grin. "A boy! God be praised." He looked at the messenger, anxiety appearing again in his gaze. "And Judith is well?"

"The messenger from Bavaria reported that the Duchess came safely through the birth and is in excellent spirits."

Henry grinned proudly, as the gathered people clamoured to congratulate him. Adelheid smiled, liking Henry more than ever for his reaction to the news. A dull pain struck her as she remembered how little meaning her own health had for Lothair, once Emma had been born.

∞ ∞ ∞

The already buoyant spirits of everyone in the entourage rose still further at this news and it was a merry bunch who arrived the next day in Pavia. As they entered the gates, the cheers for Adelheid rang out.

"The Queen! The Queen has returned."

"God be praised!"

"God's blessings on you, my lady."

The crowd grew and the cheers became louder. Adelheid smiled, forgetting her impending marriage, as she enjoyed the devotion of the people she loved. She was reminded sharply of it again as she arrived at the royal palace where it was clear the German king had made himself quite at home. But the dull resentment of the German guards who saluted them upon entry faded as she remembered how annoyed Lothair had been when her popularity had eclipsed his.

"I hope the King will not feel I am unduly courting the people's approval," she said fearfully to Henry as he helped her down from her horse. "It is natural for them to show their joy, as they have not seen me for some time."

Henry shook his head. "Otto is quite used to being outdone by his wife in popularity. In Magdeburg, the centre of Otto's power, the people used to cheer far more for Eadgyth than they did for him. He always said he regarded that as a sign of their great good sense."

Adelheid gave a tight smile, as she rested a hand which seemed suddenly clammy on Henry's arm to enter the palace. Her eyes darted around the hall, pleased to see a few familiar faces. It was of a particular delight to see Gilia again and to be able to thank her at last for her service.

"It looks as if Otto has some matters to attend to," Henry said. "Sit down and refresh yourself. I shall send a message to let him know you are here."

Adelheid did not like being bade to be seated as if she were a guest in her own residence, but she did as she was instructed, taking a cup of wine. Spiced cakes stuffed with nuts were placed before her, but she could not manage a single bite. She had to fight the urge to run from the palace, as she awaited the arrival of her betrothed, fear mingling with anger that he had not been there to welcome her. No doubt he was wasting no time in putting her in her place.

She sank into a daydream, consumed by her own fears, starting at the noise from the courtyard.

"So, a boy for you at last, Brother. You must be overjoyed," a man's voice called.

"I most certainly am," Henry called back.

Adelheid got nervously to her feet, her heart thudding with terror. She got only the most fleeting of glimpses of the tall man entering the hall, before flinging herself to her knees, bowing her head.

Footsteps swiftly crossed the hall towards her. She kept her head low, seeing only the well-made leather boots of the man standing before her. Strong hands gripped hold of hers, pulling her back to her feet. Trying to show no sign of fear she looked up into the face of the most powerful man in Christendom, Otto the King of Germany.

Chapter four

A delheid's first thought was that he looked younger than she had expected. She had assumed he would be showing the first signs of old age, but his hair was dark and abundant and if there were any grey hairs, they were not notable among the lighter streaks the Italian sun had bleached. His face did display a few lines and there was a hardness about it, which did nothing to endear him to her. Nor did his powerful looking body, enhanced by the fine green tunic. It conveyed such a regal impression, leaving Adelheid miserably aware of how drab she must appear in her grey widow's weeds.

But as Otto studied her, he did not look disapproving. The harshness of his face suddenly lit up into a broad smile bringing a sparkle to his vivid blue eyes.

"My dear lady, you must not kneel to me."

"I wish only to express my gratitude for your assistance, my lord," Adelheid stammered, dazzled by his smile.

"I regard it as a great honour that you requested it, my lady," Otto replied.

He raised the hands he still held briefly to his lips and she saw, adorning his finger, the ring she had sent. He followed her gaze.

"Ah, yes. I owe you something, do I not?" Otto opened his pouch and took out a gold band, set with a fine sapphire. With a smile he slipped it onto her finger. It was far finer than the ring she had sent him and Adelheid felt at a disadvantage as she stammered her thanks.

"Accept this as my pledge to wed you," he said.

Adelheid swallowed, realising there was nothing she could now do to extricate herself. "Of course I will honour the pledge I made to wed you."

"Thank you." Otto pressed a kiss against her lips. To Adelheid's relief it was very brief and easy enough to endure, although as he looked at her steadily for a moment, she feared she had shown some revulsion. He let go of her hands, moving fractionally away from her and gave a slight bow. "You do me a great honour. In truth I was attracted by the thought of your lands, but now I am here, I see there is a far fairer reward." He smiled again as she flushed at his words. "I would like the wedding to take place as soon as possible. How soon would be acceptable to you?"

Adelheid tried to think of an excuse to put off the inevitable. "I would like my daughter to be present if that is possible. She was sent to an abbey for her safety. I believe it is not far away, but I am not very sure where."

"I am," Otto replied. "Your priest confided in me the location and I have anticipated your request. Your brother, Konrad accompanied me here. I asked him to transport the child to Pavia. He should return some time in the morn."

"Emma will be returned to me tomorrow?" Adelheid's face lit up in a burst of radiance.

Otto's eyes widened appreciatively as her beauty glowed more than ever. "I believe so," he replied.

"I can scarce believe I will have her with me again," she breathed, the longing she had needed to keep so strictly suppressed suddenly overwhelming her, swiftly followed by excitement at the thought of holding her close. She realised Otto was still watching her with a slight smile. "Oh, forgive me, my lord, I have not thanked you. Truly I am most grateful."

"Such a beautiful smile is all the thanks I need," Otto replied. "And perhaps we can dispense with formality. You have a lovely name, Adelheid. I trust I may use it."

"Of course." Adelheid hesitated, nervous of such familiarity with this stranger. "Otto."

Otto took hold of her hands and kissed them again. "I am sure you will soon feel quite comfortable with using my name. So, can we arrange the wedding for the day after tomorrow? Assuming, of course, there is no delay with your daughter's return."

Adelheid maintained her smile, touched he had gone to the trouble to bring Emma to her. "I shall be honoured to become your wife on that day."

Otto turned to a group of men waiting by the door, Henry among them. He gestured to them and the first to come forward was a man in clerical robes who looked very like him.

"My brother and chaplain, Bruno," Otto said, confirming her guess.

"I am honoured to meet you, Fa..." Adelheid stuttered to a halt not sure how to address him.

Both Otto and Henry laughed. "We do not know how to address him either," Henry said.

"I usually just call him a fool." Otto's face was completely expressionless, but a mischievous gleam appeared in his eye.

Bruno shook his head at the other two. He was many years their junior, but his grave manner made him appear older. "Please use my name in an informal setting, my lady," Bruno said. "Or my title if you feel more comfortable with that."

The next man to come forward was Liudolf. He gave no sign of recognition as he bowed without smiling over her hand.

"My son, Liudolf, Duke of Swabia," Otto said, barely glancing at him.

"I am pleased to see you again," Adelheid said with a smile. She had not got to know him well at her wedding to Lothair, but at least he was not a stranger.

"You have met already?" Otto asked, looking faintly displeased.

"I had the honour of attending her first wedding." Liudolf gave a sideways glance at his father. "And now it seems I shall have the honour of attending her second."

"I hope Ida is well," Adelheid said. "I was so sorry to hear Hermann had died. I did not know him well, but he always struck me as the very kindest of men."

Liudolf met her eyes, the scowl fading from his face. "He was truly the finest of men and he is very much missed. Apart from that Ida is well. She has born two daughters since you last saw her."

The last of the group to be presented was a striking, red-headed man, some years older than Liudolf. "This is Conrad, the Duke of Lotharingia," Otto said, resting his hand on the man's shoulder. "My son by marriage and the father of my fine grandson."

The man bowed, but before he could say anything, Liudolf shot his father an angry look. "You never miss an opportunity to remind me of how I have failed to sire a son, do you, Father?"

Otto's face also darkened. "Do not be foolish, Liudolf. I meant no such thing."

"You are sure to have a son one day," Henry put in. "Why, look how many years Judith and I have been wed and now, at last a son."

Adelheid watched them in astonishment, noticing how close Otto was stood to his son-in-law, while Liudolf stood apart. She remembered how when she had last seen him, she had been struck by how affectionate he had been with Hermann, closer than many a father and son. Evidently closer than he was to his own father. He shrugged. "If I never sire a son, I take comfort in remembering how the one I regard as the very finest of men and indeed the very finest of fathers, sired but one daughter and always considered himself most fortunate."

Liudolf and Otto glared at each other for a moment until Adelheid leapt into the awkward silence. "I too have a daughter," she said. "Maybe it is a mother's pride, but I consider her uncommonly beautiful. I am sure your daughters are most fair, Liudolf. Indeed I do not see how they cannot be."

Liudolf looked back at her, his face relaxing once again.

"Mathilde, the youngest, is still an infant, but she has a look of Ida and so I certainly consider her fair. Regelind, the elder, is blonde and is truly beautiful. Perhaps it is wishful thinking, but I believe she resembles my mother."

"Do not be so foolish," Otto snapped. "She is not much more than an infant. You cannot possibly tell such a thing."

Liudolf returned the glare. "Given how long it is since you last saw her, I do not see how you could possibly know anything about it." He bowed to Adelheid. "Please excuse me, my lady. I have much to do."

Otto frowned as Liudolf left them, while Conrad and Bruno exchanged glances and shrugged. Conrad smiled awkwardly at Adelheid. "My lady, I am not sure if you are aware, but I have the honour of being your kinsman. My mother was your mother's sister."

"Of course," Adelheid said. "Forgive me, I had forgotten, but I remember now my mother telling me how her nephew had become the Duke of Lotharingia." She smiled brightly at them all, only too aware of the frown still marking Otto's face. "Well, I am certainly returning to my family."

∞∞∞

To Adelheid's relief, Otto had recovered his good temper by the time of the evening meal. As she entered the hall he was laughing with Bruno and Henry and she was unable to help smiling at the bond between the brothers. All three rose to their feet as they noticed her and bowed.

"Come, sit with me," Otto said indicating a chair between himself and Henry.

All of Adelheid's resentment flooded back at the presumption of this man telling her where to sit in her own residence. It annoyed her still further that he had taken the most prominent seat without asking for her approval.

"Unless, of course, you would prefer not to." The warm smile swiftly faded from Otto's face.

Inwardly Adelheid shivered at how her face had betrayed every thought. She knew she had to be more careful. "Naturally I am glad to," she said taking the chair he had indicated.

Otto filled up her cup himself with a rich smelling wine and raised his own. His smile had widened once again. "To your very good health, Adelheid."

"And to you both," Henry added. "I wish you every happiness."

"I feel sure I will be," Otto replied, laying his hand over Adelheid's. "With such a fair wife, how can I not be?"

Adelheid flushed as she murmured her thanks, wishing she could pull her hand away from the heavy one resting on it. She had to admit that Otto's manner was charming and if he was to be an acquaintance, she would have said she liked him very much. But he was to be her husband and Lothair too had been capable of being charming.

There was more laughter from the doorway as Liudolf entered, his arm flung across Conrad's shoulders. Adelheid was surprised. Earlier she had assumed the two were rivals for Otto's affection, yet it seemed they too were good friends. After polite bows to her and Otto, both men called their greetings to Bruno, stretching their arms across the table to clasp his hands. But she noted how Liudolf took the seat next to Otto without even looking at Henry, while Conrad merely nodded at him. As the lively conversation started up once again, Adelheid forced her mind away from the strange dynamics in the family, to listen attentively to her betrothed.

She was still puzzling over the family as she sat in the hall the next day when her thoughts were interrupted by the sound of horses in the courtyard. For the tenth time that day, Adelheid held her breath wondering if this would be the reunion with her daughter. She gave a cry of joy as a few moments later her brother walked in, carrying Emma fast asleep in his arms.

She ran towards them, taking in the sight of her daughter's peaceful face, her cheeks slightly flushed. "She has grown so much," she whispered. "I wonder if she will even know me."

"I am sure she will," Konrad said, gently placing Emma into her arms.

Adelheid sank down onto a chair, tears filling her eyes at the warmth of that little body tucked against hers.

"Brother, forgive me for not greeting you. It is good to see you."

"It is. So, you are to wed Otto? He is a good man. Much better than that puppy our father found for you."

"Please do not speak ill of Lothair," Adelheid said. "He had his faults, but he was Emma's father and he did not deserve to die so young or so cruelly."

"Of course," Konrad said. "I never got to know him well. I am sure as he grew older he became a fine man."

Emma stirred, saving Adelheid from having to comment on that. Sleepily she opened her eyes, a look of bewilderment flickering over her face as she saw her mother smiling tenderly down. For a heart stopping moment Adelheid was certain her daughter had forgotten her when the confusion suddenly gave way to that long missed smile. "Mother!" she cried, flinging her arms around Adelheid's neck.

Adelheid clung to her. "Oh, Emma, we will stay together now. I swear it." As she spoke those words, a chill crept upon her. She realised she had no idea whether Otto would be content with that. He might already be intending her to be raised in an abbey or with some other kin. She tightened her arms around her daughter, wondering what she would do if that was the case.

Otto came in a little while later and smiled as he saw Adelheid with the child still cradled in her arms. He patted her on the head. "Beautiful," he said. "Just like her mother. I trust this means the wedding need not be delayed any longer."

Adelheid swallowed her nerves and smiled back. "No, I shall have the honour of becoming your wife in the morn."

"Excellent." Otto sat down, pouring himself a cup of ale.

Summoning her courage, Adelheid took a deep breath. "Otto, may I make one last request of you before our marriage?"

Otto raised his eyebrows. "Of course."

"Can Emma stay with us to be raised alongside any children I bear you?"

"Naturally." Otto looked puzzled. "Where else would she be raised?"

"I did not know what your intentions were for her."

"I have no intentions," he replied, smiling at her look of surprise. "She is your daughter. Oh, I hope I may stand as a father to her, but I would not presume to make any important decisions concerning her without consulting you." His smile widened into one of amusement. "So, will we be wed in the morn?"

Adelheid nodded as the relief flowed through her. If she could keep her daughter nearby, she would somehow manage to endure this marriage.

Chapter five

The night before her wedding Adelheid took Emma into her bed, knowing it might be the last time she would ever be able to do this.

"Oh, Emma," she whispered to the sleeping child. "How I wish we could steal away, just you and I. But where would we go?"

It was a hopeless question in any case. She could hear the German guards laughing in the courtyard. She was as much a prisoner there as she had ever been.

"I wish you had been at Canossa with me," she said. "There I was truly a queen. The men did as I commanded and there was no one to control me, only to advise. If you had been there, I think it would have been the happiest time of my life."

The child stirred slightly and Adelheid lay down, holding her close. Silent tears soaked her pillow, as she lay dreading the morning.

∞∞∞

As soon as the morn came Emma was whisked away from her, as her women brought water to wash herself. They urged her to wear some of the fine dresses which had remained in the coffers at Pavia, but she was resolute in her refusal.

"Until I am wed, I am still a widow and Lothair has not yet been gone a year. It would not be fitting."

She chose a grey dress of fine wool over a cream coloured tunic. When Orsa held up a mirror, Adelheid nodded, thinking the dull colours matched the bleakness in her heart.

"You always look beautiful, my lady," Gilia said stoutly.

"It is certain the King thinks so," Orsa added.

Graciously Adelheid inclined her head and waited nervously for the summons. When it came, she gave no sign of any fear as she laid her hand on Konrad's arm. He had glanced over her sombre raiment with a slight frown, but said nothing. The flutters of Adelheid's heart increased as she suddenly wondered if Otto would be disappointed. She was dressed as befitted a widow and he could not publically complain, but no doubt in private he would find ways of showing his displeasure.

However when she reached the hall, Otto gave no sign of any anger. He was finely dressed in a red tunic, edged in bands of embroidered blue cloth. A light cloak hung from his shoulders, pinned with a fine jewel and the crown of the Lombard's was on his head. He smiled as he extended his hands to hers.

Graciously, giving no sign of her dread, she took them and waited. Around her the crowded hall stilled.

"I, Otto of Saxony, King of Germany and Italy do take you, Adelheid, daughter of King Rudolph of Burgundy and widow of King Lothair of Italy as my wife from this day until death parts us."

The panic welling in Adelheid threatened to engulf her as all eyes went expectantly to her. With a great effort she forced it down as she spoke the words to imprison herself once again. "I, Adelheid of Burgundy, Queen of Italy take you, Otto, most noble King of Germany as my husband from this day until death parts us." As she finished the slight murmur in the hall made her realise, to her consternation, she had not acknowledged his title as King of Italy. She glanced from lowered eyes at Otto, but he displayed no reaction.

Bruno, who stood before them, nodded. "Otto and Adelheid, I declare you wed."

Otto smiled, pressing a gentle kiss against her lips, which in her anguish she barely noticed.

"My Lord King, I bid you and your wife attend mass, so we may bestow upon her the title, Queen of Germany."

As they followed Bruno to the church, he glanced over his shoulder, a mischievous gleam in his eyes, which suddenly made him appear very much the younger brother. In a lowered voice, only she and Otto would hear, he said, "And I think perhaps I should crown you again, Otto, just in case any forget you are King of Germany."

Adelheid went crimson. She stole a swift look at her new husband, surprised to see him trying to control a smile. It was with a feeling of total bewilderment that she knelt before the high altar for Bruno to say the mass. At the end when everyone rose to their feet she remained kneeling.

"I anoint you, Adelheid, Queen of Germany," Bruno intoned, marking a cross on her forehead and on her shoulders. "May you bear your duties ever with grace and God's blessing." He placed a crown on her head. "Arise, Adelheid, by God's grace, Queen of Germany."

"All hail Queen Adelheid!" Otto proclaimed and in deafening tones the call was joyfully taken up.

Back in the hall Otto was quickly surrounded by well-wishers, but Konrad pulled her to one side. "Adelheid, what possessed you not to name him King of Italy? I know you had some foolish notion of reigning alone, but this must be forgotten now."

"I know not," she said. Deep down she wondered if Konrad was right. She had resented Otto for so promptly taking the title.

"He is not some foolish boy, like your first husband. You need to be careful not to offend him. First you attend the wedding looking as if you are going to a requiem mass and now this."

Before Adelheid could reply, Otto's voice interrupted them. "Where is my wife?"

He put an arm around her waist to pull her away from

Konrad, but there was no chance of any private words, as the court presented her with gift after gift. She stood stiffly, ever aware of the pressure of his arm, wondering how angry he was. It was only as Otto led her to the head of the table that she was able to glance up at him and say in a low voice, "Please forgive me for not naming all your titles."

"Do you wish to remind me that I bear the title of King of Italy only through you?" Otto's tone was courteous, but nonetheless Adelheid was certain she had detected a hint of anger underlying it.

"N... no. Of course not."

"Are you sure?" He raised an eyebrow, but his expression softened as he noted the distress in her face. "Oh, Adelheid, you try ever to be proper, do you not? It is of no matter. You have after all granted me the title I truly wished to gain this day – your husband."

∞ ∞ ∞

It was a day of feasting and merriments which afterwards Adelheid scarcely remembered. She was too busy watching her husband, laughing when he laughed and appearing to listen attentively to all he said. When night fell she took note of the expectant looks and announced she would retire. Otto too stood.

"I shall join you presently," he said in a low voice, which enough people overheard to call out some ribald comments. He sat down again, grinning as Adelheid left the hall, her cheeks red and her heart already thumping in terror.

In her chamber she quickly dismissed her women and knelt down before a jewelled cross, shivering in her thin robe.

"Blessed Father, help me endure this night and all others. Help me to be a dutiful wife, so my husband never has cause to be displeased with me."

Still shivering, she climbed into bed and waited. It did not take long for Otto to arrive. She kept her head bowed, hoping he would assume she was still at prayer. He glanced at her curiously, but said nothing as he tossed away his robe and climbed into bed.

In a panic Adelheid clutched her own robe tighter around her. His hands folded over hers. "May I?" he asked.

Adelheid's fists were clenched so tightly she was not certain she could release them, but somehow she managed it, allowing him to push the robe away from her shoulders. He muttered something appreciative, but her heart was thudding so loudly in her ears she did not hear the words. However Otto did not seize her as she had expected. Instead he put his hand under her chin, tilting up her face. He studied it in a puzzled fashion.

"You're frightened," he said softly. "When Father Warinus told me of you, he said nothing ever daunted you, but you are frightened tonight." He put a hand on her shoulder, pulling it sharply back as she flinched. "You're frightened of me."

Frantically Adelheid shook her head, furious with herself for her reaction. So many times she had angered Lothair by shrinking away from him, but clearly she had learnt nothing. Daring to look into Otto's face, she was surprised to see the sympathy on it.

"I think your first marriage was not a happy one," he said.

"Not very."

"Did he hurt you?"

"Sometimes," she whispered, but aghast at herself for complaining, she quickly added, "I do not think he meant to."

Otto's brow was slightly creased. "He cannot have tried very hard not to. It is not difficult to avoid hurting a woman."

"His father and mine had been enemies. I think it was natural for him to have little regard for me."

"I do not agree. Whatever has gone on before, a man should always treat the woman he hopes will bear his child with utmost care. I will never hurt you, Adelheid." As if to prove his words he leant forward, his lips gently meeting hers for a fleeting instant.

Her eyes widened in surprise. It seemed strange that the kiss she had barely felt against her lips was causing such stirring in her heart. He smiled and took hold of her hand. "I truly do not want to cause you any distress. Are you able to receive me this night?"

It took a moment for the meaning of his words to sink in and she was sorely tempted, but she nodded. "Naturally I can fulfil my duties."

Otto raised her hand to his lips, his face gravely respectful. "Thank you."

He pulled her into his arms at that, but for a long time he did nothing more than hold her close, one hand gently stroking her hair. Gradually the tension eased out of her, the warmth of his body surprising her with its comfort. For an instant she closed her eyes, daring to relax. The strong arm tightened around her, enfolding her even closer. As he rested his cheek briefly against the top of her head, Adelheid was stunned to realise how safe she felt. She could happily have remained like that forever, but she pulled away to look at him, wondering what he was thinking of her. Tremulously she smiled at the kindness in his expression.

"You truly do not need to be afraid. I know Eadgyth was never frightened of me."

"So your first marriage was happy?"

"Very," Otto replied. "Eadgyth came out from Wessex with her sister, so I might choose which one best pleased me. Something about Eadgyth struck me straight away, although they were both very pretty. We were married and for sixteen years she supported me in everything. When she died, it was as if the sun had gone down on my life." Otto closed his eyes against a memory which clearly still pained him. "I was not alone in my grief. I think the whole of Germany mourned a much loved queen."

"Of course," Adelheid said, ashamed to feel so jealous of that woman who, although she had not lived a long life, had been the recipient of such love.

Otto smiled at her again. "Eadgyth will always be remembered with the very deepest of love, but she has been gone now for some years. I think I could love again. What of you? Do you think you could love me or am I perhaps too old?"

There was a slight gleam in his eye which made her suspect Warinus had repeated her words to him. She flushed, but the automatic assurance which had leapt to her lips stopped. She looked at him, reaching out to wonderingly touch his cheek. "Yes, I think I can."

Never before had she wanted to touch a man, but she found herself pressing her lips against his, welcoming the arms which pulled her closer to him again. The kiss was still gentle, but there was an eagerness now to his lips. He broke away, sliding back against the pillows. With a grin he held out his arms to her. Adelheid gazed at him, bewildered by what she was feeling. The smile was hard to resist and with the candle light softening his features, he appeared younger and somehow appealing. Her heart was beating faster as she went into his strong arms, allowing them to enclose her against a muscled chest dusted in dark hair. As he pressed kisses against her face and throat, his hands drifting slowly down her body, she realised she no longer knew what to expect from their wedding night, except she was confident it would hold no terrors.

Chapter six

It was the deepest sleep Adelheid had enjoyed in a very long time. It was only as she realised Otto's body was no longer pressed against hers that she properly awoke and rolled over, surprised to see it was daylight. Otto was wrapping a robe around himself, but he sat back on the bed when he saw she was awake.

"I did not mean to disturb you," he said, smoothing back her hair. "Is all well with you?"

She nodded shyly, her face flushing at the memories of his hands and lips on her. "I did not know I could feel so happy."

Otto smiled, kissing her cheek. "I have some matters I must attend to, but you rest as long as you wish. However when you do rise, I would prefer it if you dressed as my wife. I know it is less than a year since the late king died, but do you need to remain in full mourning?" There was a hint of anger in Otto's voice and Adelheid realised she had annoyed him in her wedding attire. "After what you told me last night, I am surprised you are mourning him at all."

"I will be glad to dress finely today," she said.

"That does not answer my question. Why did you feel the need to dress so glumly for our wedding? I have got the impression on a few occasions that even though I came to your aid, you wish to put me in my place."

Adelheid flushed. "No, of course not." Even to her ears the words did not sound convincing.

"I thought so," he said wryly.

There was a tense silence and when she looked at Otto it was obvious he was still waiting for an explanation. But the humour lurking in his eyes convinced her to speak honestly. "After Lothair died I had a dream that I alone would rule Italy. Of course it was a foolish dream, but even so I mourned for it yesterday as I had to put it aside."

She waited for Otto's inevitable comments how as a woman such matters were beyond her understanding, but he surprised her. "It is unusual, but not foolish," he said. "I have heard of such a lady. She was Eadgyth's aunt and she ruled her land after the death of her husband. I am sure if you were ever called to rule, you would be skilled indeed. As my wife you will not be without influence."

Adelheid smiled. "Perhaps, but I shall come out of mourning today." She touched his cheek gently. "I have awakened now from my dream and found that reality is not so bad!"

Otto laughed. "Thank you." He kissed her again before leaving.

Adelheid lay back for a moment with a smile on her face, but the bed was cold and lonely without him. She quickly rose and delighted her serving women by demanding her finest dresses were brought from the coffer. She selected one of blue, adorned with beads around the neck and the hem which was raised to show the fine linen of a paler blue tunic.

The hall was almost empty, as the court recovered from the revels of the day before, but Henry and Conrad both rose to their feet as she entered. She knew Liudolf had returned to oversee Otto's army, which perhaps accounted for the friendlier interaction she observed between the two of them.

"Greetings, Sister," Henry said. "Is Otto not with you?"

"Otto and Bruno had some matters to discuss with the Bishop," Conrad said, as they all sat again.

"Oh dear, poor Otto," Henry said with a laugh. "This is a bit different from his first wedding."

"Why? What happened then?" Conrad asked, taking a mouthful of his drink.

"Otto and Eadgyth just about made it out of bed in time for the midday meal and then spent the afternoon making it plain they wanted to return."

Conrad almost spat out his drink at that comment. "No wonder Otto looked fed up at his early start this morn."

"It amused my father no end. Otto had not even wanted to get married."

"What of your mother?" Conrad asked. "I cannot imagine her finding it funny."

Henry considered this. "Perhaps not, but she always liked Eadgyth. I think her view was that if Otto was in bed with Eadgyth at least he was not in bed with anyone else!"

Conrad grinned. "Of course. I find it hard to imagine what a rascal Otto was before he wed Eadgyth."

"Oh, yes, he had quite a reputation."

Adelheid frowned. "I do not think it appropriate for you to discuss the King in such a manner."

Henry and Conrad both gaped at her. "Forgive me, my lady," Conrad said. "I meant no offence."

"He was not the king back then," Henry commented, but he and Conrad said no more as they hastily finished their meal and departed, leaving Adelheid deflated that Otto had not shown the same eagerness to remain in bed with her.

It was not until almost the evening that Otto returned. He gave her a long kiss and as she rose to pour him a drink, was very aware of his eyes watching her admiringly. After the festivities of the wedding, the meal that night was a far simpler one, but the conversation was as lively as ever. It was clear the Bishop of Pavia was not overly impressing Otto.

"I hope you will not be such a pompous fool once you become a bishop, Brother," he said to Bruno.

"If, Otto. If I become a bishop," Bruno replied.

"Nonsense, of course you will. And soon if I have my way," Otto replied. "William too."

"William?" Adelheid enquired.

Otto glanced at her. "Did you not know I have another son? He is a little older than Liudolf, but his birth disbars him from the succession. However he will be a fine bishop, as will you, Bruno and no arguments."

"Surely you would not appoint a bastard to such a position," Adelheid said, shocked by his casual attitude towards such matters.

"I would appoint my son." Otto withdrew his hand from where it had been lying over hers. "Do not be foolish, Adelheid. You must know that illegitimacy is no barrier to high office for a King's son. Think how your stepfather placed his illegitimate offspring."

Adelheid was outraged at Otto linking himself to Hugh. "I trust I will not be expected to regard him as a kinsman."

Otto frowned. "Whenever he is at court, which is often, I expect him to be welcomed and treated with respect."

"I intend to bring a god fearing nature to my household. I do not think it would be appropriate to consider him family," Adelheid replied.

"Eadgyth accepted him at court and indeed more than that, she welcomed him into the very heart of our family for my sake."

Adelheid did not stop to consider her next words. "Perhaps she was not as devout as I."

There was a sudden silence, as rage narrowed Otto's eyes. He pushed back his chair sharply. "You are wrong."

He left the table with no further words to anyone. Adelheid looked down, wishing more than anything she could take back her comments. Her only comfort was that at least Liudolf was not there that night to hear her words on his mother.

She looked around and awkwardly Henry met her eyes. "Take my advice, Sister," he said. "Do not say a word against Eadgyth. Otto considered her little less than perfect when she was alive. Now she is gone… no one would dare criticise her."

"No sensible man ever regarded her with censure," Conrad muttered. "Not now and not when she was alive either."

Adelheid pushed back her own chair, desperate to be alone where she could weep in peace. As she left the hall, her brother caught up with her.

"What are you trying to achieve, Adelheid?" he demanded. "You turn up at your wedding in mourning. You deny him his title. You insult his son and the wife he loved more than anything. I am disgusted by your behaviour."

"Konrad, I know. I am sorry." The list made her feel even more ashamed.

"Poor Lothair spoke to me of your manner after your wedding to him. I dismissed him as a fool, but he was right. Your manner is shocking."

"I did not mean to offend Otto or Lothair," Adelheid protested.

"Listen, Adelheid. Otto has been my most valuable ally. I will not permit you to jeopardise that. It is a great pity you were never at the German court when Eadgyth was alive. Otto was not wrong to consider her perfect. If you had seen how she supported him, you might have some idea of how a wife is supposed to act."

Adelheid wrenched herself away from him and fled to her chamber. She looked around. It was filled with so many bad memories of her marriage to Lothair, which the previous joyful night with Otto was supposed to have erased. Now she could not hope that he would not punish her and indeed she was well aware of deserving it. He had shown her nothing but kindness and she had repaid it with insults. Yet again she was failing at marriage.

It was a long time before Otto came to her. She had changed from her finery into a loose robe and had almost given up on him when he pushed open the door. Instantly she flung herself onto her knees before him.

"My lord, I most humbly beg your forgiveness. I spoke such

words without thinking and I am truly repentant."

"Get up." Otto folded his arms, scowling at her. "You had no right to say Eadgyth was not devout. You did not know her. She was truly devout, but her piety was matched by a very deep compassion." The catch in Otto's voice pierced Adelheid's heart, as she realised that not only had she angered him. She had also hurt him. "It was not easy for her to accept William, but she did so wholeheartedly. She, as much as I, made him a part of our family and it was she who encouraged the strong bond between him and Liudolf."

"Yes, of course. Please forgive me," Adelheid murmured.

"And as for William, I sired him when I was little more than a boy. It was foolish and I am not proud of my behaviour, but I am proud of my son. No one will make me anything else. He will be welcomed at court and if you cannot accept that, it will be you who has to leave, not him."

"Naturally I will welcome him." Adelheid wrung her hands as she tried to make amends. "I am truly sorry for every word I spoke."

"Good." To Adelheid's horror he began to unfasten his belt. Earlier that night she had admired the fine leather work with its jewelled buckle, but now all she could imagine was the damage it would do as the buckle bit into her flesh, particularly when it was wielded with the force Otto was undoubtedly capable of.

"No, Otto, I beg you," she cried. "Not with a belt. Of course I understand I must be punished, but please not that."

Otto's scowl deepened. "I am disrobing for the night. I assume you have no objection to that," he snapped. "And do not prate such nonsense of punishments. I am not happy with the words you spoke this night, but you have apologised and I have accepted your apology. That, I trust, is the end of the matter."

"Oh... Oh, I thought..." With her legs trembling so violently she could no longer stand, Adelheid sank onto the bed, putting her head in her hands as she tried to steady her breathing.

Otto stared at her and then looked incredulously at the belt he still held in his hands. He dropped it and sat down on the bed, putting an arm around her. She slumped against him, although the comfort made her feel guiltier than ever.

"You said he did not hurt you deliberately."

Adelheid looked piteously up at him. "Is it not natural for a husband to guide his wife on the right path?"

"I am sure it is natural for a husband and wife to guide each other, but I do not see why violence should be involved." He gave a slight smile in an effort to lighten the mood. "I hope it is not, since I have a great many faults."

"But it would not be appropriate for me to guide you."

"Why not?"

"You are my husband and my king," she stammered.

"I am a man," Otto replied. "And a flawed one at that. I do not despise guidance simply because it comes from a woman. Eadgyth had a rare good sense which few men can equal. My mother too is most wise and not afraid to voice her opinions." There was a wry smile on Otto's face at that comment. "I credit Henry's wife with how fine he has become. I have heard much of your wisdom. I cannot promise I will always follow your advice, but I shall always be glad to hear it." He took hold of her hand and shrugged. "I expect William to be welcomed at court, but if your conscience does not permit you to regard him as a part of your family, I shall respect that."

Adelheid shook her head, ashamed of her harsh judgement. "No, you were right. I should not hold a sin from so long ago over you. And in any case, William committed no sin. If he is your son, I am sure he is a fine man. I shall be honoured to regard him as my kin."

"Thank you. My mother held the sin over me for a long time. It caused many problems between us. I do not want such problems with you."

"There will not be." She looked pleadingly at him. "Otto, the words I spoke of the late Queen were not spoken out of malice, but out of envy. I have heard how she was so rightfully revered by all. I fear everyone must see me as the poorest of substitutes."

"No one is thinking that." Otto smoothed his hand over her hair. "You have been so ill-treated you no longer know your own worth."

Adelheid shrugged. "Perhaps, but it was wrong and I shall do penance for it."

"As you wish, but I have forgiven you as I know she would."

"I truly wish to be a good wife to you, but I know I am failing." Adelheid wiped her eyes. "I do need your guidance."

"Did you want to marry me?" Otto asked.

"Of course," Adelheid said quickly.

Otto smiled and shook his head. "I have told you not to be frightened of me. Did you truly want to marry me? I assume not, since you spoke of your wish to rule alone."

"I did not really even want that. After Lothair died I wished to enter an abbey. The thought of marrying again was abhorrent. But I was left with no choice but to marry Adalbert or offer myself to you. Lord Azzo and Father Warinus convinced me that you would be the better option."

"I see." Otto pushed his hand under her hair to gently cup her neck. "Adelheid, you are so beautiful and I want you as I once thought I would never again want any woman. But I will force nothing on you." He took his hand away from her to lay it against the pillow. "This is your bed. I shall lie here only if I am welcome."

He stood up and Adelheid quickly followed him, taking hold of his hands. "You are welcome, Otto. It is true I said I did not wish to marry you, but that was before we met." She smiled. "An abbey now does not seem such an appealing life."

Otto put his arms around her. "I am glad. You must know you are far too beautiful to be wasted in an abbey."

"I regard it as a great sin and vanity to consider any such thing," Adelheid replied in the full memory of how she had once angered Lothair with those words.

Otto grinned and shook his head as he removed his shoes.

Smiling herself, Adelheid climbed into bed, pushing away her own robe, suddenly impatient to feel his touch.

Snuggling in next to her, Otto took her gently into his arms. "If you will not let me tell you how beautiful I think you are, perhaps you will permit me to show you."

Chapter seven

Over the next days Adelheid fell ever more deeply in love with her husband and radiant with happiness, the court became more amazed at her beauty. In public Otto treated her with deference turning to an amused affection on informal occasions. He proved to be as good as his word, regularly seeking her opinions on how to manage situations, saying she would have a greater understanding of the Italian people than he. Often he asked her to accompany him on rides around Pavia and the surrounding area. On the first occasion she was nervous, knowing how loud the cheers would be for her. However Otto seemed to be not only unfazed by her popularity, but encouraged it. He never again referred to the occasions she had angered him. She mentioned this to Henry and a strange expression flickered over his face.

"Otto very rarely bears a grudge," he said.

When she was not with Otto she devoted her time to Emma, delighting in getting to know her again and resumed her charities towards the poor. Her friendships with Bruno and Henry grew stronger, but she struggled to become close to either Liudolf or Conrad. Both were ever polite, but nothing more. It saddened her since the two were her kinsmen quite independently of her marriage to Otto and she would have liked to be closer to them, particularly when her brother took his leave of them, saying he was needed in Burgundy.

Otto embraced him warmly before he left. "I shall take care of your sister. Do not fear."

"That is not what concerns me," Konrad replied, hugging Adelheid with an exasperated expression. "Behave."

Adelheid laughed, leaning her head against Otto's shoulder. "I try."

Konrad shook his head, although he looked pleased at how affectionate they were. "If you need assistance dealing with that one, just let me know, Otto."

Otto grinned, putting his arm around his wife, as they waved their farewells. But before they could return to the palace a messenger arrived. He knelt before Otto.

"My Lord King, I bring you word that the Archbishop of Mainz will be arriving two days hence."

Otto rolled his eyes. "How delightful."

"Let us hope he has been successful on his mission," Bruno said.

"The only thing that fool has ever succeeded in is causing trouble," Otto replied. "I would rather have sent any to the Holy Father other than him."

"He is the Elector of Germany," Bruno said. "You had to send him."

Adelheid, who had been looking forward to meeting the most prominent German churchman, was puzzled by the attitude of the brothers. "What was he discussing with the Pope?" she asked.

"I am King of Germany and Italy," Otto replied. "It is fitting he grants me the imperial title."

"Emperor?" Adelheid's eyes widened.

Otto watched her with a smile. "I think you would like to be an empress."

She blushed. "I was thinking of Willa's face if she hears I have been granted such a title. It is an unworthy thought."

Otto grinned, but squeezed her hand sympathetically. She had told him of how Willa had attacked her. "That would certainly be a bonus. Well, we shall hear the Pope's verdict soon."

Conrad overheard the comment as they returned to the hall.

"Is Father Frederick returning? I would not hope for too much, Otto. I never saw a man less enthusiastic for his mission."

"I doubt he would put in any effort, Father," Liudolf added. "His efforts have always been to take away your powers, not to increase them."

"I know," Otto said gloomily.

Adelheid was shocked by these comments. "But surely the archbishop is a fine man."

"No," Liudolf said. "He is a conniving one."

"And a trouble maker," Conrad added. "He encouraged his brother, who was wed to Otto's sister, into a rebellion."

Adelheid looked aghast at Otto. "Truly?"

"For the first few years of my reign he was nothing but trouble. He has been quiet in the last few, but I do not trust him."

"He is a very dangerous man," Henry said.

Adelheid looked around the group, thinking it was the first time she had seen them in such unity.

Otto kissed her cheek. "Prepare a welcome for him, but remain wary. I have much to do. Liudolf, will you assist me in some matters?"

As Otto moved away with his son, he rested his hand briefly on his shoulder in the first sign of affection she had seen between them.

"Did Otto's brother-in-law need encouraging into a rebellion?" Adelheid asked. "Perhaps it was the other way round."

Conrad shrugged. "Probably not. He was the Duke of Lotharingia, but he wished to swear fealty to the King of West Francia rather than Otto. He died shortly after the rebellion was put down, but the Archbishop continued his efforts against Otto."

"He tried to have him killed," Bruno said. "Not in battle, but to stab him in the back as he prayed one Easter at the grave of our father."

Adelheid crossed herself. "No, surely an archbishop would

not carry out such an act as that on sacred ground. Did he confess to this crime?"

"No, he denied it," Conrad said. "But he most certainly committed it. I was the one who uncovered the plot. I had a man spying in his household who learnt all."

"A plot from his household does not mean he necessarily had any knowledge. Truly I am sure no priest would ever commit such a sin."

Henry looked steadily at her. "He did and I know this for a fact. I was the man he plotted with."

Adelheid stared at him, convinced she had not understood his words. "You tried to kill Otto? But you are such good friends. This cannot be true."

Henry shrugged, glancing awkwardly at the others. "It is to my eternal shame that I plotted such a thing and remains the bitterest regret of my life."

"And Otto forgave you, but not the Archbishop?"

"He forgave us both," Henry said. "Otto forgives very easily. However his trust is much harder to win and I started from a low place indeed. I spent years with him in Saxony or at his side on campaigns. I asked nothing from him, but ever strove to prove my worth. When he granted me Bavaria, it was the proudest moment of my life. Not because of the powers it conferred upon me, but because it was proof of his trust."

Adelheid stared at Henry, shocked beyond all measure that the man she liked so much had once tried to kill her husband.

Henry smiled and shrugged. "I would be grieved to lose your friendship, Sister, but I have always believed I escaped too lightly from my crimes." He gave a slight bow and left them.

Adelheid looked in confusion at the others. "Did the late Queen forgive him?"

"She appeared to," Bruno said. "She was very attached to Henry's wife. I believe they both encouraged the reconciliation."

Adelheid looked at Conrad. "You do not trust him?"

"Not completely," Conrad said. "But in recent years he has

given me no reason not to trust him."

"Liudolf doesn't trust him at all, does he?"

Bruno smiled. "Liudolf was a small boy, sent away from the court with his mother and sister to an abbey for his own safety, probably wondering if he would ever again see the father he adored. He was there that day at Quedlinburg Abbey where, if Henry's plans had come to fruition, his father would have been slaughtered before his eyes on the grave of his grandfather. I would find it strange if Liudolf did trust him."

∞ ∞ ∞

Adelheid remained confused by the revelations, but eventually decided she would follow Otto's lead. He loved his brother and so she would too. She was puzzled too by Bruno's reference to Liudolf adoring Otto. If anything Liudolf seemed to dislike his father, their manner with each other ranging from formal at best to openly hostile at other times. She thought of how Bruno said it had been the friendship between Eadgyth and Judith which had helped bring the brothers together and her mind went to Ida. If she went with Otto to Germany it would be good to see her again and perhaps their friendship would reunite Otto with his son. Such a decision cheered her as she realised she might not be as lacking compared to Eadgyth as she feared.

She was sat beside Otto two days later, waiting in a mixture of fascination and fear for the arrival of the Archbishop of Mainz. He entered the hall, his face expressionless, nodding and making the sign of the cross in blessing to all he passed. There was no sign of either disappointment or triumph in his manner.

"Greetings, Father," Otto said coolly as he arrived before them. "What news?"

"Greetings my Lord King and to you too, my Lady Queen. My lord, may I say how delighted I was to hear of your marriage."

"Indeed," Otto replied. "Tell me the word of the Holy Father. Will he grant me the Imperial title?"

"No, my lord."

Otto's eyes narrowed. "Why not?"

"There were a number of interested parties in Rome, my lord. His Holiness does not consider it right to bestow such a title on you at this time."

"So, you failed to state your case." Otto's lip curled. "I suspect you did not try very hard."

"You are wrong, my lord. I made every effort." The Archbishop appeared unfazed by Otto's glare.

"I do not believe you. Do not make yourself comfortable here, Father. I do not wish to see you." Otto turned on his heel and left the hall.

There was silence as all stared at the archbishop who gave a slight smile. He nodded at Adelheid. "Should you not follow the King, my lady? Why the late Queen would always offer him comfort in his distress."

For a moment Adelheid was confused until she realised this was what he was hoping for. "As the Queen of Italy, I believe it is my duty to preside over the welcome we have prepared for you," she said, adopting a regal manner. "Please be seated, Father."

Frederick inclined his head as he sat down, turning to Liudolf. "I trust matters have improved between you and the King. It is not good for a king and his heir to be so at odds."

Liudolf shrugged and Conrad interjected, "I fail to see how that is your concern, Father."

"It merely pains me," Frederick said, helping himself to some smoked fish. "I hoped the King, in his newly married joy, would reach out to his son. I wonder why he has not. I trust no one is influencing the King against him." Innocently his eyes wandered to Adelheid.

Bruno frowned. "No one is influencing the King against anyone. It is not unusual for fathers and sons to clash on occasions, but the King's love for his son is as strong as ever."

"Excellent," Frederick said, continuing his meal.

Adelheid met Liudolf's eyes, dismayed to see the suspicion in them. She glanced at Henry, who was looking down at his plate, obviously keen to avoid the archbishop's gaze. She realised the men had all been right when they had referred to this holy man as a trouble maker.

Chapter eight

Determined to avoid the Archbishop, Otto took Adelheid with him on a visit to Turin, leaving strict instructions to Bruno that Frederick was to be gone by the time he returned. It was an emotional moment for her to stand beside Lothair's grave, not quite a year since he had died.

"Do you grieve for him?" Otto asked. "In spite of everything."

"He was Emma's father," she said sadly. "He loved her and she loved him. But mostly what I grieve for is the waste. He was so young and never had a chance to rule. Hugh was no sort of father to him, while Berengar dominated him. None showed him kindness, so he showed none to me. He did not deserve to die in such a way."

Otto pulled her close, kissing the top of her head. "You have such compassion indeed to forgive him."

"As have you. Henry told me of his crimes against you."

"He was young and easily led by men such as Father Frederick. My mother's meddling too did not help. Our father was the finest of men, but that made it all the more grievous for Henry to lose him when he was little more than a boy."

Adelheid knelt down, laying her hand against the grave. She wondered what Lothair would have made of her marriage to the German king. It was not what he wanted. "But it is not Adalbert," she whispered. "And Emma is safe."

∞∞∞

As soon as they returned to Pavia they were aware of some tension. Henry, Bruno and Conrad were whispering together and avoided Otto's eyes as they entered.

Otto had recovered his good spirits and laughed. "So, which one of you wishes to tell me that the nuisance of an Archbishop is still in Pavia?"

Bruno gave a slight smile. "He is not. He has left for Germany."

"Then what has happened?"

"Liudolf went with him," Henry said.

Otto's face darkened. "He had no permission to leave. What possessed him to do such a thing?"

Bruno and Henry fell silent, but Conrad looked firmly at his father-in-law, a hint of anger in his voice. "Liudolf said he was fed up of the contempt you showed him and he wished to return to a place where he was truly valued."

"That boy grows ever more insolent," Otto snapped. "He has been nothing but a nuisance ever since he marched into Italy without permission."

"Liudolf did not come with you to Italy?" Adelheid asked.

"No, he came in before with some foolish notion of rescuing you himself. He failed of course."

"But he tried," Adelheid cried. "I should have thanked him. Why did no one tell me this?"

"You did not need to thank him," Henry said. "He came in order to have you in his power and prevent you marrying Otto."

"You do not know this for certain, Henry," Conrad interjected.

"He did not deny it when I challenged him," Henry said. "Why else would he come? Of course the last thing Liudolf wants is brothers to rival him."

"Given how his father suffered from rival brothers, who can blame him?" Conrad said with a black look at Henry.

"Be silent, Conrad," Otto snapped. "I have more important matters to concern me than that fool. Henry, come with me."

Adelheid sat down, pulling Emma onto her knee, shaken by this latest news. Bruno and Conrad sat with her.

"Otto is making exactly the same mistakes with Liudolf as he did with Henry," Bruno said.

Adelheid raised her eyebrows. "What do you mean? I do not see how Otto is doing anything wrong? Liudolf needs to accept matters."

"Otto is too dismissive of Liudolf," Conrad said. "He has been for a few years now. He demands the whole of Germany honour Liudolf as his heir, but he treats him as a child of no account."

Bruno shook his head. "Rivalry between Otto and Liudolf could be disastrous. Adelheid, try to influence Otto towards more tolerance if you can."

"I do not see why I should, if Liudolf tried to prevent my marriage."

"We do not know if Liudolf intended that," Conrad said. "Oh, I know what he said to Henry, but Henry is the last man Liudolf would confide in even at the best of times. Henry stopped Liudolf's campaign from being a success, so the tension between them is greater than ever at present. Liudolf would have said whatever he thought would annoy Henry most. Please help Otto and Liudolf be at peace."

Adelheid was silent for a long time, thinking of the years she had lived with enemies in her court and how she had tried desperately to encourage Lothair to rid himself of them. She was determined her new life would be different. "Unless I can be confident that Liudolf is to be trusted, I shall do no such thing."

"Otto, with your permission, I too would like to return to Germany," Henry said the next day.

Otto shook his head. "No, Henry. I need you here. Besides, I do not want you dealing with Liudolf."

Henry looked steadily at him. "It is not for your son I wish to return, Otto. It is for mine."

Otto's face cleared. "Of course. You are right. I have kept you from meeting your son for quite long enough. Certainly, go as soon as you can arrange it. Conrad, you will stay here."

Conrad nodded, but did not look very happy.

"Yes, I know I have kept you from your family for too long, which is why I have sent a message to Liutgarde, requesting her presence."

Conrad brightened. "I hope I at least have your permission to ride north to meet them."

Otto laughed. "I would be most disappointed in your regard for my daughter if you did not."

∞∞∞

It was some days after Henry's departure when Conrad returned with a dainty looking young woman resting on his arm. A few strands of dark hair escaped from her mantle, but it was her vivid blue eyes which proclaimed more than anything that this was Otto's daughter.

Otto went forward to embrace her. "My dear child, I am glad you have arrived."

"Thank you, Father. It is good to see you."

"Let me present my wife. Adelheid, this is Liutgarde, the Duchess of Lotharingia."

Adelheid smiled warmly. Up close Liutgarde appeared even prettier. To her surprise she dropped into a curtsey.

"Oh, you must not do that," Adelheid exclaimed.

"I do not wish to show any disrespect, my lady," Liutgarde replied.

"But surely we are all kin," Adelheid replied, flustered by the manners of her stepdaughter – a woman only a little younger than herself.

"Of course we need no formality," Otto said. "Now where is that boy of yours?"

Behind Liutgarde a small boy was struggling to get down from the arms of his nurse. As she set him down, he started forward with a wide grin. "Grandfather!"

Adelheid smiled as Otto swung the boy into the air. "Meet young Otto," he said. "Is he not the finest boy you have ever seen?"

Adelheid nodded. "He is indeed very fine. You must be most proud," she said to Liutgarde.

"And you, young man," Otto said, setting the boy back on the ground. "Should make your bow to your new grandmother."

Adelheid shot a look of mock outrage to Otto at that, as she patted the little boy on the head. "You are about the same age as my daughter, Otto. They will keep us busy this winter, will they not?" she said to Liutgarde.

But to her dismay Liutgarde's eyes were brimming with tears and Adelheid knew she was thinking of her son's true grandmother. Conrad put his arm around her as Otto's face turned to sadness. Adelheid shivered, feeling as if a ghost had just entered the hall.

Chapter nine

The Christmas celebrations in Pavia that year were lavish, with entertainers who turned the eyes of Emma and little Otto wide with amazement. Adelheid struggled to get to know Liutgarde, never getting beyond her pleasant, polite conversation to any greater affection. She was obviously devoted to her child and she and Conrad appeared fond of each other, but Adelheid had begun to consider her somewhat cold in her manner, until she saw her talking with a group of entertainers, the men basking in her praise and watching her adoringly.

"She is so like her mother," Bruno commented. "Eadgyth had that gift of being able to make all, no matter how lowly, feel so valued."

As the Christmas celebrations progressed she often saw her laughing with Bruno and Otto and realised it was just towards her that Liutgarde was so remote. Adelheid's heart was heavy. They were a similar age, both with a young child. She had hoped they might be friends, but she said nothing to Otto. Liutgarde's manner was distant, but it was gracious enough and there was nothing of which she could complain.

∞∞∞

As soon as the festivities were over Otto, with Adelheid's full encouragement, made plans to further pursue Berengar, determined he should not be allowed to get away with his crimes. However his plans were abruptly halted by a messenger from Henry.

"My dearest brother and most noble King, Otto, I send my greetings from Regensburg and trust they find you all well. I have done as you have instructed and have had no communication with Liudolf, but I feel I must make you aware of his recent actions. He celebrated Christmas at Saalfeld, where he welcomed the greatest of the land, who did him great honour. Truly it was a celebration fit for a king and I do not doubt Liudolf is aware of how this appears. Please inform me of your instructions in this matter. Your devoted brother, Henry, Duke of Bavaria."

Otto's face darkened as he read the message. "That damned puppy. What is he playing at?"

"He wants your attention and he has it," Conrad commented. "Liudolf is popular in Germany and you cannot be everywhere at once."

"Which is why I place men I can trust in the duchies," Otto said. "It is a sad state indeed if I cannot trust my own son."

"But, Father, Liudolf is struggling to trust you," Liutgarde said. "He does not believe you regard him with any affection."

"Be silent, Liutgarde. You know nothing of these matters," Otto snapped.

Conrad thumped the table with his fist. "I would prefer it if you did not address my wife in that fashion," he said. "Do not glare at me, Otto. When you gave your daughter to me, you asked for my word that I would always defend her and I will."

Otto looked more furious than ever at his own words being used against him and Adelheid placed a hand on his arm. "Otto, you told me you did not despise advice simply because it came from a woman. Do not dismiss Liutgarde's words."

Otto's eyes narrowed at even Adelheid not siding with him and she was aware that Conrad and Liutgarde too were looking at her in astonishment. But a grudging good humour won through Otto's anger. "I think I need to stop talking since it is clear my words will always be turned against me." He took Liutgarde's hand. "Forgive me for speaking so harshly, my child. Say what you wish."

"Please do not send Henry to deal with Liudolf. He will hate it and it will make matters worse."

"Yes, you are right. It is time I returned to Germany. Bruno will come with me. Perhaps he can talk some sense into Liudolf."

"But what of Berengar?" Adelheid asked.

"Conrad can stay here and see to matters. He is one of Germany's finest commanders. He will manage as well as me."

"If that is what you wish, then I will do my utmost to fulfil your commands," Conrad said.

"Father, when you see Liudolf, please speak to him as a father to a son, not as a king to a duke," Liutgarde begged.

Otto considered this. "I need to know he respects me as a king. But sweetheart, your devotion to your brother pleases me. My sister was also wed to a duke of Lotharingia and far from urging her husband to loyalty, she encouraged his rebellions. I am glad to know, when Liudolf ascends the throne, he will not face such a fate. But Liudolf is not king yet. He needs to remember that and so does everyone else."

Conrad raised his eyebrows at the pointed look Otto gave him. "My friendship is to you both and so far nothing has happened to change that."

Otto clapped him on the shoulder. "Let us pray nothing ever will."

∞ ∞ ∞

Adelheid was not best pleased at leaving Italy before Berengar was apprehended and informed Otto in no uncertain terms of this.

"Italy still needs me. You cannot expect me to leave my land while the situation is still so uncertain."

Otto raised an eyebrow. "Do you wish to remain here without me? I need to be in Germany and I would like to present the Queen of Germany to her people."

"No, of course I do not want to be without you, Otto, but..."

He put his arms around her. "Berengar is a powerful man. It could take a long time to fully depose him. We have made a start, but for now Germany needs me and I need you."

"But, Otto, could we not just delay a little?"

"No. We are returning to Germany. Adelheid, I am insisting on this."

Adelheid glared at him as Otto stared implacably back. "What if I refuse?"

He laughed at her defiance and kissed her. "I do not think you will."

Adelheid flounced away, but knew she had to start the lengthy preparations to move from Pavia. Meanwhile Otto arranged for the transfer of power to Conrad, who was no happier than Adelheid at the situation.

"You are taking too many men," he protested. "How am I supposed to manage with what you have left me?"

"You have impressed me with your martial skills since you were not much more than a boy, Conrad," Otto said. "Of course you can manage."

"The finest of commanders are nothing without their men. I need more."

Otto folded his arms. "I cannot spare more. There is trouble in the North of the realm. I assume you do not want Germany left undefended."

"Of course not, but how do you expect me to bring Berengar down with this paltry force?"

"I expect you to do your best. I have every confidence in you, Conrad. I would not appoint you regent if I did not."

"As long as you are not disappointed if Conrad is unable to solve matters as you hope," Liutgarde put in.

Otto patted his daughter on the shoulder. "Have faith in your husband, sweetheart. I do not doubt his abilities."

With everything prepared, Adelheid and Otto mounted their horses to start their trek over the mountains. It was an emotional moment for Adelheid to leave Pavia where twice she had arrived as a bride. Although it was only recently she had found happiness there, she had always loved the city and the people had loved her. Many wept as they called their farewells, but although smiling warmly at all, Adelheid kept her face ahead to the mountains as she rode beside her husband towards her new land. Otto caught her eye and grinned.

"Come, Queen of Germany, it is time we went home."

Part Four: The Year of our Lord 952-54

Chapter one

Adelheid was glad to come down from the icy air of the mountains to get her first glimpse of her new land. On those gloomy days it seemed somewhat drab, but she imagined the meadows abloom and the trees in full leaf and guessed it would be a fair one.

"Welcome to Germany, Adelheid. This is Bavaria," Otto told her. Deciding to assess the situation before meeting with Liudolf, he had chosen a route through the mountains which avoided Swabia. "It will not be too much longer before we arrive in Regensburg. I know Henry will have planned a grand welcome."

The City of Regensburg was a magnificent one, bustling with people. Accustomed to the adoration of the people of Pavia, Adelheid had expected an enthusiastic reception, but the greetings the people called out were cordial and nothing more.

"Bavaria has never been overjoyed to be ruled by Saxony," Otto said. "That is why Henry is so valuable to me."

"Do they accept Henry's rule?"

"Henry's father-in-law was Duke Arnulf of Bavaria, so yes, they accept him. It has been grudging at times, but his wife, Judith is much loved."

In the heart of the city was a magnificent castle. The gates opened to admit them to the courtyard and many willing hands swarmed forward to take their horses. Henry came out to meet them, bowing formally before taking Otto, Adelheid and Bruno into a warm embrace.

"Welcome to Regensburg, Sister," Henry said. "Come inside. This is no day for a lady to be riding."

Inside the hall was brightly lit and the warmth from central fires brought colour to their numbed cheeks. The rich smell of roasted meats met their noses. Lent would soon be upon them and the Bavarians had the appearance of making the most of the rich dishes while they still could. A woman a few years older than Adelheid came towards them, a friendly smile of welcome on her face.

"May I present my wife, Judith, Duchess of Bavaria," Henry said.

As Adelheid looked into Judith's unusual green eyes, she took an immediate liking to her and hoped she would feel the same way. Certainly the smile Judith returned widened. "I am so pleased to meet you, my lady," she said, dropping into a curtsey. "Henry has told me much about you."

"And I have heard much of you," Adelheid replied. "Please do not be formal with me. I pray we can be sisters."

Judith looked genuinely pleased. "I am sure we will."

She turned to Otto who showed no sign of formality as he swept his sister-in-law into a hug, giving her a hearty kiss on the cheek. "It is good to see you, Judith. Now, where is this fine boy of yours?"

Beaming with pride, Henry gestured to a nurse who brought over brought over a chubby faced infant. Otto smiled, stroking the baby's cheek. "You have done well, Judith. He is fine indeed."

Judith's face glowed. "We were truly blessed with this one. But come. Many others are waiting to see you."

Otto looked surprised to see the first guest, an older lady, elegantly dressed, but he quickly hugged her. "Mother, you did not need to make the journey in this weather. We would have been in Saxony soon enough."

So this was Mathilda, the dowager queen. "I was eager to see you, my son, and meet your wife, so of course I came." She looked at Adelheid. "Welcome to Germany, my dear."

"Thank you. I am delighted to be here." She smiled at Mathilda, keen to make a good impression. The older woman had given her a measured look, but it did not seem to be disapproving. However she quickly turned her gaze to Otto and at this some disapproval did creep in. "Otto, I do not think you should have summoned Liutgarde south. She has not been well."

Otto shook his head, a rueful expression creeping over his face as his mother scolded him like a boy. "She seemed fine to me, Mother."

The next to greet them was a man in clerical robes who looked very like Otto. He bowed and Otto gave her a hesitant look. "Adelheid, this is William, my son."

Uncomfortably remembering their first quarrel, Adelheid made her smile extra wide and did not hesitate to stretch out her hands. "I am so happy to meet you."

Otto looked pleased as he embraced his son. He kept the young man in his arms for a long time, striking Adelheid by how different his manner was with this bastard son, than with Liudolf. William too seemed to be thinking of that. "Father, I have just come from Liudolf..."

"We will not speak of that this night, William. Tonight is for celebrations. Besides, I see someone else is waiting to greet Adelheid."

He put a hand on Adelheid's shoulder to turn her to where another man in priest's robes was waiting. Adelheid's eyes widened and she gave a cry of joy as she flung her arms around Father Warinus. "Oh, Father, it is so good to see you. I worried so terribly after you left Canossa."

"My journey was a smooth one, my child." Warinus looked searchingly at her. "I think you are finding this marriage very much to your liking."

Adelheid blushed, casting a beaming look at Otto. "Yes, I truly am. I have no words to thank you for arranging it."

"I agree," Otto said. "I can only add my thanks for guiding me to so fair a wife."

Warinus smiled, appearing moved almost to tears. "I need no thanks."

"I would like you to remain as my chaplain, if you have no objections, Otto," Adelheid said. "And of course as long as you are happy to remain with me, Father."

Warinus nodded. "I shall be glad to remain with you, my child."

"Thank you, Father. Your guidance sustained me through so many dark days and although I pray those are now over, I shall be glad to have you to guide me in my new role."

∞∞∞

While in Bavaria, William continued to urge Otto to reach out to Liudolf.

"The tension is bad for everyone, Father," William said. "Please meet with Liudolf. I do not see why you cannot resolve the issues."

"As long as he is loyal," Adelheid put in.

"I truly do not think you need concern yourself with that," William said. "His Christmas celebrations were foolish, but I believe they were an attempt to get your attention, nothing more. Liudolf would never stand against Otto in Germany."

"I do not doubt my stepfather, Hugh, once thought that of his son. And then Lothair always believed Berengar would acknowledge his rule. It is not good for the king of the land to be at the mercy of pretenders. Trust me, I have lived through it."

"So, in a fashion, have I," Otto muttered. Henry flushed and Otto reached out to take his brother's hand. "Forgive me, Henry. That is truly in the past, but it is not a past I wish to revisit."

"Nor do I," Henry said. "In truth I do have some understanding of Liudolf. He is of an age where he longs for more influence, but is not yet old enough to fully appreciate your judgement in such matters. I of all people know what a dangerous state it is."

"He must accept my judgement," Otto decided. "He needs to apologise to me for meddling in Italy. If he does, we shall meet."

"Otto, please be careful," Mathilda begged. "I too do not wish to return to the past. At least send someone to Liudolf who he trusts."

Otto nodded. "William, can I trust you with this?"

"Of course, Father."

"Good. Tell Liudolf if he apologises, he can join me at Easter in Magdeburg."

"You will need to be sure of his loyalty before inviting him to Magdeburg," Henry said. "He is very popular there. The city transferred much of its love for Eadgyth onto him."

"Be silent, Henry," Otto snapped. "I have made my decision."

As he strode from the hall, Mathilda looked at her other sons. "Will he still allow no mention of Eadgyth?"

Bruno shook his head. "No, still he is the only one allowed to mention her. He is the only one allowed to grieve."

"That is not true," Adelheid protested. "He told me of her. He said the whole of Germany mourned for a much loved queen."

"A much loved queen, certainly," Bruno said. "But Eadgyth was a much loved woman. We all loved her, but Otto claims the grief for him alone."

"Even Liudolf and Liutgarde cannot mention their mother's name to him," William said. "And then Father wonders why there is tension between them."

"I loved her as a daughter." Tears formed in Mathilda's eyes. "I still miss her so much, but I had to grieve away from him."

Wiping her own eyes, Judith put her arm around Mathilda. Adelheid looked around the group, seeing so clearly the sorrow uniting them. It was obvious she was an outsider there.

Chapter two

I t was on that night Adelheid first realised how a distance seemed to come between her and Otto whenever his late wife was mentioned. When he came to their chamber that night he was as gentle and affectionate as ever, but nonetheless she was aware he was not fully with her. All of her fears that she might be severely lacking compared to Eadgyth came rushing back.

After some weeks in Regensburg they prepared to move into Saxony. The land was becoming as fair as she expected with the first signs of the flowers blooming. She was pleased Henry announced he would ask his brother-in-law Arnulf to manage the duchy, so he and Judith could accompany the court into Saxony. Over the weeks in Bavaria, Adelheid's friendship with Judith had grown and she had found herself also getting on well with Mathilda. Although the older woman frequently scolded Otto as a small boy, she displayed no wish to preside over the court. There was no rivalry between them for the position of queen.

"Welcome to my home," Otto said as they arrived in Saxony. "This is the fairest of lands. Of course, Henry has become quite the Bavarian and claims that land is fairer, but he is wrong."

Judith laughed. "Bavaria is the fairest of lands, but I confess a fondness for Saxony."

Looking around her, Adelheid decided she too could become fond of Saxony and was delighted to arrive at the City of Magdeburg. But from the moment they were greeted at the gates by Lord Herman Billung, the man who acted as Otto's deputy while he was away, she felt uncertain about the place. As they rode through the streets, the cheers for Otto were deafening and she could see how this was truly the centre of his power, but the greetings called out to her were far fewer and subdued. The warm smile Adelheid had been determined to bestow upon Otto's favourite city, slipped as the people made it obvious they regarded her as an outsider.

However she had to admit the palace was magnificent, while next to it on the river banks was an abbey with an impressive looking church. The abbot greeted them warmly, bidding them enter so a mass could be said to give thanks for their safe arrival.

The interior of the abbey with its columns and frescos was more beautiful than any she had seen that side of the Alps. Adelheid smiled as she knelt, thinking this was a place she could truly feel comfortable. At the end she lingered in the building, allowing the abbot to show her the mosaics and icons, many displaying images of Saint Maurice, the patron of the abbey and the saint Otto had a particular devotion to. Otto was pleased by her reaction, the pride in his abbey obvious to all.

Before the altar lay a magnificent marble tomb. Adelheid looked at Otto, intending to ask which saint or holy man it housed, until she realised he too was gazing at the tomb and knew she did not need to ask. Of course. This was the tomb of the woman who, with Otto, had founded the abbey. It was the resting place of the woman he loved. Adelheid barely repressed her shiver. This was Eadgyth's city and Eadgyth's abbey and, judging by the faraway look in Otto's eyes, Eadgyth's husband. She turned away, knowing even there she did not belong.

As they walked to the palace she sent Otto furtive glances, wondering what he was thinking. For the first time she questioned the relationship which had sprung up so quickly between them. She had fallen intensely in love with him, delighting in his affection. Only now did it occur to her that his feelings were not as intense. He was obviously fond of her and he certainly desired her, but did it go any deeper than that? She blinked back tears as she accepted that perhaps it did not.

"I am an outsider here, Father," she said to Warinus, after changing from her travel stained clothing.

"Naturally you are at present, but you will soon make yourself at home, my child."

"No, I do not think so. This will always be the late queen's palace. How can I compete, Father? Otto fell in love with her when he was just a boy. Over the years they shared so much."

"My child, you are treating her as if she were a living woman. Naturally the King loved her, devotedly from what I have heard. You cannot expect him to forget that, but she is no threat to your position."

Adelheid shook her head, knowing he did not understand. The feast laid on for Otto to present her as his queen was lavish, served in a hall hung with banners and lined by elaborate tapestries. But as she sat in the chair which had been empty for so long, a chill pierced her heart. That chair had never truly been empty. Always the memories had filled it.

"My people," Otto said, interrupting her thoughts. "It is my great privilege to present to you my beloved wife, Adelheid, by the grace of God, Queen of Germany and Italy. I request you all drink to the good health of this fair lady."

As Adelheid smiled graciously at everyone, she took no comfort from his words. After all Lothair too, on public occasions, had always called her his beloved wife. As she ate, the food seemed to stick in her throat, making it an effort to swallow, but somehow she managed to talk in a friendly fashion with all around her.

She was glad to get to her feet at the end, bidding everyone a good night, but as she did so the hall seemed to spin around her. Those tapestries and hangings which no doubt Eadgyth had stitched, whirled ever closer before her eyes. The next thing she was aware of was Otto's strong arm around her waist, as he eased her back onto her chair. Judith was holding a cup of wine to her lips. Unable to do anything else, she took a sip, before pushing it away and looking around in bewilderment.

"What happened, Adelheid?" Otto asked, the frightened expression on his face shocking her. "You almost fell to the ground."

"I just felt a little dizzy," she said. "It is nothing serious."

"That is what Eadgyth said the night she was taken ill," Otto muttered, the fear deepening on his face.

There was a tense silence. "Truly I am fine. The journey has been a long one."

"She just needs some rest," Mathilda said with a shrewd look at Adelheid.

"Exactly," Judith put in. "Come, I shall help you to your chamber."

Despite Adelheid's protests, Judith put a supportive arm around her as they walked. Otto trailed behind, his face still tortured with worry. In the chamber Judith removed Adelheid's mantle herself, unwrapping her fair hair. Adelheid felt touched, delighting in this friendship.

"What does she need?" Otto asked. "Shall I summon one of the monks who are skilled in such medical matters? Is there some remedy they can give her? Judith, there must be something which will help."

Adelheid met her sister-in-law's eyes and could see the laughter in them. Judith struggled to keep her face solemn as she turned to Otto. "I think she just needs some rest."

"Are you sure?"

"Judith, can you excuse us a moment," Adelheid said. "I need to speak to Otto alone."

The amusement on Judith's face deepened as she squeezed her hand and left the chamber.

Adelheid patted the bed. "Sit with me, Otto," she said.

Otto sat down, pulling her tightly into his arms. "Sweetheart, please tell me if you are ill. Do not minimise such matters."

"I am not ill," Adelheid replied. "I was not going to tell you this just yet, for it is early days. But these past days I have come to believe I am with child."

The fear vanished from Otto's face and his eyes lit up. "With child? That is the most wonderful news." He kissed her gently. "We shall take the very best care of you. All must be well."

"I had no problems bearing Emma and I have told you of her birth," Adelheid reminded him.

Otto held her close. "You suffered indeed. This one will most certainly be different."

Adelheid smiled as she nestled her head against his shoulder, pleased by his reaction. This child would not be looking back to that dead queen. It would be a member of the family who was just for them.

∞∞∞

Although the pregnancy was not officially announced, the news that the Queen had fainted as she arose from the table quickly spread. As she suspected, Judith and Mathilda had guessed and both were solicitous in their attentions. Gradually she relaxed into Magdeburg, taking up charitable endeavours just as she had in Pavia. She knew she would never love it as Otto did, but it was pleasant enough.

William joined them shortly before Easter and was greeted with pleasure by his father.

"So, do you bring Liudolf's apology?"

"No," William replied.

Otto frowned. "He is refusing to apologise?"

"He says he has nothing to apologise for, but he will be glad to meet you at Easter."

"I do not think I wish to see him at Easter," Otto replied.

"I think you should," Bruno put in. "Otto, I have long told you the tension between you and Liudolf is not good for anyone. Use Easter as a time to put the past behind you."

"Liudolf tried to prevent my marriage," Otto snapped. "Why should I?"

"Try to understand his position," Mathilda begged. "Please, Otto. I should be glad to see him and his daughters."

"Liudolf needs to understand his father's position," Adelheid said. "He cannot have expected Otto to remain unwed just to suit him."

"Exactly," Otto said. "If he will not apologise, he is not welcome at court for Easter."

"But, Otto, he is your son," Mathilda cried. "To refuse to see him at Easter is a humiliation for anyone, but for your son?"

Otto put his arm around Adelheid. "Perhaps I shall soon have another son. Tell Liudolf that, William. Perhaps it will stop him taking my affection for granted."

Mathilda shook her head. "I very much doubt Liudolf does that."

Chapter three

Although Otto ordered all pomp for the Easter festivities, the celebration was a subdued one. Liudolf's absence made him more prominent than if he had been there. During the solemn mass, Adelheid stared miserably at the tomb of his mother, wishing matters were different. Although the pregnancy was progressing well, she often felt sick and tired and this was made worse by the whispers of the court as they speculated on what was between Liudolf and Otto. It was harder still to deal with the occasions when the whispering abruptly stopped and she guessed the people were blaming her for the trouble.

Shortly after Easter there was a message from Conrad, stating he had come to an agreement with Berengar and was on his way to Magdeburg.

"In truth, I do not think we have the men at present to maintain any dominance over Italy," Conrad's message stated. "But Berengar has agreed he will acknowledge your overrule if he remains King of Italy. We shall be with you presently and I entreat you to agree to this arrangement. Your devoted son by marriage, Conrad, Duke of Lotharingia."

Otto frowned. "It is not ideal," he said. "But perhaps it is the best we can hope for at present."

Bruno nodded. "With the Danes encroaching to the North, we need considerable men there. And I am not certain how much longer we can remain at peace with the Magyars."

"But, Otto," Adelheid exclaimed. "Berengar is not fit to be

King of Italy. He murdered Lothair and you know what he did to me."

Otto squeezed her hand. "I know, but I told you once before that this might take some time. I shall think on the matter. No decisions have been made as yet."

"Please do not agree," Adelheid cried. "He is evil. If you leave him in charge in Italy, who knows what he will do?"

"Do not distress yourself," Otto replied, planting a kiss on her head. "Trust me to do what is right. Bruno, come with me. I must draft my reply to Conrad."

Adelheid sank into a chair, her legs trembling at the thought of Berengar regaining his power. A hand on her shoulder made her look up.

"Take this, Sister," Henry said handing her a drink. "Otto will know what to do."

"I am not so sure," Adelheid replied, sipping at the drink. "You heard him. He thinks Conrad's solution is the best which can be achieved. I do not think I can bear it."

"I do not like it either," Henry confessed. "The stronger the king in Northern Italy, the greater the threat to Bavaria. I wonder how hard Conrad truly tried to get a better settlement."

"Otto said Conrad is the finest of commanders."

"Oh, certainly he is very fine." Henry frowned. "When I made my peace with Otto, Conrad and indeed Duke Hermann of Swabia accepted it, but we never became close allies and they remained wary of me. I do not blame them. They always had Otto's best interests at heart…"

"Did they object to you becoming Duke of Bavaria?"

"Not as far as I know and they attended my investiture in good humour, but I believe, in a way, they were both glad of a powerful leader in Italy to curtail my power."

"Do you think he wants Berengar to remain influential? Surely not. He seems a firm supporter of Liudolf and a strong Italian power could also encroach into Swabia."

"True and I may be wrong," Henry admitted. "But remember,

Liudolf is not just Duke of Swabia. He is heir to Saxony and Franconia as well as the German throne. He may be willing to accept some compromises to Swabia if it reduces my power."

"I think we must persuade Otto not to accept this arrangement," Adelheid said.

Henry raised his eyebrows. "You are intending to influence Otto in these matters?"

"Why should I not?"

"It is unusual. Eadgyth was certainly a great influence on Otto, but never would she meddle in such affairs."

Adelheid shrugged. "I have no choice. I made a vow to my late husband on his deathbed that I would do all I could to keep Berengar from power. You too have influence with Otto. Will you assist me?"

Henry smiled, raising Adelheid's hand to his lips. "I most certainly will."

∞∞∞

Over the next few days both Henry and Adelheid urged Otto to be wary about leaving Berengar too much power. Otto was non-committal, assuring them he had made no decision yet and invariably changing the subject. Bruno, however, was less impressed. He said nothing at the discussions, but afterwards he tackled Henry.

"What are you aiming for?" he demanded. "Do you want trouble between Conrad and Otto?"

"Of course I don't," Henry snapped back, scowling at his younger brother. "But I must take a stand for Bavaria and I want Otto to hold power in Italy."

"Be careful. The tension with Liudolf is bad enough. Do not alienate Conrad too. He has been a faithful supporter of Otto for a long time. Far longer than you."

Henry's face went crimson in rage. "I am aware of that. But I am supporting the Queen. She has a great understanding of the Italian situation and she believes Conrad's solution is a poor one."

Bruno glanced at Adelheid. "But does she also understand that what is right for Italy, may not be right for Germany? Sister, I mean no offense. You are new to this realm. I wish you will be guided by Otto and Conrad."

$$\infty \infty \infty$$

"Conrad and Berengar will arrive tomorrow," Otto told her one night as he arrived late in their chamber.

Adelheid had been surprised that Otto had continued to share a chamber with her, as she remembered how Lothair had used her pregnancy with Emma for wenching and debauchery. But she had come to cherish those nights, when they lay talking, free from the distractions of the court. "I do not think you should receive Berengar immediately," Adelheid said, suddenly nervous at the thought of seeing him again. "Show him how unimportant you think he is."

"You may be right," Otto replied, snuffing out the candle and climbing into bed with her. In the darkness she felt his lips against her cheek and the gentle stroke of her hair. "You must not worry, Adelheid. He can do nothing to harm you now."

Gratefully she snuggled into his arms, touched he had understood her fear without her needing to say a word.

$$\infty \infty \infty$$

Otto had made his decision by the time Conrad arrived the next day. Adelheid insisted on sitting at his side in the council chamber when Conrad was ushered in. He bowed slightly, suddenly making a deeper one as he realised she was there, although she thought he did not look pleased to see her.

"Greetings, Conrad. Welcome back to Magdeburg."

"Thank you, Otto. I thought to have a private word with you before presenting Berengar to discuss the treaty."

"Not today, Conrad. I have much to do."

Conrad's words stuttered to a halt. "But, Otto, you knew I was arriving today. We need to discuss this."

"I have said not today." Otto's eyes narrowed. "Are Liutgarde and young Otto with you?"

Conrad looked bewildered. "Of course. They are in the hall, but..."

"Excellent." Otto stood up. "I shall be glad to see them."

"I thought you were busy," Conrad muttered.

"Seeing my fine grandson is important," Otto replied. "Come."

Adelheid held back. "Is Berengar there?"

"No, my lady. He and Adalbert are at the abbey giving thanks for their safe arrival."

"Good," said Otto. "Send a message to the Abbot requesting they remain in the guest accommodation there." He squeezed Adelheid's hand reassuringly. "I do not want them in the palace at present."

Adelheid smiled back, relieved to hear it. She kept her hand in Otto's as they made their way to the hall, Conrad trailing behind them looking irritated. As they approached, young Otto slid down from his mother's knee and hurled himself exuberantly at his grandfather. The boy shrieked with laughter as Otto swung him high in the air before setting him down and embracing Liutgarde.

"I am glad to see you, my child. Are you well?"

"I feel better for being back in Saxony, Father," Liutgarde said. "Italy was pleasant enough over the winter, but it is starting to become hot. I was glad not to spend the summer there."

Adelheid frowned, feeling Liutgarde was criticising her realm. With a polite smile, Liutgarde murmured her greetings. The blue eyes were so like Otto's, it was strange to witness the hostility in them. Her gaze had flicked down to Adelheid's swelling stomach, but she made no comment.

Otto sat down, pulling his excited grandson onto his lap. With a frown Conrad also sat.

"I have done what you asked, Otto. When will you grant Berengar and myself an audience to discuss the matter?"

"Soon," Otto said vaguely.

The frown on Conrad's face deepened. "This is not good enough. I need to know when. Damn it, Otto, I have spent far too much time trying to arrange matters."

"Have you?" Otto looked firmly at Conrad. "I wished to see Berengar deposed, not in alliance with us."

"It is not a true alliance," Conrad protested. "Berengar will acknowledge your overrule."

"It is not good enough. I expected better from you."

Conrad flushed and looked down. "I did the best I could with the few men you left me."

"Did you truly try to depose him?" Adelheid asked.

Conrad's eyes narrowed. "Yes, my lady, I did. I was not aware I needed to account to you for my actions."

Otto put his arm around Adelheid's shoulders. "Do not be so rude. Your efforts have disappointed me."

"This is not fair, Father," Liutgarde cried. "Conrad has worked tirelessly for this. He told you before you left Pavia that he did not have enough men."

"You know nothing of such matters, my child."

Liutgarde shot her father a dark look and drained her cup. She stood up, holding out her arms to her son. "Come to the abbey with me, my little man."

"Leave him with us," Otto said. "I have missed him."

But Liutgarde picked up the boy with a challenging look at her father. "I wish him to pay his respects at Mother's grave."

Otto tensed, his arm slipping away from Adelheid. Since she had announced her pregnancy, Otto had been so attentive, but it seemed all it needed was Eadgyth to be mentioned and he withdrew from her once again.

Liutgarde swallowed, her gaze softening. "Why not come with us, Father?"

Otto stood up sharply. "As I have told you, I have much to do."

Chapter four

For three days the situation continued with Conrad on several occasions begging Otto for an audience, but Otto steadfastly refusing. Adelheid was delighted, imagining how powerless Berengar would be feeling.

"Thank you, Otto for doing this," she said. "I am so happy to know Berengar cannot influence you."

Otto laughed. "Did I not say you had no need to be afraid?"

However on the evening of the third day Bruno approached Otto. "How much longer do you plan to wait before seeing Berengar?"

"I haven't decided," Otto replied.

"You need to decide and soon," Bruno said. "Your actions in this matter are proving humiliating."

"Brother, you have heard of Berengar's deeds. I do not care if he is finding the wait humiliating."

Bruno looked steadily back. "If it were just Berengar you were humiliating, I would agree with you. But it is also humiliating to Conrad. The man you trusted to act for you in Italy and who you have always said you love as a son."

Otto frowned. "I do love Conrad as a son. However he did not act in Italy as I hoped."

"Brother, please be honest. Could you have done better with the men he had available to him? You should be proud of what he did achieve in such circumstances."

Otto shrugged. "It is distressing for Adelheid to receive Berengar. He will not be admitted to the palace before she is ready."

Adelheid flushed as Bruno turned his steady gaze onto her. "The Queen does not need to be present at this audience."

"True." Otto sighed. "Very well. Tell Conrad he can have his audience immediately after morning prayers tomorrow. Nothing should distress you, Adelheid, in your condition. It is probably for the best if you do not attend."

Adelheid raised her eyebrows. "Are you forbidding me from attending? Otto, I must be there."

"I do not think it will be good for you."

Adelheid drew herself up to her full height. "Are your forbidding me?"

Bruno shook his head. "So much for the Queen's distress. Otto, people are starting to talk of her influence over you."

Otto cast a somewhat annoyed look at Adelheid. "People are fools. I will hold the audience in the morn. Adelheid, attend or do not attend. It makes no difference."

Adelheid got her way and was with Otto when Conrad and Berengar were shown in the next day. Her heart thudded as she heard Berengar's voice in the passageway, but Otto's strong presence next to her and the armed guards who stood around them provided reassurance. She sat up straight, determined to look down on Berengar with a haughty disdain.

Neither Berengar nor Conrad appeared pleased to see her, giving her merely a curt bow. Otto listened courteously as the two outlined their arrangement.

"I trust you will accept it, my lord," Berengar said at the end. "I am certain it can be an amicable arrangement."

"I trust you will not," Adelheid put in, ignoring Conrad's weary shake of the head. "There should be no friendship between us."

Berengar raised an eyebrow. "Forgive me, my lord, I thought

you were the one with authority here. Have I been addressing myself to the wrong person?"

Otto frowned. "You are in no position to be impertinent. Naturally I have the authority, but this situation does not just affect me. Germany must decide on this alliance. We will convene a synod to discuss the matter."

"Why is this necessary?" Conrad asked. "You can make the decision."

"This affects us all and in particular Bavaria. The Synod will decide."

"Of course. You must let Henry have his say." Conrad smiled grimly. "But not just Bavaria. It affects Swabia. I trust the Duke will be invited to attend."

"Naturally," Otto said coolly.

"Otto, an alliance with that man is not advisable," Adelheid cried. "He is a murderer. Put a stop to this nonsense now."

The three men all looked at her in surprise as her voice got shriller. Berengar smirked. "You have my sympathies, my lord. The unfortunate King Lothair also struggled to tame her. I shall pray you have more success."

Adelheid was furious with herself for allowing her emotions to escape. It was not how she had intended the meeting to happen. As the door shut behind Conrad and Berengar, she looked defiantly at Otto, expecting to see a look of irritation on his face. But he grinned and caught her up in his arms with rather more abandon than he usually did since her pregnancy had been announced. "I rather like you untamed," he said. "Let us hope our son inherits your fire."

∞∞∞

The Synod was held at Augsburg far to the south of Magdeburg. Adelheid's pregnancy was not yet so advanced as to make travel uncomfortable, but all the same Otto insisted they make their way slowly.

They found Liudolf already in residence. He got to his feet as his father entered and stared at him for a moment, a look of both hope and defiance on his face. Otto stared back without smiling and Liudolf gave him a curt bow, his face suddenly wiped of all expression.

"Greetings, my lord," Liudolf said. He made a deeper bow to Adelheid. "And to you, my lady."

She nodded to him, deciding to show no more pleasure than Otto.

Otto's face relaxed slightly as a woman moved to stand beside Liudolf. "Ida, I did not know you would be here, my child. It is good to see you. Are your daughters here?"

Ida accepted Otto's kiss on the cheek. "No, we left them in the care of my mother."

"We are not anticipating being here very long, my lord," Liudolf added.

Ida looked at Adelheid and she smiled warmly, delighted to see her kinswoman again. "I agree. It is so good to see you, Ida. I wish I could see your daughters. You must meet Emma soon."

Ida dropped into a low curtsey. "Indeed, it will be an honour, my lady."

Adelheid's smile froze uncertainly at the polite tone, not sure how to respond, but suddenly Ida's face lit up into a beaming smile. Adelheid smiled back, filled with a relief which was swiftly dashed as she realised Ida's smile had not been directed at her. Liutgarde was standing behind her. With a cry of joy, Liutgarde threw her arms around Ida, as Conrad took Liudolf by the hands, grins lighting up the faces of both men.

Otto touched her arm. "There are many waiting to be presented to you, Adelheid."

She inclined her head. "Of course."

But as she smiled graciously, she cast a wistful look at Ida and Liutgarde sitting at the table, their fingers entwined as they started an animated conversation. Liudolf was pouring cups of wine for them all, before taking a seat next to Conrad, laughing at some comment which had just been made and beckoning to William to join them. He sat down, abandoning the dignity of a churchman as he greeted Liudolf with a mischievous smile. Adelheid blinked back tears at the relaxed manner of the group. She wanted to be sat with them. She, Liutgarde and Ida were so close in age. They should have been friends, but instead they had made it clear she did not belong.

Later she confessed her feelings to Father Warinus.

"It is not uncommon for the offspring of the first marriage to feel uncomfortable when their father marries again," Warinus said.

"I have tried to be friendly with Liutgarde and Ida, but they treat me so formally. They make me uncomfortable."

"Both the Duchess of Swabia and the Duchess of Lotharingia strike me as fine young women. Their loyalty is to their husbands and both Dukes are on uncertain terms with the King. Rightly or wrongly, they blame you."

"I have never tried to come between them and Otto, I swear it."

"I am sure that is true, my child. But have you urged the King to be closer to his sons? Or indeed make much effort yourself to befriend them? You have made plain your favour lies with the Duke of Bavaria."

"Liudolf conspired against my marriage from the start. How can I be friendly towards him?"

"My child, you forgave your late husband for far more serious sins against you. Can you not show a similar compassion towards the Duke?"

"If he supports Otto, I will. But otherwise, surely my loyalty must be to my husband."

"Of course, but my child, consider whether you might serve your husband better by encouraging a reconciliation than supporting him in animosity."

Chapter five

The synod started with a great many favouring Conrad's position. Liudolf was the first to get to his feet in support of his brother-in-law.

"I would like to thank my dearest brother for his efforts in Italy," Liudolf began. "The solution he arrived at is, in my opinion, a sensible one which will increase German influence in Italy, while allowing the majority of our forces to defend our own realm. Germany is fortunate indeed to have benefitted from such wisdom."

"Thank you, my Lord Duke," Conrad said. "As Duke of Lotharingia I am aware that in the North we need as many men as we can muster to hold the border against the Danes. I know my solution has not pleased everyone and if we did not need our forces elsewhere, I might agree with them."

However the next to stand was Henry. "I mean no disrespect to the noble Dukes of Swabia and Lotharingia," he began. "But I must disagree. The presence of enemies elsewhere is precisely why we must not allow such a power to remain in Italy. It may not be possible yet to completely topple Berengar from his position, but I am certain we can do better than the alliance the Duke of Lotharingia negotiated. While I add my thanks, I feel his efforts could have been greater."

Conrad flushed with rage and the synod descended into uproar. Conrad and Henry were openly shouting at each other, while Liudolf cheered his brother-in-law and jeered loudly at Henry. Under the cover of the noise, Adelheid whispered to

Otto, "You know Henry is right. Berengar is too dangerous to be left in power."

"Perhaps," Otto muttered, his eyes on Conrad. "But in truth Conrad did do the best anyone could in Italy. Henry could have done no better."

At that moment Liudolf got to his feet to make that exact point, but Henry was swift in his retort. "Considering how your campaign in Italy ended, I do not think you are in a position to make such a declaration, my Lord Duke."

Liudolf thumped the table. "My campaign in Italy would have been successful, if it were not for Bavarian meddling."

Uncle and nephew glared at each other, as an icy silence descended. Into that silence a new voice entered. One which up until that point had been silent. It was Archbishop Frederick of Mainz.

"My Lord King," Frederick stated. "It is clear there is to be no agreement. It seems to me that we need your wise judgement to decide the matter."

Adelheid bit her lip, with a sense of having walked into trap. Otto had just very publically been put into a position of deciding whether to side with his sons or his brother. She looked unhappily at the men, remembering how once a dislike of the archbishop had united them. But there was no sign of that now. Conrad looked at Otto from narrowed eyes, while Henry smiled expectantly. Liudolf regarded his father with a curled lip and sat down, shaking his head.

Otto stood up. "Everyone sit down. I note we are all in unity that Berengar cannot at present be toppled. I concur. I would also like to thank the Duke of Lotharingia for his efforts in Italy. His tireless actions have allowed us to convene this synod today. However I intend to build upon his achievements. I do not want an alliance with this man. Instead I will demand from him an oath of loyalty and a tribute."

Adelheid muttered a prayer that Otto's words would be enough to appease Conrad and Liudolf, but they were to be in vain. Conrad kicked back his chair and strode towards the door. "I do not know why I wasted so much time in Italy."

Liudolf also got to his feet. "When Berengar rebels against your demands, as I am sure he one day will," he said. "I do not want Swabian men wasted." He too walked away, catching Conrad up at the doorway and putting his arm around his brother-in-law in a blatant gesture of solidarity.

Otto's brow creased and he stared after them for a moment. However before he could respond to Liudolf's words, Bruno spoke. "How will you manage this, my lord?"

"The March of Verona will be added to the Duchy of Bavaria." He looked at Henry. "My Lord Duke, I am depending on you to ensure our demands are met."

Henry bowed. "My Lord King and brother, I am honoured and will not fail you."

∞∞∞

It was a triumphant moment for Adelheid when Berengar, Willa and Adalbert were brought before the synod. Adelheid wore one of her finest dresses of a pale green edged in bands of embroidered white cloth. Gold and jewels lined her throat and the crown of the Queen of Germany was on her head. Otto's eyes were admiring as she took her place next to him.

"Are you ready for this?" he asked with a grin.

"I most certainly am."

Adelheid allowed her smile to be just a fraction wider than her accustomed gracious expression for such an occasion. Willa was dressed neatly in a plain dress over a dark tunic and Adelheid was unable to help the surge of satisfaction at how drab she looked. All three looked outraged as they approached the throne. This time Adelheid was determined she would not lose control and she met the three sets of angry eyes gravely.

"My Lord Berengar, My Lord Adalbert," Otto announced. "I order you to swear fealty to me as your over-king. If you do this, I will permit you to continue to use the title King of Italy.

There will be a tribute due to me, which my chancellor will discuss with you in due course."

"And if I refuse?" Berengar asked, although his voice showed clearly he knew the matter was hopeless.

"My men will return to Italy in greater numbers than ever," Otto replied. "And will not leave until we have stripped you of your title and powers. As matters stand, you may rule Italy on my behalf. I am presenting the March of Verona to my brother, the Duke of Bavaria. You will be accountable to him, but he will not interfere unnecessarily."

Adelheid leaned forward. "It is not an unusual situation in Italy to have the title of king but little power, is it?"

Berengar's eyes narrowed. Reluctantly he knelt on the ground. "I, Berengar, swear my fealty to you, Otto, King by the grace of God of Germany and Italy."

Otto nodded approvingly. "Lord Adalbert, as joint king I require the oath of fealty from you too."

Adalbert looked around and for a moment Adelheid thought he was going to refuse. But with obvious reluctance he knelt down next to his father, repeating the words.

Adelheid smiled, savouring the sight of her bitterest enemies kneeling before them. Her eyes met Willa's. The last time they had met, Willa had been in control and how she had abused her position. Adelheid gestured to her, ordering her to kneel with her husband and son. It seemed a small gesture to atone for the bitter attack Willa had launched, but as she knelt, it was clear from her furious expression it was a fitting one.

"I can see you enjoyed that," Otto commented, as they took advantage of the cooler evening air in the courtyard.

Adelheid glanced up at him, her smile admitting his words. "I know I should show more humility, but when I think of how they treated me when I was so completely at their mercy..."

Otto kissed her. "You shall never again be treated in such a way. I swear it."

She put her arm around his waist, looking around. They were not the only ones enjoying the cool air. Liutgarde and Ida were seated on some hay bales at the edge of the courtyard, Conrad and Liudolf standing nearby. From the laughter which came from the group, it seemed Conrad and Liudolf had recovered their good tempers. Again Adelheid felt the urge to join them.

"They are your children, Otto," she said pointing in their direction. "The Italian matter is settled. Surely you can get on better terms with them now."

Otto looked at them and shrugged. "I can try."

The laughter in the group stuttered to an abrupt halt as Otto and Adelheid drew closer. Liutgarde and Ida quickly rose, dropping into curtseys, while Liudolf and Conrad bowed. Adelheid ground her teeth. There was nothing of which she could complain in such formal politeness, but it made her feel more of an outsider than ever and she suspected it was what they meant her to feel.

Otto ignored the tension, giving the group a warm smile. "I am hoping you will all remain with the court awhile. It will be good to spend some time together."

"For what purpose, Father?" Liudolf asked.

Otto frowned. "Do I need a purpose to spend time with my son? Why, we have not hunted together for an age. Truly Liudolf, I will be glad to forgive your actions of the last year and share some festivities."

Liudolf shook his head. "How kind of you to forgive me, Father. What wrong doing are you accusing me of? Oh, very well, my Christmas festivities were provocative, I'll grant you that. Do you wish me to apologise for those? Because I will. But I have done nothing else wrong. Yet you have shown your displeasure with me for far longer than that."

"I am your father. It is my place to guide you. Everyone is foolish while they are young, but you could learn much by being at my side."

Liudolf glanced at his wife. "Well, Ida, what a charming invitation this is. I am invited to remain at my father's side so he need never miss an opportunity to remind me of what a fool I am."

Otto scowled at his son. "Do not stay, then. I care not."

Adelheid tried to catch Ida's eye, hoping she could persuade her otherwise. But she remained close to Liudolf, not once glancing in her direction.

"Conrad, I have paid tribute to your efforts," Otto said. "I would very much like you and Liutgarde to remain at court."

Conrad shrugged. "If you command it, I will. But your tributes are too late. You had already informed everyone of how I failed you. And I note it is Henry who is to be rewarded in Italy, even though it was I who devoted so much time there. Everyone knows the contempt you hold for me."

"This is not true. Henry has the lands, as it is Bavaria which is best placed to supervise matters in Italy."

"Swabia is also well placed," Conrad said. "But I note Liudolf has no additional lands."

"Given how Liudolf tried to prevent my alliance with Italy, I do not see how you can blame me for that," Otto snapped.

Liudolf shook his head again. "I did nothing to prevent your alliance."

"Only because Henry stopped you."

Liudolf's shoulders slumped. "Of course," he muttered. "You must listen to Henry."

Conrad looked firmly at Otto in a way few men dared. "You have always claimed to love me like a son. I have certainly revered you as a father. But then you show me this contempt..." He rested his hand on Liudolf's shoulder. "Although I suppose you show the same contempt for your true son. Perhaps I should feel honoured to receive it."

Otto's eyes narrowed and he seized Conrad by the throat. "I have had enough of this insolence from both you and Liudolf. It needs to stop."

Adelheid gasped, as Conrad tried to pull Otto's hands away.

Liutgarde too cried out, tugging on her father's arm. "Stop this, Father. Let Conrad go."

Otto let go abruptly and Conrad stumbled back. He straightened his tunic, glaring at Otto. "I am returning to Lotharingia, my lord. I do not think I care to be at court."

Liutgarde was still holding onto Otto's arm. He glanced down pleadingly at her. "There is nothing to prevent you from remaining at court. Will you, sweetheart?"

Liutgarde looked up at her father, tears forming in her eyes. "Are you asking me to choose between you and Conrad? Of course I will return to Lotharingia with Conrad. A wife's loyalty must always lie with her husband. Who do you think it was who taught me that?"

The colour drained out of Otto's cheeks and he shoved Liutgarde towards Conrad. "You ungrateful child," he snapped. "Do not dare use Eadgyth's memory in such a way."

Conrad caught hold of Liutgarde and glared back at Otto. "If any other man pushed Liutgarde around, you would expect me to kill him. And quite frankly, Otto, I am highly tempted."

Adelheid felt like bursting into tears. She had wanted to forge some friendships, but instead Conrad and Liudolf were both glaring at Otto, while Ida had pulled Liutgarde into her arms, comforting her as the tears flowed. Otto's face was still white and suddenly he looked much older. She stepped closer to him, but he did not appear to be aware she was there.

"We scarcely dare remember Mother at all when you are present," Liudolf said.

Abruptly Otto turned and strode away from them with no further words. Adelheid let out a shaky breath. "I am sorry," she whispered. "I truly wanted him on amicable terms with you. I want no tension in the family."

"Really, my lady," Conrad asked. "Given how you have stirred matters, I find that very hard to believe."

Liudolf looked at her, a bitter smile on his lips. "I believe you truly love my father. But what does this say for your newly married idyll, when the mere mention of Mother's name makes him react like that?"

Adelheid turned away with tears in her eyes. It would have been easier for her if Liudolf had spoken those words with contempt, but he hadn't. The tone in his voice was pity.

Chapter six

Liudolf and Ida took their leave of Otto with only the most formal of farewells. Adelheid's eyes went from Otto's stern face to Liudolf's scornful one. They looked so alike even down to the misery in their expressions. Conrad too was distantly polite, with Liutgarde composed but pale standing beside him.

"Otto," she said in a low tone as they turned away. "Do not let them leave like this."

Otto stared moodily after them. As Conrad stopped to consult with his entourage, he strode over to Liutgarde.

"Forgive me, my child," he said. "Your mother was always so proud of you and she would be prouder still if she could see you today."

"Oh, Father." Liutgarde stood on tiptoes to embrace Otto.

"I hope it will not be too long before we meet again, sweetheart. Take good care of this one." Otto bent to give his grandson a kiss.

"I hope so too, Father." Liutgarde looked at Adelheid, a faint, but genuine smile hovering on her lips. "I hope all goes well with your child. You will be in my prayers."

Adelheid smiled back, feeling a sudden liking for her stepdaughter. "Thank you. I too hope we see you again soon."

∞∞∞

Adelheid and Otto made a leisurely return to Saxony so Adelheid could prepare for the birth of their child. She managed to dissuade Otto from returning to Magdeburg, claiming it was too far. However Liudolf's words often rang in her ears and the truth was that the last place she wished to give birth was in the city which was so bound up in his mind with his dead wife.

As the summer drifted into autumn, she began to become uncomfortable but even so she insisted on joining Otto and Henry whenever they discussed Italy. While Otto was cautious, she found Henry determined to do whatever was necessary to keep Berengar under control. With her deep friendship with him growing ever stronger she was pleased he remained at the court and even happier when Judith informed her she would be with her during the birth.

"As, of course, shall I," Mathilda added when she too joined them.

"Assuming you want us," Judith said, looking at the stunned expression on Adelheid's face.

She reached out to take their hands. "Oh, I do," she said. "I was thinking of Emma's birth, when I had only two trusted maidservants with me and dared not make a sound. This will be so different."

"It will be," Judith said. "Second births are usually easier in any case. My first seemed never ending. I often felt it was only Eadgyth's support which allowed me to survive at all."

"Otto was my first," Mathilda said with a reminiscent smile. "He took a long time, but the moment he was born he was ever impatient with life. The boy has not changed much."

Adelheid's confinement began as the first hint of winter hit the air, but as Judith had predicted, it was easier than Emma's birth had been. The ability to cry out as she paced her chamber, combined with the tender care from Mathilda and Judith helped. She was comforted too by the knowledge of the prayers being said for her in the church and of Otto, undoubtedly striding around the hall, longing to hear good news.

It was with great delight that Mathilda finally placed an infant into her arms. "A boy," she proclaimed.

Adelheid looked at the tiny baby, wondering anxiously if Emma had ever been that small, as she cradled the precious child close. When Otto entered the chamber his face was lit in a joy greater than Adelheid had ever seen. He sat next to her, tenderly kissing her.

"Are you well? Was it hard?" he asked.

"Childbirth is always hard, Otto," Mathilda said, somewhat impatiently. "But as births go, it was not so bad."

"I am fine, Otto," Adelheid whispered, resting her head wearily, but happily against his chest.

Otto kissed the top of her head and took the child into his arms. "A fine boy. Shall we name him Otto?"

Adelheid straightened herself. "No. His name is Henry, since it is Henry who is managing the Italian situation as I wished."

Mathilda raised her eyebrows at this blatant defiance, but Otto laughed. "Henry was my father's name. I shall be glad to name my son for the very finest of men." He kissed Adelheid again. "But I cannot play favourites with my brothers. If we are ever blessed with a second son, he will have to be called Bruno."

It was a swift recovery and soon Adelheid was able to re-join the court. Otto honoured her more than ever and her status was obviously high. It was a merry Christmas that year, as Adelheid enjoyed the festivities with her new baby on one arm and little Emma snuggled against her. As she and Otto laughed together, she was certain it was the happiest time of her life. For the most part Otto too seemed relaxed, but occasionally she caught a wistful look on his face and she wondered if he was remembering happy Christmases when Eadgyth was alive and all his children had been around him.

As the festivities drew to a close, William and Bruno urged

Otto to try again to reconcile with Liudolf and Conrad.

"Father, there are rumours that Adelheid and Henry have encouraged you to name your new son as your heir," William said. "If these reach Conrad and Liudolf…"

"Or indeed if anyone believes them," Bruno said. "The nobles and churchmen of the realm were glad to accept Liudolf as your heir and have sworn loyalty to him. He is very popular. They will not be happy if they think you will ask them to overturn that vow."

"What fool would believe such rumours?" Otto asked. "How could anybody think I would displace my eldest legitimate son, a fully grown man and replace him with a baby?"

"It is what the rumours are saying," William replied. "And for them to spread, some must be believing them."

"Who started the rumours?" Otto demanded. "If they came from someone in the court, I wish to know."

"It is impossible to say." Bruno hesitated. "But William and I have our suspicions."

"The Archbishop of Mainz," William said. "He was here for the baptism and has undoubtedly seen how high the queen is in your esteem."

Otto put his arm protectively around her. "Of course she is high. She is my devoted wife and has recently born me a son. But Liudolf is my heir."

"We know that, Otto," Bruno said. "But the people do not. Does Liudolf know it?"

"I hope Liudolf has more sense than to believe such nonsense."

"Father, you have barely spoken to Liudolf this last year except in the most formal terms," William said. "I have seen him more informally and his belief is that now you have a new wife, you no longer care for the offspring of your last wife."

"How dare you repeat such a thing, William. Be silent," Otto snapped.

"Father, please listen," William begged. "Liudolf needs to hear some words of affection from you, if you truly still feel any."

"Of course I do," Otto replied. "But his attitude is annoying me. In truth I do not care if he does believe my new son is to be my heir. It might teach him a little humility."

"You do not mean that," Bruno said.

"Do I not? If Liudolf is fool enough to believe such a thing, I feel it serves him right."

∞∞∞

In the spring they moved across the realm, intending to be at Ingelheim on the River Rhine to celebrate Easter. Both Bruno and William had begged Otto to invite Liudolf to the celebrations. Otto was non-committal to them, but alone with Adelheid he had confessed how much he missed his son.

As they drew closer to Ingelheim, the weather had grown warmer, but the mood among the people they passed was cool. In Saxony Otto was greeted with cheers wherever he went, but as they left, the cheers became subdued and half-hearted. Adelheid assumed this was a natural reaction as he left his Saxon heartland, but the confused whispers of the court made her realise this was not at all normal.

"What is up with these people?" Henry muttered.

"I know not," Otto replied. "It is certainly strange. Let us break our journey for a while and send out scouts."

Otto did not seem unduly concerned as they rested at an abbey, but the mood swiftly changed when the scouts returned.

"My Lord King, you cannot enter Ingelheim."

"Why not?" Otto demanded.

"This region is in the hands of the Duke of Swabia and the Duke of Lotharingia, my lord. They will take force if necessary to prevent you."

Chapter six

"Those boys, how dare they?" Otto cried, running his hand through his hair. "What do they hope to achieve? We ride on and demand entry. If they refuse, it will be very much the worse for them."

"My lord," started one of the scouts.

But Otto was in no mood to hear them. "I will not be defied by my own son. And Conrad, I never believed him capable of such betrayal. I have loved him as a son for years. I loved him so much, I gave him my only daughter and this is how he repays me?"

"Otto, calm down and listen," Bruno said.

"Why should Otto calm down?" Adelheid cried, her whole body trembling. Her worst nightmare was that yet again she would find herself a powerless queen and it seemed to be coming true. A future where her household was dictated to her by Ida and Liutgarde flashed before her. "They have to be stopped."

"They will be," Bruno replied. "But we must plan carefully. We have all seen the mood here. Both Liudolf and Conrad hold considerable influence in this region."

"That is true, but we do have a large force," Henry said. "I agree the ladies and the children must be got to a place of safety, but I believe the remainder of us should march on."

"My lord," the scout cried. "I have further information. I beg you permit me to speak."

Otto nodded, calming himself with an effort. "Of course. Tell us everything you know."

"It is true they wish to prevent you from celebrating Easter at any of the churches here, and the holy Archbishop of Mainz is supporting them in this but that is not their main aim. Their plan is to seize the Duke of Bavaria. They feel he has a sinister influence over you and the Queen."

"They have no idea what they are talking about," Henry muttered.

"But it is true that since his marriage, Otto has drawn closer to you and further from his sons," Bruno commented.

"Do you blame me for that?" Henry demanded.

Otto frowned. "Quiet, everyone. There are enough problems in the family. We will not add to them. We must decide our next move."

"I do not blame you, Henry," Bruno said. "Otto, I have been urging you for months to talk to Liudolf as a father to a son. I wish Liudolf had not forced you into this position, but perhaps now you can meet and agree some common ground."

"Why should Otto agree anything with so traitorous a son?" Adelheid demanded.

"Because he is Otto's son and his heir," Bruno said firmly.

Otto sighed. "Yes, you are right, Brother. We will go to Mainz, where I do not doubt Father Frederick has been stirring matters. What possessed Liudolf and Conrad to side with him? I thought they hated him as much as I."

"Perhaps they do," Bruno said. "That could be the start of the common ground between you."

"You will come with me, Bruno. Henry, I want you to escort the ladies back to Saxony. To Magdeburg, I think. It will be the safest place."

"My place is with you, Otto," Henry protested.

"No, Brother. You heard the scout. I'll not deliver you to those boys. I am depending on you to defend Adelheid and my son."

"I'm not leaving you," Adelheid said. "I shall be at your side in Mainz."

"That would not be a wise move," Bruno said. "Liudolf and

Conrad have both expressed concerns about your influence with Otto. Standing with him will only antagonise them further. It is for the best if Otto faces them without you or Henry."

"I agree. Adelheid, return to Magdeburg with our son. I shall join you there soon."

"No, I shall not. I must be with you." Adelheid's voice rose, as her terror escaped her.

"That is an order, Adelheid. Do not argue," Otto snapped, but his face softened as he took in her trembling lips. "I need to know you and our little Henry are safe in Saxony. We will not be apart for long."

"What if they harm you? What if they try to kill you?"

"That is a risk I must take, but I do not think they will."

"Are you sure, Otto?" Henry asked. "The hatred they bear you…"

"You are wrong." William spoke up for the first time. "Father, Liudolf loves you, I know it. He would never wish to kill you."

"Let us hope so," Otto muttered. He pulled Adelheid into his arms and gave her a long, but gentle kiss. "Do not worry."

"Perhaps you should return to Saxony and let me deal with Conrad and Liudolf," Henry said. "It is me they want."

"Which is why they shall not get you," Otto said, clapping his brother on the shoulder. "I shall go to Mainz. You will escort my wife and yours and indeed, Mother, back to Saxony." He smiled at the expression on the faces of all three ladies. "I suspect you will have the harder task."

It was a long and anxious journey back to Magdeburg, through the sullen settlements. Once they had arrived, there was an even longer and more worrisome wait for news from Otto. Every day passed so slowly with Mathilda alternating between cursing Liudolf for his actions and blaming Otto for all the trouble. Adelheid began to feel she would go mad with the waiting. She suspected she was with child again and at night she often wept that what should be a joyful time had been overshadowed.

When eventually Otto re-joined them, he looked exhausted, but his tired face brightened as he saw Adelheid and he pulled her into his arms for a long kiss.

"Is all well, Otto?" she asked, looking up at him, trying to remember if the few grey hair at his temples had been there when she last saw him.

He smiled. "Yes, all is well."

Adelheid tugged him to the table and poured him a cup of wine. He sank into a chair and sipped at it. Some of the tension eased out of him.

"Is all truly well, Otto?" Henry asked.

"Yes. I met with Liudolf and Conrad. There was much posturing, but Bruno helped us to come to an agreement. I must say I thought Father Frederick would encourage more dissonance but he too was most helpful in the mediation."

Adelheid frowned. "What sort of an agreement?"

"Well, they are no longer demanding Henry's immediate surrender to start with."

Henry laughed. "I am glad to hear that. But what else did they want?"

"Liudolf wanted an assurance he would remain my heir. I have given him that." Otto looked challengingly at Henry. "That always was my intention. I do not consider that a concession."

"Does he still deserve to be your heir?" Henry asked.

Otto frowned. "I have two other sons. One is disbarred from the succession, while the other is an infant. If Liudolf is not my heir, who do you suggest?"

Henry's eyes dropped. "You know I renounced my own claim many years ago. Very well, I accept Liudolf is the only heir for now."

"Did you make any concessions?" Adelheid asked.

Otto sighed. "Yes, I made one. I agreed to reinstate Conrad's treaty with Berengar. Both Liudolf and Conrad are happy and this will be the end of the trouble."

Adelheid leapt to her feet. "An end? Otto, you fool. This will be just the beginning."

Otto frowned. "Do not talk nonsense, Adelheid. Of course this is the end. I have told you. They are happy."

"For now they are," Adelheid cried. "But when they are once more unhappy they will act again and again. Trust me, Otto. I have seen how this works."

"Liudolf and Conrad are honourable men," Otto said. "They will honour the agreement we made, as will I."

"You cannot be certain of that," Henry said. "How could you go back on the will of the synod? You said you will not surrender me to them, but you might as well have done."

"If I have trouble in the German lands I cannot manage the Italian situation in any case," Otto replied. "Conrad's treaty is a fair one for now."

"A fair one?" Adelheid shrieked. "Nothing about this is fair. Otto, you need to be a king. You need to put those two in their place. This is how it starts. They will soon control everything and you will be powerless against them. It will be how Berengar ruled Lothair all over again. I cannot go back to that."

"Control yourself, Adelheid. This is completely different."

"When I begged for your aid I thought you were the strongest of men. How cruelly I was mistaken."

Otto narrowed his eyes. "I see. You are telling me I am a disappointment to you."

Chapter seven

"**N**o, of course you have not disappointed me, Otto," Adelheid cried, unnerved by how anguished Otto looked. "But you must see how foolish this is."

"I have come to an agreement with my son. Do you find that foolish? Adelheid, families must stand together."

"I saw how Lothair treated his father and I saw how that ended for Hugh, in exile. I could not bear for this to happen to you."

"Liudolf wouldn't exile me. He has made no claims on the kingship."

"Not yet," Adelheid muttered.

"Can you be sure of this, Otto?" Henry asked. "Do you think our father would ever have believed how I would behave in the years after your accession?"

"He knew you were ambitious," Otto replied. "As of course Liudolf is. Indeed I encouraged his ambitions, as our father most certainly did not encourage you."

"Exactly," Henry replied. "Even with no encouragement, I had pretensions. Liudolf has reason for his impatience. He is of the same age you were when you ascended the throne, but for Liudolf such an event is hopefully many years off. You were ready to rule. Do you not think Liudolf also is?"

Otto ran his hand through his hair looking wearier than ever. "You may be right."

Adelheid put an arm around him. "Otto, I speak purely out of concern for you. Indeed if Liudolf took power, I would go into exile with you and remain proud to be your wife. My dearest, never think you have disappointed me. But I do not think you could bear it. It destroyed Hugh. Is it truly what you want?"

"Of course it is not," Otto said sharply. "I intend to rule both Germany and Italy. I intend to wear the crown of the emperor if God is willing."

Henry shrugged. "You will get none of this if Liudolf and Conrad prevail."

∞∞∞

Otto took a few days over his decision before talking with the family in the abbey.

"I am going to void the treaty. Liudolf and Conrad will be named as outlaws until they swear their loyalty to me." Otto spoke solemnly, looking many years older than he had over the merry Christmas tide just a few months before.

"Are you sure of this, Father?" William asked. "I thought the treaty you agreed with them was a fair one. I hoped it would lead to an improvement of your relations."

"The treaty was forced on him," Henry said. "I think Otto has made the right decision."

"What if Liudolf does not accept the decision?" William asked. "He raised a powerful army at Mainz."

"Liudolf needs to remember it is his father who is God's anointed, not him," Adelheid said sharply. "And Otto has pledged not to desert Italy."

Otto held up a hand. "There must be no quarrels here. I need to know every one of you here supports me in this."

"You know I do," Henry said.

Bruno gave a solemn nod. "With a heavy heart, I concur. You are God's anointed and everyone must honour that, including Liudolf. But I shall pray for a speedy resolution to this matter."

"William?" Otto asked.

Tears welled in William's eyes. "My father or my brother?

What sort of a choice is that?" He shook his head. "Bruno is right. You are God's anointed and it is not as if I could take up arms. But Father, please when Liudolf swears loyalty, make some amends. He remains my beloved brother. I am struggling to see you so willing to fight him."

Otto pressed his lips tightly together to contain his emotion. "I am not willing, but it is necessary for the good of this land. Nothing will please me more than to accept both Liudolf and Conrad back into my affection."

"What if it is too late for that?" Mathilda said. "What if there is fighting and either Liudolf or Conrad are slain? Can you accept that, Otto?"

Otto's face crumpled and Adelheid flung herself into the silence. "This quarrel is not of Otto's making."

Mathilda's gaze was steady. "No, it is not." Adelheid frowned at the insinuation as Mathilda looked pleadingly at Otto. "I do not condone Liudolf's actions, but to fight against your own son? This is wrong."

"Are you going to again side with my enemies?"

"Your enemies?" Mathilda cried. "Liudolf is your beloved son. What do you think she would make of this?" She pointed at the tomb before the altar.

The lines of pain on Otto's face deepened. "Eadgyth supported me always," he cried, almost running from the abbey. "Do not use her name against me."

Mathilda shook her head as she sank to her knees at the grave. "Yes, she always supported you, but this would have broken her heart."

Henry and William went after Otto, but Adelheid remained frozen to the spot, knowing Otto would not wish to see her.

"When has Mathilda sided with Otto's enemies?" she asked Bruno.

"She sided with Henry in his pretensions to the crown. Her relationship with Otto in those days was poor indeed. It was Eadgyth who brought them to a reconciliation," Bruno replied.

Adelheid turned away, not wanting to hear any more.

Eadgyth had brought harmony to Otto's life, while she had brought only strife.

∞ ∞ ∞

Adelheid broke the news to Otto that she was again with child before he convened a synod at Fritzlar. He was delighted and kissed her tenderly, declaring it more important than ever for him to keep control of the realm.

The synod supported Otto's wishes and this news was swiftly sent to Liudolf. As an additional measure, Otto sent messages to the Lotharingian nobles, encouraging them not to support Conrad.

"Conrad is a Frank," Otto said with satisfaction. "The Lotharingians have never fully accepted him. Let him see how he likes a rebellion."

The Lotharingians did indeed pledge their support to Otto, driving Conrad from his duchy but their glee was short lived as Franconia and Swabia reacted angrily. Before long the first reports of skirmishes arrived.

Adelheid began to feel she barely saw Otto. He was mostly away, campaigning against the rebels and even when he returned to court he was in continuous consultation with Henry or Bruno. At night he came to their chambers looking exhausted.

"Is it very bad, Otto?" Adelheid asked one night.

Otto shrugged. "I could bring it to an end at any time. All I have to do is promise to abandon Italy, but I will not do that. The imperial crown is to be mine and everyone will have to accept it."

"But if you lose control of Swabia and Franconia will it even be possible?"

"Franconia and Swabia will have to be brought to my will." Otto shook his head. "My God, how I miss Hermann. There were never problems in Swabia while he was alive."

Adelheid was struck by the memory of Hermann with his arm around Liudolf, the son he never had. Otto sat on the bed staring into space and as he sank his head into his hands, she wondered if he was thinking the same thing. If there was anyone who could have turned Hermann or indeed Eadgyth from their unwavering loyalty to Otto, it would surely be their beloved Liudolf. Suddenly feeling protective of him, Adelheid put her arms around him, thinking it was just as well he had her to support him, but at that he tensed.

"I am going to the church for a while." He kissed her. "You need your rest."

∞ ∞ ∞

Henry appointed his brother-in-law, Arnulf to oversee matters in Bavaria so he was free to support Otto in his campaigns. They proved to be stronger than Liudolf and Conrad, who retreated to Mainz, but they did not surrender and for two months Adelheid rarely saw Otto as he and Henry laid siege to the city.

In June Otto returned briefly to court. Adelheid, now growing great with child, struggled to her feet to greet him, looking at him anxiously. Each time she saw him he looked older and wearier. He greeted her swiftly, enquiring to her health and asking after their little Henry, but he turned quickly to Bruno.

"Archbishop Wigfried of Cologne has died," Otto said solemnly.

"I am sorry to hear that," Bruno replied. "He was a fine man. I shall never forget the first time I met him at your coronation. He was the one who greeted Eadgyth and myself when we arrived at the church."

"That was a long time ago," Otto snapped, before taking a deep breath to calm himself. "But yes, he was a fine man as I am certain the next Archbishop will be. It is time, Bruno."

"Me?"

Otto took his brother's hands. "I shall greatly miss you at court, but there is no one finer I could appoint as Archbishop. Lotharingia will be in your diocese. You can do much to bring peace to the region. Please, Bruno. You are needed."

Bruno nodded slowly. "You are right. I think God is indeed calling me to this. With your permission, Otto, I shall go immediately to Cologne."

"Permission most certainly granted," Otto replied.

Adelheid smiled, delighted to see one of Otto's most faithful allies in such a position. "You will truly be the finest of bishops," she said.

"I endeavour only to do God's work. Once I have been invested, I shall return to your side, Otto. And I shall continue my efforts to bring peace between you and Liudolf."

Otto smiled. "Of course. I would not expect anything else."

Chapter eight

Otto maintained the siege of Mainz, but Liudolf and Conrad held fast. Matters had become worse as the rebellions in Swabia increased, so Otto's latest message was welcome news to Adelheid as she neared the end of her pregnancy.

"My dearest Adelheid," his message started. "I send my greetings and pray they find you in good health. I am intending to start negotiations for peace with Liudolf and Conrad. This situation is intolerable and bad for Germany. Lend your prayers that the negotiations are successful and, God willing, our separation will soon be at an end."

Adelheid did indeed pray earnestly for their success. She was joined in this by both Mathilda and Judith and Adelheid wondered whether elsewhere Ida and Liutgarde were in a similar prayer. However Bruno returned alone to court.

"What has happened?" she asked. "Is the trouble at an end?"

Bruno shook his head. "I did my best. I thought the negotiations were going well, but Henry provoked Liudolf and Conrad. They stormed from the meeting saying they would not talk to Otto while he listened to such counsel."

"What did Otto do?"

"He declared them stripped of their duchies. He has named me as Duke of Lotharingia, although it is not an office I seek. Not that any of this makes much difference. Lotharingia was already siding with Otto, while Swabia will remain loyal to Liudolf, regardless of whether he holds the title." Bruno shook his head. "I truly thought we had a chance of peace. Sister, I know how you favour Henry, but be certain that it is in Otto's interest."

"What do you mean?"

"If Liudolf and Conrad are slain or exiled, who will be Otto's heir? Your son is too young. Henry coveted the throne once before."

Adelheid felt sick, but Judith glared indignantly at Bruno. "You are wrong. Henry is completely loyal to Otto. I know this for a fact."

"I hope you are right, Judith, but why did he prevent the peace? I do not want to believe ill of my brother, but I do not think his actions have served Otto well."

Judith shrugged. "Henry is not always wise, I know that. But if he has urged Otto to continue the quarrel, it is because he genuinely believes it is in Otto's best interest. Please believe me, Bruno. Henry still feels so guilty for his own lack of loyalty. It makes him protective of Otto. That is why he is so harsh on Liudolf and Conrad."

"Perhaps," Bruno replied. "But I think in this case his loyalty is misguided. How would Henry like to fight against his son?"

Judith looked down. "I know. He would hate it."

"Adelheid, I know you too mistrust Liudolf and Conrad. I know you favour Henry," Bruno said. "But even so I beg you to urge Otto to reconsider."

However when Otto returned he refused to listen to her. "You must not worry yourself at such a time," he said, laying his hand gently against her swollen stomach. "Concentrate on keeping yourself well."

Determined to preserve some normalcy, Otto maintained his tradition of receiving petitioners. Despite feeling highly uncomfortable, Adelheid sat beside him, bestowing her smile on the favoured, although her mind was elsewhere. She watched idly as a woman, her hood drawn low over her face, knelt before Otto.

"How may I assist you, my lady?" Otto said jovially.

"My Lord King, I beg you to call a truce in your quarrel with the Dukes of Swabia and Lotharingia," the woman said in a low voice.

Otto stiffened. "Liutgarde?" He pushed back her hood to stare at his kneeling daughter. "My dear child, please rise."

Liutgarde remained on her knees. "Please, Father. I am feeling torn in two. I must support my husband and brother, but I cannot wish you to be defeated. Surely you cannot wish for this war to continue. Please do not tell me I know not what I say. I understand more than you think."

"I know you do, sweetheart," Otto replied. He looked at the petitioners still waiting to talk to him. "I cannot discuss this with you now. Adelheid, take Liutgarde to refresh herself. I shall finish swiftly and then we shall talk."

Adelheid hauled herself from her chair to lead Liutgarde to the great table, calling for wine and honeyed cakes. She sat down with her, not sure what to say. They had never been friends and she found it hard to maintain her normal light conversation.

Liutgarde took a sip of her drink before looking directly at Adelheid. "I hoped to have the chance to talk to you alone. I have a request."

Adelheid shook her head. "I can guess what you wish to ask, but Otto is not listening to me. He says I must prepare myself for the birth and not think of such serious matters."

Liutgarde smiled sympathetically. "I can imagine that. But I am not asking you to urge my father towards peace. What I wish to ask you will be much harder for you."

"What is it?"

Liutgarde hesitated. "Liudolf believes you truly love Father. I have never been so sure. If he is right, what I have to ask will be so hard for you, but if you do truly love him, you will do it."

"I do love him. I swear that."

"Father and Liudolf used to be so close. Never was a father and son so affectionate. Perhaps you find it hard to believe."

"I have seen no sign of such closeness."

"No. It all changed when Mother died. Father was devastated by her death. I think it nearly destroyed him. The only way he coped was by controlling his grief. That is why only he is allowed to mention her name. If others mention her, he is not prepared for it and so he reacts with anger. You have seen it yourself. We hoped when he married you, this would change."

"But it has not," Adelheid whispered.

"No. Because he has never fully faced his grief, he cannot recover from the loss as the rest of us have. After Mother died he sent Liudolf to Hermann in Swabia, saying Liudolf must prepare himself for the duchy. It was a sensible plan. Perhaps he would have done that if Mother was alive, but to be sent away so soon after her death was hard. I know Hermann was a great comfort to him, but Liudolf needed his father. He feared Father no longer cared for him."

"I do not believe that," Adelheid said. "I am certain, in spite of everything, he loves Liudolf."

"So am I. It is strange. I resemble Mother more, yet my appearance has never bothered Father. But Liudolf has Mother's eyes. Every time Father looks at Liudolf, he sees our mother and he cannot control his grief if he sees her looking at him from Liudolf's eyes. In the end it became easier for Father not to look at him at all."

"I had no idea," Adelheid said.

"I hope you can understand how hard that is for Liudolf. As a boy he was so close to Father." Liutgarde looked at her apologetically. "I do not mean to give you too bleak an impression. It was not always bad. Often Father would greet him affectionately. When he officially named Liudolf his heir, no father could be prouder. After Liudolf and Ida were wed, they remained with the court and all seemed well. But then abruptly he sent them to Swabia. I think seeing them together reminded him too much of when he and Mother were first wed, but Liudolf was furious." She took a sip of her drink and wiped her eyes. "Of course this made it even harder for Father to look at him. I was never aware of any quarrels between my parents, so seeing Mother's eyes look so angrily at him, widened the gap."

"I do understand how hard all this was for Liudolf and Otto too, but what can I do?"

"You have to convince Father to open his heart to his grief. Yes, he will suffer. It will tear him apart, but he will know no peace until he faces it. And perhaps only then can he fully reconcile with Liudolf."

Adelheid stared at her stepdaughter, shifting her aching back against the chair.

Liutgarde gave a wry smile. "Perhaps I ask too much. You love Father. You do not want him to express his love for another woman, even if she is dead. Liudolf believes you love him, but he thinks your need to be always first with Father is too much. He does not believe you love Father enough to give him that peace."

Adelheid had still found no words before Otto approached them, pouring his own cup of wine and taking his daughter's hand. "Sweetheart, I will not discuss this war with you. Not because I think you do not understand, but because I already know what you wish to say. I will consider it, but I cannot promise anything. So let us talk of other matters. Tell me of young Otto. What escapades is he up to?"

Adelheid struggled to her feet. "I shall leave you two to talk. Truly, Liutgarde, I am glad to see you."

Liutgarde nodded, her eyes conveying her gratitude at being allowed some time alone with her father as Adelheid sought the one man she could always talk freely to.

"Father, am I too needy of Otto? Should I do what Liutgarde asks?"

Warinus smiled. "As his wife, it is right you come first with the King. Perhaps you feel needy because you fear he does not love you enough."

"How can I compare to Eadgyth? Father, I am afraid to encourage Otto to open his heart to his grief. I fear he only cares for me because he does not allow himself to think of her."

"But if you care for him, can you deny him an emotion which may in time bring him peace?"

Adelheid tried to find the words, as a pain shot through her. She cried out, clasping onto the priest's hand. Any decisions would have to wait. Her child had decided to arrive.

∞∞∞

As Otto had decreed, they named their second son, Bruno. Adelheid clutched her son to her breast, alarmed as he struggled to latch on. He was even smaller than Henry had been and Henry's health often concerned her.

Otto did not look as delighted as she would have liked. "Let us hope with good care he grows stronger," he said. "Liudolf and Liutgarde were far bigger. So was little Otto and Liudolf's daughters too."

Sensing criticism, Adelheid retorted sharply. "So was Emma."

Catching his mother's frown, Otto kissed her. "I am sure he will quickly grow. You have done well. Take care of yourself. I need you to recover."

∞∞∞

Adelheid did not see Liutgarde again before she re-joined her husband and Otto too quickly returned to Mainz. He said nothing of his intentions, but Adelheid prayed he was going to make another attempt at peace.

When she heard Otto had lifted the siege of Mainz she was hopeful, but the messenger who brought the news quickly dashed that hope.

"Count Arnulf is encouraging rebellion in Bavaria," the man said. "He claims the duchy for his own."

"Could he be successful?" Adelheid asked.

It was Judith who answered. "Arnulf is my brother. He is named for our father, Duke Arnulf of Bavaria. The Bavarians reluctantly accepted Henry as their duke because of me, but in truth they would prefer a son of Duke Arnulf over a son-in-law."

"It seemed they accepted him when I was in Bavaria," Adelheid said.

"With the support of Otto, they had no choice but Otto is now weakened so it seems Arnulf is seizing his chance."

"Oh, why must Otto always fight against his family?" Mathilda said with a shake of her head. "Does he not have enough enemies to contend with on the borders?"

"None of this is Otto's fault," Adelheid said sharply.

Mathilda and Judith exchanged glances. "Otto must take some responsibility both for this rebellion and Henry's," Judith said. "After their father died, Otto treated Henry with such suspicion. Oh, he had some justification, I know that, but..."

"But Otto made no attempt to win Henry to loyalty," Mathilda continued. "He was a young, foolish boy grieving for his father, but Otto turned to men such as Duke Hermann of Swabia, rather than his own brother. Even in the family he made it plain how much fonder he was of Bruno. Henry resented it."

Judith nodded. "And now he has done the same with Liudolf. He treated him as a child of no account, belittled him for his efforts in Italy and has made it plain how much higher in his regard you and Henry are."

"Liudolf tried to prevent my marriage," Adelheid said. "Why should Otto not condemn that?"

"If he tried to prevent your marriage," Mathilda muttered. "Liudolf has never stated this."

"Even if he did, Otto could have shown more understanding

of how Liudolf felt his position threatened," Judith said. "No harm was done and some reassurance would have eased the situation considerably."

Mathilda sighed. "Otto considers himself so far above everyone, he gives little understanding to others. And since Eadgyth died, he has become worse."

Adelheid felt like weeping as she listened to this, following so soon after Liutgarde's revelations. It had seemed a simple matter to support Otto, but suddenly she understood this rebellion was not as clear cut as she had thought.

For the three women there was a tense wait, until they got Otto's message in the late autumn to return swiftly to Saxony. It was a stormy evening when Otto and Henry joined them in Magdeburg, Otto's face white with exhaustion.

"The nobles of Bavaria have turned against us," he said. "Franconia and Swabia are still in revolt and even here in Saxony, the very centre of my power there is unrest." Otto sank into a chair. "My God, I could lose everything."

Chapter nine

"**O**pen negotiations for peace, Otto," Adelheid urged. "Concessions may be necessary to save your position."

Otto shook his head. "Now I have seen how popular Liudolf is, my position will always be vulnerable. I need to be victorious or die."

"Please, Otto, I need you. Do not speak of dying."

Otto pulled her tightly into his arms and kissed the top of her head. "I hope it will not come to that. In the spring I shall renew my efforts."

Adelheid made preparations for a glum Christmas, while continually worrying about her children. Both Henry and Bruno went from ailment to ailment. Only Emma threw off her occasional sickness with ease.

As Advent came upon them they received a message from Conrad. "He begs for a temporary truce, my lord," the man said.

"A temporary truce?" Otto said, looking up morosely from the game Henry was playing with him to try to distract him from his woes. "What does that mean?"

"He wishes to talk to you, my lord," the man said. "He wants your oath you will not attack or imprison him if he makes a private visit to your court."

Otto looked more hopeful. "I wonder if he and Liudolf have fallen out. Very well. Inform him if he visits court, he has my word he will be at complete liberty to leave at any time."

Adelheid alone was with Otto when Conrad was ushered in.

Like Otto, he looked exhausted and she shook her head sadly at the strain this quarrel was placing on the men. As she poured him a cup of wine, she muttered a prayer that he and Otto might reach an agreement.

"Greetings, Otto," Conrad said, taking the hands of his father-in-law.

"Greetings, Conrad. In spite of everything, it is good to see you."

Conrad gave a tortured smile. "You will not think that when you hear what I have to say." He looked Otto in the eye and Adelheid was shocked to see tears in his own. "Otto, there is no easy way I can say this. Liutgarde, my beloved wife, your beloved daughter, has died."

Otto fell back into his chair, staring at Conrad, his eyes wide in shock. Feeling completely numb herself, Adelheid reached for his hand. He gripped it tightly, almost crushing her fingers as his knuckles whitened. "This cannot be. She is so young."

I know." Conrad sank into his own chair.

"I thought her mother was too young to die," Otto whispered. "But she had years on Liutgarde." He sank his head into his hands. "My little Liutgarde. How did it happen? Did she suffer?"

Conrad shook his head. "For some time she has had a sickness. But it always seemed a trivial matter. She would be unable to stomach food and take to her bed for a few days, but it would soon be over and she would be herself again. When she sickened this time, I thought it was the same. The night she died I took young Otto in to bid her good night. She was in good spirits. I thought she would rise from her bed in the morn. But when they went to wake her... I think she knew nothing of it. I pray she did not."

Adelheid put her arms around Otto, shocked beyond words by this news. Just a few months before Liutgarde had sat with her, confident and charming. It seemed impossible that attractive woman could be so suddenly taken from them.

His face drained of colour, Otto looked again at Conrad. "Did you love my daughter?"

"I came to," Conrad replied. "At our wedding, no. I cared only that she was pretty and compliant and she brought me closer to you. But she came to mean so much to me. I relied so much on her calm good sense. I think I realised how much she meant to me on the day young Otto was born. When they brought me the news of a son, all I felt was impatience that they had not told me how she was. The birth of a son meant little if she did not recover."

Otto gave a faint smile. "I am glad she knew that."

"So am I, but it hurts so much more that she is gone."

"I know," Otto replied.

"Yes, you do. But you and Eadgyth had years together that were denied to me and Liutgarde."

"It was not enough," Otto replied. Adelheid looked unhappily at him, not certain he even realised she was there. This was a grief for him and Conrad. She shared their shock, but could not share their grief. She had barely got to know Liutgarde and for that she was overwhelmed by regret.

Conrad reached out to take Otto by the hands. "She wanted us to be friends, Otto. You know that. I know she came to see you. Is there any way we could reach a peace? For her sake?"

"Will you stop the rebellion?"

"If you will listen to our wishes," Conrad replied. "Otto, neither Liudolf nor I are out to depose you."

"Conditions? So, Liutgarde's wishes do not mean that much to you."

Conrad recoiled as if Otto had struck him. "Nor to you either, apparently. I do not think Liutgarde wished for me to desert Liudolf. He needs to know someone in the family still reveres him. I know I could make my peace with you this day, but where would that leave him?"

"Does he know of Liutgarde's death?"

Conrad nodded. "He attended her requiem. He grieves deeply."

"Oh, Conrad, do you see what this quarrel has done? I am

denied a place at my own daughter's requiem. I beg you to make peace."

"Will you listen to our demands?"

"I cannot give in to such a rebellion."

"Then there can be no peace. Liudolf is my brother, as much as he ever was. You always hoped I would support him, after your experiences with your own brother-in-law."

"I did, but I did not expect you to support him against me."

"Nor did I. Liudolf and I love you. We have both learnt from you. If we have a point of view, is it not worth listening to? Otto, I was your loyal man for years. I once saved your life from Henry and now you side with Henry against me. And Liudolf was your beloved son. From the first time I came to court, I was struck by the bond between the two of you. I thought nothing could ever break it. Do you have any idea how it feels for you to turn against us?"

Otto narrowed his eyes. "Stop the rebellion."

Conrad stood. "No, of course you do not. You never now consider the feelings of any other than yourself. I first swore loyalty to you as my king, but over time it was the man I revered, just as Hermann did. We both loved you. We would have done anything for you, died for you if necessary."

Otto was silent but Adelheid could see the pain in his expression. "You need to swear loyalty, Conrad," she said quietly. "It is the only way to end this."

"The man I swore loyalty to no longer exists. Liutgarde always believed he would return one day, but I fear she was wrong. Perhaps it is a mercy she will never know that. I came to break this sad news in person. I have done that and shall depart now. You gave me your word that I can do this."

His face frozen, Otto nodded. "Yes, you are free. Where is young Otto? Why not send him to court to be cared for safely?"

Conrad gave a half laugh. "You expect me to place my son as a hostage in the care of your wife? I think not."

"I would care for him as my own," Adelheid said, realising this was the one thing she could do for Otto at this time.

"No, I do not trust you. He is with Ida. I trust her to care for my son as Liutgarde would have cared for him. If you want to see your grandson, if you want to see Liutgarde's son, you will make peace."

$$\infty\infty\infty$$

There was nothing Adelheid could do for Otto that winter. Liutgarde's sudden death had affected him deeply, but if he wept, he wept alone. With Otto determined not to accept comfort from her, Adelheid tried to console Mathilda who was devastated by the death of her granddaughter, but there was little she could say. In any case, Mathilda seemed to gain more solace from kneeling at Eadgyth's grave or sharing tearful reminiscences with Judith, memories which Adelheid was not a party to. There were no Christmas festivities and Adelheid spent much of the day weeping bitterly for everything which had gone wrong. But the winter was only to get worse.

Little Henry came down with one of the winter infections which were so rife, but could not throw it off. For days Adelheid sat at his cradle watching his tiny body wracked with coughs, the only food she could get into him, quickly brought back up.

She and Warinus knelt beside him, earnestly uttering every prayer she could think of. But they were to be in vain. Little Henry expired just a few months after his half-sister. Looking older than ever, Otto attended his requiem mass and held Adelheid in his arms as she wept for her precious first born son.

But the comfort Otto offered was short lived. Learning of the chaos in Germany, both Slavs and Magyars mounted their own attacks. With an effort Otto put the deaths of his children from his mind and left to defend the border, commenting that at least Conrad and Liudolf would have their hands full with the invasions.

"Otto, there can be no shame in calling for a truce at such a time. Contact Liudolf and Conrad, ask for their aid in defending the border. Perhaps a common enemy will bring you closer together."

"A truce?" Otto demanded. "Do not be foolish, Adelheid. You yourself pointed out how vulnerable I would be if I give into the demands of rebels. They should surrender, pledging their men to my forces. That is all I have to say on the matter."

"But if Liudolf and Conrad were to be reasonable…"

Otto shook his head. "I do not know what you want any more. You were the one who urged me to take a firm hand and now you urge me in another way. Can I ever please you?"

"Of course you do," Adelheid replied. "Can I ever please you?"

Otto frowned. "Support me, Adelheid. That is all I ask."

"I do support you. Otto, I think I am with child again."

Otto brightened and kissed her. "That is excellent news. Stop worrying about the rebellion. I will sort those fools. You keep yourself well and try to deliver a fine strong son."

Chapter ten

Adelheid tried to do as Otto had commanded. She did her best to forget the joys of cradling her first born son in her arms. She tried not to think of his sweet smile, his first toddling steps and his arms outstretched for her. Most of all she tried to forget the sight of his tiny body wracked by illness. Instead she concentrated on little Bruno, giving thanks as he flung off his illnesses and rejoiced as her body swelled again.

News from all over Germany was of revolt and invasion. Otto tried desperately to keep the Slavs from Saxony, sending as many men as he dared to strengthen the border. He rejoined Adelheid to celebrate Easter at Magdeburg. There was no mention of either Liutgarde or little Henry, but Adelheid noticed unhappily how his eyes lingered on Eadgyth's grave. Often she remembered Liutgarde's last request of her, to encourage Otto to open his heart to his feelings, but feeling sick with the pregnancy, she lacked the energy to deal with such emotion.

Soon after Easter news reached them of Liudolf's own celebrations at Worms and how he had invited the Magyar chiefs to celebrate with him, giving them costly gifts in welcome.

"Why is he doing that?" Adelheid cried. "I always thought he would be loyal to Germany."

"He is being loyal," Otto replied. "He is buying them off, so he can concentrate his efforts against me. How did it come to this, that my own son would rather fight me than the Magyars?"

"Is there no hope for peace?" Adelheid asked wearily. She was so tired of the war. She hated only seeing Otto briefly, before he rode away again, only to return with the lines of worry etching his face more deeply than ever.

"Not until Liudolf surrenders," Otto replied. "I will not let that boy beat me."

"We could turn this to our advantage," Henry said. "Suppose the people believed Liudolf was paying the Magyars to attack Germany? They would turn against him."

"Do not be foolish, Henry," Otto snapped. "Liudolf would never do such a thing."

"We know that, Otto, but the people do not. Let us accuse him of this and the heart will go out of his rebellion."

Otto looked disgusted. "This is no way to fight a war."

"But if it brings an end to the rebellion," Adelheid said. "Surely it is worth it."

"I suppose so. Very well, Henry. Spread what rumours you wish." Otto turned away. "I am not sure I am fit to be king if the only way I can triumph is in such an underhand way."

It was William who comforted Otto for this latest action, as Henry got to work. But while Otto remained distasteful of the actions they proved to be effective. The rebellions in Saxony died away as everyone rallied behind their king against the Slavs. Even in Franconia and Swabia support for the rebels waned. As the summer began, Conrad again contacted Otto, asking for peace.

To Adelheid's relief Otto was willing to listen, summoning Conrad to come immediately. He came and in a further welcome development Archbishop Frederick and Liudolf also agreed to the truce while the negotiations took place. There was tension when the synod was convened at Langenzenn, but both Frederick and Conrad appeared sincere in their wish to bring the conflict to an end. Conrad even accepted he would lose his duchy, while Frederick swore he had never born

Otto any ill will. Otto's lip curled, but he did not refute this statement. Liudolf looked wary, but he agreed to listen.

"I remain willing to accept you all back into my affection," Otto stated. "There will be no imprisonment or any further punishment beyond the loss of the duchies."

Adelheid held her breath, praying this would be enough, but Liudolf's eyes narrowed. "Do I remain your heir?"

Before Otto could reply, Henry got to his feet. "You tried to form an alliance with the Magyars," he cried. "Germany does not need a traitor king."

"That is a lie," Liudolf shouted. "Just like all the other lies you have told about me. I demand you take back that statement, Uncle. I tried my utmost to keep them from Germany and when that failed, I tried to bribe them. Nothing more."

"I do not believe you," Henry said. "You are a friend to the Magyars and no friend to the King."

Liudolf turned his eyes to Otto and even though she had never met the woman, almost Adelheid could see his mother looking from them. "My lord, say you refute the Duke of Bavaria's comments. State publically that I did not form an alliance with the Magyars."

Otto's face was pale and Adelheid knew he too was seeing Eadgyth looking accusingly at him. "Stop this, Liudolf. This is not the time to discuss it."

Liudolf stared longer at his father, a bitter disappointment setting over his features. "Very well, my lord. Inform me when it is time to discuss it. As far as I am concerned the truce is at an end."

"No, Liudolf," Otto cried. "Do not be so foolish."

"And yet again you do not miss a chance to remind me what a fool I am." Liudolf turned away from his father to look at Conrad and Frederick. "Are you two still with me?"

"I have never intentionally stood against the King, my lord," Frederick said.

Liudolf sent the archbishop a withering look. "Conrad?"

"Liudolf, we are here for peace. Do not give up. He is your

father."

Liudolf turned his scornful gaze to Otto. "I have no father. My true father was Duke Hermann of Swabia - the man who never failed to love me as a son. Fine, Conrad. Stay here with those who will treat you with contempt. I care not. The truce is ended."

Liudolf stormed from the hall and Otto slumped his head in his hands, Liudolf's words clearly hurting him. Conrad ran after him, imploring him to come back.

Adelheid rounded on Henry. "Why did you say such a thing? We had a chance at peace."

"I do not like to see Otto with so ungrateful a son," Henry replied. "I was standing up for him, as you also should, Sister. Let Otto name your little boy as his heir."

"My son is a baby and a frail one at that," Adelheid said. "How can he be Otto's heir?"

"Be silent," Otto said. "I alone decide these matters. Henry, you should have kept quiet. Peace was within our grasp."

"But I notice you did not refute my words," Henry said. "You could have done what Liudolf asked."

Otto shook his head. "The matter should never have been raised. Once you had raised it, I could not deny the rumours we spread." He looked hopefully at Conrad who had returned to the hall. "Has Liudolf calmed down?"

"No, Otto. He is gone. I wish you would go after him. You alone could persuade your son."

Otto gave a bitter smile. "You heard him. He is no longer my son."

"Oh, Otto, you should not listen to that." Conrad shook his head as Otto remained seated. "Very well. But let me make one point clear. I swear loyalty to you. Not to him." He pointed at Henry. "He is a poor advisor. I am not sure even now if he is truly loyal to you. He certainly benefits from your animosity towards Liudolf."

"I am loyal," snapped Henry.

Conrad turned to Adelheid. "If you truly love the King as

Liutgarde believed, you will advise him to be wary."

∞∞∞

Otto and Henry spent days in frantic planning, ignoring Adelheid's pleas to pursue a peaceful solution.

"Go to him without Henry," she suggested. "Talk to him as a father to a son as many have so long begged you to do."

"He is no longer my son," Otto snapped. "That is his choice, not mine."

"Whose side are you on?" Henry demanded.

"I am on Otto's," she cried. "Would you want to be encouraged to fight your son?"

"Stay out of this, Adelheid. It need not concern you," Otto said.

Sighing, Adelheid left the men to their plans, hoping William could talk some sense into him. It was late when Otto came to their chamber and he took her tightly into his arms. "I thank God I have you. I would be bereft indeed if I did not." His hands drifted to her stomach where the baby stirred against him. Some of the tension eased out of his face. "This feels like a strong one. Let us hope it is not an ungrateful one."

Adelheid said nothing. The joy she would once have felt in Otto's words, meaningless at such a time. His last words chilled her. Otto had turned so completely against Liudolf. Could she be certain her child would fare any better?

As Otto drifted off to sleep, she tried to relax her own body. But the child inside her was restless and Otto was more restless still. In the dark of the night he sat upright. "Thankmar! Thankmar! No. Please, God, no."

Adelheid put her arms around him, trying to pull him back down again. As he pressed his face against her shoulder, she stroked his hair, desperately trying to calm him.

"Oh, Eadgyth," he muttered. "I do not know what I would do without you, my sweet."

Adelheid froze, as Otto stilled at last. Tears rolled down her cheeks, as she realised how easily Eadgyth had been able to comfort him. Even now she was the one he turned to.

Chapter eleven

"Who is Thankmar?" Adelheid asked Mathilda the next day.

"Thankmar? That is a name not mentioned in a very long time," she replied. "He was Otto's older brother."

"Older brother? But you said Otto was your firstborn."

"He is. My husband had a previous union. It had been declared illegal, as she had taken holy vows. Thankmar was disbarred from the succession, something he bitterly resented. It was sensible of Otto to encourage William into the church, so that such a situation did not again arise."

"What happened to Thankmar? Otto called out his name in his sleep."

Mathilda paled. "I am not surprised it is playing on his mind. Thankmar rebelled against Otto after his first year on the throne. He surrendered, but Otto's men stormed the stronghold and slew Thankmar in the chapel. Otto blamed himself and the grief nearly tore him apart. I think it was only Eadgyth who kept him going at such a time. She was ever a support for Otto."

"Are you implying I am not?"

Mathilda shrugged. "I mean no criticism. Eadgyth was older than Otto by a few years. When they married, he was not much more than a boy. He looked up to her and depended heavily on her support. It is different with you. He is very protective of you in a way I rarely saw with Eadgyth."

Adelheid was not sure whether to take comfort from this or

not.

"So, Thankmar is playing again on his mind," Mathilda continued. "He fought against his brother and his brother died. Now he fights against his son. Thankmar's death nearly destroyed him. I do not think he could cope with being responsible for Liudolf's death."

"I do not think he can either," Adelheid whispered. "But what can I do? I am urging him to peace."

Mathilda's face crumpled. "Only one can win – Otto or Liudolf. I do not think Liudolf could cope with the responsibility for his father's death either, yet it seems both are determined to fight until one of them dies. My son and my grandson. I love them both so much. I hate seeing them try to destroy each other."

∞∞∞

Word quickly came that Liudolf had taken control of much of Bavaria with the help of Arnulf. Otto and Henry followed them and messengers brought news of a fierce battle at Nuremburg. Adelheid no longer knew what to pray for. She needed Otto to be victorious, but the thought of his grief if his son was slain was unbearable. Mostly she prayed for a peace which would content the men, although it seemed an impossible wish. As Mathilda had said, father and son seemed intent on destroying each other.

Although Otto had gained the upper hand in the battle, it was not decisive. When he and Henry returned briefly to court, Henry was in a furious mood.

"That boy has given away treasure after treasure. The brat has made sure I can never regain my full splendour," Henry told her.

Otto put a hand on his shoulder. "Calm down, Brother. Treasures can be replaced. Indeed Liudolf will replace them. I will make sure of that."

"He had better," Henry replied.

"Never mind this," Adelheid said. "Is there peace now?"

"No. Liudolf has taken refuge in Regensburg. My men are besieging it. I would like to move the court closer so I can supervise this personally. Are you well enough to move, Adelheid?"

"Yes, I think so. If we move slowly."

"Good. This will not take long."

However Otto proved to be over optimistic as the siege dragged on throughout the summer. There was a glimmer of hope when Otto reported that Liudolf had asked to open negotiations.

"That is wonderful, is it not?" Adelheid cried.

"I want an unconditional surrender," Otto said. "I am not interested in negotiations."

"But Otto, this is your son."

"He is not my son," Otto almost shouted at her. "Adelheid, do you have any idea how close he came to beating me? I will show no weakness."

Liudolf requested peace a second time, informing them that the people of Regensburg were starving, but still Otto held fast. Adelheid was disappointed Otto was proving so stubborn, wishing he would show forgiveness to his own son.

"Henry, these are your people who are dying," she implored her brother-in-law. "Can't you stop this?"

Henry had been injured in the arm which did nothing to improve his temper. "The people could kick Liudolf and Arnulf out at any time. If they choose not to, they deserve to starve."

The next time she saw them, both men were in better spirits, reporting gleefully that Arnulf had been slain. "Hopefully the Bavarians will turn against Liudolf now," Henry said.

"Prepare a victory celebration," Otto instructed. "We must

celebrate this advancement."

Adelheid did as she was bidden, aided by Judith. But as they arranged the cups to be filled with the finest of wines, Judith suddenly broke down.

"Arnulf was my brother," she sobbed. "How can I celebrate his death?"

Adelheid put an arm around her. "You cannot. In truth I have no heart for the celebration either. I feel sick, wondering if Otto would throw a similar celebration for his own son's death."

"I hate this conflict," Judith said. "I hated it when Henry was fighting Otto and I hate it now they are both fighting Liudolf."

Adelheid set down the cup. "I think I have been taken ill," she said. "And I think you must care for me. Come, we shall not be part of this celebration."

Otto came to their chamber in concern as soon as he heard the news, but stood frozen in the doorway upon seeing Adelheid still fully dressed and standing, instead of in bed as he had expected to find her. Adelheid and Judith stared defiantly back.

"There is nothing wrong with you," he said.

"No, but I do not think you should expect Judith to celebrate the death of her own brother."

"Why not? He fought against her husband. This is no time for sentimentality. You are either with us or not. So, where do you two stand?"

"I no longer know," Adelheid snapped.

Otto narrowed his eyes and folded his arms. "What does that mean? Are you saying you no longer support me? Eadgyth supported me in everything."

"Would she have supported you in this?" Adelheid asked. "Would you have asked her to support you against her own son?"

"Be silent," Otto bellowed. "You did not know her. You do not get to talk for her."

Judith flinched at Otto's rage, but Adelheid looked at him,

realising Liutgarde's words were true. Otto did need to confront his grief. "I did not know her, that is true. But like her, I am a mother. I know how a mother thinks. Look into your heart, Otto. Did you truly love her? Your determination to destroy her son is a betrayal of her and her love."

Otto froze, his whole body tensing. His eyes narrowed in what appeared to be pure hatred. "Do not ever say such things to me again, do you understand, Adelheid?"

There was a jug of ale on a table. He picked it up and hurled it against the opposite wall. Adelheid cried out as it shattered into tiny fragments. Otto turned on his heel and left the room, slamming the door on his way out. Shakily Adelheid sank onto the bed, her body trembling. Judith put an arm around her. "Adelheid, what have you said?"

"What I had to. Somebody needed to say it," she replied, wondering if she had lost Otto's affection for ever. "I can no longer support him, because what if one day he expects me to support him against my son?"

∞∞∞

Over the next days Otto barely spoke to her, giving only curt instructions. At night he left her to lie alone and she had no idea where he went until Judith told her he was often in the church. That next night she went there herself. At the doorway she paused, her breath catching in her throat as she saw her husband dressed all in black, kneeling at the altar with William sat on a chair beside him.

"Why did God take her from me? I loved her."

William laid his hand on Otto's shoulder. "Father, it is not for us to question God's will. Eadgyth lived a virtuous life and she is assured of God's salvation."

"But I needed her. I still need her. William, she has been gone for years but still I struggle without her. I fear I am no longer the man she loved."

"All you can do is remember the love she bore you and the love she gave so freely to others. She was always an inspiration. Let her memory inspire you to be the man she was so proud of."

"It is not enough. I do not know if it ever will be." Otto sank his head in his hands, his shoulders shaking as Adelheid went quietly away with tears in her own eyes, not knowing whether she should be hopeful or heartbroken at what she had witnessed.

$$\infty\infty\infty$$

After the death of Arnulf matters changed quickly. Deprived of support, Liudolf left Bavaria for Swabia with Otto swiftly in pursuit. He left instructions for Adelheid and the court to make their way to the Palace of Illertisson. Otto was hunting nearby, but he rode to meet them as they rested not far from their destination.

"Are you ready to ride on?" he asked. "If anywhere is still loyal to Liudolf, it is here."

Adelheid struggled to her feet, looking up at Otto astride his horse, the dogs panting at his heels. "Please, Otto, do not remain so angry with me."

"The way you spoke to me was unacceptable. I am justified in my anger. Are you ready to apologise? Will you swear never to speak to me in such a fashion again?"

"You said I could always freely speak my mind to you."

"Do you have any idea how those words hurt me?" Otto leaned down slightly, his voice low, but she could hear the rage boiling in him.

"Yes, but I did not say them lightly. My dearest, you once told me it was my place as a wife to guide you on the right path. If you no longer believe that, please say and naturally I will never voice my opinions to you again."

"Of course that is not what I want," Otto replied, looking

exasperated. "Damn it, Adelheid, I need to know my wife will not deliberately hurt me."

"I never wished to hurt you. I hurt Lothair once with my words, when I told him I was ashamed to be his wife. He responded by beating me senseless. I did not say such hurtful words to either of you to be cruel, but because I truly believed they were needed. Please, Otto. I think I would rather you beat me senseless than treated me coldly for the rest of our lives."

Otto's face softened and he slid down from his horse. "Oh, Adelheid, I can never be angry at you for long." He took her into his arms and she clung tightly to him. "Of course you should always speak your mind to me. I promised you that, but remember I did not promise to always listen to your words."

"I know, as long as you know I would never say any words to you in malice."

"I do. Come, let us get you to shelter. We are on the border with Swabia. It could be dangerous."

They rode on, when a company of armed men emerged from the trees. Leading them was Liudolf.

Chapter twelve

Liudolf slid from his horse as Otto gestured to men to surround Adelheid and the other ladies.

"My lord, I beg for a truce," Liudolf said, kneeling on the ground.

"Archers, raise your weapons," Henry called.

Adelheid cried out, wondering if Otto was about to see his son slaughtered before his eyes. Liudolf made no attempt to defend himself, but threw his sword down, bowing his head.

"Fire!" Henry yelled.

"No," Otto shouted.

Henry frowned as the archers lowered their weapons. Liudolf said nothing, but stared at his father.

"Get up," Otto snapped. "I do not want a truce. I want you to surrender. Send away your men and come willingly with me."

Liudolf hesitated and Adelheid expected him to refuse, but then he nodded, gesturing to his men to turn back. He stepped out of his shoes. "I surrender, my lord."

Adelheid's body sagged with relief, while Henry grinned triumphantly. He strode over and picked up Liudolf's sword. "Arrest him," he ordered.

A few men stepped forward, but Otto held up his hand. To Adelheid's surprise there was only pain on his face, no triumph. "That is not necessary. Henry, give him back his sword."

Henry looked at Otto in shock, but grudgingly handed the sword to Liudolf.

"Thank you, Uncle," Liudolf said. He turned to Otto and gave a slight bow. "What are your orders, my lord?"

Otto's eyes narrowed. "Follow me."

"Yes, my lord."

"He learnt that trick from Eadgyth," Judith whispered, as she urged her horse next to Adelheid.

"What do you mean?"

"Eadgyth was devoted to Otto. She always supported him and-"

"Yes, I know," Adelheid sighed. "In sixteen years there was never a cross word between them."

Judith looked puzzled. "Who told you that? Eadgyth was a strong and intelligent woman. Of course she and Otto disagreed on occasion, but Eadgyth kept their rare quarrels behind closed doors. It was her policy to always support Otto in public. If she was ever angry with him in front of others, she displayed it by treating him very formally. Just as Liudolf is doing now."

"Did this often happen?" Adelheid asked, amazed to hear of Eadgyth as less than perfect.

"Not often. She and Otto had a rare bond which left them mostly in accord, but yes, it happened at times." Judith sighed. "In truth I do not blame Liudolf, but I wish he was not doing it. He will not put Otto in a good mood by reminding him of those occasions when Eadgyth was angry with him."

At the Palace of Illertissen Otto sat on his throne with Adelheid on one side and Henry on the other, ordering Liudolf to stand before him. Adelheid felt a grudging respect at how Liudolf tolerated this indignity, simply staring back at his father. His blue eyes were steady and again Adelheid was certain it was Eadgyth Otto was seeing.

"I would lose the insolence if I were you," Henry said. "You have lost everything."

Liudolf gave a slight smile. "Not everything. I have lost much. That is true. First I lost my mother, then I lost the man I revered as a father. I lost the love of my true father and I dare say I have lost my duchy and my status as heir to the throne. But I still have the fairest wife any man was ever blessed with. I still have two beautiful daughters. And I have the finest of sons."

Otto looked sharply at Liudolf. "You have a son?"

"Yes, my lord. My wife presented me with a son just three months past."

"Why was I not informed of this?"

"You have your own family, my lord. You have no interest in mine."

"I agree with Henry. Lose the insolence," Otto said. "The distance between us was not of my making."

"Really? In many ways I lost my father when I lost Mother."

Otto leaned forward, his eyes narrow. "Be silent, Liudolf."

"No, I will not. I am tired of needing permission to mention my own mother. The memories I have of her love are one thing you never will take from me. Even if you imprison me away from my family, I shall still have those memories. And know this, my lord, I shall be thinking of her every day." Liudolf paused, but Otto said nothing. "After Mother died I never knew whether you would be affectionate or distant. And in the last years it has become worse."

"What did you expect? You tried to prevent my marriage."

"I did not try to prevent your marriage," Liudolf said. "That was an invention by Henry and you chose to believe him, rather than talk to me."

"Then why did you go ahead of me to Italy?" Otto shouted.

"Why? Because Regelind begged me with tears pouring down her cheeks to help her unfortunate granddaughter. Everyone in Swabia was horrified when they heard how the widowed queen of Italy was treated. No one knew if you would arrive in time. I could not refuse Regelind. Not after she and Hermann took me so wholeheartedly into their family as a son." He glanced at Adelheid. "Hermann promised you Swabian aid at your first wedding. I did not forget that promise, even if you did."

Adelheid stared at Liudolf. There was no doubt in her mind that he was telling the truth.

"If Henry had not meddled, I would have succeeded in rescuing her," Liudolf continued, addressing his father once again. "She suffered for longer under siege because of Henry's actions. She was separated from her daughter for so much longer than was necessary. But still she favours Henry."

Adelheid's mouth went dry as she remembered those terrible days when food had shortened and she had prepared herself to marry Adalbert. She could have been free those days. Henry flushed and tried to catch her eye, but she looked down. She did not blame Henry. It was to her shame that she had never shown any gratitude to Liudolf.

"Was that the only reason?" Otto demanded, looking stunned.

Liudolf shrugged. "Obviously I hoped for some spoils of war. Perhaps additional lands and influence. But it was never my intention to prevent your marriage, my lord. Quite the opposite."

"The opposite? You wanted me to marry Adelheid? Do you truly expect me to believe that?"

"Oh, I admit I was not overjoyed at the prospect of half-brothers, but I always knew you would remarry one day. A kinswoman of Ida was better than any other. You forget I had already seen her. I knew you would admire her beauty and her piety. I hated the distance which had grown between us, my lord. I thought if I delivered her to you, you would be grateful. But I failed. Henry delivered her to you and it was him who was rewarded. You are right. I am a fool." Liudolf knelt, bowing his fair head. "My Lord King, I beg humbly for your forgiveness for my actions this last year. I swear undying loyalty to you, Otto of Saxony, as my king." He rose and shrugged. "I am returning to Ida now. Punish me as you wish."

There was silence as Liudolf turned away unhindered, even Henry raising no objection. He walked towards the door.

"Liudolf," Otto called. "What have you named your son?"

Liudolf turned back, his bitter expression giving way to a weary smile. "I named him for the man who, in spite of everything, I still love more than any other. He is called Otto."

Otto's mouth dropped open as Liudolf kept walking. "Liudolf, come back."

"Is that an order, my lord?"

Otto got up and took a step towards him. "No. It is a request from a father to a son."

Tears were escaping Liudolf's eyes as Otto caught his son up in his arms and for a long time the two clung together. Otto's cheeks were wet as he looked up. "Everyone out. I wish to be alone with my son."

The room swiftly emptied. With a frown Henry, was one of the first to leave, but Adelheid remained seated. She was not certain what she made of Liudolf's revelations. With his arms still around his son, Otto nodded at her. "You too, Adelheid. Liudolf and I have much to discuss."

Avoiding Liudolf's gaze, Adelheid left the room, wondering what this meant for her position. Outside the door she took a seat, determined to hear everything which was said. The first sound was one of sloshing liquid and she guessed one of them was pouring drinks.

"Your mother would have a few choice words for me, I think," Otto said.

"For us both, perhaps," Liudolf replied.

Otto laughed. "She would have kept us in order."

"Yes, she would."

"By God, Liudolf. What happened to us? We should not fight."

"I did not know if you still cared for me. When I heard you intended to make another son your heir..."

"I never intended that. You always remained my heir. You

still remain my heir."

"I believed that back in Mainz, but then you voided the treaty. I thought we had an agreement. What was I supposed to think after that?"

"You should have known I have more sense than to name a baby as my heir."

"You should have known I would not have interfered in your marriage plans." There was a tense silence. "You voided our treaty because of the influence of Henry and your wife. Do not deny that, Father."

"I have never been pushed into any course of action that I do not wish to follow. Do not blame Henry and Adelheid. Yes, they encouraged me, but I voided the treaty because I resented you forcing it on me."

"We had an agreement and you went back on it. That was dishonourable."

"Yes, it was," Otto agreed.

There was another long silence and then Liudolf burst out laughing. "Damn you, Father. You should not say that so smugly."

Otto also laughed. "No, I should not. In truth there has been little for me to feel proud of in all this. I have ignored agreements and exploited rumours which I knew to be false. But I had to triumph. A weakened king is no king at all. Such a situation would be bad for Germany."

"While I suppose killing your heir is not a bad thing at all." Liudolf's voice remained good humoured, but Adelheid was certain there was an undercurrent of hurt in it.

"No, Liudolf. Killing you would be a very bad turn for Germany. There is one thing I have been proud of this last year, although I shall deny saying this. I cannot tell you how proud I am of your skill. I am an old soldier. I should not have found you so hard to beat. One day you will out match me."

"But not yet," Liudolf said.

"Not yet," Otto replied. "Perhaps mainly because you still have the idealism of youth. I care nothing for treaties or exploiting rumours if they bring me an advantage. When you are as experienced as I, you will understand that. But, my God, Liudolf, you are skilled."

"I learnt from you and Hermann. How could I not be?"

Otto laughed again, sounding more carefree than he had in an age. "Why did you side with Frederick? I thought you loathed him."

"I do," Liudolf replied. "But I knew it would annoy you and you were siding with Frederick's old ally – Henry."

"A fair point," Otto conceded. "Did you really have to give away so many of Henry's treasures? You know he is furious about that."

"Good." Liudolf's tone was defiant. "Do you know what I was thinking when I did that? I remembered those days when I was at the abbey while you fought Henry. Mother was so brave. She was so positive you would be victorious. She bore everyone along with her, so no one ever thought you could be defeated. All Liutgarde and Ida spoke of was the dresses they would wear for the victory celebrations. But one night I could not sleep and I went to the chapel. Mother was there, on her knees, sobbing as she begged God to spare you. I knelt with her, but there was nothing I could do to comfort her. She was terrified she would lose you. I am glad to have finally got my revenge."

"Oh, Liudolf. I had no idea. I am proud of you for defending your mother. Do you truly not object to me marrying again?"

"I have a wife. I know how much I would miss Ida if I lost her. I would not wish to spend the rest of my life alone. Why would I begrudge you some happiness? I do not begrudge her happiness either. I was at her first wedding. None of us thought much of her husband. I was only young and all I knew was that I did not particularly like him, but I know others felt more strongly. When we returned to Swabia, Hermann told me he loved me like a son, but if I ever treated Ida the way he suspected that fool Lothair was treating Adelheid, he would kill me."

Otto laughed. "Oh, I miss Hermann. I was so lost in grief for your mother, I did not grieve for him as he deserved."

"I grieved for him and still miss him. Always he was a second father to me."

"He was truly the best of men. I know he had no fears for Ida in marrying you. He told me that at your wedding. He said he had always expected to feel fearful on Ida's wedding day, but as she was marrying you, he had no worries, only great pride."

"I was certainly blessed on that day," Liudolf said. "I am glad you have a wife again and I am sure you treat her well. If you had asked me, I would have given you my blessing."

"Thank you. Perhaps it is late, but I shall ask for it now."

"You have it, but Father, do you still think sometimes of Mother?"

"Think of her? Liudolf, there is not a day which goes past when I do not miss her as much as the day she died. Did you think otherwise? Because of Adelheid?"

"I suppose so. You seem happy," Liudolf said.

"I am happy, but it is different," Otto replied. "Adelheid loves a king, but Eadgyth loved a man."

Adelheid could listen to no more. She fled awkwardly to her chamber, tears streaming down her cheeks. It was obvious that yet again she had failed.

Chapter thirteen

Otto and Liudolf agreed a truce to last until a synod could be convened. The mood of everyone was hopeful that peace could be achieved at last and even more so when they received the news Archbishop Frederick of Mainz had died. Otto was more carefree than Adelheid had ever seen him, but she struggled to match his mood as she repeated his words to Warinus.

"I do not understand what he meant," she whispered. "I sometimes doubt whether he genuinely loves me, but truly I love him."

"It is obvious to all that you do," Warinus replied. "But, my child, you came from a marriage where you were treated ill. You bravely faced imprisonment and then the King swept in and rescued you. It has often seemed to me that you almost worship him."

"And the late queen?"

"She knew him before he came to power. She first met him as a boy and saw him grow into a man. You have only known him as a king. Naturally it is different. You should not take it as a criticism. I do not doubt the King enjoys your adoration."

"Perhaps he does, but you did not hear his words. He was able to rely on her in a way I think he does not rely on me. Even though he has my love, he still struggles without hers."

"But are you there for him, my child or do you just expect him to be there for you? When his son rebelled, did you reflect on the pain he must have felt as a man or were you just considering the impact on him as a king?"

Adelheid dropped her eyes, mortified to realise she had only considered the shame of a defeated and exiled king, never comforting him for the pain of a father who believed his son no longer loved him.

"And what of Liudolf? Did you ever truly try to understand his position?" Warinus asked.

"I... I tried to. But I thought Liudolf had tried to prevent my marriage, to keep me from the greatest happiness."

"Could you not have forgiven him even if that had been the case? Forgiveness and mercy are fine qualities."

"I know," Adelheid said sharply. "Did I not forgive Lothair for his treatment?"

"You did when he was dying. It is easy to forgive the dying. They can do nothing more to harm you. But to forgive the living, who may still bear you ill will – that is very much harder."

Adelheid bowed her head, begging for God's forgiveness. She had felt so noble in forgiving Lothair, it had never occurred to her how easy it was. Her mind went to Berengar, Willa and Adalbert. She knew she must try to forgive them.

∞∞∞

Although the synod could not yet be convened, Otto summoned Conrad, Bruno and William to join them, bringing the whole family together at last.

"Whatever decisions are made, the synod will need to ratify them," Otto said. "But if we are in agreement, it will be ratified without objection."

Bruno stood. "Brother, I wonder if I could say a few words. We are a family, but that does not mean we all agree or even like each other. However I truly believe everyone here loves the King and loves this land. Let that bind us."

"I agree," Otto said. "I truly love everyone here, although

I know I have not always shown this. For that I wish to apologise. I have come to some decisions, but if anyone objects, I wish you to voice this here today. Never again must resentment be allowed to fester."

Heads nodded as Otto turned to look at Liudolf and Conrad. They were sat together, Conrad's arm resting on the back of Liudolf's chair, their friendship clearly as strong as ever. "Since the beginning of my reign I have made it my policy to reward for skill and loyalty, not kinship. I will not change that policy for anyone, not even my sons. And Conrad, you do remain my son. Please do not doubt that."

"I do not," Conrad replied.

"Your duchies are forfeited. Bruno remains as Duke of Lotharingia and I intend to appoint Burchard as Duke of Swabia."

"You wife's uncle," Liudolf commented, although his tone remained even.

"Your wife's brother," Otto retorted. "However you keep all lands. It is merely the titles which are gone. It has also always been my policy to allow for redemption. Both of you can regain such honours, once you have proved your worth to me as your king."

Adelheid watched Conrad and Liudolf anxiously, half expecting them to object, but they both nodded their acceptance.

"I do not want any to think this in any way shows lack of affection. These two are my beloved sons. Conrad is still the most prominent Frankish nobleman and retains the titles he inherited from his father. Liudolf remains the heir to the Duchies of Saxony and Franconia, as well as the throne of Germany. If any treat them with lack of respect, it will be the worse for them. I expect them both to regain full honours in due course."

Again everyone nodded. "I am truly a reluctant duke," Bruno said. "I would prefer to concentrate on my diocese. So if one day Otto restores it to you, Conrad, I will most certainly not object."

"Our main focus must be the enemies of Germany," Otto continued. "The Slavs have become a problem once again. Conrad, I am tasking you with their subjection."

"Give him an army? Otto, are you sure?" Henry burst out.

"I need a fine commander and Conrad is one of the finest. I promised him a chance to prove himself and this is it." He rested his hand on Conrad's shoulder and grinned. "Naturally he will keep all spoils and glory, which knowing him will undoubtedly be considerable."

Conrad clasped his father-in-law's hand. "Thank you, Otto. I will not let you down."

"Now to Italy. I still intend to rule both. I am determined that the imperial crown will one day be mine. Berengar is quiet at present, but I do not trust him. I feel sure that one day he will rebel against my rule and when that day comes, I need another fine commander ready to move into Italy." He gestured to Liudolf. "My son, this is a role for you."

There was a gasp and Henry got to his feet. "Now I know you are mad," he said. "I understand you do not wish to punish Liudolf for his actions, but to reward him? How can you trust Liudolf with this? I am the one who has always supported you in Italy. This role should be mine."

"No, Henry. You are needed in Bavaria. Your people lost faith in you as they saw how involved you were in Italy. You need to concentrate on restoring order there and be ready for any Magyar incursions. A duchy is an honour, but it is also a responsibility. Liudolf is now unhindered by that responsibility and his abilities at the head of an army are impressive."

"I cannot believe the Queen is happy with this," Henry muttered, as he sat down.

All eyes went to Adelheid. She flushed. "I support whatever Otto thinks is best." She met her stepson's eyes for the first time in an age, surprised to see no hostility in them. "Liudolf, may I belatedly thank you for your attempts to aid me. I know this time you will be successful."

Liudolf nodded in a friendly fashion. "Thank you. I will not fail you."

Otto put his arm around her. "While we are on the subject of the Queen, she not only keeps all dower lands bestowed upon her, I intend to increase them. Even if they are in territories which conceded to you, Liudolf."

"Naturally," Liudolf replied. "I have no objections to that. But may I ask one thing, Father? Are you sending me to Italy because you want me out of Germany?"

"No. I hope Berengar behaves so you do not need to go for some time. I want you at court for a while."

"So you can keep an eye on me?"

Adelheid held her breath, afraid tempers might fracture yet again, but Otto shook his head. "No, because you are my son and I have missed you." He stretched out his hands to Liudolf, who took them, gripping them tightly. "But when the time comes, I must send a fine commander to Italy. I will trust you to manage any territories you take there on my behalf. You are clearly ready to rule, but I am afraid I am not quite ready to retire to the grave and allow you Germany just yet, so please content yourself with Italy for the time being."

Liudolf gave a sheepish grin as everyone laughed.

"Moving on to the Archdiocese of Mainz. Frederick has been a thorn in my side since almost the beginning of my reign. I feel no grief at his death, although of course we shall all pray for his soul. But there will now be a new and very fine Archbishop. William, I am appointing you."

"Me?"

"An excellent decision, Otto," Bruno said and every head at the table nodded.

"I need you there, my son," Otto said, putting his hand on William's shoulder. "I do not doubt we will disagree on occasions once you are in such a position, but the affection between us has always been great and I know I can trust you there."

"I shall pray I can fulfil your trust," William said.

"Does anyone have any other matters they wish to raise? If there are any objections or further requests, I wish to hear them now."

"I do," Henry stated. "Many have said I urged you against Liudolf out of ambition. This is not true. I am aware I may not have advised you wisely, but always it has been from my heart."

"I do not doubt that," Otto replied. He gave a pointed look at Liudolf. "And nor should anyone else."

"And I wish it to be known I was never in alliance with the Magyars," Liudolf added. "Father, I asked you once before to refute that and you would not. I am true to Germany and I want you to publically state it. If you do not, I am sorry, but I will resent it."

"I would not blame you," Otto said. "I hope everyone here will accept your word on this matter. I certainly do and I will state that publically at the synod."

"What of the treasures he gave away?" Henry demanded. "Will they be repaid?"

Otto looked at Liudolf with a glimmer of a smile and then back at Henry. "No, Brother. You will accept that as the revenge of a very brave, but very frightened boy, who was kept in an abbey for his own safety, powerless to protect his mother from distress."

Henry lowered his eyes. "I have always said I escaped with too light a punishment for that."

Otto looked again at Liudolf. "Forgiveness must come from the heart and I cannot order you to forgive Henry for those dark times, but my son, do consider what your mother would want you to do."

Liudolf swallowed and slowly extended his hand across the table. Henry gripped it and everyone let out a shaky breath as they prayed this was truly the end of the family strife.

"I wish to say something about William's appointment," Conrad said. He grinned and shook his head as all eyes went incredulously to him. "No, not to object. Liutgarde is buried in the abbey at Mainz. I hope you will take over the prayers for her soul."

"You do not need to ask that," William replied.

"I am sure I do not, but I would like to ask this. Once you are invested, will you make one of your first acts to say a mass for her? And please will everyone attend? She loved everyone here."

"I add my pleas to Conrad's," Liudolf said quietly.

"As do I," Otto said. "If all of us had followed Liutgarde's example we would not have fought these last years. She gave so much to us all, never realising how privileged we were simply to know her."

"Like Mother," Liudolf added.

"Yes, like Eadgyth. They both left our lives so much poorer by their deaths, but so much richer for being in them at all."

William nodded. "To say such a mass will be a privilege, albeit a sad one. And, Father, with your permission, I would like to mention Eadgyth in the prayers."

Otto smiled. "You do not need my permission to mention Eadgyth. I do not want her to be forgotten."

There was silence for a moment as everyone struggled to keep back their tears. Otto cleared his throat. "There is one last wish I have and there will certainly be resentment if it is not granted. Liudolf, I wish for entry to your residence."

Liudolf raised an eyebrow playfully. "Is that an order?"

Otto grinned. "No, I do not want entry as a king. I wish to come as a father. I have heard I have a fine grandson who I am longing to meet."

"Request most certainly granted," Liudolf replied. "I shall send word to Ida to expect us."

∞∞∞

Henry and Judith returned to Bavaria to start restoring

order, while Bruno and William headed to their respective dioceses, as Otto and Adelheid went with Liudolf and Conrad into Swabia. Although she rode much of the way in a litter, for Adelheid it was an uncomfortable trek.

"I do not think you should be making this journey in your condition, my dear," Mathilda said. "Why not tell Otto you need to stop?"

"Because I fear he would insist on staying with me and he should see Liudolf's son," she replied. "I know I have not supported Otto enough, so I will do this." She looked ahead to where Liudolf and Otto were talking as they rode.

Mathilda followed her gaze. "It is good to see those two like this again. My dear, Judith told me what you said to Otto. That took courage."

"I had to say it. I could not bear to think of Otto's pain if he killed his son. And if it helped bring this truce, I am glad. Liudolf is being friendly. He seems to bear me no grudge."

Mathilda looked again at Liudolf, who was laughing as he challenged Otto and Conrad to a race. As they sped ahead, Mathilda smiled. "He is Otto and Eadgyth's son. What did you expect?"

∞∞∞

When they arrived at Liudolf's home, they found a magnificent welcome had been prepared. Conrad was almost bowled over by the exuberant greeting of his son, who crowed with delight at also seeing his grandfather. Otto picked him up and held him tightly, visibly affected at holding Liutgarde's son in his arms. Ida got anxiously to her feet.

"Liudolf, is all well?"

Liudolf kissed her. "Yes, my love. There will be changes, but they are not for the worse. All is well."

Otto too hugged Ida. "Yes, all is truly well. I am here as a father, nothing more."

Liudolf bent over the crib at Ida's feet and lifted out the infant. "He has grown even since I last saw him." He handed the baby to Otto.

Adelheid stood back, noting with a pang how sturdy the baby was compared to how her boys had been as infants.

Otto gave a proud grin. "Oh, Liudolf, this is a fine boy. He looks so like you. If I did not know better, I would swear I was back at Quedlinburg with you in my arms."

"I thought you considered it impossible to say who an infant resembles," Liudolf said.

"I say a lot of foolish things," Otto retorted. "But I prefer not to be reminded of them." He handed the baby back to Liudolf and looked at the two little girls clinging to Ida's skirts. "You were right about these two." He laid his hand on the dark hair of the younger. "Mathilde does indeed resemble Ida." He picked up Regelind, tears shimmering in his eyes as he gave his granddaughter a kiss. "Eadgyth must have looked just like this as a girl."

Adelheid stared at the pretty little girl, who looked so like Otto's lost love, feeling an outsider again. Ida seemed to suddenly remember her and came forward, a polite smile of welcome on her face.

Adelheid smiled uncertainly back, hoping Ida would not curtsey to her. But Ida stopped and stared at her.

"Adelheid, you should not have been travelling in your condition. Sit down. Take some refreshment. Is there anything you need?"

Adelheid's smile widened at Ida's informal manner. "Truly, I am fine." But she swayed slightly as Ida pulled a chair towards her.

Ida rounded on her father-in-law. "Why did you make her come in such a condition?"

"I didn't," Otto protested. "She should have said if it was too much."

Ida shook her head, muttering a few comments under her breath. "It is just as well my mother is not here to see how you treat her granddaughter. I hope you are not planning on her travelling again for a long time. She is having her child here. Is that clear?"

"Yes, Ida," Otto said meekly, evidently knowing when he was defeated.

Ida's words proved to be right, as Adelheid went into labour just a few days later with Ida and Mathilda at her side. The baby was a sturdy looking one, but it was a girl.

"Are you disappointed, Otto?" she asked.

Otto smiled and shook his head. "No. I am glad to have a daughter again. Shall we call her Adelheid after her beautiful mother?"

Adelheid hesitated. "If you wish, Otto, but your mother has looked after me so well in my confinements…"

Otto looked down again at the baby. "Matilda. Yes, the name suits her."

Part five: The Year of our Lord 955-58

Chapter one

A delheid remained with Ida, while Otto, Liudolf and Conrad attended the synod. With her new baby so strong and her friendship with Ida growing stronger, it proved to be a pleasant recovery. The synod went smoothly. Conrad and Liudolf formally surrendered all territories they held to Otto, while Otto made it plain to all that he regarded them both with the strongest of affection. The synod ratified all of Otto's arrangements and the men returned in friendship.

The Christmas of that year was the merriest she had ever spent. Emma struck up a firm friendship with Liudolf's two daughters, while Conrad's son took a definite liking to little Bruno and although the lad was only just toddling, he took to following young Otto everywhere. As there were no further bouts of the illnesses he had suffered the previous year, Adelheid dared to believe he was growing stronger. With their babies cradled on their laps, she and Ida laughed together at the merriments held in a hall bedecked with greenery. She was pleased to find Otto too was more relaxed than she had ever seen him, spending many happy days hunting with Liudolf and Conrad. As Adelheid watched them return, his arms around the two younger men, it seemed impossible to believe the three had so recently been in the deepest of animosity.

It took some time for the troubles in Bavaria to be completely settled, but Otto eventually announced they would return to Magdeburg, so he could keep a close watch on the Slavic border. At Otto's request, Liudolf and Ida remained with the court as it moved back across the realm.

There was some uncertainty when the family arrived at the city gates, as the people wondered how to greet them. Adelheid remembered hearing of how popular Liudolf was in the city and the people seemed pleased to see him, although unsure whether cheering him would anger Otto. Liudolf and Otto exchanged glances and both slid down from their horses. They entered Magdeburg on foot with Otto's arm around his son's shoulders. The people burst into cheers of joy at this sign that the trouble in the land was truly over.

Once settled back into Magdeburg, Otto spent much time with Liudolf at the abbey, discussing how to improve it.

"I wish to make it truly worthy of your mother," he said. "The abbey is fine, but Eadgyth is deserving of the very finest resting place. We had such dreams for it."

"If you are intending for marble columns, that will certainly be very fine," Liudolf replied, staring at his mother's grave. "It will be as beautiful as she was."

Otto rested his hand on his son's shoulder. "Nothing can be as beautiful as she was, but we shall make it more worthy. She should not lie in a mere abbey. I want a cathedral for her."

Liudolf raised his eyebrows. "You intend to make Magdeburg a bishopric?"

"An archbishopric if I have my way," Otto replied. "Only that is worthy of her city."

Adelheid turned away, frowning to herself as she left the abbey. She knew she had been right to encourage Otto to face his grief and was glad to see him so at peace with his memories, but she remained unsure where that left her.

Ida glanced at the downcast expression on her face. "Please do not begrudge Otto and Liudolf this time together," she begged.

"I do not," she said. "Indeed I am happy to see them on such terms. It is the woman who binds them together..."

"Eadgyth?" Mathilda exclaimed. "You begrudge them discussing Eadgyth?"

Wearily Adelheid ran her hand over her face. "Not begrudge. But I find it hard. He loved her so much."

"He loves you," Ida said. "I am certain of it."

"But it is not the same. I see you and Liudolf together and it is clear that you are the first and the only woman Liudolf has loved. You shared your childhood and now you are sharing your youth. I did not love my first husband and I know what a sinner that makes me. Otto is the only man I have loved, but I am neither the first nor the only for him. So much of his life is nothing to do with me."

"My husband was many years older than me," Mathilda said. "But we had a long and happy marriage. The years before need be of no consequence unless you let it. You cannot deny Eadgyth's existence and it is good that Otto and Liudolf can speak of her together."

"I know and of course I will do nothing to hinder it, but it reminds me of the years I was nothing to Otto. What was Eadgyth like?"

"Eadgyth was brave and compassionate. Her unwavering support of Otto was the greatest of blessings," Mathilda said. "I mean no criticism, my dear. Eadgyth had no other realm to consider as you do. Her situation was less complicated."

"And she was so very beautiful," Adelheid sighed. "No wonder Otto loved her so much."

"Beautiful?" Mathilda looked puzzled. "She was certainly very pretty, particularly when she first arrived and remained most attractive, of course. But I would not describe her as beautiful."

"But Otto says..."

Mathilda smiled indulgently. "Oh, in Otto's eyes she was the most beautiful of women. He was smitten the moment he set eyes on her and has remained that way ever since."

"Eadgyth seemed beautiful to me," Ida said. "I remember when I first knew them, they seemed almost as if out of a fable. Otto, so young and handsome with his lovely wife always at his side. The next time I met them Liudolf and Liutgarde were present, all of them so happy and in such a bond. I could scarce believe it when my father told me I was to join their family."

"Eadgyth had such charm," Mathilda said. "I do not think she realised how much, but she made everyone she met feel so welcomed. Yes, in that way she was truly beautiful. It was no surprise that Otto succumbed so fully to that charm and she was truly worthy of his devotion."

"I can never compete," Adelheid said with tears in her eyes. "And indeed I am not certain I am worthy of his devotion."

Ida put an arm around her. "Nonsense. Otto values you truly. I know he does. You do not need to feel inferior."

Adelheid smiled at her words, but the certainty of being a poor substitute clung on to her heart, growing greater as Otto enthused over his plans for the abbey.

∞ ∞ ∞

However Otto's plans to make Magdeburg an archdiocese were opposed from a surprising source. Having been named Archbishop of Mainz, William had travelled to Rome to receive the Pope's blessing. Upon his return, he joined them briefly in Magdeburg.

"You will need to be careful if you have any dealings with this new pope, Father. Pope John has not struck me as the holiest of men," he said. "He has already hinted strongly that I am to keep a close eye on you and report all to him."

"I believe he is my stepfather, Hugh's grandson, is he not?" Adelheid said. "It does not surprise me if he is a trifle tricky."

Otto grinned. "Are you going to spy on me? Well, I do not mind if you pass this news onto him. Tell him I am hoping for an Archdiocese of Magdeburg. See what he has to say to that."

William frowned. "Magdeburg is currently in the diocese of Halberstadt, which is under my jurisdiction. I do not want that changed. I hope you do not expect me to urge the Pope to this."

Otto stared in surprise at his son. "Mere months into your

appointment and already you are opposing me. I thought it would take longer than that."

"So did I, Father."

"Surely you do not forget who appointed you to such a position," Adelheid put in, determined to show her support for Otto's plan. "Is it appropriate for one such as you to oppose the King?"

Otto looked less than grateful. "What do you mean by that, Adelheid? Are you referring to his birth?"

"No, of course not," Adelheid protested, trying to work out exactly what she had meant. She was certain she was with child yet again and inevitably it seemed to make her blurt out such comments without thinking.

"I am sure she meant no such thing," William said. "But it is God who appoints me and I must maintain the office he has entrusted to me."

"Eadgyth was ever kind to you, William. You should do this for her."

"I shall never forget her kindness," William replied. "Indeed I hope you make her resting place magnificent, but she was never one to court great glory. She would have been content to rest in an abbey."

"Perhaps she would have been, but I am not and one day Magdeburg will be my resting place. Think on that, William."

Otto turned away, leaving Adelheid dismayed. She had never given any thought to where Otto would one day be buried, but should have realised he would want to lie beside his greatest love. With an effort she smiled at William. "Truly I meant no offence."

"None is taken," William replied. He looked at Liudolf. "I hope you have taken no offence at my stance."

Liudolf shook his head. "No, I agree with you. Mother would have been content to lie in the abbey she helped Father found. But you might as well agree. You know Father will get his way in the end." He looked amused. "He'll be emperor one day and then no doubt the Pope will be powerless to refuse him."

∞ ∞ ∞

But further plans for Magdeburg were forced to wait as messengers from Bavaria brought news of increased Magyar raids. Otto summoned Bruno and Conrad back to court, but before they could take action even more frantic messengers arrived from Augsburg and Regensburg. Otto spent a long time talking alone with them, before hastily assembling the family.

"We must act quickly," he said. "Augsburg is under serious attack."

Chapter two

"Bruno, I want you to return to Lotharingia immediately. If the Danes or West Francia know we are under attack, they may seize their opportunity. Keep your men there, ready for defence."

"Agreed," Bruno replied.

Adelheid exchanged dismayed glances with Mathilda and Ida at this news. To deal with raids was normal enough, but it was clear from Otto's expression this was much more serious.

"We must be careful on all borders," Otto continued. "Most Saxons must remain here in Saxony, as the Slavs too are being troublesome. Like the Magyars, they have already taken advantage of the troubles of the last few years."

"Do you blame me for this, Father?" Liudolf asked, his expression clearly conveying that he blamed himself.

Otto shook his head. "We both bear responsibility for this. But we shall not dwell on blame now. Our priority is to stop the attacks."

"You know I am with you, Otto," Conrad said.

"I am glad to hear it. You are one of the finest of commanders. You are at the head of the Frankish forces. Bring them to Augsburg at all speed."

Conrad nodded. "I should be able to muster a good number of Franks. I know the Franks have not always been loyal to you, Otto, but this time they will truly prove their worth. You can rely on me."

Otto smiled, gratefully clasping his son-in-law's hand. "I

know I can. The Bavarians are already in position, of course and I shall send a message to Burchard to bring the Swabians," Otto continued. "There is some good news from the Bohemians. They have no more liking for the Magyars than we do and are marching to aid us. Of course I do not completely trust them, but they will be useful to back us up."

"What of me?" Liudolf asked.

Otto hesitated. "This is not your fight, Liudolf. You are to remain here."

There was a shocked silence and Liudolf stared disbelievingly at his father. "Is this because you do not trust me?"

Ida moved to swiftly stand with her husband and Adelheid clamped her hand over her mouth, horrified at how easily trouble could flare up again.

"No, my son. I do trust you."

"Then let me fight. You do not need to give me a command if you do not fully trust me," Liudolf said. "Let me fight at your side. Father, I swear I will be loyal."

Otto shook his head. "I know you would. This has nothing to do with trust. I trust you completely, but this fight will be dangerous."

Liudolf looked even more incredulous. "Do you think I am a coward? Or do you wish to portray me as one?"

"Oh, Liudolf, no one could ever think you a coward."

Adelheid reached for Otto's hand, hearing the catch in his voice. "What is wrong, Otto? Tell us truly why you do not want Liudolf to fight."

Otto sighed and got to his feet. He moved round the table to stand beside his mother. "The attack of the Magyars is not the only bad news I received," he said, putting his arm around Mathilda's shoulders. "The message from Regensburg was not from Henry. It was from Judith. Henry is grievously ill. I am so sorry, Mother, but she fears the worst."

Mathilda cried out. "No, Otto, tell me it is not so."

"I only know what Judith has told me. Of course we shall all pray he recovers."

"I must go to him," Mathilda said.

"Mother, Bavaria is very dangerous at present."

"I do not care," Mathilda cried. "I must be with my son. I have lived long enough already."

Otto started to protest, but Adelheid put her arms around her mother-in-law, as tears trickled down her cheeks. "Otto, help her get to Henry. As a mother she needs to do this."

Otto squeezed his mother's hand. "Very well, Mother. I shall do my best to bring you safely to Regensburg."

Adelheid wiped away her own tears as everyone absorbed this news. Liudolf cleared his throat. "Father, in spite of everything which has gone before, I am truly sorry to hear about Henry. I too shall be praying for his recovery. But why does this prevent me fighting?"

"This fight promises to be a bloody one. If Henry succumbs to his illness and you and I fall in battle, what happens then to Germany? My son is too young to rule and so is yours. What is to stop an ambitious man forcing Adelheid or Ida or even Judith into marriage, taking control of our sons and Henry's? Conrad's boy too would make a valuable pawn for such a man."

"Such matters happen, Liudolf. I know that better than anyone," Adelheid said, nestling closer to Otto as she remembered the terrible days after Lothair's death. Such a forced marriage would be many times worse now she knew of what joy a marriage could bring.

Liudolf nodded slowly. "If this fight is so dangerous perhaps it is I who should fight the Magyars, not you, Father."

Otto clapped his son on the shoulder. "I am not that old, thank you, Liudolf. No, this is my fight. These last years the people of Germany have feared my interests lie elsewhere. I need to prove my devotion to this realm. You are a fine commander. I wish I could put you in command of a flank. If I had a son or grandson just a little older, I would like nothing more than to have you fight with me, as I fought with my father the last time we faced a serious Magyar attack."

"I understand, Father."

"Just do not think I do not trust you. I do. If the worst happens, I am trusting you with the future of everyone I hold dear."

∞∞∞

Anxious about the situation in Bavaria, Otto planned quickly and the day of his departure approached far too soon. The night before, after the last prayers were chanted in the abbey, Otto lingered a little longer, kneeling before Eadgyth's grave to entreat Saint Maurice for his aid. As he rose, he looked solemnly at Adelheid and Liudolf who had remained with him.

"If I fall in this fight, bury me there." He pointed at the space next to Eadgyth.

Adelheid hid her pain at both the thought of Otto's death and his wish to return to his first wife. "Of course, but I shall pray it will not yet come to that."

Liudolf tried to smile when Otto put one arm around his shoulders and the other around Adelheid. "But naturally, Father, I will have to make this much more splendid for you."

Otto's face relaxed and he laughed. "Indeed. Make sure that you do." He tightened his arm around his son's shoulders. "Liudolf, if I should fall..."

"If you should fall," Liudolf interrupted, "Adelheid and her children will be safe in my protection. I swear that by Mother's grave."

∞∞∞

The next day, as the men gathered to depart, a solemn procession left the abbey. The abbot bore towards Otto a battered looking lance, which it was said Saint Maurice himself had once held. Everyone fell to their knees as it passed and even Otto knelt when the abbot reached him, crossing himself and closing his eyes in a brief moment of prayer. Adelheid knelt beside him, awed at the presence of Holy Lance, the one once used to stab Christ on his cross. Hope surged in her. This lance had brought victory over the Magyars once before.

"Lord King of Germany, bear with you this sacred relic," the abbot said. "Use it to keep our fair land safe from the heathens who threaten it."

Otto kissed the lance. "I swear to defend this realm." He got back to his feet. "Who here joins me in this sacred cause?" There was a deafening cheer from the men and Otto grinned, already appearing triumphant. "Then to your horses, my men. Let us ride!"

In the chaos which followed, Otto laid his hand on the heads of his children and grandchildren, before giving both Liudolf and Ida a warm embrace. Finally he turned to Adelheid, holding her very close. He pressed his hand gently against her stomach. "If this one is a boy, name him Otto."

Adelheid nodded, feeling the tears come to her eyes as she imagined naming her son after his dead father. Otto shook his head and kissed her. "Do not worry about me. I shall be fine."

"I shall be praying for you, my dearest," she said. "May God send you victorious."

Otto gave her a last kiss. "I am confident he will. He cannot want the heathens to triumph. Farewell."

Otto's spirits were buoyant as he mounted his horse. Adelheid stood back with Liudolf and Ida, terrified this would be the last she would see of him. He waved his hand at them, urging his horse into a brisk trot, followed by his personal guard. She tried to take comfort from the sight of their keen lances and quivers full of arrows. She knew those men would do anything to protect Otto, but equally she knew Otto would not hide behind his men.

Liudolf glanced at her. "I know matters have not always been good between us, but I truly meant my words to Father last night. Whatever happens, I shall keep you and your children safe. There will be no repeat of what happened to you in Italy."

"I know you will," she replied. "This is a hard day for you too."

Liudolf looked after the army. "Yes, I should be with him. A son should always stand with his father." He glanced at his own son in his nurse's arms, the faraway look in his eye clearly telling her that he was imagining the boy fighting alongside him. He made the effort to smile. "Do not worry about Father. He'll be fine. If I couldn't kill him, no one can!"

Adelheid and Ida exchanged glances, as Liudolf caught little Bruno into his arms, chasing playfully after Conrad's son. "It is strange," Ida said. "I spent so long praying for a boy, but once he was born, all I felt was dread of the day he would grow to fight. Almost it is easier to have daughters."

Adelheid gave a sad smile. "Except you may one day have to give them in marriage and you cannot be certain their husbands will treat them with the same tenderness as their fathers."

"Adelheid, the morning after your wedding to Lothair, I asked if the marriage bed had been truly bad for you and you said it wasn't. That wasn't true, was it?"

Adelheid squeezed Ida's hand. "No, it wasn't. But it was a long time ago and I forgave him."

Chapter three

The days following Otto's departure were long and empty. Adelheid and Ida busied themselves with the children and their charities, while Liudolf paced around, obviously restless. Otto's messengers returned frequently, bringing news of their movements, but given how long it took messages to reach them she was unable to take comfort from his words of good cheer, knowing that already the situation might be very different.

She spent many hours on her knees in the abbey with Father Warinus, praying to Saint Maurice for victory and Otto's safe return. As she knelt, she was always aware of Eadgyth's grave and imagined the many occasions that woman must have whispered the same prayers.

It was some weeks after the departure when a message told them their wait was over. "I send my greetings to my beloved wife, Adelheid and my dearest son, Liudolf and pray this message finds you well. I am camped this night near the Lech River and all men are now in position. In the morn we shall mount our attack. The force here is a splendid one and I shall bear the Holy Lance, so believe me when I say you must not fear. I know you are praying for us and I am confident my next message will be to report our victory."

"The battle will be already over by now," Adelheid said smoothing her stomach, where her child suddenly seemed livelier than ever. "Anything could have happened."

Liudolf shrugged helplessly, his clenched fists betraying his wish to be at the fight. "I have the Saxon men ready if matters have gone ill. All we can do is pray. Father will know how we long for news and hopefully in the next day or two we shall hear from him again."

That day was the longest of all and the night longer still. Once Adelheid lapsed into a doze, but her dreams were so terrifying that upon awakening she lit candles and lay tensely awaiting the dawn.

She was in the abbey with Liudolf and Ida when the next messenger arrived. He knelt before them.

"What news?" Liudolf asked.

"The King sends his greetings," the messenger began and Adelheid felt joy flood through her. Otto was still alive. She would bear whatever came next. "He bids me to tell you that his victory was a glorious one. The fighting was hard, but the victory over the heathens was decisive. The King orders a thanks giving to be said in every church in the land."

Liudolf grinned. "I knew Father would prevail."

"At the end the men hailed him as Emperor," the man continued.

"He must have been so proud," Adelheid said. "I wish I had seen it."

"So do I," Liudolf said. "Well, I shall have to start my preparations for Italy. After this Father will be more eager than ever for the imperial crown."

"Yes, he will," Adelheid replied. "Oh, we shall have such a celebration here when he returns."

Around them the people chattered excitedly, overjoyed at the news of this victory.

"Is there any news of when the King will return?" Ida asked.

"It will not be yet," the man said. "He wishes to pursue the Magyars to ensure they never return but first..."

Adelheid stared at the man, shocked by the solemn look on his face. "What have you not told us?"

The man gave a half smile. "The news I bear is not all good. I shall deliver the King's exact message to you, my lord," he said to Liudolf, who nodded tensely.

"Go on."

"My dearest son, glorious as my victory has been, it has come at a high cost. Conrad made the ultimate sacrifice. The man you revered as a brother and my beloved son by marriage gave his life on the battle field. He dies a hero of Germany. I beg you to pray for his soul."

Ida cried out and Liudolf stumbled backwards, his face draining of all colour. "No," he whispered. "Not Conrad."

Adelheid's eyes filled with tears. She had never got to know Conrad particularly well, but she could imagine Otto's pain. She put her arm around Ida as her tears fell.

Liudolf remained white faced as he glanced at the abbot. "Start the prayers for my brother," he said, his voice breaking on the last word. He took a moment to compose himself, forcing a note of pride into his words. "He died defending both Germany and Christendom from the Heathen hoards."

"He is to be buried at Worms, my lord," the messenger said. "The King commands you to go there at all speed, bearing with you young Otto so he may bid his father a final farewell."

∞∞∞

Liudolf broke the news to young Otto as gently as he could and then watched helplessly as the boy sobbed in Ida's arms.

"First Liutgarde and now Conrad," Adelheid whispered. "The poor child."

"I felt unfortunate when my mother died, but at least my father still lived," Liudolf said. "And I had years of her care denied to this little lad."

"We must all love him as Conrad and Liutgarde would have wished us to," Adelheid added. "It is all we can do for them."

The next day, dressed all in black, Liudolf prepared to bear young Otto to join his father's funeral cortege. He kissed Ida tenderly and even gave Adelheid a tight embrace, Conrad's sudden death bringing them all closer together.

Adelheid wished she could accompany them, guessing how Otto would be in need of comfort, but the ride would need to be too swift to be advisable in her condition. She had to content herself with giving young Otto a kiss and sending a message of love and comfort to Otto, while she and Ida attended the prayers in the abbey at Magdeburg.

"I cannot believe he is gone," Ida whispered.

"Nor I and I know it is worse for you. You knew him so well."

Ida nodded. "He was my kinsman, but it was more than that. Conrad first came to Otto's attention when the Duke of Franconia rebelled. Otto was very impressed with his skill and despite his youth, he appointed Conrad to act as his deputy in Franconia after the Duke died."

"Yes, I had heard that."

"My father's duchy bordered Franconia and of course Conrad was my mother's grandson. Whenever he needed advice in managing matters in Franconia, he turned to my father. I know my father loved me, but like all men, he always longed for a son. I think Conrad became as a son to him, almost as much as Liudolf did. When he wed Liutgarde and I wed Liudolf, I already viewed him as an elder brother." Ida's face crumpled. "I hate war. Always it takes the best from us."

After the funeral Otto and Liudolf headed to the Marches, to ensure the border was secure and the last of the Magyar threat was settled. However, the threat was no longer great and Otto was soon able to leave Liudolf in charge there and return to a joyous reception in Magdeburg. Adelheid met him at the doorway seeing instantly how this battle had changed him. As the cheers of the people rang out, he stood even taller, his victory making him more powerful than ever. But there were more lines on his face, deeply marking his grief.

She hugged him tightly. "I am so sorry about Conrad," she whispered.

Otto forced a smile. "Such a glorious victory always comes at a price, but I wish it had not been that one. In many ways I owe the victory to him. It was his manoeuvre which trapped the Magyars. It was not the easiest of attacks and only a man as skilled as Conrad could achieve it." Otto shook his head. "It was a hot day, not the day for full armour. I was told he loosened his helmet straps just for an instant to cool himself and it was in that instant the arrow struck."

Otto's voice had broken and Adelheid's own cheeks were wet as she held him close once again. "We shall never forget what we owe to him and we shall love his boy as if he were our own. Is there any news of Henry?" Adelheid prayed that at least he was much recovered.

Otto's face fell further. "No, he was so weak when I saw him. I cannot remain long at Magdeburg. I must go to him."

"I shall come with you," Adelheid said, knowing she could not let Otto bid farewell to his brother alone. Mathilda and Judith too would both be in need of comfort.

"Not in your condition," Otto said. "I am sure it would not be good for you."

Adelheid shook her head, aware of how, as usual, Otto was not allowing her to support him. His arms around her felt strong. As ever he was her protector. "Please, Otto. Henry was my first friend in this family and I love him as my own brother. I too wish to see him again."

"I suppose I cannot dissuade you? Very well, but you must proceed carefully. I want no ill coming to you."

Adelheid nodded. Her words were not a lie. She did want to see Henry again, but it was clear in going, she would be as a burden to Otto and not the support she so longed to be.

Chapter four

Fortunately Pohlde Abbey, where Henry lay, was not too far from Magdeburg and even riding slowly they managed the journey in three days. It had been an uncomfortable trip, but Adelheid displayed no sign of that. Otto was often restless at night, his grief for Conrad and the impending loss of Henry making sleep impossible. It was a sombre arrival at the abbey, as Otto clasped Judith's hands.

"I had hoped there might be better news," he said. "But I can see from your face, there is not."

Judith's eyes filled with tears. "No, he is weaker even than when you last saw him. The priests think he does not have long."

"I must see him. Adelheid, you rest a little first."

Judith looked shocked to see Adelheid. "You should not have made such a journey. Sit down and let me send for some refreshment."

Adelheid caught hold of her hand. "No, Judith. I am here to support you. Truly I am fine. Please do not worry about me and devote yourself to Henry and your children."

The sight of Henry was shocking. He lay in bed, not even able to lift his head from the pillow as she came towards him. Adelheid took a seat next to him, trying not to show her emotion at his appearance. The muscular body had wasted to a skeletal form swathed in blankets, while his once handsome countenance was tinged with yellow. Gently she took his hand, allowing it to lie limply in hers. Only his vivid blue eyes remained the same and he managed a smile as he saw her.

"I did not think to see you again, Sister," he whispered.

With an effort Adelheid kept back her tears. "Of course I came, Henry. How could I not want to see my dearest brother and best of friends?"

"We have been good friends, but you have been a better friend to me than I to you," he said. "Eadgyth became fond of me, but I do not think she ever thought highly of me, as you do. Thank you for that, Adelheid. You have been the best of sisters."

Adelheid swallowed the lump in her throat as she realised she was losing the one member of the family who revered her more than Eadgyth. "In Italy I knew so little of friendship, other than from my priest and my serving women. When you came to Canossa, I could scarce believe how friendly and solicitous you were towards me. Thank you, Henry. It was your care which first made me realise how much happier my second marriage would be."

Henry smiled faintly and closed his eyes, even such a brief talk as that exhausting him. Adelheid sat beside him for a long time, horrified by how quickly a vital man had deteriorated to such a state. Then she rose and gently kissed his cheek. She left the room with tears streaming down her cheeks, knowing she was likely never to speak to him again.

∞∞∞

Only Judith and Mathilda were with Henry as he slipped from the world. Otto had earlier that day made his own final farewells and the priest had administered Last Rites. Adelheid sat in the hall, holding Otto's hand as they waited for the news.

Eventually Judith and Mathilda came to them. Judith's eyes were red rimmed with weeping, while Mathilda's white face was frozen into a mask of grief. Swiftly Adelheid put her arms around Mathilda as Otto pulled Judith into an embrace. Adelheid watched with tears streaking her own cheeks as she sobbed against his chest.

"I am sorry, Otto," she whispered at last. "I knew the end was coming, but still this day is so much harder than I expected. I know I was fortunate to have had sixteen years with him and mostly they were happy ones, but it was not enough."

Otto's face contorted. "No, it is not enough."

"Of course, Otto," Judith whispered. "You understand that better than anybody."

"Twenty-five years I had with my husband," Mathilda said. "And still it was not enough, but at least he lived to be an old man. Henry and Eadgyth were too young." Her voice broke as tears came to her at last. "My beloved son. I do not know how to bear it."

Otto released Judith to put an arm around his mother, his own face wet with tears. As Judith sank to a bench, Adelheid sat beside her, holding her hand. Judith wiped her eyes. "You too must understand this, Adelheid," she said. "Your husband was younger still."

Adelheid forced a smile and nodded, ashamed of how little she had grieved for Lothair. However cruel he had been, he was her husband, yet she rarely thought of him, often almost forgetting Emma was not Otto's daughter. She resolved that when she returned to Emma, she would talk to her of her father. If nothing else, he had been a loving one.

∞ ∞ ∞

"What will become of me and Bavaria now?" Judith asked as they prepared to accompany Henry's body to Regensburg. Adelheid was ordered to remain in Saxony and wearied by her grief, she was glad to agree. "Who will you appoint as Duke?"

Otto took her hand. "Henry's last request to me was that his son inherit the duchy and it is one I am glad to fulfil."

Judith gave a faint smile. "Oh, Otto, I am grateful for that. But my son is too young to rule. Who will you appoint to manage the duchy for now?" She bit her lip. "Otto, I wish you to take my son into your protection. Whichever man you appoint is bound to have his own ambitions for Bavaria."

"That is why I am not appointing a man," Otto said. "Oh, your son will be under my protection, do not doubt it. But it seems to me that a mother is the person best trusted to manage matters for her son."

Judith gasped. "You want me to manage Bavaria?"

"Why not? Judith, you are one of the wisest women I know and I have been privileged to know several. In truth I think you have been ruling Bavaria for a long time. I loved Henry. He was brave and kind, but he was not the wisest of men."

Judith smiled through her tears. "No, he was not."

"You will rule Bavaria until your son is old enough to reign and he is a fortunate lad to be learning from someone as wise as you."

Adelheid squeezed her hand. "Otto is right. There is no one better than you to keep Bavaria safe for your son."

∞∞∞

When Adelheid re-joined the court, which had moved to Meresburg, it was only Ida who was there to greet her, as Liudolf was still in the Marches.

"Yes, I know I should not be travelling," Adelheid said, correctly understanding Ida's expression.

"No, you shouldn't. You must take care of yourself. We have lost too many recently."

Otto had not yet returned when the familiar pains struck some weeks later, so it was only Ida who was there to share her joy when her baby boy was placed into her arms. She gazed at him for a long time, delighted to see how strong he looked and murmuring a heartfelt prayer of thanks.

"Otto," she whispered. "His name is Otto."

When Otto did return a few days after the birth, he sat down on the bed, taking the boy into his arms and the strain of the last months visibly fell away from him.

"Oh, Adelheid, you have done well. This is truly a fine boy."

Adelheid's eyes stung at the thought of little Bruno who still had the tendency to be so sickly, as well as her little Henry who Otto seemed to have completely forgotten. "I think he looks like you," she said.

"Really? I think he looks like you which is why he is such a handsome lad." He leant over and kissed her gently. "How are you? Are you recovering as expected?"

"Yes, I am fine. I would get out of bed, but Ida will not let me."

"I am glad someone has some sense," Otto replied. He looked again at the baby, his smile spreading wider than ever. "It is good to have some happy news at last. Let us pray our sorrowful times are at an end."

Chapter five

Christmas that year was an odd one as everyone's mood vacillated between the continued celebrations of the glorious victory over the Magyars and their sorrow at the bitter losses. They kept Conrad's young son at court as Otto declared he should be raised with their own children. He had become even more of a favourite with Otto, taking the place of both Liutgarde and Conrad in his heart. Liudolf and his family too were now often at court, joining them whenever he was not needed on his own lands. Father and son were closer than ever, as the two monitored the progress on the abbey at Magdeburg.

"This is looking truly splendid, Father," Liudolf said on his latest visit in the summer.

"Splendid enough for your mother?" Otto asked with a sideways look.

Liudolf shook his head. "You know Mother cared nothing for that. For her it would be enough to lie here on the sacred ground she had founded." He looked speculatively at Otto. "But perhaps it is almost splendid enough for you."

Otto grinned and cuffed his son lightly about the head. "I am not dead yet, my boy."

"Good," Liudolf replied. "And if you keep improving the church, perhaps by the time you do die, it will be magnificent enough for you, even in your eyes."

Adelheid laughed. "But Liudolf, I think he would have to live for more than a hundred years to make it magnificent enough in his eyes."

Otto looked suitably outraged at that comment, as Liudolf's smothered grin told Adelheid he completely agreed with her.

"So, Liudolf, have you just come to court to insult me or have you some other purpose?"

Liudolf flung his arm around his father. "As if I would dare insult you!" But his face became serious. "Father, I have heard that Berengar and Adalbert are rebelling against your overlordship in Italy."

Otto nodded. "I have heard it too," he said. "Indeed their tribute this year has been... delayed."

"I think they view us as weakened by the Slavs and Magyars," Adelheid said. "But they will learn of their mistake. For are we not well prepared?"

"We are," Liudolf replied. "Do I have your permission to march, Father?"

Otto laid his hand on his son's shoulder. "Yes, you do."

Liudolf turned to Adelheid. "Do I have your blessing? I know the plan to put me in charge of the Italian campaign was foisted on you."

"Do not think that. Of course you have my blessing. I am proud so fine a commander as you will liberate my land from those pretenders."

"Liudolf, if you need assistance on the campaign, you must send word," Otto put in.

Liudolf raised an eyebrow. "Do you think I cannot manage?"

"He knows you can manage," Adelheid replied. "He's just itching to take part."

Otto gave a rueful grin. "Yes, that is true. I wish I could go with you. You and I campaigning together again, as we did so many years ago in West Francia. But this is your fight and I know you can manage. After all, you learnt from me and Hermann."

"Exactly. And Conrad too gave me some most useful advice before that first campaign, although his was of a slightly different nature!"

Otto, the man whose own first campaign had resulted in a bastard son, looked somewhat disapproving. "I thought you faithful to Ida."

"I am, but we were not wed then. It was only once I had even kissed her."

"Don't talk nonsense, Liudolf. Just because your mother only caught you once, does not mean that was the only occasion. Hermann and I were well aware of what the two of you were up to."

An awestruck expression swept Liudolf's face. "Hermann knew? And I am still alive?"

Otto laughed, regaining his good humour. "Oh, he trusted you and we were all pleased to see the affection growing between you. Naturally we kept a close watch and would have brought the marriage forward if necessary." The mischief faded from Otto's face. "When Eadgyth died, I wished we had brought it forward. She loved Ida and would have been so pleased to see her becoming truly her daughter."

Liudolf glanced back at his mother's grave and shrugged. "So, Father, Italy? I am ready as soon as you give the word."

"I have already given orders for the men to gather near the mountains. I shall ride with you as far as that, if you not object. I am not eager for us to be parted.

"Nor I, Father." He looked at Eadgyth's grave once again. "I must make my farewells here too."

He returned to kneel by the grave. Otto watched him. "My God, she would have been so proud of that boy." He smiled slightly at Adelheid. "Return to the palace. I shall stay a while with Liudolf."

Through tears she watched Otto kneel beside Liudolf, before the woman they both loved. Then slowly she turned away.

∞ ∞ ∞

The gathered force was a splendid one. As Liudolf

marshalled them, the cheers and smiles of the men showed clearly the extent of their adoration for him.

"Berengar and Adalbert will not stand a chance," Otto commented. "The boy will sort them out."

"Good. They have ruled for far too long already," Adelheid replied.

Liudolf and Ida stood beside them during the prayers for victory. At the end Liudolf knelt solemnly before his father.

"Permission to depart, my lord," he said.

Otto laid his hand on his son's head. "Permission most certainly granted."

"Our prayers will be with you, for your victory and your safe return," Adelheid spoke the formal words of blessing.

As Liudolf rose back to his feet, his men scrambled for their horses and Liudolf relaxed into an informal grin. "Any message for Berengar and Adalbert when I catch up with them?"

Adelheid considered this for a moment. "Tell them how glad I am that Italy will now be in the hands of a man worthy to rule as they were not. But tell them I forgive them for their treatment of me and for the death of my husband."

Adelheid felt a weight lift from her at those words. She had carried her hatred of those men for too long. The memory of how that hatred had once poisoned her relationship with Liudolf made her fling her arms around him. "Look after yourself. I know you will be victorious."

Liudolf smiled and turned to his father. "Farewell, Father. I shall send word on my progress."

"I shall be glad to hear of it," Otto replied. He laid his hands on his son's shoulders and kissed him. "You were the pride of your mother's heart and you are the pride of mine. Never forget how proud I am of you, my son or how much I love you."

"I love you too, Father," Liudolf replied. "And I am proud to be your son."

Adelheid hugged Ida, who was riding some way with Liudolf to be close to him for when he needed to set up court. Excitement was sparkling in her eyes and it was clear that despite the danger of this expedition, she was glad to be part of it. Jealousy flickered through her. She had come to make Germany her home, but she missed Italy. She hoped that at some point she and Otto would join them there.

Otto kept his arm around Liudolf's shoulders as he walked to his horse. He kissed Ida on the cheek.

"Look after Liudolf for me, my daughter," he said.

Ida laughed. "If he will let me. You know how he hates being fussed over."

Liudolf laughed too, as he helped Ida onto her horse and Otto pulled him into his arms for a last embrace. For a long time Otto held him, as if he never wanted to let him go. But at last Liudolf mounted his own horse and Otto stood back beside Adelheid.

She looked up at Liudolf, his fair hair sparkling in the sunshine. Above him banners fluttered in the breeze, the light glinting off the golden threads.

"Fight for the glory of King Otto and in the name of Saint Maurice," he cried. "To Italy!"

Around him the men broke into deafening cheers. Liudolf waved his hand at them.

"God's blessings on you, my son," Otto cried.

"And on you too, Father," Liudolf called back, his dazzling smile widening as he urged his horse into a brisk trot.

Otto put his arm around Adelheid, staring after his son for a long time as they rode towards the mountains.

"Look at that army, Adelheid," he said, turning away at last. "There is no way he can fail."

Chapter six

T he first reports of Liudolf's successes filtered back almost as soon as he could have arrived in Italy and his messages confirmed that the Italian nobility were supporting him.

"With Liudolf's charm and Berengar's complete lack of it, I am hardly surprised," Adelheid commented.

Otto sent a message of pride and support back to Liudolf and another to William, asking him to be ready to go to the Pope to demand the imperial crown. "I would also very much like it if you could reconsider the matter of the Archbishopric of Magdeburg," he added. "After the trouble with the Slavs, a strong diocese on the Marches can only be an advantage in our aim to bring salvation to these heathens. I wish you would not oppose me in this matter."

"Otto, please do not quarrel with William over this," Adelheid begged. "It is good not to have strife in the family for a change."

Otto arched an eyebrow. "You have never commented on whether you think Magdeburg should be made into an archdiocese."

Adelheid froze, not wanting to put on the spot. If she were honest to herself, she had to admit she still resented Otto's attachment to Eadgyth's city. "I am sure it is a fine plan, but not one worth a quarrel with your son."

Otto raised his eyes to the ceiling, but he turned to the messenger. "Please assure the Archbishop I remain ever his affectionate father."

"The emperor's crown is within my grasp," Otto said as they retired that night. "I can feel it."

They celebrated Christmas in Bavaria, which Judith was managing as well as everyone had expected.

"Otto, my eldest daughter is old enough to be wed," she said. "I had thought of arranging a marriage between her and Duke Burchard of Swabia, with your permission."

"Have you raised the matter with him?" Otto asked.

"Yes and he says he would be honoured to wed your niece. I would like this alliance. Bavaria and Swabia have been in conflict for too long."

"If you are to rule in Italy, peace in Southern Germany would most certainly be an advantage," Adelheid put in.

"Yes, it would," Otto replied. "I knew you would rule wisely. Tell Burchard this union most certainly has my blessing."

∞∞∞

It was the summer before they returned to Saxony, making their way to the various palaces until they arrived back at Magdeburg as the autumn approached.

Otto grinned as he entered the gates. "It is good to be back. Nowhere else feels quite so much like home."

Adelheid wished she could share his love for the city, but she nodded, agreeing how good it was to be back. However they had only been there a little while when little Bruno sickened.

Day after day Adelheid sat helplessly by his cradle, wishing she could coax some food into him. Steadily the little boy grew thinner and she feared for the worst.

"He has never been the strongest of children," Otto tried to comfort her. "Remember we still have little Matilda and Otto."

Adelheid buried her head against his chest, knowing his words were true. But still the sight of her son's frail body as he clung so desperately to life, pierced her to her heart.

There was better news from Italy, as Liudolf's latest message came to them.

"My Lord King and beloved Father, I send my greetings from Pavia. Resistance from Adalbert these last months has been fierce, but I have prevailed at last and he has fled. I am pleased to inform you that Lombardy is now in my control, to swell your empire. With your permission, I would like to return now to Germany so we may plan how best to proceed. Your loving son, Liudolf."

Otto grinned triumphantly. "I knew the boy would prevail. Take this message in return. My dearest son, I send my greetings from Magdeburg. Please know I have rarely felt such pride as I did to get your message. Your triumph is a glorious one indeed. I shall be glad to see you back here, my son. We have been parted for too long and I shall anticipate eagerly our reunion. Your devoted father, Otto." He turned to Adelheid. "I shall be able to reward him. Perhaps an Italian title to give him the right to rule there in due course."

"But you are King of Italy," she replied.

"True, but with such a large realm I will need a regent in Italy. I cannot think of a better choice than Liudolf."

"I know, but..."

Otto frowned. "Adelheid, Liudolf is ambitious. We know that. We also know we need to live in harmony. He is now several years older than me, when I took the throne. Liudolf is like me. He is more than ready to rule."

"Yes, of course. I have no objection," Adelheid said quickly. "Indeed you need someone to manage matters in Italy and Liudolf would be an excellent choice. It is just that I hoped I might one day return there."

"Really? I had thought you always unhappy there," Otto replied.

"Not always," Adelheid said with a smile.

Otto grinned and pulled her into his arms. "I confess to fond memories of Pavia myself. Certainly I shall be in Italy on occasions, but I cannot be always there. However we will wait for Liudolf to return and discuss the matter with him. The celebrations must be magnificent."

Liudolf's next message confirmed he was on his way back and glad to have something other than her own son's poor health to dwell on, Adelheid began to give some thought to the victory celebrations.

Little Bruno was still clinging onto life when another messenger from Italy arrived. Otto was amused when he was told of the man's arrival.

"What does the boy want now? No doubt making sure his celebrations are magnificent enough for him."

"Well, he is your son, so I am not sure why you are so surprised," Adelheid replied, taking his hand as they entered the hall.

However their mirth was short lived as the messenger turned to them, the grave look on his face clearly proclaiming he bore bad news. The man knelt.

"My Lord King, I beg you forgive me for the news I bring. Truly it is the most grievous message I have ever born."

Otto stared at him, his fists clenched. "No," he gasped, the colour fading from his face as fast as his smile.

"Your noble son was called from this world as he prepared to start his journey over the mountains."

Otto was frozen and Adelheid could scarce believe the words she had heard. "Was it a battle?" she asked, thinking surely it was impossible for Liudolf to have been slain.

"No, my lady. It was a fever. The illness was mercifully brief and Lady Ida was with him throughout. He received Last Rites and is assured of God's salvation."

"A fever?" Otto whispered. "Like his mother. No. This cannot be. Both of Eadgyth's beautiful children gone."

There were shocked whispers around the hall, with tears from many. The charismatic young heir had been popular at court. From the corner of her eye Adelheid saw Mathilda collapse into a chair, Emma putting her arms around her as the sounds of her harsh sobs broke the silence. Otto too sat, his head sinking into his hands. Still feeling completely numb, Adelheid put her arms around him, knowing there would not be enough comfort in the world to console him for this.

Otto looked up at her, suddenly pushing her arms away. "You never liked Liudolf."

"Oh, Otto, I did. Truly I considered him the finest of men."

"You were the one who encouraged me to void the treaty I agreed with Liudolf at Mainz. I fought my son, my beloved, precious son a whole year longer than was necessary."

Tears spilled from Adelheid's eyes. "I know. I have always regretted it. But, Otto, we were reconciled."

Otto turned away from her, running from the hall. Adelheid stared after him for a moment, wiping her eyes before following him. The shocked people parted to let her through. There was no sign of Otto as she left the great doorway, but she knew exactly where he would be.

In the abbey the soft sound of prayers for Liudolf's soul was already echoing throughout the building. Otto was where she had expected him to be, sprawled before Eadgyth's grave.

"Our son, our beloved son." Otto could scarcely get the words out, as his tears came at last. "I am so sorry, my sweet. I failed you and I failed our beloved son."

Adelheid ran to him, wrapping her arms around his shoulders. "Please, Otto, I did care for Liudolf. Truly I did."

Otto did not even look at her. "Eadgyth treated William as if he were her own son. Did you ever do that for Liudolf?"

Adelheid stared at him. She and Liudolf had been the same age. It was impossible for her to care for him as a son. "Not as a son, no. But as a friend and a kinsman. I swear to you, Otto, this news grieves me. Truly it does."

Otto looked at her and Adelheid almost cried out at the desolation in his eyes, as the tears streaked his cheeks. He shook away her arms once again. "Leave me, Adelheid." He slumped against Eadgyth's grave. "Leave me with the one woman who would understand."

Chapter seven

The court was plunged into the deepest mourning as everyone absorbed the terrible news of Liudolf's death. A message from William, the grief clear in every word, said he had ridden to meet the funeral cortege and that he wished his beloved brother to be laid to rest in Mainz, so he might personally see to the prayers for his soul.

Crushed by the news, Otto agreed and made his own plans to head to Mainz.

"He and Liutgarde will lie together," Mathilda said, her lined face soaked in tears. "They were always close, so it is fitting. Those two beautiful children. I cannot bear it. I have lived too long."

Adelheid simply put her arms around her, unable to comfort either her or Otto. But even then death was not yet done with them, as little Bruno, already weak and unable to stomach food suffered a fit, which left him weaker than ever.

Adelheid knelt by his cradle begging God not to call another of Otto's children from the world, as the child gasped helplessly for breath.

"We ride in the morn," Otto told her. He was composed, but deathly pale.

"I cannot go, Otto. How can I leave our son like this?"

Otto did not give even the most fleeting of glances into the cradle where the little boy lay. "You are not coming?"

"I wish to come. Truly, I want to pay my respects to Liudolf and mourn at his grave. As soon as little Bruno is recovered or…" Adelheid's voice broke and she could not get the words out. She wanted Otto to put his arms around her. She wanted to put her arms around him, to allow their grief to mingle. But he turned from her and left the chamber with no further words.

"You need to go with Otto." Mathilda's voice startled Adelheid from her bleak thoughts. "You cannot let him ride alone."

"I cannot leave my son."

Mathilda put an arm around her. "My dear, it is hard to lose a child. I understand that. But Liudolf was no longer a child. To lose a child you have raised to adulthood is so many times harder." Her voice broke and Adelheid guessed she was remembering Henry as well as Liudolf. She stroked little Bruno's soft hair. "He is barely aware of you. He does not need you, Adelheid. Otto needs you."

"I do not think Otto does need me," she replied. "The only woman who could offer him any comfort, died long ago."

$$\infty \infty \infty$$

A long night followed as she agonised over her decision. "I feel so torn," she whispered to Warinus. "My husband or my son. I think this is a judgement on me. How many times did Otto feel torn between me and Liudolf?"

"In truth, my daughter, I think you should accompany your husband. A wife's first duty is always to her husband."

"I know, but he does not need me. He has made that plain."

"My child, the pain he feels for his loss is great. He may not show it, but I think he will be glad of your comfort at such a time." He smiled gently as Adelheid looked doubtful. "I think his need for comfort is greater than your need for him to prove his love."

Adelheid flushed, suddenly aware of how petulant her words must have seemed. But as Bruno's fragile body shook from the efforts of his faint gasps, she turned back to him, trying to sooth the little boy. She knew it made her a poor wife, but she could not leave her son.

However in the end the decision was made for her, as Bruno suffered another fit. In the flickering light of a candle, Adelheid could do nothing more than hold his tiny body as his lips contorted with the effort of drawing breath. Eventually his thrashing stilled, but so did his lips. Tears flowed down Adelheid's cheeks, as she realised he was gone. She cradled his body in her arms until dawn, before laying him back on the bed. She looked at his face for the last time then turned to Warinus, wiping her eyes dry of tears.

"Pray for him, Father. I ride this day with my husband. Pray also that my presence can ease his heart a little."

∞∞∞

The hall was filled with the clatter of departure, as the entourage prepared to move with Otto to Mainz. Dressed for travelling, Otto sat at the head of the table, an untouched cup of ale before him. He got to his feet and bowed to her, as if she were a mere acquaintance.

"It is good of you to bid me farewell. There is no need for it."

Adelheid swallowed. "Can you delay your departure just a little, so I may prepare myself? I will ride with you."

Otto's face remained unchanged. "Your son needs you. Stay here."

Tears filled Adelheid's eyes. "No. My son needs me no longer. He is with God now."

"I see." A ripple passed over Otto's face, but there was no other reaction. Adelheid was not even certain he had registered that he had lost another son. "Then make your preparations quickly. I wish to ride soon."

Otto returned to staring into his ale, his face expressionless. She noticed suddenly how thin he had become and wondered if he had eaten since hearing the news of Liudolf's death. In the slump of his shoulders, it was obvious he had barely slept.

Gently she laid her hand on his arm, pushing down her own grief. "I will make myself ready as quickly as I can."

Otto's face contorted, but he quickly brought it under control, shrugging away her hand. "I must see to the horses."

He pushed back his chair, staggering to his feet. But he made only one step towards the door before collapsing senseless to the ground.

∞ ∞ ∞

Otto lay in his chamber for days. The monks of Magdeburg prayed for his recovery as his attendants managed to feed him on sips of mead and occasional spoonfuls of porridge. Adelheid felt helpless as she sat by his bed, terrified by the heat coming from his brow. A fever. Just what had killed his wife and son.

"Eadgyth," he muttered in a delirium. "You have done so well, my sweet. Look at our fine boy."

Tears streamed down Adelheid's cheeks as she listened to him, hating the pain which would strike him afresh when he recovered from this fever. If he recovered.

"I am the luckiest of men. The most beautiful wife." He laughed, reaching out as if to take a hand. "Do not shake your head, Eadgyth. You are so beautiful. And now Liudolf. Never was there so fine a child."

Adelheid shivered as Otto's eyes opened, fixing joyfully on a point beyond her. She looked over her shoulder, almost expecting to see the wife and son who had loved him, returned from the grave to comfort him. But of course the chamber was filled only with attendants. Unable to bear it any longer, she stumbled from the room.

"Adelheid?" Mathilda was sat outside. She struggled to her feet, her eyes widening in horror at Adelheid's tear streaked face. "Is Otto...?"

"He is unchanged," Adelheid said quickly. Feeling foolish she described the scene to her mother-in-law.

"That must have been hard to hear," Mathilda said quietly. "I know you love him very much. But do not take it to heart. It is natural, perhaps, that in his grief he is returning to happier, simpler days."

"I do not blame him," Adelheid replied. "I blame myself for not bringing him the same happiness she did."

"Do not blame yourself. Back then Otto had fewer responsibilities and no cares. No tragedies had yet occurred. He and Eadgyth were both so young and in love. And then came the children. A fine son, a beautiful daughter. Never was a father as proud as Otto, not much more than a boy himself, when Liudolf was born." The voice Mathilda had managed to keep calm up until that point broke into choking sobs. "Oh, those days were the happiest of his life, they were such happy days for us all. Once he assumed the throne, it was impossible for him to ever return to such a happy, carefree existence. Eadgyth did her best, but so do you. And in truth it is harder for you."

Bruno was ushered in at that moment and Adelheid was glad of an interruption as Mathilda struggled over her words. He stretched his hands out to them both. "Mother, Adelheid, I came as quickly as I could. How is Otto faring?"

"He remains so ill," Adelheid said. "But you should see for yourself."

"I will." Bruno put his arm tightly around Mathilda. "To lose Liudolf... the only mercy is that at least they were reconciled."

"But they fought for so long. Otto blames me and he is right to do so."

Bruno shook his head. "Many bear the responsibility for the quarrel, Sister. Not just you. If Otto is blaming you, it is because he cannot yet face blaming himself."

Adelheid gave a bitter smile. "Then it is as well he is blaming me. I do not think he can cope with any more pain at present."

As always in times of trouble, Adelheid sought out Warinus.

"Otto will never love me as he loved Eadgyth. I know that. She deserved his love. Why should he love a poor sinner such as myself?"

"My child, I am certain he truly values you. Do not take to heart the words he speaks at such a time."

"I do not. I have accepted now what cannot be changed. I ask only that God spares him. If he lives, I shall ever strive to be more worthy and never again complain that I am the very poorest of replacements."

Chapter eight

Otto continued to sink to such a point that Bruno told her if he became any weaker, he would have to administer Last Rites.

"What will happen if Otto dies?" Adelheid asked with tears streaming down her cheeks. "What will happen to Germany? He has no other son or grandson yet able to succeed him."

"I know," Bruno said solemnly. "A synod will decide. God blesses a land when he sends wise rulers, as he did when he sent my father and then Otto. Perhaps we took that blessing for granted, thinking that with Otto in good health and Liudolf to succeed him, our prosperity would continue. Whatever happens next, we must remember it is God's will."

"I have never questioned God's will, but if he takes Otto..."

"If he takes Otto we must all pray for acceptance. It is in these times of hardship that he truly tests us. I know how difficult it is. Do you think I did not question God's will when I heard Liudolf had died? I may be a priest, but I am still a man." Bruno clutched at the cross on his breast. "Liudolf was not much younger than me. We were boys together."

Adelheid squeezed his hand, with no comfort to offer him on the death of his nephew. She returned to Otto. Thin and white, he was barely recognisable. She took his hand and it lay limply in hers. "Oh, Otto, you must recover. Not for my sake. Not even for your children and grandchildren. But for Germany. It still needs you."

∞ ∞ ∞

To everyone's relief, Otto did recover and prayers of thanksgiving were said in the church. However as Otto refused to rise from his bed, simply lying motionless, staring upwards, Adelheid wondered if she had done him a wrong turn in coaxing him back from the shadowy world. The joy she remembered filling his blue eyes when he had thought he had seen Eadgyth and Liudolf in his chamber made a heart breaking contrast with his eyes now so empty and she wondered if he would ever again know such joy.

Adelheid was tireless in her efforts to persuade him to rise, but he responded listlessly, turning his head away from her. Otto had ever been a man of action, hating to lie abed. It was terrible to see him in such a state. Eventually she asked Bruno to talk to him. Bruno spent a long time alone in the chamber with Otto. When he came out, he too appeared many years older and Adelheid did not dare ask what words had passed between them.

"The King will dine in the hall this night," Bruno said.

Adelheid nodded and muttered her thanks, but she felt no joy. Bruno's words told her everything she needed to know. It would be a king who rose from his bed, to take his place in the hall. The man was gone.

Her worst fears came true as Otto sat back at the head of the table. He greeted her courteously, extending his greetings to others nearby, graciously accepting their joy in his recovery. During the meal he conversed politely, even smiling at some comments. The people were overcome with admiration that they had a king who could behave with such fortitude in such times. But Adelheid could see the truth. In many ways Otto was no more present at that meal than Liudolf.

∞∞∞

Otto's recovery, poor weather and other matters which needed attention prevented Otto and Adelheid from travelling to Mainz until the spring. Adelheid glanced at Otto, mounted on his horse, as they neared the city. He was staring directly ahead, his face drawn. Over the winter his hair had greyed still further, but it was the dullness of his eyes which seemed to have truly driven away the last of his youth.

Although the hour was drawing late, Otto did not go to the palace in Mainz but instead urged his horse to the Abbey of Saint Albans, just south of the city. Pain settled ever more deeply across his face and Adelheid guessed he was remembering the time he had come there to reach an agreement with his rebellious son – an agreement she had urged him to overturn.

They dismounted at the abbey and Adelheid put her arm around him, although he seemed barely aware of her. However that was no longer of any importance. All that mattered was that she offered comfort. It was up to him if he wished to accept it.

William greeted them at the door, embracing his father warmly. For once Otto responded to the comfort, allowing his son to lead him into the building. Liudolf's grave was a fine one, before the altar. Otto stared at it and the one beside it, where Liutgarde lay.

"I am a poor father that this is the first time I have visited their resting place," Otto said quietly. "I shall make some gifts to the abbey while I am here so Liudolf may have a place that is truly worthy of him."

"Thank you, Father," William replied. "I am grateful, but in truth I would prefer to have my brother back."

"So would I," Otto whispered. "It does not seem so long ago that Liudolf was teasing me about how magnificent he would make my tomb. Now that is all I can do for him, for my beloved son."

As Otto's voice broke, Adelheid stepped towards him, tears in her own eyes at the sight of the tombs which housed the remains of those two vibrant siblings. However it was William who put his arm around him.

"Otto?" a voice said.

They turned to see Ida coming towards them, dressed all in black. If there was any part of Adelheid's heart which had not broken at Otto and William's grief, it shattered at the sight of Ida, her beauty now wreathed in shadows and regrets.

Otto broke away from William, taking Ida tightly into his arms. "Oh, Ida. Forgive me for not coming before."

"I heard you had been ill. I am glad you have recovered," Ida replied, her toneless voice sounding so much like Otto's own.

Ida and Otto looked at each other, then with no further words they went together to kneel before the grave. Adelheid started to join them, but William put a hand on her arm.

"Let them have this time alone," he said in a low voice.

"I must support Otto," Adelheid protested.

William shook his head. "You will support him better by allowing him this time with Ida. You do not grieve as they grieve. There will be a mass in the morn when it would be appropriate to show your respects."

Adelheid hesitated, knowing there was no right action she could take. If she knelt with Otto and Ida she would be seen as intruding, but if she left now she would be accused of not showing proper respect. However as Otto put his arm around his daughter-in-law, both of their bodies shaking with grief, she realised the truth of William's words and allowed him to conduct her to an abbey guest chamber.

∞∞∞

She did not see Otto again that night and when she went

to the abbey church the next morn, she found him there, dressed as he had been the day before. Ida was with him and she suspected they had both been there all night. Otto looked exhausted, but more at peace than he had done for a long time. She lingered back, not wanting to intrude on his conversation with William, but Ida noticed her and came towards her.

"Oh, Ida." Adelheid took hold of her hands. "I am so sorry."

Ida pulled her hands away. "I hate Italy. The first time Liudolf went there it stretched the affection between him and Otto. The second time it removed him permanently, so now you have Otto's devotion solely for your children."

"No, Ida, truly I never wished for this. I too grieve for Liudolf. He was the very best of men."

Ida gave her an incredulous look and Adelheid knew she had lost Ida's friendship, probably forever. As a soft toll of the bell signalled the start of the mass, she and Ida moved to stand with Otto, pausing before they reached him. Ida looked at her, but Adelheid indicated for her to stand next to Otto. It seemed the least she could do.

Throughout the mass Adelheid kept her tears back with an effort, knowing many would view them as false. The service seemed to go on for ever and she wished it would end so she could weep in peace for everyone they had lost.

At the simple meal afterwards, Ida led her children to Otto. He knelt down, gathering all three into his arms.

"Your children will be under my protection now, Ida. I swear I will defend them with my life," Otto said. "With your blessing, I would like them to be raised at court. I will stand as a father to them, loving them as Liudolf would have done."

"I will be glad of your protection," Ida replied. "But… Otto, may I speak freely?"

"Of course."

"After Eadgyth died, Liudolf found it impossible to speak of his mother to you. I do not want that for my children. They must know of their father."

Otto looked down at the little boy who so resembled Liudolf.

"You are wiser than I, Ida. I swear to you, I will tell them often of their brave father. They shall know I am the poorest of substitutes. And Ida, you too must be at court. You remain my daughter, just as you have been since you were the age of your own daughters. You know how Eadgyth and I always loved you. When you were at court with Liudolf and Liutgarde, we were so proud of our little family."

Ida smiled through her tears. "Those were happy days, Otto. And now only you and I are left. I shall be glad to be at court with Otto and Regelind. But with your permission, Mathilde would like to take her place at the Abbey of Essen. It was Liudolf's wish that she one day be the Abbess and she wants to honour it."

Otto laid his hand on Mathilde's dark hair. "Your father would be most proud of you, sweetheart. You have my blessing."

Taking Liudolf's children into his heart as his own seemed to bring further peace to Otto and he returned to Adelheid's bed for the first time since Liudolf's death. Gladly Adelheid held out her arms to him, hoping he had come back to her at last. Almost immediately she realised what a false hope that had been when he pulled her down without kissing her. His hands were gentle as they had always been, but looking into his eyes in the candlelight, she could see the vast distance still looming between them.

Afterwards he quickly moved away from her, not holding her in his arms as had always been their custom. Knowing Otto was as lost to her as ever, Adelheid lay still, tears falling silently down her cheeks until she drifted into an uneasy doze.

The sound of the door closing jolted Adelheid from her sleep. Instinctively she reached across the bed to find it empty. Swiftly she pulled on a tunic and made her way to the abbey where she knew Otto would be.

It was dimly lit by flickering candles, but she found Otto easily enough before the graves of his children.

"I wish you could see our grandchildren, Eadgyth. You always longed for another boy so we could name him Otto. Now you have two grandsons named Otto. How that would make you smile. You would be so proud of Mathilde. She is very wise even at such a young age and little Regelind looks just like you, my sweet. Just as beautiful as you."

Adelheid froze, remembering how Otto had returned to happier times in his delirium. It was many times worse to see him doing it in full consciousness. Again she wondered whether Otto had truly been pulled back from the brink of death.

"Oh, Eadgyth, I failed our children. I failed them so badly. But our grandchildren will be a different matter. Liudolf, Liutgarde, my dearest, sweetest children, I swear I will not fail yours."

Part Six: The Year of our Lord 960-62

Chapter one

Over the next years Otto focussed solely on ruling his realm, throwing himself into defending the northern marches and returning to court looking almost disappointed to have survived another campaign. He seemed to have abandoned his plans for Italy, even when Berengar managed to take back control of the March of Verona, besieging her old friend, Azzo there.

"Who do you suggest I sacrifice now?" Otto asked coldly, when Adelheid raised the matter with him.

Although she hated the thought of her people in Italy back under Berengar's rule, Adelheid knew she had no chance of persuading him otherwise. Otto had remained distant from her, treating her with all the respect due to a queen, but never turning to her as a woman, let alone a woman he loved. She mourned that distance with all her heart, often sobbing at night, while praying for acceptance by day. She did her best to keep busy, concentrating on the household, children and her duties to the church, but pain was never far from her heart.

"This is how Otto was after Eadgyth died," Mathilda said, when she found Adelheid weeping one day. "He insisted on grieving alone. I pray that sooner or later something will restore his appetite for life."

Mathilda had found her own solace in devoting herself ever more to Quedlinburg Abbey, spending much time there with little Matilda, who Otto intended would one day be the abbess. The child seemed happy, delighting the nuns with her piety and Adelheid came to almost envy her daughter, thinking how much simpler her life would have been if she had been permitted to enter an abbey.

"What restored him to life after Eadgyth died?" Adelheid asked.

"You," Mathilda replied.

Adelheid was astonished. "Me?"

"I remember when the messenger brought your plea for aid. It was as if Otto suddenly woke up. The chance to expand his lands into Italy was certainly a draw, as it would be for any king. But the thought of a beautiful young woman in desperate need... Yes, that was what appealed to him as a man."

Adelheid managed to smile at that, although she did not know what would help this time around. It was only the children and in particular the boys – The Three Ottos, as they styled themselves, who seemed to bring a genuine smile to Otto's face.

∞∞∞

In the autumn of 960 they were once again in Magdeburg, as Adelheid started lacklustre plans for some festivities which Otto would give only the show of enjoying. To all outward appearances, Adelheid was in as high status as ever and she was sat beside her husband when a papal envoy was ushered in.

"Most noble King Otto of Germany, I bring the greetings of the Holy Father, Pope John the twelfth of that name. I bear the grievous news that the pretender to the throne of the Lombard's, Berengar of Ivrea is attacking our lands. I beg you, Otto, King of Germany to proceed with that most solemn of Christian duties and aid us in liberating ourselves from these terrible sinners."

Adelheid had her eyes on Otto as the man spoke. A strange expression flickered across his face, before it returned to his usual impassivity. Adelheid blinked, trying to work out if she had imagined that flicker. She was certain he looked more alert as the man finished his words with a respectful bow of his head.

"I am honoured the Holy Father entrusts me with such a mission," Otto replied. "It may be possible for me to aid him, but obviously my absence could hinder the stability of my realm."

"An attack on the Holy Father hinders the stability of all Christendom, my lord," the man pled.

Otto regarded the man speculatively with a hint of amusement. "It would indeed. We must talk more, but perhaps we can come to an arrangement which will benefit us both."

Otto spent the rest of the day talking to the men, the conversation even continuing throughout the evening meal. They were still talking when she retired for the night.

Adelheid was almost asleep when she heard Otto preparing himself for the night in the antechamber. She sat up, listening hard, as her ears caught a faint noise. Was Otto whistling?

A few moments later he pushed open the door, clad just in a tunic, the light from his candle brightening the room.

"The imperial crown, Adelheid. This time it will be mine."

"Is that what the Holy Father is offering?" Adelheid asked cautiously.

"Not yet, but he will. He will have to if he wants my help. Is this not how it happened for the great Frank emperor, Charles?"

Adelheid stared at him, afraid to give in to the hope that this would be the event which would restore Otto's zest for life. Otto flung his tunic aside and climbed into bed, pulling Adelheid into his arms. He lay down, keeping his arms around her, gently running his fingers through her hair. Adelheid held her breath, realising the last time he had simply held her in this way was before they had heard of Liudolf's death.

Otto pressed his lips to the top of her head. "You have been very patient with me, Adelheid."

Adelheid let out her breath, relaxing against him. "Oh, Otto."

"I do not learn from my mistakes. I pushed my children away after Eadgyth died and after Liudolf... I pushed you away. Please forgive me, sweetheart, for the blame I placed on you. Nothing was your fault."

With difficulty Adelheid held back her tears. "I think I must bear my share of the blame, but it is so easy to know how to act after the event."

Otto continued to stroke her hair, pulling her even tighter against him. "I know it has not seemed like it, but I have grieved also for our little boys. I hoped for so much for them."

The tears spilled over. "They were so little, holding the mere promise of life. I know losing an adult child is very different."

Otto released Adelheid and rolled onto his back, staring upwards. "Yes, it is. And it was not just losing Liudolf. I felt as if I was losing Eadgyth all over again in the loss of those two precious children she gave me." He turned his head to look at her. "I have achieved power beyond my wildest dreams, but what is the use, when I cannot keep those I love with me?"

"You are a king, not God."

Otto stared upwards once again. "I know."

There was a forlorn note in his voice and Adelheid suddenly realised her mistake. "And you are also a man with no more power over life and death than any other man. But unlike other men, you have to remain strong, unable to display the weakness of grief."

"I know," Otto said again, sounding lonelier than ever.

"But not here, Otto. Alone with me, you can grieve like a man, weep like a man, fear like a man, knowing I will never think any less of you." Adelheid pulled him back to her, drawing his head against her breast. Otto tensed for a moment and then relaxed, for the first time allowing her to comfort him. She felt his tears wet against her skin. "We have lost so many these last years."

Otto clung tighter. "We have lost too many."

"But we still have many." Adelheid stroked his hair. "William,

Matilda, Emma, Regelind and Mathilde. Not to mention The Three Ottos."

The sob which had clearly been building up in Otto's throat was suddenly overwhelmed by laughter. "Ah yes, The Three Ottos. They are proving a force to be reckoned with, are they not?"

Otto raised his head to look down at her, the smile of genuine amusement causing Adelheid's heart to lift in joy. Not sure what his reaction would be, she brushed a kiss against his lips. "And we still have each other."

Otto returned the kiss, his lips eagerly seeking hers in a way they had not done in a long time. "Yes, we still have each other."

The next morning Adelheid awoke with an unfamiliar sense of warmth and she realised Otto's arm was still around her, just as it always used to be. The light streaming in the chamber told her it was already day. She had slept deeply and so too had Otto with none of the restlessness and nightmares which so often plagued his sleep. She turned to look at him, smiling as she saw he was already awake. He leant over to kiss her, before pulling her so her head rested against his chest.

"Will you come with me?" he asked.

Adelheid laughed. "Of course, Otto. Where to?"

"Italy."

Adelheid jerked upright, staring at Otto. "Italy?"

It was Otto's turn to laugh. "Naturally not this day. Indeed it will probably take some time before I come to an agreement with the Holy Father. But soon."

"And you want me there?"

Otto nodded. "I would like you at my side. I do not forget that you were Queen of Italy before I was King. Your understanding of the land and your skills with the language of the Romans would be useful indeed. But it may be dangerous. The children will all stay here, so I will understand if you do not wish to go."

Adelheid did not hesitate. Aware she had not always supported Otto as he deserved, she knew this was the time to truly prove herself worthy of being his wife. Besides, it would be good to leave the sadness of Germany behind and return to the place where she had first learnt to love. "I will miss the children, but of course I will come to Italy with you. I would go to the ends of the Earth with you if you wished for it."

Otto sat up and kissed her. "I do not think it will come to that, but who knows?" He pushed back the covers. "I cannot lie abed all day. I have much to do."

Adelheid smiled as she watched him wrap a robe around himself, delighted to see him in such spirits. His hair was now more grey than brown and the tragedies of the last years had left their marks on his face, but with his blue eyes sparkling with life, he appeared younger than he had in a long time.

Chapter two

O ver the winter many messengers travelled between Germany and Rome as bishops from Milan, Como and Navare added their pleas to the Pope's. When they made their way to Bavaria to celebrate Christmas, Judith welcomed them at Regensburg and William too joined them as they prepared for a particularly sacred occasion.

With word already spreading throughout Christendom that Otto was close to achieving the imperial title, Adelheid's brother was keen to display his alliance and sent a treasure Otto had long coveted, the relics of Saint Maurice himself.

With Adelheid on one side of him and William on the other, Otto waited to receive the relics. Around them was a grand assembly of bishops as well as the most prominent of the Bavarian nobility, awe filling the faces of all as the procession drew closer.

As the casket was placed in front of Otto, he knelt and closed his eyes. Around him everyone also fell to their knees as William spoke the sacred words of the mass. For all the familiarity of the words, never had they felt so hallowed as they did at that moment.

"Most noble King Otto," the envoy said at the end. "On behalf of King Konrad of Burgundy, I commend to your care these sacred relics of the blessed Saint Maurice."

Otto kissed the casket and rose to his feet. "Please thank my dearest brother, King Konrad of Burgundy. I command these sacred relics of Saint Maurice be transported to the abbey which bears his name in my beloved city of Magdeburg."

He was jubilant over the Christmas celebrations, more certain than ever he would soon be emperor. Watching him in animated consultation with the bishops and nobility, Adelheid was overjoyed, but nervous that something would overturn his plans.

"I do not think you need to worry," Judith said. "I do not see how this can fail. The Holy Father needs him."

"I hope so. I never thought to see Otto again in such spirits. He needs this challenge."

Judith gave a thoughtful nod. "I can understand that. When Henry died, I felt so lost. But in ruling Bavaria, I have learnt to live again." She glanced at Ida, who was talking to William. "I wish Ida too could find a new purpose."

"Mathilda suggested she take religious vows as she would quickly rise to high office, but she will not."

To Adelheid's great regret, Ida had adopted a cordial manner with her, but they had never regained their friendship after Liudolf's death. Adelheid suspected that Ida's refusal to enter an abbey stemmed mainly from her wish not to place her children into her care. Dressed always in dark colours and rarely smiling, she remained a tragic figure at court.

When news came from Rome that in return for liberation, the Pope would indeed crown Otto emperor, the mood in Bavaria was jubilant, an emotion which was soon echoed throughout Germany. Considering the matter already settled, Otto sent orders and a vast quantity of gems to the skilled metal smiths at the Abbey of Reichenau, ordering them to make him a crown of such magnificence the like of which had never been seen.

It was William who raised a few concerns when Otto announced he would be leading the campaign himself.

"Father, after what happened to Liudolf, I am sure I do not need to mention the dangers of such an expedition. As Elector of Germany, I need you to consider what is best for the realm.

What will happen to Germany if you die on campaign?"

"I have thought on this many times since we lost Liudolf," Otto replied with a sad smile. "Even if I do not campaign, I am well aware I may not live to see my son grow to manhood. I want him crowned before we leave for Italy."

Adelheid and William both gaped at him. "But he has not yet seen seven years," Adelheid protested.

"The King of West Francia was just a boy when his father died," Otto said. "Bruno and my sisters have managed the realm for him."

"This has never been done in Germany," William said. "Always it is a man to rule."

"I agree and until my son is of age, it will be a man to rule. William, you and Bruno are to be regents while I am away." He took hold of Adelheid's hand. "But do not forget a mother's wisdom. If I fall, you must work with Adelheid to keep the realm secure for my son."

Adelheid squeezed his hand, remembering how once she had wished to rule free from the influence of a husband. It was the last thing she wanted now. "I pray you live to see our son become a man," she said. "But if you do not, know your son will be safe. We will not let you down."

"The nobles will have to agree," William said. "But if they do, I have no objections to crowning him."

Otto grinned. "The nobles of Saxony and Franconia will most certainly agree. Bruno will ensure the Lotharingians agree and Judith will bring the support of Bavaria. If Burchard of Swabia does not agree, it will be the worse for him." His face turned sadder once again. "I want Liudolf's son to have Swabia one day in any case. I owe that to Liudolf and Hermann."

Adelheid squeezed his hand. "I feel sure Burchard will support you, but I agree that Liudolf's son should certainly one day gain every honour."

∞∞∞

After celebrating Easter at Wallhausen, the court travelled across the realm to Worms, where Otto convened a synod and presented his son as the heir to Germany. Many were taken aback, but as Otto had predicted there were few detractors. Just a few weeks later the court moved on to Aachen where Otto himself had once been anointed. There the boy could be crowned by William, Bruno and the Archbishop of Trier.

In the magnificent domed church, Adelheid stared at her young son, thinking how tiny he looked as he processed towards the three archbishops, kneeling solemnly before the altar.

"Otto of Saxony, son of the noble King Otto, do you swear to uphold your sacred duties to this realm?" Bruno asked, smiling in a kindly fashion at his nervous nephew. "Do you swear to defend this land, to uphold God's holy laws and maintain the authority of His Holiness, the Pope?"

"I swear by almighty God to ever defend this realm from its enemies." Little Otto's high voice echoed uncertainly in the hall. "I swear that, while there is breath in my body, I will uphold God's holy laws and the authority of the Pope."

Archbishop Henry of Trier fastened the braces to his arms and clasped a cloak around his shoulders. "I bestow these upon you so you may defend your realm from its enemies."

William anointed him on his forehead and arms with oil. "I anoint you King by the grace of God."

Bruno placed an orb and sceptre in his hand. "I grant you these so you may uphold the authority of His Holiness the Pope in this realm."

Lastly Bruno and William together lowered the crown onto his head. "Arise King Otto, son of King Otto."

The little boy's head bowed slightly with the weight of the crown and Otto stepped forward to stand beside his son, laying a hand reassuringly on his shoulder as the boy rose to his feet. With a smile, Otto led him by the hand to climb the steps of the white marble throne of Charles the Great, sitting with his son beside him.

"All hail King Otto of Germany," Otto proclaimed. "I command all to show their loyalty."

The nobles processed solemnly to the throne to kneel and kiss his hand, until at last the two could leave the church together. Although there would be a celebration, the formality was relaxed and it was with a look of relief that little Otto joined the other two Ottos.

Adelheid slipped her hand into her husband's, guessing this was difficult day for him. "I know it should have been Liudolf."

Otto smiled slightly, but his eyes were moist. "I shall never understand why it is not Liudolf. He would have been so fine, but our son has been crowned by the grace of God. It is God's will that he rule and I have to accept it. I am proud of him."

Chapter three

At the feast afterwards Adelheid found herself seated with Ida. She remained in high favour with Otto, who made it plain he regarded her still as a daughter, perhaps all the more precious for the two children he had lost. He always commanded her to be seated with honour on such occasions, but on this day Adelheid wished Otto had not been so insistent on Ida taking a prominent place at the festivities. If it was a difficult day for him, it was many times harder for Ida.

"Your son is king. You got what you wanted," Ida said the moment she sat down.

Adelheid bit her lip, guessing she felt her own son had a better claim. "I do not know if it is what I want. Being king has brought Otto to within the grasp of his greatest ambition, but he has had to sacrifice so much and always it has strained the affection between him and those he loves the most. My first husband was crowned young, yet it brought him nothing but grief. Yes, I am proud of my son, but I am also afraid for him."

Ida swallowed. "My son will always be loyal. I know it."

"I know," Adelheid said. "They are closer than many brothers. You know Otto loves your children as his own." She looked to where Otto stood talking with his eldest granddaughter. If he had a favourite among the children, it was this one. Adelheid tried to tell herself it was only because Matilda was more often with her grandmother at Quedlinburg than at court, but she suspected there was another reason why Otto doted on the girl.

"Regelind looks so like Eadgyth," Ida said, reading her thoughts. "Now she is older, she must be starting to look like Eadgyth as Otto first knew her."

Adelheid had remembered her vow to keep all jealousy at bay, so felt the merest pang at the sight of the pretty girl who always reminded Otto of the woman he had so deeply loved.

"Ida, you know I am to go to Italy with Otto. I have a favour to ask of you."

"What is it?"

"The children are all in the care of William and Bruno. Of course I trust them completely, but they are so young. They will miss a mother's care. Please, will you be a mother to Emma, Matilda and my little Otto, as well as your own and Liutgarde's."

"Do you trust me?"

Adelheid smiled warmly. "Completely. You are the daughter of Regelind and Hermann and the daughter of the heart of Otto and Eadgyth. Could there be any one more trustworthy?"

"Oh, Adelheid." Ida flung her arms around her. "I shall fulfil that trust. Your children will be loved, I swear it." She frowned slightly. "At least, I will if Otto is happy with this arrangement."

"Of course he will. Why wouldn't he be?"

Ida shrugged. "I need to talk to Otto in the morn. I think you should be there when I do."

∞ ∞ ∞

Adelheid did not have to curb her impatience long before finding out what Ida wanted to say. She approached him immediately after the morning's first prayers in the church.

"Otto," she said with her usual directness. "I would like to marry again. I beg you for your blessing."

Otto looked taken aback and so was Adelheid. It seemed strange to imagine Ida loving anyone other than Liudolf.

"Who?" Otto demanded.

"His name is Adalbero. He is a count with lands in Saxony and-"

"I know who he is," Otto snapped. "Why do you wish to marry him? Did you not love my son?"

"Did you love his mother?" Ida bit back.

"You know I fell in love with her when I was seventeen. You have not answered my question."

Ida narrowed her eyes. "I fell in love with Liudolf when I was seven and I never stopped loving him."

Otto's face darkened. "Do not speak to me in that fashion, Ida." He turned and left the church with no further words.

Ida clamped her hand over her mouth. "Oh, dear God, I should not have said that to him."

"No, you should not, but I do not blame you." Adelheid slipped an arm around her. "Everyone knows how you loved Liudolf. He should not have suggested you did not. Do you also love this man?"

Ida gave her a sideways look and nodded. "Is it wrong of me? When they laid Liudolf to rest in Mainz, I wanted to crawl into the grave with him. I shall always love him, but is it truly so impossible for me to love again?"

Adelheid glanced in the direction Otto had left. "I have always hoped it is not."

"I know Mathilda thinks I should enter an abbey. My mother too suggested it before she died, but I do not think such a life is for me."

"Perhaps it is because you were so happy in your marriage that you wish to marry again. My first marriage was miserable and I longed for an abbey after he died."

"You may be right, but I do not know what to do. It seems Otto also thinks I should enter an abbey. I wonder what Eadgyth would say if she were here. Perhaps she too would chide me for my infidelity to her son's memory."

"If Eadgyth were here, she would tell me not to be so unfeeling," Otto said from behind them. "And she would be right."

Ida went slowly to Otto and put her arms around him. "I am so sorry, Otto. I should not have said that."

Otto gave a sad smile. "You were right. You never stopped loving him and I know what a support your devotion must have been on those dark days. I did not always do right by my son, but when I chose you to be his wife, I did him the very best turn any father could do for their son. Just as my father did for me when he arranged for Eadgyth to come to Germany. At least I can be proud of that."

Tears were trickling down Ida's cheeks. "I will not marry again if I do not have your blessing."

"You do have it. Will you wed him before we go to Italy? I would like to be present. You remain a daughter to me."

Ida nodded, smiling through her tears. "And you will always be a father to me."

Otto held her tightly for a moment, kissing her on the cheek. "You marry this man, sweetheart and you be happy. I do not know anyone who deserves that more than you."

∞∞∞

As the summer warmed up, the troops began to assemble at Augsburg. Adelheid and Otto returned to Magdeburg where they celebrated Ida's wedding quietly but with great joy. Ida's happiness was touching to see, while Adelbero, the Saxon nobleman clearly could not believe his luck in gaining the beautiful daughter-in-law of the King as his wife.

While in Magdeburg Otto transferred power to Bruno and William, allowing them to issue commands in the names of the kings and the three spent many days in consultation on how the realm should be managed. On the day of their departure Adelheid bade a tearful farewell to the children, commending them to Ida's care before making her way to the abbey. In a solemn ceremony the two archbishops prayed earnestly for the successful liberation of the Pope.

"You have God's blessing on your mission, Otto," Bruno said, embracing his brother and Adelheid. "You will both be in my prayers."

"Thank you, Brother." He turned to William. "You know if I am successful, Magdeburg will become an archdiocese?"

William grinned. "Of course and I do not doubt I will soon receive the Pope's command on that matter."

"I do not want ill feeling between us," Otto said.

"Do not fear, Father. All will be as well with us as it always has been." He embraced Otto tightly. "It is only as a bishop that I have opposed you on this. As a son, I hope you are successful. I shall never forget Eadgyth's kindness to me. She is truly worthy of the finest of resting places. But, Father, this Pope is an awkward one. Do not assume anything just yet."

Otto nodded, kissing his son. He turned to Adelheid. "We must be on our way." He gave a slight smile. "Just grant me a few moments."

Adelheid watched as he went over to Eadgyth's grave and knelt there, placing his hand against the cool marble. She turned away. They were returning to Italy, but Eadgyth would undoubtedly accompany them in Otto's heart.

"I am glad you will be with Otto," Mathilda said, taking Adelheid's arm as they left the abbey. "Try to persuade him not to do anything reckless."

Mathilda was starting to look very frail and Adelheid felt a lump come to her throat as she prayed Otto's mother would live to see their return. "I shall take care of him."

As Otto too followed them from the abbey, he clasped Mathilda's hands in his, kissing her on each cheek. "May God keep you, Mother. I shall send word of my progress."

"God's blessings on you, Otto. I am so proud of you, my dearest son. Your father always envisioned you would be emperor. In truth I did not believe him, but you have fulfilled his dream."

Warmly Otto embraced his mother. "Thank you, Mother. I

feel proud to be fulfilling his vision."

Otto and Adelheid mounted their horses, taking a last look at the family. Firmly forcing down the grief of farewells, they exchanged smiles, as their entourage formed behind them. Otto raised his hand.

"To Italy!"

Chapter four

They joined the army at Augsburg before starting the climb into the mountains. Adelheid often glanced back as she rode to admire the splendid sight which followed them. The columns of horses, carts laden with supplies and the banners fluttering above them stretched as far as she could see, while the sounds of battle songs filled the air. Otto frequently asked if she needed to rest, but she simply laughed, urging her horse even faster through the mountain passes. They tried to find abbeys and residences no matter how humble to rest at night, but when on one occasion that was not possible, the men erected great tents and sat late around blazing fires. Morale was high and as she surveyed the sheer numbers of men in the army, Adelheid shared their optimism. It would be impossible for Otto to fail.

It was as they came down from the mountains into the warmth of an Italian autumn, that they were brought word of Berengar's forces mustering against them. Otto halted at an abbey, ordering Adelheid to remain with Warinus and the other clergymen who had accompanied them while he prepared his forces for a fight.

"If matters were to go badly for us, I shall send word and you must return to the mountains immediately," Otto said. "I do not want you falling into Berengar's hands again." He frowned. "Perhaps it was a mistake to bring you here until I had the land more under control."

"Of course I came with you," Adelheid said, frowning herself.

"Otto, must you be the one to lead the men into battle?"

"Do you think I am too old?" Otto asked, looking faintly annoyed.

"Of course not, but it could be dangerous."

"I have faced danger before," Otto replied, the annoyance deepening.

Adelheid let out an exasperated sigh. "Very well. Be as reckless as you wish. But remember, the Pope cannot crown you emperor if you are dead."

Otto laughed at that. "You are very wise. I shall most certainly do my best to return alive."

Adelheid's fears turned out to be unfounded as Otto faced mere skirmishes, returning very much alive and delighted by his progress. Throughout the autumn they made steady progress southwards, arriving at Pavia just as the winter was beginning. Otto put on a great show of strength, fearing they would have to besiege the city, but they needn't have worried. The gates of the city opened willingly and they entered in triumph.

Adelheid had always been popular in Pavia and despite the many years of absence, she was greeted with cheers by the delighted people. As they settled into the palace, Otto gave orders for magnificent Christmas celebrations.

"Fit for the King and Queen of Italy," he commented with a grin.

Adelheid was happy to oblige, thinking of how angry Berengar and Willa would be when they heard of them assuming the royal status. It soon became obvious just how unpopular Berengar had been as nobles from across Lombardy arrived at court to pay homage to the man they were happy to call king.

Otto was in good spirits, accepting graciously the

protestations of loyalty. But when he arrived in their chamber on Christmas night, she noticed a wistful look on his face. Until that point he had always made some smiling reference to their wedding night which they had spent in that very chamber, but that night he was in a more solemn mood.

"Is all well?" she asked, putting her hand on his shoulder, as he sat on the bed, making no effort to disrobe or turn to her.

Otto nodded. "I was remembering our last Christmas here with Conrad and Liutgarde. I never again celebrated a Christmas with my beautiful daughter."

"I know." Adelheid wondered once again if he was blaming her, but there was no anger on his face. Just sadness.

"And Liudolf's last message to me was from here."

"Do you have regrets, Otto? Do you sometimes wish you had remained in Germany and never ventured south of the Alps to rescue me?"

Otto pulled her into his arms. "No, do not think that. How could I ever regret our marriage? And I have long aimed to be Emperor. The only regret I have is how I allowed such a distance grow with my children. It was my fault. Eadgyth kept me always rooted in our family. I never properly appreciated her influence until she was gone. Nothing could have avoided Liutgarde's death. Illness can strike at any time. I only pray she knew how I loved her."

"I am sure she did."

"And as for Liudolf, I know I could have protected him, kept him safely in Germany and away from battles, but he would not have thanked me. The lad was born to be a warrior, as I was and my father before me. We all know the risks of campaigns. Injuries can be severe and illnesses are rife, but we face them anyway. I was so proud of him. Did he know that?"

"Oh, Otto, of course he did. Your last words to him were to tell him that and every message you sent to him in Italy told him again. Try not to dwell on the years of separation, but remember the happy times. Your mother told me much of their childhood. I know you feel you were not a good father to them, but so often you were."

"I hope so. In any case, the sacrifice made by Liudolf and indeed Conrad shall not be in vain. In the next days we press on for Rome."

Adelheid smiled at his brighter mood. "I have so longed to see Rome. I can scarce believe I will soon be there."

"It is still some distance. I do not know how much resistance we will face, but I hope to be in Rome before the winter is out. Can you be ready to move in the next few days?"

Adelheid leant over to kiss him. "As soon as you give the word."

∞∞∞

The march to Rome was far easier than any had dared hope as scouts reported that Berengar, Willa and Adalbert had retreated to their strongholds in the south. The weather too seemed to be blessing them with a winter so mild, it felt almost as if spring was already upon them.

They moved swiftly down the well-trodden pilgrim route, with cheers from the many who knew why they were there. Often she rode with Warinus, reminiscing how long ago they had claimed to be pilgrims as they sought refuge from their enemies, but now they truly were. Little more than a month after Christmas Otto reined in his horse, a smile of both triumph and awe on his face.

Before them lay a city of towering basilicas and fine residences. The pinnacle of an obelisk reached into the sky, marking the most sacred place of all – the Basilica of Saint Peter. Adelheid crossed herself, suddenly wondering if she was worthy to enter such a hallowed spot. She could scarce believe she was witnessing the site of the Saint's martyrdom and burial.

Otto tore his gaze away from the city to look back at his army. "My people," he cried. "We have arrived at Rome."

Chapter five

Having ordered the men to set up camp just outside Rome, Otto dispatched a messenger informing the Pope that he was there and requesting permission to enter the city. It was with a flourish of horns that the answer came.

Adelheid took her place alongside Otto as the man in flowing white robes proceeded towards them, surrounded by a large group of men all in clerical dress. Around the neck of the man hung a magnificent jewelled cross and further jewels sparkled on his fingers as he made the sign of the cross to all he passed in blessing. Adelheid noticed a faint resemblance to Hugh and Lothair in his thin, but not unattractive, features. However it brought her no distrust. If anything it reminded her of how her first husband's death had remained unavenged. As the Pope drew closer, Otto knelt on the ground, Adelheid kneeling beside him. It was strange to see Otto kneeling to any man, but particularly one as young as this even if he was the Pope.

"State who you are and your intentions in this holy city," Pope John said formally.

"Greetings, Your Holiness. I am Otto, King by the grace of God of Germany and Italy. I am here to serve you."

At a nod from the Pope, the priests set up a wooden cross in front of the kneeling king and beside it they placed jewelled chests, which bore the relics of many a saint.

"Your service is most welcome, King Otto. Speak the words to pledge your true intent."

"Lord Pope John, I, Otto, by the Grace of God King of Germany and Italy do swear by the Father, son and holy spirit, by this life-giving cross and by these sacred relics, that if God is willing for me to enter this holy city of Rome, I will ever honour the Holy Roman Church and you, its ruler and never will I command any to cause you harm or the loss of the sacred honour you possess. Unless you grant me your consent, I will make no regulations within the Holy City which affects you or its people. If any territory of Saint Peter comes into my possession, I will return it to you. I speak not only for myself, but whoever I trust with the Kingdom of Italy shall also be required to swear to aid you in defending the lands of Saint Peter."

"Please rise, King Otto. I bid you welcome to Rome."

Otto got to his feet and strode forward to take the hands of the Pope, towering over the younger man. His humble attitude had completely faded as he spoke his own greetings. "And may I also present my wife, Adelheid, Queen of Germany and Italy."

Adelheid dropped into a low curtsey. "It is an honour to meet you, Your Holiness," she murmured, overawed to be in the sacred presence of the highest churchman in Christendom.

Pope John's eyes flicked over her. "Please rise, my dear lady. Are we not kin by marriage? My poor uncle, King Lothair. That was a bad business."

"Indeed it was," Adelheid said. "Your family has suffered most grievously at the hands of the evil traitor, Berengar."

"We most certainly have. Tell me of my dear kinswoman, your daughter, the Lady Emma." The Pope smiled. "She must be quite the young lady by now."

"It is true she is nearly full grown," Adelheid replied. "She is considered to be most fair."

"And like her mother, Lady Emma is an inspiration to us all in her purity and virtue," Otto put in. There was a frown on his face which surprised Adelheid.

"Of course, my Lord King. Well, I do not doubt that you and your fair Queen are wearied of rough living. I invite you to stay at my own residence." He smiled warmly at Adelheid. "I shall ensure you are most comfortable there, my lady."

Adelheid smiled back. "You do us a great honour, Your Holiness. We will be truly grateful for your hospitality."

She was surprised to see Otto's frown deepen and she wondered if he had planned to refuse the Pope's invitation. However he nodded, adding his thanks to Adelheid's.

It was a wondrous moment as they entered the gates of the Holy City with marvels to be seen on all sides. Riding through the ancient streets, the Pope pointed out the many wonders. There were churches worn with age, as well as some magnificent new basilicas, but Pope John seemed equally proud of some of the crumbling pagan temples they passed, commenting on the revels which must have taken place in the days when the Emperor of Rome ruled all.

∞ ∞ ∞

The Papal Palace was magnificent with a luxurious splendour Adelheid had not anticipated.

"Of course I know how a bishop lives," she said to Warinus. "Both Bruno and William have most comfortable residences and preside over their congregations in some state, but this opulence is something else."

"It is indeed," Warinus replied, looking at the luxury with some disapproval. "It is many years since I was last in Rome and indeed I was far too lowly to be welcomed to the Papal Palace, but I heard no tales of splendour such as this."

Adelheid paused to look at one of the tapestries adorning the wall. It was normal enough to see tapestries glinting with silken threads in the highest residences, but she had expected to see one depicting the tale of a saint or some such matter. This one was of a far more worldly nature, with even some lewd scenes depicted in the tale it told. It seemed very strange to see such a thing side by side with gilded icons.

∞∞∞

A lavish banquet was laid on to welcome them, with spiced meats, honeyed pastries and rich wines among the many delicacies on offer. However Otto ate sparingly as he talked to the Pope on religious matters. Adelheid was left with the impression that he was testing the Pontiff and several times she tried to catch his eye, certain his attitude was not proper.

However the Pope did not appear offended, simply urging more food on his guests and responding intelligently to Otto's questions.

"It is time you retired, Adelheid," Otto said in a low voice, as the wine grew low in the jugs.

Adelheid looked at him resentfully. She would have liked to linger longer over the table to enjoy more of the learned discourse. But it was rare for Otto to issue a direct order at her in this fashion and when he did, he expected it to be obeyed. With a charming smile at everyone, she thanked their host and bade everyone a good night.

To her surprise Otto was not long in joining her in the luxurious bedchamber.

"Did you not wish to stay longer at the feast?" she asked.

Otto shook his head and kissed her, holding her tightly for a moment. "I would much prefer to be with my beautiful wife."

"I hope you did not offend the Holy Father by retiring so early," Adelheid said as she pulled herself free from Otto's arms, still irritated by his strange attitude at dinner.

Otto gave a wry smile. "No, he was not offended. Indeed he was most understanding."

Adelheid snuggled under the covers, watching him disrobe, even more puzzled by that reply. But as he climbed into bed, he seemed to have recovered his good temper.

"So, Adelheid, we have made it to Rome at last. And in just two days I shall be emperor. Is that not splendid?"

"Yes, it is splendid indeed."

Otto lay down with her, pulling her into his arms, pressing his lips against hers. Forgetting herself for a moment, Adelheid responded just as eagerly, then once again she pulled herself away.

"Otto, is this right? To give into our carnal desires in such a sacred place?"

Otto gave a derisive laugh. "You do not need to concern yourself with such proprieties here."

"What do you mean?"

"Nothing. Truly, Adelheid, there is nothing improper in such desires between a husband and a wife, even here." He kissed her lightly. "But if your conscience requires you to remain chaste while here, you know I will respect that."

Adelheid returned the kiss. "No, you are right. There can never be anything improper between us. Besides, if you must spend tomorrow night in prayer, is this not the last time I will lie with a king? The next time we share this chamber you will be an emperor." She pulled Otto back into her arms. "My dearest, I am so proud of you."

Chapter six

The next day Otto was busy planning for the crowning, taking the crown which he had kept concealed from all during the journey from Germany to the Basilica of Saint Peter to be blessed. The following day would be Candlemas and Otto was pleased that his crowning should take place on such a significant day.

"The great Frankish emperor, Charles was crowned on Christmas Day," he commented. "But Candlemas is also a sacred day."

"Besides," Adelheid said, kissing him as he left. "You do not want to wait any longer."

Otto grinned, but did not deny her words.

Adelheid shook her head as she felt herself caught up in the excitement, scarcely able to wait for the moment when Otto would be anointed. She took up some stitching, wishing to present the Pope with some more fitting hangings for his walls, but she was too excited to concentrate and eventually cast it aside, preferring to talk to Father Warinus, as they speculated on what the following day would bring.

"Otto will not even tell me what he intends to wear," Adelheid complained. "He is determined to make an entrance none will forget."

"I do not think any would forget this day however the King appears," Warinus replied. "But truly it will be a splendid occasion. I am privileged indeed that I shall witness it."

"So am I," Adelheid replied. "Oh, Otto has worked so hard for this day through such trials and suffering. Everything must go well tomorrow. It is what he deserves."

Suddenly consumed with the fear that something would occur to spoil Otto's triumph, she and Warinus made their way to the Pope's private chapel, where they knelt in lengthy prayers that all would be well.

Just as they were about to leave the chapel, Adelheid was surprised to see the thin figure of the Pontiff dressed in his familiar white robes. His face lit up as he saw her and she dropped into a curtsey.

The Pope laid his hand on her head in the customary blessing, although it seemed to last a little longer than usual. "Please rise, my dear lady." He barely glanced at Warinus. "And you too, my brother."

"I had thought you would still be in talks with Otto," she said.

The Pope let out a sigh so faint Adelheid was not sure if she had imagined it. "I have spent long in talks with the King."

Adelheid repressed her own sigh. She did not know what was wrong with Otto, but never had she expected him to show so little deference to the Holy Father. She gave the Pope an understanding smile.

As he met her eyes, his own lips stretched wider than ever. "But now it would be good to have a talk with you, my lady."

"Of course, Father. It will be an honour. Shall we be seated?"

"Oh, I think we could converse somewhere a little more comfortable than this. Please come with me, my dear lady."

They made their way along the passageway when the Pope suddenly stopped. He glanced back at Warinus. "There is no need to trouble yourself, my brother. I can speak to the Queen alone."

To Adelheid's surprise Warinus froze. "My lady, I have little else to occupy myself at present. I shall be glad to remain in attendance."

Adelheid smiled and shook her head. "There is no need, Father."

Warinus swallowed, sending the Pope a nervous glance. "Did

the King not say he required your presence at this time? I think I should accompany you to him."

Adelheid's brow creased in concern, wondering if Warinus had been taken ill. "Father, is something amiss? The King made no such commands. I think you should rest yourself. These last days have been so busy."

"But, my lady…" Warinus said, a note of desperation creeping into his voice.

"I am commanding that, Father. How terrible it would be if you were too ill to attend the crowning in the morn."

Adelheid squeezed his hand, resolving to send someone with some refreshment to the priest. He had been a presence in her life for so long but he was becoming old. Such a long journey and the emotions of being in Rome must be wearisome indeed for a man of his years. She would need to take care of him to ensure he would remain with her for some time yet.

"My lady, I shall inform the King you are in audience with the Holy Father," Warinus called, as she moved further along the passageway.

Adelheid paused. "You know Otto is far too busy to be disturbed. Please, Father, take some time to rest." She turned back to the Pope, still looking worried. "Forgive me, Your Holiness. I do not know what ails him this day. He is not himself."

She thought too of Otto's strange behaviour and wondered if he might be similarly ailing. Again a fear struck her that something might hinder the crowning, dashing Otto's greatest dream.

"Shall we step in here, my lady," the Pope said, interrupting her thoughts.

The chamber they entered was small, but lavishly furnished with finely carved benches bedecked with soft coverings and cushions. He gestured to a bench and poured two cups of wine. Adelheid looked around the room. Like most chambers it was hung with fine embroidered cloths and tapestries. But the content of the hanging was astounding, depicting scenes of an even more worldly nature than the previous one she had seen. Adelheid blushed, ashamed the Pope might have caught her staring at it, although she wondered why he would have such a thing in what was clearly his private space.

To her surprise he took a seat beside her on the bench, ignoring the other chairs nearby. It was barely large enough for two to sit on, forcing Adelheid to shift herself uncomfortably against one end. The Pope gave her a sly smile and she guessed he had seen her looking at the hangings. The long ago memory of Warinus telling her that a religious path should never be an easy one suddenly increased her respect for the Pope, as she realised he had undoubtedly chosen to make his own path even harder by surrounding himself with images of the carnal desires he had set aside.

Sitting up very straight, she smiled warmly at him. "How may I be of assistance, Father?"

The Pope gestured to the table. "Please, take a drink." He took several mouthfuls of his own wine, refilling his cup while she had barely sipped at hers.

"Thank you, Father. Please, can we conclude our business? In truth I am concerned for my priest."

"Of course you are, my dear lady. Your loving heart is truly inspirational. Your friends are all most fortunate to experience it."

"Thank you, Father," Adelheid said again, wishing he would get to the point. "What did you wish to say to me?"

The Pope smiled. "The King is, I am sure, a fine man..."

"Yes, he is," Adelheid said sharply, suddenly afraid the Pope was changing his mind about the crowning. "He is the finest."

"But he is not a young man," the Pope commented.

Adelheid smiled in relief that this was all that worried him. "Oh, you need have no concerns about that. The King is in good health and is as strong as he ever was. He will defeat Berengar."

"I am sure he will. But he has seen nearly half a century. You look so young and beautiful beside him."

Adelheid laughed. "I am not so young. I have seen three

decades now."

The Pope moved closer, bending his head towards hers. "But still, it must be a dull time for you. The King so moralistic and so old..."

Adelheid caught her breath, bewildered by his meaning as the holiest of men rested his hand on her knee, squeezing her leg through the fine fabric of her tunic.

Chapter seven

"Your Holiness, I... I am not sure what you mean. Truly my life is far from dull. My marriage has brought me great happiness." She pressed herself against the carved arm of the chair in her efforts to get away from the Pope, while his hand edged further up her leg.

"My dear lady, I do not think you truly know how dull your marriage bed is."

"Father, it is most inappropriate for you to speak to me in this fashion." With difficulty she stood up. "I shall take my leave of you."

The Pope also stood, catching her around the waist. Adelheid pulled back, but the indolent pontiff was far stronger than he looked. "Oh, I hear the voice of your dull husband as you mouth such proprieties. It is sad to hear them from a fair lady such as yourself."

"My husband is not dull or old," Adelheid cried. "He is the finest of men. I would never betray him."

The Pope gave a laugh and pressed a wet kiss against her cheek. "My dear Adelheid, do you think you are the first lady who has not fully understood what pleasures I can offer until I have shown her? Come, my dear. There is no need to fight this."

Feeling truly terrified, Adelheid pushed against him. She opened her mouth to scream, although she burned with shame that anyone would witness this, but the Pope swiftly clamped a hand over it.

"There is no need for that, besides none is around. I made

sure of that. Why, I have considered everything. After the King has been crowned, he will leave Rome in search of Berengar. You can remain here as my very special guest. Once I have finished with you today, you will understand how fine that will be."

She shook off his hand. "No. I would never stay with you, no matter what you do to me today. Nothing would stop me leaving with my husband." Tears filled her eyes. "Or if he despises me for my actions, I shall enter an abbey."

Adelheid's heart broke at the thought Otto regarding her with such disgust. Again the words of Warinus telling her how a religious path should never be an easy one filled her mind. For the first time she truly understood what he meant.

"An abbey is an excellent plan, my dear. I frequently stay in abbeys."

Bile rose to her throat at the thought of this man appearing in his papal splendour in the church before defiling the nuns in their cells. "No. Please, let me go. I know I am a sinner, but I would never willingly betray my husband. Even I am not so great a sinner as that."

The Pope laughed, tightening his arms around her, his lips pressed against hers. It was impossible to escape no matter how hard she tried. "But my dear," he whispered. "There is no sin. I am the Pope. I shall absolve you of everything."

She cried out as he pulled the mantle from her head, exclaiming on the beauty of her fair hair. Terror had brought such a thud to her heart, she did not even hear the door crashing open. The first she realised was when the arms which had so tightly held her were released. In a blur she saw the Pope flying to the ground and heard the voice roar, "Remove your hands from my wife."

The next thing she knew, she was in Otto's arms, still breathless and sobbing, hardly able to believe he was there.

"Are you harmed?" he whispered, his arms tightening around her.

"N... no." Adelheid clung to him. "I do not know what you

must think of me. Otto, I swear I did not encourage this."

Otto stroked her hair, soothing her trembling body. "Hush, sweetheart, I know you did not. I do not think any worse of you." He lifted his head from where it had rested against Adelheid's to stare at the Pope from narrowed eyes. "You, on the other hand, disgust me as no man has ever disgusted me. I had heard such tales, but never did I think you would sink to the level of molesting a guest in your house."

The Pope struggled back to his feet, straightening his robes. He glared at Otto. "And I did not think you would sink to the level of breaking your sacred oath, my Lord King. The one you swore not to harm me."

Otto ground his teeth. "I can live with breaking my oath to shove you. Indeed after what I just witnessed, I do not think my conscience would overly trouble me if I killed you."

Pope John took a step back at the anger in Otto's eyes, the menace in his voice clearly conveying that he meant every word.

Otto gave a mirthless laugh. "In any case, you can consider my oath set aside. I came here at your invitation to aid you and you have repaid that by attacking my Queen. We will be leaving your residence this day and Rome as soon as it can be arranged."

"But... Berengar..."

"You and Berengar can kill each other for all I care. I shall send a message to Berengar informing him that if he leaves my lands in Lombardy alone, he is welcome to take as many of your lands as he wishes."

"My lord, you cannot do such a thing," he cried. "Forgive me if I misunderstood the Queen's wishes. I did not mean to cause her distress. I was sure she wished for this."

"You did not misunderstand me," Adelheid cried. "I told you many times to let me leave."

Otto's lip curled as he glared at the Pope. "Your sin disgusts me all the more that you have tried to apportion blame onto the Queen, a woman whose soul is pure."

He turned away, pulling Adelheid with him.

The Pope's voice broke. "Please, my lord. I beg you, do not leave me to Berengar's mercy."

"Otto," Adelheid whispered. "You have long dreamt of being emperor. Do not give up now." Tears filled her eyes as she realised she had unwittingly endangered Otto's dream.

"He does not deserve my aid," Otto replied.

"I know, but you deserve to be emperor. Besides, if Berengar triumphs, it is not just this pope who will suffer. It will be every pope until the Second Coming."

Otto frowned. "True." He turned back to the Pope. "Very well. I have a number of conditions. Firstly, Magdeburg. I want it made an archdiocese."

"Of course, of course," the Pontiff cried eagerly. "I have every intention of honouring the city."

"Secondly, you will learn the error of your ways. You will give up your licentious lifestyle and live in the chaste manner befitting your office." Otto threw a look of disgust around the room. He wrenched one of the hangings from the walls and flung it to the ground. "These should be removed immediately."

The man's face fell. "My lord, please stop. I may be the Pope, but I am still a man. I know you are familiar with such desires."

Otto turned from pulling down another of the hangings. "I know nothing of such desires you express."

The Pope gave a sly smile. "Really? I do not doubt the mother of the noble Archbishop of Mainz could tell a very different tale."

Otto scowled. "The mother of the Archbishop of Mainz, may God have mercy on her soul, could tell the story of a brief, but passionate liaison with a foolish boy, away from the watchful eye of his mother for the first time. Little more than a year later I married and learnt there could be far greater joys in desiring, with a pure heart, just one woman. You are no longer a boy, so do not compare my actions to yours. Give up your licentious ways. If you are unable to remain chaste, it is not illegal for you to wed."

The Pope's eyes dropped. "Of course, my lord. I will make every effort to improve my ways."

Adelheid did not believe him and from Otto's incredulous shake of the head, she suspected he did not either. He folded his arms with a sardonic look. "Lastly, in the morn, when I am crowned Emperor, you will also anoint my wife as Empress."

Adelheid gasped. "Otto, I am not worthy of this."

Otto ignored her, his gaze fixed on the Pope. "Well? I am waiting for your agreement. You will do this if you want my aid. For perhaps the first time in your life, you will bestow honour upon a woman rather than dishonour. Before the eyes of Rome, before Christendom itself, you will show how highly you can elevate a woman of such pure character. I shall enjoy seeing you do that as much as my own crowning."

The Pope shot Adelheid a resentful look, but nodded. "Very well, my Lord King. I agree to your conditions."

Otto nodded curtly, and keeping his arm around Adelheid, slammed the door behind him with no further words. They remained silent until they reached their own chamber, where Otto pulled her tightly into his arms.

"Oh, Adelheid, I should never have brought you here. I should have left you safe in Germany. Please forgive me."

Tears came to Adelheid's eyes, aware of how again she had proved to be such a burden to Otto. Almost she had cost him everything. "I wished to be with you. This was not your fault. It was my own foolishness. Otto, do not feel you must have me crowned. Truly I am not worthy of it."

"Adelheid, how did you come to be alone with him? Father Warinus tried so hard to warn you, but you dismissed him. Why?" A note of anger had entered Otto's voice. His arms fell away from her and she bowed her head to hide the tears trickling down her cheeks.

"How could I know the Pope would be capable of such actions? He is Lothair's nephew, my nephew by marriage. I assumed he viewed me as an aunt."

Otto looked at her, his voice rising in his disbelief. "Have you truly not heard what he is capable of? They say he surrounds himself with beautiful women. His own sister and niece are said to have been among them. Boys too have featured in his debauchery. He would not care that you are his aunt by marriage. He would not care that you are my wife. All he cares is that you are a beautiful woman."

"I am sorry," she cried desperately. "I know you must find such foolishness hard to forgive. Yes, I was aware of some rumours, but I did not listen to them. It is a sin to judge men harshly on false words. He is the Holy Father. I believed the best of him."

"But after everything you have suffered in your life, how can you reserve judgement in such a way?"

"Because once I did not and I believed ill without justice of a fine man. I condemned Liudolf on the words of others. Because of what I had suffered at the hands of Berengar and Adalbert, I found it easy to believe the worst of him. I have no words to express how bitterly I now regret it." Ineffectually Adelheid wiped her eyes. "I would prefer now to believe the best of a wicked man until he demonstrates his wickedness to me than ever again harshly judge a good man."

Adelheid managed at last to stop the tears from overflowing, her body still trembling at all the shocks of the days. She could not bear Otto's impatience with her, but she looked firmly at him, knowing he was right to chide her for her foolishness. If he was disgusted with her, it was a punishment she would have to bear. But Otto was looking at her in awe. Gently he pulled her towards him.

"You are an inspiration to us all. Without suffering half as much as you, I find myself suspicious of everybody. I could learn so much from your faith." He wiped the tears from her cheeks, smiling tenderly. "No one is more worthy than you to be Empress. My lady, I regard it as a great honour to be crowned alongside you."

Chapter eight

Candlemas dawned bright, but cold. Across Rome nobility and clergy alike hurried to the Basilica of Saint Peter, eager to claim a good spot to witness the crowning. Now she too was to be crowned, Adelheid had spent much of the night in prayer with Otto as they prepared for their sacred roles, but the excitement bubbling inside her prevented any exhaustion as she robed herself for the coronation.

Her dress was of a deep blue, embroidered in silvery threads with the hem raised to show the pale linen of her tunic. Her head was covered in a white mantle, although as Otto had requested, just enough of her golden hair escaped to frame her face. Around her shoulders was a cloak lined with ermine fur and she clutched it to her, shivering with a mixture of cold and nervousness, as she knelt for some last prayers with Father Warinus.

"You are in my prayers this day, my child. I know God will guide you well in this new role."

"I hope he will," Adelheid murmured. "I am honoured that Otto wishes me to be crowned alongside him and I shall always endeavour to serve God to the best of my poor abilities, but is a sinner, such as I, truly worthy?"

"We are all sinners, my child. I have watched over you for years, seeing how you struggled through hardship and sorrow. Of course you have made mistakes, but from each mistake you have emerged stronger. And throughout I have not once seen your faith waver. You are worthy."

Adelheid smiled. "Thank you, Father. You have watched over me well. I pray you will continue to watch over me for some time to come."

Warinus rose to his feet. "You are the daughter of my heart and I shall watch over you until the day I draw my final breath. I am certainly privileged to watch you this day."

Unable to speak, Adelheid embraced him in love and gratitude, as he took his leave of her to go ahead to the Basilica. Left alone she continued to stare at the altar, unable to believe she was about to be elevated to such a position.

"Adelheid."

She started, not having heard anyone come in. Turning, her mouth dropped open in awe. Otto was dressed in a red tunic, studded with jewels around the neck. From his shoulders hung a cloak of a darker red, lined with fur and encrusted with golden threads. His body, as muscular as ever, filled out the tunic, presenting a vision of such power and wealth, Adelheid found herself speechless.

"Oh, Otto," she breathed at last. "You look magnificent."

Otto grinned, his smile as dazzling as it had ever been and his blue eyes sparkling with excitement. "And yet none will be looking at me, as all eyes will be on the beautiful woman at my side."

Adelheid remained solemn. "No, Otto. Everyone will be looking at you."

"Perhaps," Otto replied, taking her by the hand. "Come, it is time."

∞∞∞

The soft chanting of monks was the only sound they could hear, but upon entering the Basilica there was a faint rustling as the gathered people turned to watch them. Adelheid had been told much of the magnificent frescos and mosaics adorning the walls, but these passed in a blur of jewelled hues as she walked beside Otto. The chanting rose to surround them on all sides, floating on the cloud of incense drifting from the altar. Having been required to fast that morning, Adelheid began to feel lightheaded, almost as if she were floating herself.

Otto moved slowly up the central aisle, his head high and his gaze fixed on the sacred altar. His face showed nothing beyond the gravity of the ceremony, but despite this, he had an air of making the most of his entrance.

At the altar the Pope awaited them. He was in white robes, encrusted with jewels. It was the first time Adelheid had seen him since her terrifying encounter, but she looked at him serenely, knowing he was far too afraid of Otto to ever attempt to harm her again.

At they arrived, Otto let go of her hand and sank to his knees. Crossing herself, Adelheid knelt beside him, bowing her head before the sacred shrine of Saint Peter.

"Lord God, be with thy servant, Otto, King of Germany and Italy this day," Pope John began in a prayer for the long life and strength of the Emperor.

The Pope was assisted in the service by a number of bishops, their heads lowered. The Bishop of Milan came forward bearing a sword. "I stand here all unworthy in this place of the apostles," the bishop proclaimed. "But on their behalf, I grant you, Otto, this sword to defend the Empire in the name of His Holiness and God our father. Do you swear to honour this obligation?"

"I do," Otto proclaimed, taking the sword and holding it before him as a cross.

"I grant you this orb as a symbol of imperial authority." Pope John took over once again. "Do you swear to uphold this authority with honour and piety?"

"I do."

"Otto, King of Germany and Italy, accept this ring as a symbol of your royal dignity." Otto extended his hand, still grasping the sword, to allow a fine jewelled ring to be placed on his finger.

The Pope dipped his finger in oil and marked a cross on Otto's forehead. "I anoint you, Otto, King of Germany and Italy, Emperor of the Romans. May God our father, son and holy spirit aid you in this task."

He placed a mitre on Otto's head, before turning to the altar. He crossed himself, then removed the cloth covering an object which had been resting on it. There was a gasp at the sight and Adelheid had to restrain her own surprise. The crown was the most magnificent she had ever seen. It was octagonal in shape with panels reflecting the dancing candlelight in a writhing mass of gold. Each panel was studded with jewels. Adelheid could see pearls, emeralds and amethysts, but so many she could not possibly count them all. A flicker of satisfaction crossed Otto's face at the reaction of the crowd, but he bowed his head again as the Pope raised the crown aloft. Slowly it was lowered onto Otto's head.

"I proclaim you, Otto, Emperor of the Romans. All hail Emperor Otto!"

The cheers in the Basilica were deafening, but Otto remained on his knees, waiting for them to die down.

"As Christ is wed with his church which ever honours and obeys him, so our noble Emperor Otto is accompanied on his sacred path by his wife, Adelheid, Queen of Germany and Italy. Adelheid, accept this ring as a symbol of your devotion to your new role."

Adelheid stretched out her hand, allowing him to slip a ring over her finger. She would not have put it past the Pope to keep hold of her hand longer than necessary, but with Otto's eyes boring into him, he behaved impeccably.

Again the Pope dipped his finger in the oil, this time to mark the cross on her. "I anoint you, Adelheid, Empress of the Romans."

Lastly he raised a golden circlet and placed it on her head, her neck bowing with the weight of it. She had worn crowns before, so she was sure it was her imagination that this one seemed heavier. "All hail Empress Adelheid."

Again the cheers rang out and together she and Otto rose to face their people. Otto took her hand to lead her to the throne. There they sat as one by the one the nobles of Rome came to kneel and swear their loyalty.

∞∞∞

The solemnity of the service was to give way to a magnificent banquet. Awed by the occasion, Adelheid had been glad of a brief rest in a small chamber while everyone took their places. Otto too appeared overwhelmed, his brow creased in thoughts Adelheid had no wish to interrupt. When they were informed everything was ready, he took her hand without smiling.

"You have done it, Otto," Adelheid said as they left the chamber. "You are emperor, as once the great Charles was."

"I am," Otto agreed, moving swiftly along the passageway. "But there is still much to do. This Pope is most certainly a tricky one. I suspect he will remain friendly only as long as it suits him. Then there is Berengar. He is still at large. He must be dealt with at all speed. No doubt he will attempt to take back the Italian throne. It must not happen. He must be punished for how he treated you."

"Otto, I have forgiven him," Adelheid protested, trying to keep up with him. "It is enough for me that he no longer occupies the Italian throne. I no longer bear any hatred."

Otto gave no sign of listening. "I must also deal with the Emperor in Constantinople. He will undoubtedly be displeased with today's events. I may have to work hard to gain his recognition and-"

"Otto, stop." Adelheid pulled Otto to a halt beside her, just before they reached the door to the feasting hall. "For one day, just stop. In there, everyone is waiting to celebrate your coronation." She smiled. "Enjoy it and not just for yourself. Back in Germany, think how proud your mother, Bruno and William will be when they hear of today. And Judith, Ida and all the children. Celebrate it for them."

Otto nodded ruefully. "Yes, you are right."

"And not just for them, Otto. Celebrate it for those who helped you achieve this day and who too would be so proud, but who have not lived to see it. Celebrate for Henry, Conrad and Liutgarde." She took hold of his hand. "And most of all, celebrate for Liudolf."

Otto's eyes glistened. "Yes, for them. It is my greatest regret that they are not here with me this day." For a moment she thought Otto would be overcome with emotion, but he managed to control it. "There are others too who helped me. It was my father's wisdom which first set me on this path. And Hermann, my dearest friend... I do not think I would have managed more than a few years on the German throne without him to aid me. This day is for them."

Adelheid swallowed. "And it is for Eadgyth."

Otto's reminiscent smile lit up his face, telling Adelheid how no longer did memories of his first wife pain him. "Her support saw me through so many dark days, her love enhanced every occasion. I know I would not be the man I am today without her devotion. Yes, this day is most certainly for my beautiful Eadgyth."

Adelheid felt no jealousy, although a lump rose in her throat. "Exactly," she said. Eadgyth had been a few years older than Otto. If she had been beside him that day, her hair would have been streaked with grey and her face lined, but Adelheid knew in Otto's eyes she would have been as beautiful as the day he first laid eyes on her.

Otto looked at her quizzically. "Are you not forgetting someone?"

Adelheid shook her head. "Who?"

He laughed. "Why, you, of course. This day is for you."

The lump threatened to choke her and she shook her head.

"No, Otto. I know I have not been the wife to you that she was. She supported you unquestioningly and never defied you as I have so often done."

"Eadgyth was with me when I was little more than a boy. She was at my side as I became king, helping me through those terrible days when I did not know if I could hold on to power. I needed her unquestioning support and one day it will be my privilege to lie again beside her." He smiled, pushing back a few strands of hair from her face. "But I am no longer that untested boy. It is right I have someone at my side who is not afraid to challenge and guide me. I am honoured to call you my wife." There was a long pause as Otto's intense blue eyes looked into hers in a way which made it impossible to doubt his next words. "You are very different from Eadgyth, but you hold no lesser place in my heart. My love, do not doubt my devotion to you for I have never doubted yours."

"Oh, Otto." Adelheid flung her arms around the first, the only man she had loved, no longer caring that she was not the first or the only for him. All that mattered was that she would be his last love. Eadgyth had been at his side as he emerged into manhood and taken his first steps to power, but she was the one with him as he realised his greatest ambition. And although she prayed it would be many years yet, it would undoubtedly be her hand he held as God called him from the world. When that day came, Adelheid knew she would return him to Eadgyth without bitterness, feeling only a sense of kinship with the other woman who had loved him as devotedly as she did. It would be right then to entrust Otto back to her.

Otto pressed his lips to hers in a long, lingering kiss. "So, my Lady Empress, shall we dine?"

Adelheid smiled back. "Yes, my Lord Emperor, we shall."

Hand in hand they entered the hall, where everyone rose to bow before the couple making their way to the head of the table or, as it seemed to many, to the head of the whole world.

Notes on the characters

Pope John XII: There is no evidence that the Pope tried to molest Adelheid, but if he didn't, she must have been one of the few women who escaped him. He really was quite as bad as described here. Otto's motivations for crowning Adelheid were probably political – he was claiming Italy through her. But, Otto did seem to have a deep respect for women, so it is not impossible that he gained some satisfaction from seeing the licentious pope honouring a woman in such a way. Certainly he gave the Pope a lecture on the error of his ways – one of those historical moments I would love to be a fly on the wall at. It must have been excruciating!

Often in history people do not get their comeuppance, so the end of Pope John is satisfying. He died young, either of an apoplexy sustained during some alfresco sex or, more probably, was killed by the husband of one of his victims.

Berengar, Willa and Adalbert: Berengar was finally apprehended by Otto a couple of years after his coronation. He ended his days as a prisoner in Germany, while Willa was forced to retire to a nunnery. Adalbert fled Italy after Otto's coronation, but made several attempts to regain his kingdom. None of these were successful and eventually he retired to his wife's estates in Burgundy.

Lothair: Not much is known about Adelheid's first husband. Even in Adelheid's history he receives little mention. He was a powerless king of Italy, very much under Berengar's domination. Did he respond by domineering someone even less powerful than himself? At the very least he must have been an unhappy figure and not easy to live with and Adelheid is the patron saint of abuse victims.

Azzo: As so often in historical novels, one of the problems I have come up against is several characters having the same name. In this book I have tried to find various ways around this to avoid confusion. I have used different spellings such as Mathilda, Matilda and Mathilde for Otto's mother, daughter and granddaughter or Conrad and Konrad for his son-in-law and brother-in-law. I let The Three Ottos themselves make a joke about Otto in the space of a few years having a son and two grandsons all with his name. Azzo's true name was Adalbert Azzo, but to avoid confusion with Adalbert son of Berengar, it seemed easiest simply to drop the first part of his name.

Liudolf and Ida: It is not clear exactly how many children they had. The definite ones are Mathilde and Otto. Regelind appears in later records as Otto's daughter. But as she was born too late to be Eadgyth's and too early to be Adelheid's, some historians consider her to be Liudolf's, possibly adopted by Otto after Liudolf's death. That blurring of the relationships can be seen elsewhere – Otto II, for example, referred to Liudolf's son as both his brother and nephew. The name Regelind, perhaps for Ida's mother, suggests a connection to that branch of the family. She may have been married to the man who became Duke of Swabia after Liudolf's son and if so the names of her children include Liudolf, Hermann and Ida, making an even stronger case for her identity. Although it is by no means certain, I have included her here as Liudolf's daughter simply because Hermann, Liudolf and Ida have been much loved characters across two books and as Mathilde became Abbess of Essen and Otto died without children, it pleases me to think those three do have descendants alive today. Not much is known of Ida after Liudolf's death other than her death date many years later. But as she does not seem to have entered an abbey it seems likely that Ida, described in the records as beautiful and feminine and presumably also rich, would have married again.

Otto: It is always emotional to say goodbye to my characters as I finish a book, but Otto, who has been a major character over two books, is particularly hard to leave behind. History views him as a triumphant figure, but at times I have found him a tragic one. After the troubles of the early years of his reign, it seems each decade resulted in some significant losses. Eadgyth and Hermann in the 940s; Liutgarde, Conrad, Henry and Liudolf in the 950s; and Bruno and William in the 960s, with William and Mathilda dying a few weeks apart in 966. He is described in the records as a restless and vocal sleeper. Some of this was undoubtedly the active mind of a man who was endlessly busy, but perhaps there were also memories and regrets which haunted him.

Despite his autocratic nature he has mostly come across as a likable figure. He enjoyed two happy marriages and seems to have regarded both women with a deep respect, not always granted to women in those times. He was also unusually merciful towards those who challenged him. Other kings would not have hesitated to punish their rebel brothers and sons with physical and even fatal consequences, while Otto forgave his. I wonder, was he unable to change his overbearing nature, but at the same time very aware of how provoking it was to his family?

He reigned as Emperor for eleven years, dividing his time between Germany and Italy. He eventually died after a short illness at Memleben, the same palace where his father had died, at the age of 60 and was buried, as he had wished, beside his beloved Eadgyth in Magdeburg Cathedral, where his grave can still be seen today.

He was succeeded as Emperor by Otto II and then his grandson, Otto III. After that the title went to Henry, the grandson of Otto's brother Henry of Bavaria, before returning to a descendent of Otto's through Liutgarde and Conrad.

It is possible that the wife of this emperor and therefore the next emperor was a descendant of Liudolf, through the above mentioned Regelind. I would like to think this is true. Otto's treatment of Liudolf is the one point where I do not understand him and Liudolf's son did indeed lose out in the succession to Adelheid's. It would be fitting if eventually his descendants gained control.

However, while this is a goodbye to Otto as a main character, I do wonder whether I have really seen the last of him. The Ottonian women were a formidable bunch, so it seems distinctly possible I will see him again.

Adelheid: Adelheid's life remained eventful after Otto's death. She was influential in the early years of the reign of Otto II, but Otto's tragic history with Liudolf was repeated with Adelheid and Otto II. Adelheid's relationship with her daughter-in-law, the Empress Theopanu was poor and Otto II, perhaps forced to choose between his wife and his mother, chose his wife. Adelheid was exiled from court, estranged from her son. They were reconciled, but like Liudolf, Otto II died not long after in his late twenties.

Otto III was at this point very young and Henry of Bavaria, the son of Henry and Judith, claimed the regency for himself. However Adelheid joined forces with Theopanu and her daughter Matilda, Abbess of Quedlinburg, to safeguard the young emperor. Henry of Bavaria was no match for these three Ottonian women and Theopanu took the regency.

But Theopanu also died young, propelling Adelheid to the greatest heights of her power as regent of the Empire, one of the most powerful people in Europe. When Otto III came of age, Adelheid retired to an abbey where she described herself as "Adelheid, by God's gift an empress and by herself a poor sinner and God's maidservant" which is, of course, where this book gets its title. I am always pleased if I can allow my characters to speak with their own voices and for Adelheid's own words to form the title is a particular privilege.

Of course she wasn't really a poor sinner, but, despite her subsequent canonisation, I don't think she was exactly a saint either. She must take some responsibility for the quarrel between Otto and Liudolf, as well as her poor relationship with her own son. As a mother-in-law she comes across as difficult. When Theopanu died, Adelheid was said to have been very pleased that 'that Greek woman' had died. Hardly saintly behaviour! But she lived through dangerous times and no doubt reacted to them in the best way she could. Who is to say if we could have done any better? Ultimately she emerges as someone who was neither saint nor sinner, but simply very human.

Women of the Dark Ages

More than a thousand years before today was a fabulous period where history and legend collided to form what is often known as the Dark Ages. Peering through the mists of time figures emerge, often insubstantially becoming as much legendary as historical. And if the men are hard to see, the women are even harder. But they lived, they were loved, they mattered and they should be remembered. Each of the books in the Women of the Dark Ages series tells the stories of the forgotten or uncelebrated, but very remarkable women who lived through these tumultuous times.

The Saxon Marriage

The story of the woman whose memory haunted this book – Eadgyth of Wessex.

Dawn Of The Franks

Bitter betrayal, forbidden love and the visions sent by the Gods as Queen Basina of Thuringia seeks her destiny.

Kenneth's Queen

The tale of the unknown wife of Kenneth Mac Alpin.

The Girl From Brittia

The curious tale of the warrior princess, known only as The Island Girl.

Three Times The Lady

A Frankish princess, a Wessex queen, stepmother to Alfred the Great, a scandalous widow – the exciting true story of Judith of Flanders

Quest for New England

It is the 1070s, England is reeling from the Conquest and an epic voyage is about to begin...

1066 is probably the most famous date in English history and we all know what happened. Duke William of Normandy invaded England, winning a decisive victory at the Battle of Hastings, bringing as end to the Anglo-Saxon era.

But not all Anglo-Saxons were quietly absorbed into the regime. There were rebellions and when these failed, some preferred exile over submission. The Quest for New England trilogy is based on a true story, following a large group of Anglo-Saxons in their search for a place to call home.

Rising From The Ruins

After the defeat at Hastings, the failure of rebellions and the devastation of the North, England desperately needs a new hero. Will Siward of Gloucester be that man?

Peril & Plunder

Siward and his Anglo-Saxon exiles have escaped England, but can they escape the ghosts of the past. Can they even escape the Normans?

Courage Of The Conquered

Sinister secrets lurk beneath the splendour of a fabulous city. Will Siward's Quest for New England end in heart-breaking tragedy?

Tales of the Wasteland

Follow in the footsteps of Arthurian heroes to the Wasteland of 6th century Britannia...

The year 536 has been called the worst year to be alive, spanning a decade of cold, famine and disease. The world was a wasteland.

But like all good wastelands it is also a spiritual wasteland inhabited by disreputable and damaged kings.

These are their stories...

Tyrant Whelp

Custennin was King of Dumnonia.
Legend names him a kinsman of King Arthur.
So why did a monk write the words to damn him for all time?

Fisher King

Told around firesides, retold into legend, his anguish echoes down the centuries... The tale of the Fisher King – the man behind the myth.

About the author

Anna Chant was born and spent her childhood in Essex. She studied history at the University of Sheffield, before qualifying as a primary teacher. She currently lives in Devon with her husband and three sons. In her spare time she enjoys reading, sewing and camping. 'God's Maidservant' is her fifth novel. Her first novel published in 2016 was 'Kenneth's Queen', telling the tale of the unknown wife of Kenneth Mac Alpin. Anna has fallen in love with the Dark Ages and in particular the part played by the often unrecorded and uncelebrated women of the time. She plans to tell the stories of as many as possible!

I hope you have enjoyed reading God's Maidservant. As one of the most remarkable women of the age, telling Adelheid's story has been a fascinating experience. Good reviews are critical to a book's success, so please take a moment to leave your review on the platform where you bought the book. I look forward to hearing from you!

For more news, offers, upcoming releases and all things Dark Age please get in touch via
My Facebook Page
https://www.facebook.com/darkagevoices/
Check out my blog: https://darkagevoices.wordpress.com/
Or follow me on Twitter: https://twitter.com/anna_chant

For more information on the characters, places and events of this book take a look at my Pinterest board, where I have pinned many of the sites and articles I used in my research.
https://www.pinterest.co.uk/annachant/adelaide-of-italy-st-adelaide/

Made in the USA
Las Vegas, NV
30 July 2023

75436519R00219